MW00674863

PRA[I

WALKING ON THE SEA OF CLOUDS

"*There is a very rare and special pleasure that comes from reading a beautifully written book from a true expert in his field. In reading* Walking on the Sea of Clouds, *it immediately becomes apparent that Gray Rinehart is intimately familiar with the field of near-future space exploration. He understands what it will take to get mankind to the moon and beyond. He writes about the military as only someone who has been in the military can. He writes about bureaucracies and funding in the way that someone who has struggled with them does. When it comes to astronauts and space exploration, his characters ring undeniably true. He understands that some people are motivated to give all that they have in order to go into space simply because he has devoted so much of his life to this great endeavor.*

"*This book will be treasured by anyone who has ever dreamt of visiting the Moon, walking on another world, or bathing beneath the light of a distant star.*"

—David Farland, author of the
NYT-bestselling *Runelords* novels

"*You've always wanted to go to the Moon. You've always loved hard science fiction. You've always gravitated toward believable characters. You've never found a way to get all three in the same place, at the same time. Well, now there's a way. Here's how:*

"*You pick up Gray Rinehart's* Walking on the Sea of Clouds, *the most faithful and gritty 'you are there' novel of early lunar settlement I've ever had the pleasure to read. This is hard SF at its hardest—by which I mean that not only is the science spot on and largely off-the-shelf, but the characters conform to the emotional and psychological limits of folks we interact with every day. There are no galactic crises to be overcome, no interpersonal conflicts that erupt into homicidal rage, and no cast of quirky tycoons, femme fatales, or wise-cracking test-pilots. This is the Moon as it's likely to be in the early* days of colonization, where even the smallest problems have impacts far beyond what living on Earth has trained us to anticipate.

"Annoyed you haven't been to the Moon yet? Then pick up Walking on the Sea of Clouds; you'll feel like you're there."

—Charles E. Gannon, author of the award-winning *Fire with Fire*

"Two things are immediately clear. First, Gray Rinehart knows his field(s) inside out; and second, he writes with grace, skill, and professional polish. What more could any reader ask?"

—Mike Resnick, multiple Hugo-award-winning author

"Gray Rinehart knows that real engineering is messy, and that Murphy was an optimist. When whatever can go wrong with constructing the first Lunar colony does go wrong, teams on the Moon and on Earth struggle to save the project—and their lives. This is meat and potatoes for the hard science fiction fan."

—Martin L. Shoemaker, award-winning author of "Today I Am Paul"

"From the science to the science fiction costume party to the one scientist's African accent, everything about Walking on the Sea of Clouds feels amazingly authentic. They say an author should write what he knows, and based on this book, I'd say that Gray Rinehart has been in outer space, walked on the moon, thrown up in a NASA-approved barf-bag, fired thruster engines, and driven an LVN (gotta read the book if you want to know what that last one is). You can experience all that and more for yourself, too; just jump in on page one and don't stop until you get the end."

—Edmund R. Schubert, award-winning editor and author of *This Giant Leap*

WALKING *on the* SEA *of* CLOUDS

WALKING *on the*
SEA *of* CLOUDS

A saga of the first colony on the Moon
GRAY RINEHART

WordFire Press
Colorado Springs, Colorado

WALKING ON THE SEA OF CLOUDS
Copyright © 2017 Gray Rinehart

ISBN: 978-1-61475-521-0

Cover design by Janet McDonald

Cover artwork images by Adobe Stock

Edited by Bryan Thomas Schmidt

Kevin J. Anderson, Art Director

Book Design by RuneWright, LLC
www.RuneWright.com

Published by
WordFire Press, an imprint of
WordFire, Inc.
PO Box 1840
Monument CO 80132

Kevin J. Anderson & Rebecca Moesta, Publishers

WordFire Press Trade Paperback Edition July 2017
Printed in the USA
wordfirepress.com

DEDICATION

for Jillian

CHAPTER ONE

Wisdom Has Nothing to Do with It

It should have been a perfect Santa Barbara Sunday.

It *seemed* like a perfect Santa Barbara Sunday, but all day Stormie carried a ticklish feeling in the pit of her stomach that something was about to go wrong. As the day progressed she let herself relax, but when the crisis came she rushed in—"ahead of those frightened angels," as her grandmother used to say—and learned how badly doing the right thing can backfire.

The morning started perfectly. They woke early to watch the colony setup team launch on the Asteroid Consortium feed, and Frank distracted her in his not-so-subtle way. Sweaty and spent, she lay with her head on his chest and dismissed the nervous tickle as a sympathetic reaction, anticipating their own launch still six months away. It was low in her gut, as if she could feel the subsonic rumble when the engines ignited even though they were 7500 kilometers away from the French Guiana launch site.

The afternoon offered its own version of perfection. They strolled down the TechnArt alley along East Beach, invigorated by the clear, cool day. Musicians vied for their attention as they passed ingenious tech-infused artwork and multisensory productions; they paused frequently but bought only a three-in-one piece the artist called a "digital triptych." Stormie credited the twinge in her belly to disappointment that the only art they could take with them was digital.

She relaxed enough to enjoy their early supper at Bucatini—superb, if a little pricey compared to the restaurants they frequented back home in Houston—and did she feel a bit of indigestion when they came again to the beach to catch the last of the sunset?

The winter solstice was still eight weeks away, so the Sun wasn't as far south as it would eventually go, but it sank into a magnificent ocean vista, turning the low, thin clouds vivid orange.

"Red sun at night," Frank quoted.

The cool breeze massaged Stormie's bare arms. Frank had offered her his coat, and Mother Mac's voice in her head—"Don't wanna catch cold, child"—urged her to accept. But with Frank's arm around her she had warmth enough.

"I hope they're okay," she said, the tickle inside her a counterpoint to the thought of "sailors' delight." By now the team should be close to boosting out of Earth's orbit into cis-lunar space.

"Should we check?" Frank asked, though he did not reach for his CommPact. He traced a pattern on her upper arm, his fingers strong and gentle.

She wanted to, but said, "No, if something had gone wrong someone would have called."

Frank nodded. With his free hand he scooped up some sand and squeezed it; Stormie enjoyed the smooth tension of his muscles as he involuntarily held her a little tighter.

"Yes," he said, "I am certain James would let us know."

Stormie smiled at his formal speech; his teachers had emphasized very proper English, and Frank always learned his lessons well.

The breeze strengthened, and brought a heavier hint of winter cold. Stormie dug her toes deeper into the rapidly cooling sand to get them out of the wind. She huddled closer to Frank, more for company than for comfort.

"Would you like to go in?"

"No, let's see the Moon come up."

They talked about the day, the art and music and dinner, always circling back to the lunatic dream—in the purest sense of the word—they had been pursuing together. Gradually stars emerged in the twilight, but only those bright enough to shine through the high haze and penetrate the ambient light from the city behind them. The old oil wells in the Channel provided their own version of romantic illumination from the still-burning platform lights and gas flares, but that didn't help with seeing the stars.

The last vestiges of twilight fell away into night, and the waning gibbous Moon, just two days past full, crept upward behind the cloud layer. It should be close to lunar high noon over Mercator Crater, their eventual home on the southern edge of Mare Nubium.

As the silence lengthened, Frank recited from Noyes' "The Highwayman." "The Moon was a ghostly galleon—"

"That's what you always say."

"That is what I always think, when the Moon is in clouds like that. Have you found another verse, a better one?"

She shook her head. "No, and not for lack of trying. I should be able to come up with something, but I can't." It was a game they played from early in their dating life—

Motorcycles tearing up and down Cabrillo Boulevard drowned out whatever reply Frank made. They faded in the distance, and Stormie closed her eyes and listened to the gentle, soothing waves.

"A shekel for your thoughts," Frank said. The words rumbled through his chest; Stormie felt as much as heard them. She didn't mind his interrupting her reverie.

"I'm just listening to the water. It's nice to sit here—out in the open, I mean. It'll be hard to leave this behind."

In his slow, rolling cadence, with the distinct Kenyan rhythm that comforted her, Frank said, "Yes, it will. But even if it is hard, I do not think it will be so very bad. We are committed now."

Or we ought to be. "Do you really think we're doing the right thing?" she asked.

"I have no doubt. How many people get to be pioneers?" His words blended into the rolling waves, and he dropped the remains of more sand she had some moments before dribbled into his hand.

3

"You didn't always sound so sure," Stormie said, wondering as she often did if she had asked too much of him. To some degree her passion for the project had influenced his.

"That is true. But ... it is one thing to tend to plants and trees on a living world, to help sustain it, and quite another to try to bring a dead world to life." He brushed his hand on his pants.

Stormie smiled. "We should go back soon. Then let's get up early to see the sunrise."

"I think we can do that, and still meet James for breakfast. And even if we are late, I am sure he will not begrudge us—after all, we will soon use up our allotment of sunrises. I hope our new ones are splendid enough to make up for having only one a month."

"I just want to be done with all the prep," she said, and her stomach tightened. In a few weeks they would undergo one final test to see if they had what it took to live on the Moon: ninety days in long-term isolation, buried with other trainees in an underground center. Anticipation and frustration swirled together inside her; she wanted to launch *now*, not wait any more or go through more training. After so many months of preliminaries, to have to go through one more phase seemed almost impossible. Maybe that was the point: it was a marathon rather than a sprint. But she'd always been a sprinter. "I can't believe it'll be almost two years by the time we launch."

Frank laughed. "Imagine how much longer it would have been if we worked for the government. But even so, it has been much longer than two years, my love."

Stormie counted back the months, and shook her head. "Maybe if you count setting up the company, two years ago next month. Then, if we launch in May, that'll be twenty-eight months." *Although we started talking about it right after Jim's accident, and that was over three years ago.* "I was counting from last August, when we won the contract, so it'll only be twenty months."

Frank shook his head, and swayed with the motion. "No, my love, you have forgotten. I am sure we have been talking about this as long as I have known you—six years or more. On our second date, if I recall, you talked about some nanoparticle breakthroughs in one of the orbital stations. And I believe you mentioned on our third date how much you wanted to fly away into space."

She smiled, but only at his lilting diction. She had forgotten both of those conversations; if they had just started dating, that would've been when they were in that astronomy elective together. She vaguely remembered the station experiments as being one of the more profitable ventures for either Low-Gee or OrbiTech; that would've been a reasonable topic, just an extrapolation from their coursework. But ... she gave Frank a soft jab to the ribs. "No, I didn't."

"Oh, yes, my dear. And on the one-month anniversary of our first date, which I still do not comprehend the meaning of a one-month anniversary, you gave me an article about the move to enact a new Space Treaty—"

"I don't think so, Frank."

"And you wanted to write it into our wedding vows...."

Stormie looked up into Frank's face. In the shadows only the whites of his eyes were visible. *If you felt like I was badgering you, why'd you ask me to marry you in the first—*

Frank smiled then, and his teeth were almost bright enough to blind.

Stormie leaned in and kissed him. The evening seemed warmer still, and the flutter in her stomach was anything but apprehension. Her enthusiasm buoyed her, and she held on to Frank for fear she might float away to the Moon without him.

O   O   O

A little later, they walked east along Cabrillo toward their hotel. Frank had insisted that Stormie wear his sport coat, and it hung on her almost like a short dress.

His words were drowned out as two black-clad daredevils on crotch rockets sped past them up Cabrillo.

"What did you say?"

"I said, perhaps we should go dancing." To emphasize his point, he raised her hand and, touching it lightly, revolved himself around her like the Moon around the Earth.

Stormie didn't break stride, but she chuckled at him and shook her head. "It's been a long time," she said. "And I don't know where we could go."

"That is fine, my love. We can dance right here." He danced another turn around her as she walked, and started a third as the motorcycle jockeys came roaring back the other way.

Just in front of her, Frank slowed, with a puzzled look on his face, as her mind registered unexpected sounds: brakes; an impact and then another, louder one; the crunch and groan of crumpling metal; the distinctive crackle of breaking glass. Puzzlement turned slowly to surprise on Frank's face and his momentum carried him halfway around her.

Stormie turned with him, and the tickle in her stomach solidified into jagged granite.

A little silver Ford—one of the new fully-automated Dragonelle turbine/flywheel models, just like their rental—and a black or very dark blue older model Nissan had hit headlight-to-headlight a dozen meters away. A thousand sparkling bits of glass littered the street around the cars. To the left, a minivan was up on the sidewalk, resting against one of the palm trees lining Cabrillo. A black-clad figure lay unmoving on the pavement.

By the time Frank came to a stop, he had pulled Stormie halfway around. She glanced at him, looked back at the crash, and took a step toward the vehicles. Frank tightened his grip on her hand to hold her back.

She pulled against his hold. "Come on," she said, "we have to help."

He kept his grip on her. "Do you think that is wise? We have to—"

Stormie shook her head. *Wisdom has nothing to do with it.* "We have to help, if we can. Now. I'll see if that biker is okay, and you call 9-1-1." She tapped her right foot, twice, then pressed it down a little behind her as if she were settling into her old starting blocks.

Come on, Frank. If we don't help, no one will. No one ever helps.

"Very well," Frank said. He held Stormie's hand a second longer. "Be careful. No unnecessary risks." He kissed her hand; she squeezed his, trusting him to move when she did.

She sprinted toward the dark shape on the street.

CHAPTER TWO

The Problem with Theory

The ride had been just as kick-ass as Van Richards had dreamed it would be: a bass rumble deeper than the physical vibrations that shook the vehicle around him, the feeling of being alternately bounced in random directions with bone-jarring force and being compressed into a vaguely human-shaped pancake, and then the whispery silence that settled around even the routine noises like fog around a streetlight.

Which would all be good if his stomach would cooperate.

They had all eschewed the anti-nausea meltaway strips, though he suspected a couple of the crew had used them secretly. In theory, the preflight meal should've been well digested by the time he reached orbit, and certainly too far along his gut now to threaten to come back. But that was the problem with theory: if you weren't careful, it didn't quite match up with reality.

The first hour had been fine: no worse than the parabolic flights in the Consortium's retrofitted KC-10. But as the hours dragged by in maneuvers to raise the orbit while avoiding a multitude of satellite and space junk paths, it seemed that time might not be his friend.

He tried to concentrate on the fact that he'd won the first round of the puke pool. He'd picked Henry Crafts to blow first, and the little man had obliged before they'd completed three orbits. Van wasn't sure what Henry had eaten, but it didn't smell very appetizing now. At least Henry had caught almost everything in the barf bag.

"Thruster firing in thirty seconds," Shay Nakamura said from his command seat. "Secure your shit."

Van had strapped down his helmet as soon as he took it off, and now checked it again to be sure it was secure. He looked around and patted his acceleration couch and the outside of his suit, even though he hadn't gotten anything out since they reached orbit. He fingered the pocket where he had his sick sack.

"Ten seconds," Shay said. Van counted down himself, glad that Shay didn't run the count over the intercom for every maneuver.

The thruster engine firings were gentle nudges compared to the launch, but without his helmet on they were louder than Van expected. Not ear-splitting, but resonant, like being inside a barrel while someone beat on it with a hammer, or threw rocks at it.

"Okay," Shay said, "we're in the clear. Next big boost is a little over an hour away, and we'll be on track to catch up to the transfer rig. How's everybody doing?"

Everyone reported in order of position or seniority. Oskar Hintener, the setup crew engineer, and Roy Chesterfield, the crew foreman, sounded fine. Jovelyn Nguyen, the number one grunt, said she was fine but didn't sound so. Van grinned; he had his money on Jovie losing her breakfast next. Refusing to admit that he was fighting sickness himself, he tried to put some cheer in his report. "Richards here, A-OK."

After Van, Henry grunted a reply, but Grace Teliopolous and Scooter Mast both sounded good. Van's grin dropped a little; he needed Grace to get sick third if he was going to win the trifecta.

"So," Shay said, "who's up for some lunch?"

Van wasn't the only one who groaned, but he slapped his thigh for giving in to the impulse.

From Shay's voice, it was easy to hear that he was smiling like a teenager after his first French kiss. "Let's see what we have ... the tuna casserole is pretty good ... maybe some sweet and sour pork—"

Van wrinkled his nose as wafts of the pork concoction reached him. On its own, it might smell vaguely like food, but mixed with what Henry contributed to the cabin it did not improve the atmosphere.

A minute or so later, Jovelyn retched into her bag. Van pumped his fist but said nothing: his teeth were clenched, and he was afraid to open his mouth.

"Who was that?" Shay asked. "And is your ECS secure?"

Van shook his head at the acronym: Emesis Containment System. As if a plastic-coated baggie could legitimately be considered a "system."

A few seconds later, Jovelyn said, "It was me. And yes, you sick bastard."

"That seems like a poor choice of words, Jovie," Shay said, "and checking the pool, it looks like Van picked both the win and the place. Who do you have for the show, Van?"

Van feigned disinterest. "Hmmm?" As the odor of Jovelyn's breakfast mixed with Henry's and with Shay's lunch, Van found himself clawing at his pocket to retrieve his bag.

"Cat got your tongue, Richards? Sound off, Airman!"

Van swallowed, and immediately regretted it. "I bet on Grace to show."

"In your dreams, Van," Grace said. "My money's on you."

"Now, play nice, children," Shay said. "I'll admit to you that Oskar is looking a little peaked up here. He may blow any minute. You had a very traditional breakfast, didn't you, Oskar? Western omelet, bacon, hash browns?"

Van tried to shut out Shay's voice, but was no more successful than he was at blocking out the smells. The cabin had a faint air that he could not identify … something like corned beef hash, if it had been fermented in malt vinegar. Van laid his hand on his stomach, but the layers of pressure suit stripped all comfort from the gesture.

Oskar's laugh cut through Van's concentrated aloofness. "No, sir, nothing like that," the engineer said. "Today I had an English breakfast: baked beans, tomato slices—"

Van's stomach turned one notch too far, and he didn't hear what else Oskar listed. As his system emptied what little it had in it, he heard a good bit more cheering than he appreciated.

"Yeah, yeah," he said a moment later. "Congratulations, Grace. Shay, tell the designers that they need better air scrubbers on these things."

"They sure do now," said Grace.

Shay laughed. "I suppose it would help if we actually turned the filtration system on."

Van laid his head back. He licked his lips and grimaced at the aftertaste. "Go ahead, have your fun. At least I won the exacta."

"Okay, gang," Shay said, in as smooth a transition to "command mode" as Van had ever heard, "time to start getting serious. We've got a long way to go and a lot of work to do when we get there."

More than we should. The previous setup team hadn't so much left a "punch list" of things to fix as they'd left a lot of their own tasks undone. But that was okay for Van: it was exactly what he'd signed up for. He'd dreamed of this day for as long as he could remember, and after this three-month mission he had his sights set on a long-term colony stint with Barbara at his side. It wouldn't matter what job they had for him, either; he'd take the grubbiest duty they had to offer. If they only gave him a wrench to turn, he'd be happy.

Van brought his attention back to Shay.

"—so settle down, enjoy the ride, and we'll be back on solid ground before you know it."

Van tried closing his eyes, but that made him feel worse, so he focused on the blank flex display in front of him. He would eventually get used to freefall, but for now he was glad their flight profile was as direct an insertion as possible so they wouldn't have to screw around with a stop at the Clarke station.

At the moment, "before you know it" couldn't come soon enough.

CHAPTER THREE

Some Barbaric Ritual

Sunday, 29 October 2034

Stormie marked fluids draining away from the smashed front end of the minivan—a green Toyota hybrid. The liquid stained the sidewalk and formed a little puddle at the base of the curb. She didn't see any other obvious dangers: no fires or other hazards. People were starting to climb out of the van—parents and one, two, three children. They were going to be okay.

Stormie knelt by the biker. Long, shiny, coal-black hair fanned out from underneath the woman's helmet. Collision avoidance systems and automatic brakes in the other vehicles must surely have protected their passengers, but she had had no such defenses.

Recollection pushed at Stormie's brain and pulled at her guts. For an instant she was a child again, in the early days of summer heat, deep in the concrete-and-asphalt of Charleston where the harbor breeze never reached. Involuntary tears formed and burst from her eyes before she seized control. She had no time for that.

The woman—girl?—lay on her left arm; her legs were set as if she were sleeping and had dreamed of running. She lay in a shiny puddle of urine and blood. Tanned and torn skin showed through abrasions on her pants and flimsy windbreaker—no one had taught this girl about motorcycle leathers, or she hadn't had sense enough to listen. At least she'd worn a helmet; it was dented and the faceplate was badly scratched.

"Excuse me!" Stormie called toward the minivan. A small crowd had gathered there, and some of them started toward her. "Do you have any gloves in your van?" That was probably too much to hope for; even bags over her hands would keep her away from the blood. "Or plastic bags?"

"Huh?" The father, possibly still dazed from the collision, shook his head quickly and violently the way a cat does when you blow in its ears. The airbags inflating may have damaged his hearing. "What?"

"Plastic bags. Do you have any?"

He put his right hand to his ear and held up his left for an instant, but he nodded. "I'll check." He headed back to the van, a little wobbly but quickly.

Stormie pulled off Frank's coat and dropped it behind her. She touched the girl's throat, under the helmet, and found a pulse. She counted three beats before, with the new angle of light, she realized the puddle of blood under the girl's hips was becoming a pool.

Possibilities flew through Stormie's mind like butterflies, and it took her a second to catch and examine them. They were ugly.

She felt the back of the girl's neck, gently. She closed her eyes and concentrated on the skin under her fingers, under her palm, trying to block out other sensations at least for a moment. She knew she couldn't detect a mild injury, and maybe not a gross one, but it was important to try. She satisfied herself—or maybe just convinced herself—that the rider's neck wasn't broken.

Supporting the girl's neck and head, Stormie rolled her onto her back. She didn't remove the helmet, but pulled open the faceplate. The girl looked Indian, with heavy dark brows that matched her dark hair, and very pretty. Her left arm resembled ground chuck and was broken in at least two places. Stormie took its condition in with a glance: the blood was coming from lower down.

A jagged tip of the girl's right femur stuck out from her inner thigh. Bright red blood erupted from the wound, subsided, and erupted again with each heartbeat.

Stormie pondered for two of the woman's visible heartbeats. She needed to stop the bleeding, but the bone was a problem: as long as it protruded, the wound would stay open. She couldn't straighten the girl's leg, to pull the bone back in, and apply pressure to the wound all on her own.

The man from the Toyota wasn't back yet, but Stormie couldn't hesitate. He might be back any second, he might never come back, or he might come back empty-handed, but the girl's face had already lost some color. Stormie didn't have time to wait for gloves or bags, and couldn't debate the issue any more: the pool of blood was spreading. But she still needed help.

A few more people had wandered over from the minivan, mostly silent but some whispering to one another or into the air, those with phone earpieces. A few had whipped out microcams, and Stormie ground her teeth at them. Sirens in the distance grew louder, but slowly.

Stormie knew that she should single out whomever she wanted to help her: put the onus on them personally in order to get them out of bystander paralysis. She made eye contact with one man who didn't appear preoccupied with commenting on the scene. He was as likely a candidate as any.

"You!" she said. The man looked around to see if anyone else acknowledged her, though he must know she meant him. He looked back again. "Yes, sir, you. We need your help."

He took a small step forward, about half what his normal stride would've been. He wasn't a tall man, but he bent down and said, "With what?"

If he'd been within arm's reach, Stormie would've grabbed him—instead she worked her way down the woman's body from the shoulders, trying as best she could to palpate her shoulders, arms, and rib cage for additional injuries. "I need you to grab this girl's right foot," Stormie said. "First, check to make sure her lower legs aren't injured, then when I tell you to you'll pull her foot gently while I put pressure on this wound." The thought of shock occurred to her; the girl had certainly lost enough blood already for shock to be an issue. "Once that's done, roll up your jacket and put it under her feet."

"No way," the man said. He shuffled back a little. "This is real leather."

"Well, if she dies from shock and blood loss you can be real proud of your damn leather jacket. Get the hell out of the way." Stormie picked up Frank's coat and tossed it toward the girl's feet. "You, ma'am! Will you help? We need to set this leg as best we can, and then we need to keep her warm. Thank you. That's right … thank you very much."

Stormie counted to three and the helpful woman pulled. The jagged stub of bone receded into the girl's leg. Her blood was warm and gushed against Stormie's bare palm as she got her hand over it.

Stormie kept pressure on the wounded leg. The woman helping her elevated the biker's other leg and put Frank's coat under her foot. Stormie hoped having only one leg raised would be enough to stave off shock.

She put more pressure on the wound, willing it to stay closed under her hand. She glanced down at herself and almost laughed at the realization that she was covered in a stranger's blood in the middle of Cabrillo Boulevard: not at all how she had expected this day to end. But she didn't afford herself the luxury of even that release of tension. Loss of blood had left the girl very pale now.

Without prompting, another man from the crowd laid his coat over the injured girl. Something in Stormie's perception changed and the chill breeze on her bare arms cut through the heat within her body. At least the girl had on a jacket, even if it wasn't leather. Hopefully the pavement wasn't too cold, or it would leach too much heat from her body. And hopefully the ambulance would show up soon.

Stormie looked around. Frank had extracted a boy maybe eight or ten years old from one of the cars. He was up the street a little, kneeling next to the boy who sat on the curb and stared, wide-eyed, at Stormie, at the prone woman, at the blood.

Without much else to do at the moment, Stormie considered how this scene would be different for her and Frank once they were in place on the Moon. Vehicle collisions would be rare, and a good thing because response would be much harder. With all of them in pressure suits, Stormie would be compressing suit layers into the girl's wound; the fabric would almost certainly be torn and she would be relying on clamping baffles in the suit to limit oxygen loss, and probably calling for duct tape instead of a bystander's jacket. Inside her own suit, she'd smell … what, her own sweat, instead of antifreeze and fuel? She wondered if she would've been able to see the girl's pallor through her helmet. If the girl went shocky, Stormie could adjust her suit's heat exchanger. And she would have access to the suit's monitors to check the girl's vital signs.

The blood flow slowed, but the girl's color was too pale. Stormie tried to find the pressure point on the inside of the girl's thigh, to compress the femoral artery and slow the flow to her leg; she didn't even know if it would work, with the leg so badly broken. She might be doing more damage, tearing tissues deep inside, but she had to try—

She had to try. Had to. Had to make up for not being able to save Erick when he drowned, for not being able to save her mother when she lay broken and bleeding in the gutter under the hot Carolina sun. Waves of heat from the pavement, waves of tears in her eyes—tears in her eyes now, that she blinked away in embarrassed fury. She had to try.

"Come on," Stormie said through half-gritted teeth, pushing down harder on the girl's flesh. A siren wound down and she realized she hadn't even heard it approach. She glanced around.

A fire truck threaded its way through the traffic and as soon as its wheels stopped responders swarmed out of it like ants from an anthill. Frank ran to one of the firemen and gestured toward the old Nissan, near the curb where the young boy still sat.

Stormie looked back down at the girl. Her own heart seemed to slow within her chest, to have trouble pumping blood that suddenly thickened and chilled. Hope faded that the rider hadn't lost too much blood, that anyone would be able to save her.

Motion around her, next to her. A uniform-clad young man with a big red-and-white tackle box—not a fireman—leaned in, poking and prodding her patient. Another joined him, his expert hands dislodging Stormie's inexpert ones and with practiced motions applying a tournipack to the girl's shattered leg.

Hands on her shoulder, pulling her back. She sat back on her heels, clasping her sticky hands together, and Frank knelt beside her. "You did well, dear," he said. He put one hand on her back and with his other grasped both of hers. She was still as a statue, watching the EMTs work.

One of them tapped his earpiece and began calling for a life-flight. The other muttered, "Don't know where they're going to land," but kept working.

"Sir? Ma'am? Could you come over this way, please?"

Stormie glanced up at a big woman in firefighter gear. Frank stood, and gently pulled Stormie after him. All her motions seemed sluggish, unreal, as if she was watching someone else make them. She vaguely registered that her cheeks were itchy and her nose runny, and realized that she was crying. She turned toward Frank, who leaned in and gently kissed her.

O O O

Frank pulled Stormie a little closer and led her away from the scene. Tears had left salty trails down her ebony cheeks. Around them the chaos of response continued, with clusters of medical technicians and firefighters and now police officers moving with urgent purpose. Frank noted that Augustus, the boy he had pulled from the back seat of the Nissan, now had a blanket around his shoulders. In the opposite direction, a team huddled around the prone form of the second motorcyclist; Frank had forgotten there had been two.

"Here we go," said the lady firefighter. "Let's get you folks cleaned up."

Frank looked down at Stormie's hands in his, and beyond to the bloody streaks on his wife's cream-colored slacks. He slowly traced his gaze back up from her knees to her hands and the blood that trailed away toward her elbows. It looked as if Stormie had dipped her hands into a bucket of blood and raised them to heaven in some barbaric ritual.

Sweet baby Jesus in the manger.

His own hand now sticky with a stranger's blood, Frank pulled gently to turn Stormie toward him. He smiled softly, but her expression was guarded, as if she was not quite sure whether he might chastise her. Tears pooled in her eyes, and though they could be so hard when she radiated determination, in them now he didn't see his adult wife: he saw the frightened thirteen-year-old girl who had watched as her mother was struck and killed by two teenagers fleeing their abortive bank robbery—and behind that the nine-year-old who had seen her brother drown. Frank was certain that if she had it to do over again, she would do the same thing, because to fail to do so would be false, a rejection of everything she believed about herself.

"I had to try," she said. "I had to."

"I know," he said, and pulled her close to him.

O O O

Strangers and emergency vehicles moved in and out of Stormie's vision, and gradually she became aware that she had moved. Frank had gotten her up and steered her over to the sidewalk, a few meters away from the wide-eyed boy she'd noticed before. The boy was swaddled in a blanket, holding hands with a college-aged girl, probably his sister. Stormie nodded at him, and he nodded back.

She turned to Frank. She said, "This isn't exactly the way I had hoped our evening would end."

He chuckled, and kissed her temple. "Well, you have always been able to count on me for an exciting time."

Stormie snuggled a little deeper into Frank's embrace, and wished they were still down on the beach. She looked back out to sea. When they'd sat on the beach earlier, she had tried to imagine the oil well flares as candles for the two of them. The feel of cool sand in her fingers had been so much more pleasant than the sticky blood.

It seemed only moments ago that she had scooped up a handful of sand, said, "Hold out your hand," and drizzled some into Frank's palm. She had held her fingers together like the throat of an hourglass, and let the grains trickle through.

"And what is this for?" he'd asked.

She'd shrugged, and picked up another scoopful and let it drain out of her hand into his. "I don't know. This sand feels different from the sand back home. Heavier, maybe. But it's basically the same stuff. And I know we're not going to find 'sand' where we're going, and the whole concept of 'outside' will be gone, but I guess I hope it's not going to be such a different place."

"Well, that will be up to us, will it not?"

"Yeah." The colony's air and water supplies would be their responsibility; every breath of air, every drink of water would be dispensed from their hands as she was dispensing sand into Frank's. But it wouldn't be like picking it up off the beach and dropping it like milk and honey into the others' palms. As excited as she was at the prospect, sometimes the sheer scope of the effort daunted her. "I hope we're up to it," she'd said.

He had kissed her forehead. "We will be, my sweet."

The big firewoman interrupted Stormie's memory. "Folks, we have some bleach solution over here, and we need to make sure you wash your hands. You did a good thing, ma'am, but ... you don't have any open wounds on your hands, do you?"

Stormie resisted the urge to tell her she had been trained on the precautions and had tried to abide by them. She shook her head and said, "No, I don't think so."

Frank's embrace suddenly tightened. "What is it?" she asked him.

He leaned back and opened his hands. "I slipped, after I checked on the driver of that Ford, and put my hand down in some of the broken glass. I think I may still have some splinters." He shrugged. "My dress shoes were not made for running."

Frank's palm was coated in blood, but dotted here and there with glints of silver-white.

"Then I'll have an EMT come take a look," the woman said. "Meantime, Victor here will take care of you."

Stormie and Frank stayed next to the puke-yellow tanker for a long time. Stormie washed her hands until they hurt, washed up her arms to the elbows and beyond. Frank borrowed a tweezer from one of the firemen, plucked shards of glass from his palm, then scrubbed his hands as thoroughly as she had hers. They did not joke, they did not make small talk, and Stormie knew it was because he was afraid of the same thing she was: that the barest hint of a possibility of catching a major illness might invalidate their contract with the Asteroid Consortium and ground them forever.

The medical technician brought Frank's coat, itself darkened with the rider's blood, when he came over to look at Frank's hand. The two of them stepped away from the fire truck, but Stormie stayed and scrubbed her hands again.

The blood was gone, Stormie could see that under the bright lights, but she kept scrubbing. The backs of her hands were glossy, wet-looking and nearly as dark as dyed leather. She had scrubbed her palms almost pink; she studied the lines of her palms to ensure no speck of blood darkened them.

Her eyes and nose stung from the bleach, but to her it wasn't a strong enough solution. It didn't burn, and it needed to burn, to burn away her arrogance, her stupidity, her pride.

"That should be enough, ma'am," the fireman said as he doused her hands with clean water for the fifth time.

Stormie shook her head. "Have to be sure."

"I'm sure," he said. His voice was clear and firm, and when she looked at him so were his eyes. "You keep going at this rate, you won't have any skin left on your hands."

The fireman—Victor, she remembered—was young, blond and tanned, as opposite from her as he could be. Did he spend his off days surfing? She'd never tried. If they kicked her off the mission, maybe she'd get to.

Stormie shut down that line of thought. She wouldn't give up hope, not after coming this far. She would do anything to stay in the program, scrub her hands down to the bones if she had to.

Stormie looked her hands over once more. They were clean. Nothing she could do would get them cleaner. If she were a surgeon, she could do an open-heart procedure without gloves.

A few meters away, the EMT bandaged Frank's hand. If he hadn't held her hands, if she hadn't needed to hold on to him … if he caught something because of her impulsiveness, could she forgive herself?

She resisted the urge to wash her own hands again. She was afraid they weren't clean enough, and never would be.

CHAPTER FOUR

The Rumorsphere Has Picked Up on It

Sunday, 29 October 2034

Frank touched Stormie on the arm. "It appears the police want to speak to us," he said.

Vertigo stabbed Stormie in the back. She felt alternately as if everything had happened in an instant, and then that they'd been working at the scene for hours. Time was fluid, and the thought of talking with the police distorted her internal clock until it seemed like one of Dali's melting timepieces. Who needed Einstein and relativistic speeds to achieve time dilation?

A grey-haired police officer walked up and spoke briefly to Victor, the young blond fireman. Idly Stormie wondered if Victor was his first or last name. By the time the policeman got to Stormie and Frank he had his datapad ready to take their statements. Frank held out his own device, one of the newer-model CommPacts they had laid in for the mission, and as it transmitted his personal information the policeman looked at his readout for a long moment. "Pastorelli? You don't look Italian."

It was a comment they heard from time to time, usually with levity. Frank normally laughed it off, but now his voice sliced the air with a sharp edge. He said, "No, I suppose not." He leaned in and studied the policeman's nametag for a second. "In America, I find that heritage is not always apparent. Just as, Officer MacNeil, you do not sound Scottish. Our—"

"Okay, then, smartass. You don't *sound* Italian, either. Maybe I should be asking you for a green card."

"I do not understand why," Frank said. "You can verify with that data store that I am a citizen of the United States."

"Yeah, we'll see about that—"

Stormie pitched her voice in as close a match to her grandmother's as she could—one of the things she had picked up from Mother Mac that she most appreciated. "Officer? I presume your pad is recording our conversation—I'm certain my husband's is. You seem surprised that my husband would have an Italian family name. You don't mean to indicate any latent prejudice by that, do you? That would be … inappropriate, don't you think?"

Actually, she wasn't sure Frank was recording but it was worth the bluff. Officer MacNeil looked back and forth between the two of them, and snuck a look down at Frank's datapad as well.

The policeman said, "No, ma'am, that was just a poor joke on my part. I didn't mean anything by it."

Frank shook his head, and Stormie said, "No, I'm sure you didn't. My husband's father was a missionary. How they came by their name is a long story, but Frank came to this country when he was a teenager and his family still lives up in San Luis Obispo.

"We'd like to keep this interview brief, if possible. We're staying at the hotel down the street, and we're supposed to meet our business partner tomorrow morning."

"Your partner's name?"

Frank said, "James Fennerling, of The Paszek Group."

The officer made a note on his computer. He asked for Stormie's information, and Frank transmitted it from his CommPact because hers was in their hotel room.

Officer MacNeil asked, "Gale Pastorelli? That right?"

"Yes. But people call me 'Stormie.'" She hoped Frank wouldn't chime in with one of his many variations. Sometimes it was "Abbey Gale," sometimes "Gaelic," sometimes "Gale Force"—but Frank stayed silent.

The officer looked as if he wanted to ask about the spelling. Stormie clenched her stomach a little, and Frank tensed as well, but she took a deep breath and willed herself to relax. She'd told the story a thousand times, that she was born when her mother had evacuated from Charleston because of yet another hurricane, and one more telling wouldn't hurt. But Officer MacNeil just shrugged and said, "I guess I can see that." He made another notation on his datapad.

"Did either of you see the accident?"

Stormie and Frank said, "No," and "Yes," simultaneously. She looked at Frank, who shrugged.

"I was dancing around you, and watched it happen," he said. He described the action with quick movements of his hands. "I saw the first motorcycle swing into the oncoming lane—it was trying to pass the silver Ford. The second motorcycle followed, but the blue car was approaching. The car started to its right, to give them room, but the lead motorcycle sped up and went the same direction, toward the sidewalk. The car turned back, but the trailing motorcycle had split off and the car caught it in the rear wheel.

"I lost sight of the motorcycle then, because the blue car hit the Ford almost head-on. Then it looked as if the lead rider turned back to see what had happened. In the process, it pulled right into the path of that small van. The van tried to swerve, and after it hit the rider it ended up on the sidewalk there."

Officer MacNeil made another notation and asked what happened next. They explained what they had done, and the policeman was proper and polite through the rest of the interview. Relief sighed out of Stormie when Officer MacNeil said, "Okay, I think that's about it. The address and numbers are current, right? I heard you say you go back to Houston in a few days. If we have any more questions, I want to be able to get in touch with you."

"We had meetings earlier this week in San Diego," Frank said, "but we will be here in Santa Barbara until Wednesday."

"San Diego, huh?" The officer raised an eyebrow and began accessing his datapad faster. After a few seconds, he said, "Well, hell, if I'd checked the newsblogs I would've known who you were sooner." He turned his pad in their direction, so Stormie could see the screen.

MacNeil had pulled up an image of Stormie with her hands on the motorcycle rider's leg, over a caption that read, *Lunar Colony Candidate Molests Injured Motorcyclist.*

O O O

Jim Fennerling, Stormie and Frank's partner in Lunar Life Engineering and the primary champion and backer of their crazy venture, set aside his book and rubbed his eyes. Fatigue crept over him like a crawling insect, and though he couldn't quite fathom why, his stomach writhed as if something had crawled into it.

He closed his eyes, and the quick nausea spread up and down from just below his breastbone. Around him his home produced only its usual noises: the refrigerator hummed, the escapement of the old clock on the bookshelf ticked its mechanical tick. He breathed deep and nearly gagged on a waft of Kung Pao shrimp from the kitchen counter. Gradually the nausea spread enough that it thinned a little, the way ripples die out as they move across the surface of a pond. He took another deep breath and the nausea dissipated, and left him with only a general unease.

He looked around his living room to see if he could spot something wrong. Frozen faces stared back at him from all the same pictures, his retirement plaque from the Jet Propulsion Laboratory silently lauded his quarter century of service, his near-antique books and discs and magazines stood regimented in their precise, orderly rows.

A click, the furnace kicked on, and in the blast from the vent Meredith's Moon wobbled in its frozen orbit.

Jim wheeled over to the fake fireplace and looked up at the half-meter-wide silver-and-gold model spacecraft. Its gossamer web spread out from a silvered sphere, a pea-sized Sputnik, at its center; that central core crouched like a legless spider, ready to crawl out and snag some unsuspecting twenty-first century fly.

Tiny plastic dewdrops shimmered along the web's slender gold threads; the sheer veil suspended from the threads caught the breeze. The model strained against its moorings, anchored to the fake wooden ceiling beams and the cup hook screwed into the wallboard. It rocked back and forth and the thin film billowed in places, as if the craft flew while motionless. In a way, the real spacecraft did fly motionless: elevated above the Earth's orbit, suspended by light pressure, it led the Earth in its path around the Sun but always moved in lock step with the planet's motion. The real spacecraft's meter-wide central core controlled thousands of power collectors and sensors arrayed across the kilometers-wide solar sail web, as the vehicle maintained vigilant watch over the near-earth orbital environment.

Only Jim referred to the Solar Levitated Out-of-Ecliptic Forward Orbiter—"Forward" in the sense that it preceded the Earth as they orbited the Sun, and in tribute to the twentieth century space pioneer who originated the idea—as Meredith's Moon. Meredith worked out most of the orbital insertion and station-keeping routines as part of her doctoral work, with partial differential matrices and other advanced mathematics that Jim could never fathom. She took him once to see the vehicle under construction: the thin anti-static coveralls itched against his arm hairs, the papery booties crinkled as they walked, and the antiseptic isopropyl alcohol smell permeated the El Segundo factory. Meredith's pride shone in her eyes as she showed him the open silver globe and explained its mission in terms even an accountant could understand. Jim smiled so much at the wonder of seeing his daughter's dream made real before their eyes that his face hurt at the end of the tour.

Meredith never saw the launch. The brain tumor took her before the spacecraft even got into sine-vibration testing. Jim had brought the model of her artificial Moon back home when he cleaned out her student apartment.

The model shuddered in the air currents. Some dust dislodged from its lacy webbing, and the falling motes sparkled like tiny snowflakes in the light. Jim's eyes swam as dust fell into them.

He looked away, right into Meredith's happy eyes in her picture as Gale Pastorelli's maid of honor. She was only weeks away from dying, then, but she radiated joy all the same. If Meredith were still alive, Jim knew, she'd find a way to ship out with Gale and Frank. She'd stow away in their luggage if she couldn't wrangle a colony position for herself. So what if the Consortium only let married couples apply? Meredith would've snagged a suitable husband in order to land a spot in the program.

Maybe if Meredith was alive, Alyson wouldn't have gone the way she did.

Jim smacked the arm of his wheelchair. Where did this sudden attack of melancholy come from? What was he worried about? About seeing Gale and Frank tomorrow? He couldn't remember the last time he'd lost himself in pointless contemplations.

Meredith and Alyson smiled at him from inside another frame. From the time Meredith was fifteen, people who met them mistook them for sisters. They both enjoyed that, for altogether different reasons. And then Meredith faded, and Alyson followed.

Jim opened his eyes wide and stared at the blank television screen, to keep from envisioning Alyson's pallid face and vomit-coated blue lips. He gradually looked back at the picture and focused on the image of her, alive. He wondered why he kept the things he did; he hardly noticed them anymore, and when he did notice them they invariably hurt.

Maybe if Meredith was still alive, her mother would be, too. But maybe Alyson would have gone the same way, just at another time.

At least neither of them had to see me in this damn chair.

The furnace cut off. Jim watched the spacecraft model settle down until it hung still from its moorings as if it floated above his head.

How remarkable it would be to float so far above the Earth, to look down on the marble-sized globe and watch the silver clouds coalesce and dissolve over the blue surface, to be a sentinel guarding all of humanity instead of a wheelchair-bound paper-pusher living vicariously through his dead daughter's best friends. Nothing really floated in space, he knew: everything moved, ellipses in ellipses in ellipses without reference to any single, fixed point because there were no fixed points.

He was still thinking about that when the phone rang. His gut clenched; whatever was wrong was on the other end of the line. He steered himself over and picked up the receiver—he could not abide the room-filling phone pickups that some people had in their homes. Frank's name was on the little ID screen.

Not now. Not this late in the game.

"Hey, Frank," he said immediately. "Not getting cold feet, are you?"

"Hello, James," said Frank. "We may have a problem, my friend." Frank's voice was calm and his speech as formal as ever, but Jim sensed that he was serious.

"What kind of problem, Frank?"

"There was an automobile accident. The emergency crew has gotten us decontaminated and we have answered the police officer's questions, but the rumorsphere has picked up on it—"

Frank was still talking, but Jim's brain was stuck trying to process what he'd just heard. *Accident? Police? Emergency crew? Contaminated?* The phrase "breach of contract" ran through his head, and embarrassed him that he thought of money first, before the welfare of his friends. The habits of an accountant turned venture capitalist. And they *were* his friends now; at first they had only been Meredith's, but now he claimed them as his own.

"Frank, are you and Gale alright? Are you hurt?"

"I had some small pieces of glass in my hand, but otherwise I am unhurt. Stormie also is unhurt."

"What happened? How'd you get in an accident?"

Frank told him the story from the beginning. Jim's first impulse was to pace about the room; instead, he wheeled his chair one-handed into the kitchen and filled a glass with ice water from the refrigerator door. He drank while he listened.

"Where is Stormie now, Frank?"

"She is next to a fire wagon, talking with the police officer. She suspects whoever took her picture ran it through a face-recognition algorithm which matched her to the Asteroid Consortium. She is quite upset about the implications. She looks as if she may begin to wash her hands again."

Jim rubbed his face, trying to prioritize the potential problems; in school and in business he'd learned to consider all possible scenarios. Internet gossip was annoying but probably harmless; he would call Claire tonight and they could have some positive spin out in short order. "Decontamination," on the other hand, implied "contamination," and even though that might sound worse than it really was, it was likely to cause more trouble. He was no doctor, so he wasn't sure if his list was complete, but the scenarios that ran through his mind had frightening names like SARS, hepatitis, plague. He closed his eyes and tried to concentrate. If he could eliminate the worst-case scenario, then they could work their way to the no-problem scenario.

"Okay, Frank," he said. "Do the police or the hospital types have any reason to think that the lady Stormie was helping had a disease? HIV, maybe, or something worse?"

"I do not know. They moved her away and a few moments ago a helicopter arrived to transport her."

"Okay, I can call my brother-in-law and get him to dig into that. Did you ever meet Bruce? He's a detective—he should be able to detect something for us. Meanwhile, ask one of the EMTs to take blood samples from you and Stormie. It's too soon for anything to show up, but we'll have it analyzed independently, just to make sure. Better yet, see if they'll take two samples: one for us to analyze and one for them to keep in an official chain of custody."

"Is that necessary?"

"I don't know. Maybe not. I hope not. What I do know is that the contract is pretty specific about timing and disease exposures and incubation periods and such. I'll have to dig into the details, but if we don't make the milestones we forfeit our payments, and it's clear that you both have to be in good health before we send you to Utah. I figure they'll poke and prod you again when you get down in the mine. It may help to have some test results of our own, even if we don't need them. It's best, of course, if the woman Gale was helping was clean. Pity you don't know her name."

"I am sorry, my friend," Frank said. "We did not intend to cause so much trouble."

Jim laughed, a little. "Oh, no, of course not. I guess you had to step in and help, didn't you?"

After a slight pause, Frank said, "Yes, of course. We could not stand by and do nothing."

"Couldn't? You mean, 'wouldn't.' I don't guess many people stepped out of the crowd. Were you two the first ones to help?"

28

Another slight hesitation on Frank's part. "I do not know. Perhaps there were one or two others."

The pauses told Jim everything he needed to know: Frank wouldn't have claimed to be first on the scene even if he was—he was the most humble person Jim had ever met—but it was almost certain that Frank wasn't actually first. Gale was, and probably in such a way that she earned her "Stormie" nickname. She would've seen what needed to be done and jumped in to do it while Frank was still taking stock of the situation. That's why they made a good team: his tendency to deliberate usually kept her from leaping too far before she'd looked. Usually.

"Right," Jim said. "It's a pretty safe bet you were the first. I've known you a long time, Frank, and you've never been one to stand idly by when someone needed help. Although in a case like this I bet you were just trying to keep up with that crazy wife of yours."

Jim took the silence on the other end of the line for assent. "Don't worry about it, Frank. It'll all work out. Meanwhile, get that blood sample. If the EMTs won't do it, ask them where the nearest Urgent Care is and go there. Then try to get some sleep, and I'll see you at breakfast as planned. Right now I've got to call my no-good brother-in-law about checking that woman's test results."

"All right, James. Thank you, and again I am sorry."

Jim said good-bye and put his water glass on the counter. He got a beer out of the refrigerator and took a long drink before he scrolled down to his sister's number.

CHAPTER FIVE

Picophages Ready for Delivery

Tuesday, 31 October 2034

Stormie and Frank spent Monday and Tuesday in videoteleconferences with Asteroid Consortium contract managers and engineers from the Long Beach headquarters and smaller contract engineering offices. From a conference room at UC-Santa Barbara that Jim had booked, they reviewed plant life growth projections, water reclamation rates, and the schedule for the current lunar setup mission, in addition to air and water system maintenance schedules and some negotiable elements of their statement of work. She smiled at every agenda item they ticked off.

"That looks like it," Antonio Harter, the engineering director, said. "Glad you hobnobbin' hero-types were able to condescend to help us out these last two days."

Stormie shook her head, but had given up responding to the jibes. They derived from a minor media coup Jim had shown off at breakfast Monday morning, when *Lunar Contractor Saves Princess's Life* had beaten out the more salacious interpretations that had permeated the Net. Jim seemed inordinately pleased that the girl Stormie had helped turned out to be royalty, albeit from a small province in Pakistan.

"Good work today," she told Frank after they signed off.

"And you," he said, gathering her in for a kiss. "Though the day is not yet over."

"I know. Do you think Jim will miss us if we don't go?"

Not that she wanted to offend the VCs who were bankrolling their lunar venture: their money magic bought and paid for the dream, and she wondered sometimes how Jim had gotten them to invest in it. Those would-be tycoons squeezed turnips until they bled and then sold the blood to the Red Cross. She wasn't sure she wanted to spend the evening schmoozing them.

"I think you should check your messages. He seemed quite insistent."

She wrestled her CommPact out of her bag once they got in their rented Dragonelle-T/F to go back to the hotel. Jim's e-mail was titled, "The invitation I told you about." It started with "There's a surprise for you at the hotel," followed by a montage of images from perhaps a dozen movie and television franchises, each image followed by a similar one featuring costumed partygoers.

"You've got to be kidding," she said.

Frank grinned. "I am sure it will be an enjoyable affair."

At the bottom of the final screen listing the party time and location, Jim had added "Don't let me down" in faux script on a virtual Post-It Note. Stormie paged back through the images.

"Very retro," she said.

"I suspect James would say, 'vintage.'"

O O O

Almost an hour late, thanks to crushing traffic on the 101, they pulled into the parking area. When Frank opened the car door, the night air ran cold fingers up Stormie's thighs. *Damn '60s mini-dress.*

Stormie stopped for a moment and savored the faint smell of eucalyptus, mixed with traces of scrub pine. She put her hand on Frank's arm and they walked up the long driveway already lined with vehicles.

"Had we been on time," Frank said, "we would not have to walk so far."

Stormie put her thumb against his side and pressed; his tickle reflex kicked him into a little hop. "It's your fault," she said. "You had to be different."

They rounded the last curve before the house, a Georgian-style home with a columned portico that sported strands of electric jack-o-lantern lights. Elaborate real jack-o-lanterns flanked the steps.

They stepped onto the walkway up to the steps, and someone called, "The Pastorellis are here!"

A couple of seconds later, the theme from the original *Star Trek* began playing through hidden speakers.

"I don't know which is worse," Stormie said, "this costume Jim sent, or that I let you talk me into wearing it."

Frank laughed, and exaggerated his accent a little. "You will be the hit of the party, my dear. Listen to the music—you are the star of the evening, and you have not even walked in the door."

She tried to smile, tried to display the joy that Frank's precise diction and gentle manner usually elicited, but the gust of cool wind that found its way up her costume prevented her. She would have preferred a longer skirt, but tonight she was Lieutenant Uhura, from the authentic earpiece down to the shiny boots. Frank stood for a second and admired her; she tugged the uniform's hem down as far as it could go.

"Besides," he said, "you look better than Nichelle Nichols ever did."

Now she did frown—she was too tall and too thin and too dark to compare to the original or the 21st century Uhura.

Frank tilted his head and bowed slightly. Then he stepped back, opened his arms, motioned theatrically toward his chest, and said, "And you have the whole of the galaxy at your command."

She shook her head at her handiwork, and the reason they were late to the party: a fair representation of the Milky Way galaxy, painted in several hundred white dots that spread from the base of his throat to his belly button. Above his heart, where most people put the nametags they got at conferences, she had added yellow lettering that declared, "You are here," with an arrow pointing to a yellow dot on the outer edge of one of the spiral arms.

Frank made a decent canvas, even if his skin was not as dark as space, and she was glad he wanted to wear her amateur artwork. He would have looked great in the Captain Sisko uniform that Jim had sent for him, but Frank wanted something original. And Stormie had taken special pleasure whenever she painted a spot that tickled him.

"Yeah, but it's such a backward galaxy," Stormie said. "Nobody else wanted it."

She started up the steps, and turned around when he didn't follow. Frank wore the expression of a scolded puppy, but it didn't fit him: he was bad at play-acting.

"Cut it out, Frank. Galaxy at my command? Right. First of all, I'm just a lieutenant. Second, I think you really want the co-eds to ogle your bare chest."

He smiled. "That never occurred to me, but it does seem like a nice fringe benefit." He stepped up and took her hand to lead her into the house. With her other hand she poked him about where his appendix was. He jumped and laughed.

Stormie said, "You watch yourself, Mr. Galaxy, or you'll see how commanding I can be."

Frank looked up toward the second story of the house. After a moment he smiled and quoted,

"Thou art my life, my love, my heart,
The very eyes of me;
And hast command of every part,
To live and die for thee."

"Come here, galaxy man," Stormie said, and kissed him as the last bars of the *Star Trek* theme played.

The small crowd in the living room and down the hallway clapped as they entered. Stormie tugged again at her hem.

They exchanged pleasantries with and accepted drinks from people they hardly knew, and looked for their host. Most of the guests were Jim's friends, either from his years at the Jet Propulsion Laboratory or from the venture capital firm he had joined in '29. One of The Paszek Group partners owned the house, which was built on what had been part of Gaviota State Park until the state of

California sold some of its public lands to extricate itself from yet another budget crisis.

They moved from room to room, admiring the costumes and chatting. Most of the costumes would fit in at any science fiction convention: primarily vintage *Star Trek* like Stormie's, plus characters from the other iterations, with a few *Star Wars* and *Firefly* and *Vorkosigan Chronicles* costumes as well. A few people had been more daring, like the stunning Shiva with fully articulating multiple arms or the understated but elegant anime princess who smelled of cinnamon. Everyone recognized Frank and Stormie, and either congratulated them for saving the princess or made small talk about how exciting it would be once they were working on the Moon. Stormie tried to be gracious, but the guests were too obsequious for her taste.

After nearly an hour, they found Jim in one corner of an office in the back of the house.

Jim Fennerling looked hideous. His normally salt-and-pepper hair was pewter grey and half his face looked melted. He had only one eye open, and that had a filmy cataract over the iris—an eggshell-colored contact lens, probably. His wheelchair was covered with a shiny black plastic housing that encapsulated him from his shoulders to the floor. On the front of the carapace, three large lights nestled close to his chest in a horizontal row.

"Great costume, Jim," Stormie said. "Whoever did your makeup is a pro."

Jim kept his head stiff; he didn't turn or otherwise acknowledge her. The center light on his chair lit up for a second, accompanied by an audible tone.

"Now I get why you ordered this uniform for me," she said. "So how's it going?"

Jim did not respond. Stormie started to ask again, but Frank stepped forward and said, "Please excuse the lieutenant, Captain Pike. She forgot that your responses are limited to yes and no. Are you well?"

The light lit again.

"Once for yes," Frank said.

"I know how it works," Stormie said. "I just didn't think he was going to stay in character the whole time. If we have to play twenty questions, that's going to get old really quick." She turned to the ersatz Captain Christopher Pike, late of his encounter with the mysterious delta rays, and said, "What about it, Jim?"

The corner of Jim's mouth twitched, as if he wanted to smile. Stormie admired his self-control, but only for a second.

"Are you going to talk to me, Jim? With your mouth?"

The light blinked, twice: no.

"Have it your way," Stormie said, and started out of the room.

"Okay, Stormie," Jim said. He accented the words with great exhalations to highlight his disappointment. "You're no fun."

Stormie turned, and a smile formed on her lips. It was unusual enough for Jim to use her nickname, but she was thrilled to hear him talk about fun. The multiple miseries he had endured the past few years had taken their toll.

"Nice party," she said.

Jim smiled through the makeup. "Glad you think so. Might be nicer if people would wear the costumes that were picked out for them."

"I thought it went against the canon," Frank said. "Now, there was the crewman from 'The Man Trap' episode—"

"Dear God, I forgot how seriously some of you take this stuff."

Stormie and Frank looked at each other; Frank tilted his head, furrowed his brow, and gestured to Jim's elaborate wheelchair costume. Stormie struggled not to smile.

"Would that be considered irony?" Frank asked.

"A Freudian slip?" said Stormie.

"Okay, that's enough." Jim might have been blushing underneath the makeup.

"Projection, maybe?" asked Stormie. Yes, Jim's ears were definitely red.

"Power it down, you two," Jim said. "I give up. How did the meetings go today?"

"Pretty well," Stormie said. "We should finish up early tomorrow, which is good because we need to get back. We've got a lot of closeouts on the Huntsville contract before we shut down to go underground—"

"I need to talk to you about that," Jim said. His tone didn't change, but he spoke with an authority that stripped Stormie of her smile. "It seems we have a problem."

Jim popped open a panel on the right side of his wheelchair's "costume," and carried a drink to his lips. Ice clinked in the wide glass as he drained the cocktail. The half-melted cubes settled on top of what looked like a slice of orange.

Stormie fumbled with the drink in her hand, and then finished it in one gulp. It had been fruity and flavorful, but now it was just cold.

Frank asked, "What kind of problem, James?"

"The kind that will keep you out of training, and ground you if we don't take care of it." He rolled over to the desk. "Get that door, will you, Frank? Gale, would you reach my tablet out of this bag?" He bumped the front of his chair gently against the dark blue canvas case.

Stormie propped up the tablet where Jim could reach it—his Christopher Pike costume kept him from being able to roll under the desk—and he typed his password in one-handed. He talked while he opened documents.

"Actually, we have two problems." He pulled up a picture of Princess Sinta Varramull, the girl Stormie had helped. "Both related to your patient. It seems she has left the country."

Stormie asked, "Why is that our problem?"

"Because it makes it damn hard to get additional blood samples from her."

Stormie looked at Frank, but he seemed as puzzled as she was. "Why do we need more blood from her?"

Jim opened a file with some tabulated figures on it, slid it out of the way and opened two more in quick succession. "Because she seems to have been one very sick girl, and I'd rather this be a case of 'false positive' than 'positive.'"

With every word Stormie's world collapsed a little, like a star becoming a black hole, her dreams slipping along the event horizon on the edge of oblivion. Frank stepped toward her and took her hand.

"What does she have, James?" Frank asked.

"My brother-in-law is trying to get us some of her blood, enough to run our own tests," he said. "If we can, we'll run tests all the way down to electron micro ... microscopy, if we have to.

"Bruce did some digging on the heiress or princess or whatever she is, and found out she'd spent time in some very odd places. Apparently she was some sort of jet-setter. We may be lucky that she wasn't carrying some kind of Madagascar jungle flu.

"But what she *does* have is a strain of HPV—human papillomavirus. That normally wouldn't be a show-stopper, lots of people have it, but this variety is different. Somewhere in this file they specify what kind it is, but I can't find it right now. All I know is it's a mutation, pernicious and drug-resistant, and because of that, if either of you got it, it would keep you out of the training Cave. And that would mean you wouldn't make your launch, which would mean we'd default on the contract and the game would be over for us. I don't know what the AC would do—it's not as if they could find another company right away to run the environmental setup—but we can't afford to pay the penalties they'd impose."

Laughter and voices trickled in under the door jamb, but otherwise all was silent.

After a minute, Stormie said, "You said there were two problems."

"Yeah, as if one wasn't enough. The other thing Bruce found is that the princess's husband has hepatitis." Jim opened a couple of reference windows on his computer. "I've done a lot of reading on infectious diseases over the last few hours. Hepatitis isn't so bad compared to other things that can be transmitted by blood. Here's one—Rift Valley fever—and there's American ... hell, I can barely say it ... trypanosomiasis. Those are real nasty, whereas millions, maybe billions, of people have hepatitis and live okay lives. But those people aren't trying to colonize the Moon, and don't have contracts that make them accountable to the Asteroid Consortium."

"How about our blood tests, Jim?"

"So far, your panels are clean. Whether that's going to make a difference is anybody's guess."

"What do you mean? It's got to make a difference. If we're not sick—"

"They may not care," Jim said, and held up his free hand. "I'm sorry, Gale, but that's the truth of it. We have test results that may be accurate but may not be conclusive. They have photos of you practically lathering your arms with this woman's blood, and your own statements that Frank had a cut on his hand and got some of the same blood on that hand. That's not an equitable transaction.

"I don't know what else to tell you. It's a risk management decision, and even though you, Frank, and I may be willing to take the risk I'm not sure the rest of them will be."

Stormie wished for a fresh drink.

Frank said in a soft voice, "Is there anything we can do, to allay their concerns?" Stormie smiled at the loyalty, dependability, and love in his question.

Their partner looked back and forth between them, his face unreadable beneath his makeup. "I've talked to the contract managers about getting you both pico-scrubbed. They may want to couple that with a series of interferon treatments." He pulled up a new set of documents on his tablet. "I took the liberty of getting picophages ready for delivery from Low-Gee to San Diego. I've got all the paperwork ready for your authorizations, and then it'll take a week or more to get the shipment processed and de-orbited.

"I know this isn't a happy prospect, and it's coming down all at once. While you two were ironing out technical details today, this is what I was doing: trying to keep our contract alive. And if we're going to do anything, we need to do it soon. Do you two want to step out on the porch, or take a walk to talk about it?"

Pressure built in Stormie's chest, but words would not come. Frank's eyes radiated strength and resolution that she didn't feel she deserved. She shook her head.

Frank said, "I believe Stormie means that talking about it is unnecessary, if we have no choice about the course of action."

She nodded.

"Are you sure?"

Stormie wanted to shout at Jim for even asking the question. They'd already given so much, mortgaged everything, to earn their way into the colony; how could they stop now? Whatever it would take to stay on the roster, to build a better future together, she would do it. Jim should know that by now.

Frank put his arm around her shoulder, and she snaked her own around his waist. He said, "If I recall from the news stories about Low-Gee's pico-cure, James, this new treatment is still experimental."

"Yeah, and break-the-bank expensive, and intensely painful."

Stormie trembled a little, not so much in fear of whatever experimental technological treatment Jim had in mind, but in fear of sabotaging the plans they had worked so hard to achieve. She compressed the fear, in hopes of turning it into diamond-hard resolve.

Stormie looked up at Frank. "What do you want to do?"

He knew what she wanted. She would never easily give up their crazy dream of stepping out toward the stars together. She would face this challenge and suffer the consequences, whatever they might be. She hoped Frank would, too. She needed him to, for so many reasons.

Frank deliberated for only a moment. He hugged her a bit closer, and turned to Jim. "Will an electronic signature be sufficient?" he asked.

CHAPTER SIX

The Maddening Desire

*Wednesday, 8 November 2034
Lunar Setup Mission II, Day 8*

Van Richards couldn't see the stars, but he knew they were there and that was enough.

It should've been dark enough in the lunar night, even with the Earth glowing up above, to see the stars—but the worklights all around were too much. Even the head-up display in his helmet washed out any ambient light from the distance of space.

Van didn't care: he loved it, whether he ever saw any star except the Sun again. He was convinced he was in the right place, with the solemn assurance of a recent convert to the religion of his choice. This was his purpose, his calling.

Okay, maybe not this particular job: opening what, at the moment, was essentially a shipping crate bigger than a Greyhound bus. He was unscrewing the dozen bolts that held down the man-sized access cover: an unglamorous task by any standard. But the fact that the crate was on the surface of the Moon aligned it with his purpose. The thing that solidified his confidence that this was what and where he was meant to be, however, was knowing that within a year he and Barbara would both be here.

Van's partner at the moment was Roy Chesterfield, the crew foreman. Roy had been a crewmember on the first setup mission before being selected as foreman for the second; his North London accent came through louder and clearer over work channel one than his words. "How are we doing, Van?" he said.

"Gooder 'n snuff," Van said, putting as much of a drawl in as he could. "Best laydown yet."

"You think we've topped out the learning curve, finally?"

"No, pretty soon we'll be measuring our errors in microns."

It had been the cleanest installation yet of the prefabricated shelter units. The shelters had semi-circular cross-sections, so that those that were entrenched close to the surface and covered over with lunar soil for radiation protection looked something like Quonset huts. The exceptions were the central dome about eight meters across and six high that the first setup mission had erected, and the garage units that had big airlocks along their sides.

"Keep it up, Van, and we'll have you digging all the trenches."

"Alright by me, boss. I like driving the big machines."

"Don't we all," Roy said. "But the rest are going to be even harder. Coming up behind you now. Spot me while I back up, if you don't mind?"

Van hopped up the slight incline to the top of the trench. Calling anything that was only a meter-and-a-half deep at its deepest point a "trench" seemed overly generous, but that was the convention. The incline to the surface was so slight that it took three hops to cover the length of it. There would be more digging out and even some rock hauling for the next few shelters, since the Consortium hadn't gotten the best real estate in the lottery/buyout the U.N. had brokered. They bought some of the less desirable pieces of property and spent more to develop theirs fast, rather than buying better property that they'd have to wait longer to develop. It made the work harder, especially if they had to do any blasting— setting the little shaped charges to break up boulders was tedious enough, but setting up shields to keep the fragments contained was the worst—

But the signature element was that they were further along in getting established on the Moon, and that made all the difference.

Van counted down the meters until Roy had the flatbed MPV—multi-purpose vehicle—in place with plenty of maneuver room. Roy climbed down from the "cab," which was little more than a roll cage. Only the big truck had a pressurized cabin.

"Ready to open 'er up?" Van asked.

"We'd better be. Henry and Jovelyn should have the junction hooked up to the other end in an hour, and have power up a little after that. It'll take a few more hours to hook up the ductwork and piping, so pressure check and systems check will have to wait until next shift. Still, we'll have to work fast to get a path cleared in there."

"Fair enough," Van said, and unscrewed the last two bolts.

Roy tugged on the access cover but it didn't come free. "It's stuck," he said. "Give me a hand."

Van grabbed one handle and pulled when Roy counted three. The access cover resisted, the way a vacuum-sealed lid didn't want to come off a jar. But that didn't make any sense, because the cover had vacuum on either side of it.

The cover vibrated through Van's glove as it came free a second later. Roy carried it to the side; they would find a good use for it somewhere.

Van looked inside. As expected, the stack of transit cases blocked the narrow corridor up to the low ceiling. The shelter was packed from end to end along its entire length, just like all the others. Heavy webbing held all the gear in place against the stresses and vibrations of launch, landing, and emplacement. Van adjusted a worklight for a better look.

Everything—the stacked crates, the straps, even the floor—reflected back shimmering white. He cursed.

"What's the matter?" Roy asked.

"Looks like it snowed in here," Van said. He hung the worklight on the inner pressure door—open for shipping, it would seal against the hatchway when the shelter was aired in—and stepped inside. He wiped a thin film of ice off the nearest transit case. "We've got ice."

"How much?"

"Can't tell. Very thin layer, all over everything. Not whiskers like rime ice, just a thin sheet of crystals." He started releasing the webbing straps. "I don't think it'll slow us down any, I just wonder where the water came from. Shouldn't be from the plumbing, unless some idiot charged the system before they sealed everything up."

"Didn't you read the inventory?"

Van didn't bother answering. Of course he didn't read the inventory; why clog up his brain with what was packed in the thing when they were just going to empty it and rearrange everything anyway?

"This prefab's another farm module," Roy said. "It has some tooling for the garage that we can take out and stage, some crates of spare suits, and a few other small things, but it's supposed to have four water tanks. Not bladders, but tanks, filled. Do you suppose one of them cracked?"

"Don't know what else it could be," Van said, "or how much we'll lose when this ice sublimates away." He had the webbing undone and pulled the first transit case down from the stack. He composed a litany of complaints as he pulled the case backward through the hatch. "Damn low-bid outfit. I bet they didn't assemble the tank right, left a weak weld or something. Or are they composite tanks, filament-wound?" Roy grabbed the other end of the crate and together the two of them made their way up the incline. Van barely paused in his diatribe; he didn't leave time for a response. "Maybe a thin spot, or some other defect. Then I bet when they filled the tank they didn't leave enough ullage in it. Who knows how many times that water froze and thawed since it launched? Tank probably busted when the water froze and expanded, or when the whole package heated up in the sunlight—"

"Are you quite finished?" Roy asked as they swung the case onto the back of the flatbed.

"No. These things always make me wonder what else we're going to find messed up." Van hadn't been impressed with the general workmanship of some of the equipment they used, and it wasn't as if all of the Consortium's plans had worked without a hitch. The third set of prefab shelters had crashed instead of soft-landing; the AC built another set and worked it into the supply launch schedule, but that original set remained a twisted hunk of scrap about forty kilometers northwest of the colony on the north rim of Campanus Crater. Eventually it would be salvaged; maybe when Van came back as a colonist. "I bet one of those water tanks cracked. Water couldn't escape like from a comet. It got deposited and stuck by surface tension, then froze—"

"Enough, please, Mr. Richards." Roy's sigh carried over the radio. "We've a lot of work to do, so let's get to it."

Van frowned. Frustration simmered in his gut—this time ice in the shelter, the time before a broken tool, before that a defective control unit. He knew one day something big would go wrong, and hated giving in to the thought because it smothered little bits of his enthusiasm. He took a deep breath and forced himself to smile. "Aw, Roy," he said, "why d'you want to take all the fun out of work?"

O O O

"Good work today," Shay Nakamura said as he stepped through the hatch. His slight Japanese accent echoed in the dome that most of the setup crew had taken to calling "Grand Central." Grace Teliopolous, for some reason, preferred to call it the "pimple."

Van looked up from his bowl of reconstituted potato soup. It was thick, the way he liked it—he never added as much water as the instructions called for—and a few good shots of Texas Pete gave it enough flavor to make up for the slightly pasty taste and feel. It helped overpower the usual stale locker-room-and-sewer-gas smell, too. He hoped once more of the farm units were up and running the air would clear; and he'd have to make sure some hot peppers got planted, as backup.

"Thanks," Van said. Despite the way he'd dogged Van during their first orbits, Shay was a good guy, even if he was the setup mission commander. "Didn't run into too many rocks, so the trenching went pretty easily."

Shay pulled a packet out of the cabinet, tore off the cover, and tossed the pack in the oven. He sat down opposite Van while his dinner heated, picked up a deck of cards, and without shuffling began laying out a hand of solitaire.

"Why do you do that?" Van asked.

"What?"

Van sighed. He reached into the side pocket of his coveralls and withdrew his datapad. "See this? I know you have one, and if you like I can transfer about a hundred different versions of solitaire or any other game you want to play."

Shay shook his head. "I like the feel of shuffling cards. I like the sound they make."

"I bet I can find that sound on here, too, and you can program it to play the sound whenever it starts a new game."

Shay laid the three of hearts on the four of clubs, with a little thwack as he released the corner of the card. "Yeah, that'll be authentic."

"I bet you still read books on paper, too, don't you?"

"I have one or two," Shay admitted. "You might try it sometime. Expand your horizons."

"I've got the widest horizons of anybody I know," Van said.

"I don't even know what that means."

"Neither do I."

Shay glanced up toward the high windows. "Whatever."

Van didn't like the emptiness in Shay's eyes. "Something eating at you?"

Shay played two more cards before answering. "They lost one of the one-way-trippers yesterday."

"Anybody you know?"

"No."

"Still," Van said, "I'm sorry to hear about that." If Van had been single he would have thrown in with that bunch, but he'd known better than even to apply. Barbara would have skinned him alive if he'd volunteered to go to Mars knowing he would die there. He didn't understand her reluctance; you had to die somewhere. "What happened, do you know?"

Shay shook his head and played another card. "No, they just posted the notice. Kind of brings the issue of risk into the spotlight."

Van nodded, but only out of courtesy. He refused to dwell on risks. Risk management was Barbara's specialty.

"Probably best to concentrate on what's front and center, things we can control. Which reminds me: you were just telling me what a good job I did today."

One corner of Shay's mouth twitched upward; not much, but enough. "Yes, I was," he said. "And as long as you keep laying down shelters as smooth as that last one, we might even get back on schedule."

Van grinned a little in response, but he shook his head. "Don't count on it."

"I'm not. Even if we weren't starting to creep up on the crater's edge, Murphy always shows up to 'help.' Like losing that water tank—that's going to hurt."

"How many times you think it froze and thawed?"

"Many. A few times while it was en route, and it's been on the surface for four months. Do you recall how it was oriented before we split it?"

Van hadn't been on the split crew for that module. Each habitat had been launched and soft-landed as a set of two, joined base-to-base with another habitat, to form a complete cylinder; the setup crews split them apart—like splitting a big log into two perfect halves, except of course they had to be a lot more careful—so they could be rotated and planted flat side down. It was a delicate maneuver, even with the support cradles and rigging, because the prefabs were monstrous big. They were small enough on the inside—especially filled as they were with everything the Consortium could cram into them—but they were still a little over five meters wide and nearly thirty meters long.

"I wouldn't know, Shay," Van said. "Even if I'd been on duty for that split, I probably wouldn't remember. Everything's starting to run together in my mind."

"Is that why you didn't take down your observations of the ice today? I didn't see any details in your log."

"No," Van said, "it was more important to get the unloading done." He didn't add that he hated the "typing mode" built into the suits; the gloves had feedback sensors that let you do touch typing by just wiggling your fingers, but Van had trouble getting it to work. Especially trying to contort his fingers for the SHIFT function—

•

that was the worst. "I took a couple of images, and I'll write up a report before I rack out."

They had been on the Moon just over a week, but Van was tired enough that sometimes it seemed like a month. Murphy's Law had conspired, among other things, to temporarily shut down the furnaces in the unit that processed metal-oxide-rich layers scraped from Mare Nubium into alloys and oxygen—officially the Automated Regolith Processor, Oxygen Extraction and Smelting—which put them behind schedule on pressurizing the habitats. They were also behind schedule because they were still finishing up the first setup team's unfinished tasks. That was no surprise: all the corporate-built schedules were so ambitious that they weren't just success-oriented, they assumed success. It produced a near-impossible workload and added to Van's creeping sense of frustration. Nobody minded pulling extra duty, least of all Van, but it was easy to get discouraged when their progress still left so many things to do. And when he had to write reports about every little thing.

Van yawned. "So tell me some good news, Shay. How're Oskar and Scooter doing?" Two days ago the pair had flown to Faustini Crater at the lunar south pole, where the first survey team had set up the Lunar Ice Collection and Extraction Operations Module: an automated processor that extracted ice microgram by microgram from dust collected from the crater floor, and compressed the ice into blocks for later recovery. There were no polar oases of ice like people back in the 20th century had hoped, and again the AC had not gotten the best of the available sources, but the surveys showed they would be able to process enough to keep the colony going. The LICEOM, pronounced "lyceum," was powered by an Advanced Radioisotope Generator—officially Lunar Power Plant, Nuclear, number 2—installed on the crater floor in perpetual darkness. Since the Lunar Suborbital Vehicle—LSOV—wouldn't always be available for ice runs, and everyone hoped the loads would mass more than its capacity anyway, Oskar and Scooter were surveying and blasting a route so teams could drive down into the crater to collect the ice.

"Oskar's last message said he thinks it'll take five or six days to do the main blasting. Then they should be able to grade and fuse a path at least partway up from the crater floor. He's not sure they'll get to the top, and they definitely won't get started on the outer wall."

Van nodded. "If there's a way to make it happen, Scooter'll find it. He's the best. Hope he waves at the yokels on the Shackleton rim while he's down there.

"On another subject, you gonna make us draw straws again to see who gets to go next time? I'm still happy to volunteer."

"I'm sure you are," Shay said. He checked on his food, stirred it around a little, and put it back in the oven. Van coughed; Shay was warming up the tuna-like casserole that Van always avoided. It smelled like tuna the way a dairy farm smells like milk.

Shay came back to the table and said, "What's that about, anyway? You trying to score points with the bosses, always volunteering for things?"

Van wasn't sure how to express his sense of urgency, the maddening desire to get each job done quickly and right. Sometimes his hands itched to be put to work, and he knew from past experience that when that happened he had to do something right or he might end up doing something wrong.

"As cute as I think you are, Shay, I'm really not trying to kiss up to you. I just get antsy sitting around for too long. I feel like I need to be doing something, so I may as well work. Never mind. Got any other news?"

"Heard that all is well on the *Forty-Niner*. They're on track to rendezvous with Aten-Galliani in early December."

Van nodded. *Forty-Niner* was the second of the Asteroid Consortium's prospecting ships; the first, with the comfortably uncreative name *Prospector*, had already rendezvoused with Aten-Ichijouji and was on its way back to the Earth-Moon System. The ships were originally supposed to be named *Prospector I* and *II*, until elementary school students in San Francisco collected thousands of signatures on a petition asking the AC to name the second ship after those who went west during the Gold Rush. The asteroids' double names at least made some kind of simplistic sense. They combined their type—Aten asteroids crossed the Earth's orbit from time to time—and their discoverers.

Van had considered trying for the asteroid mission, but after taking over a day to get used to freefall on the way to the Moon he was just as glad to be on the ground support side of things for now. Plus, *Prospector* had been out almost eighteen months—a little too long to be cooped up with just three other people. Their first shipment of ore and ammonia, sent back on a different orbital track than either the ship or the asteroid itself, had been captured a month before.

"*Prospector* still due back next month, too?" Van asked. The ship was supposed to return just before the new year; the Aten-Ichijouji asteroid was supposed to be captured—or near enough—near L-4, the Earth-leading Lagrange point, five months later.

"Haven't heard anything different." Shay pushed aside his game, retrieved his meal, and sat back down. They ate in silence.

Van had just scraped the last of his soup from the bowl when the hatch opened and Henry Crafts came in. He was a compact, powerful fellow from Tullahoma, Tennessee. Like Van, Henry was another "grunt" on the lunar setup mission. Nominally, the five grunts—Van, Henry, Jovelyn Nguyen, Grace Teliopolous, and Scooter Mast—worked for the three bosses: Shay, Oskar, and Roy. Everyone deferred to Shay but he didn't stand on ceremony; in practice, what hierarchy existed didn't come into play very much except when Oskar was in charge of something. Of all the setup crew, though, Van got along with Henry the best: he didn't take himself too seriously, the way some of the others did.

"Hey, Henry, Shay was just telling me the *Forty-Niner*'s flying true. Didn't I hear from Grace that you were going into the mines once we're all done?"

Henry sat down and looked skeptically at Shay's meal. "Not if I can help it," he said. "I like flying too much to become a mole. I'm hoping to run one of the ferries."

"So you're just going to sit on your hands for the time being? They won't be making regular runs for two years or more."

"No, it'll be sooner than that," Henry said. "If the government was running this show, maybe it would take so long. They could drag things out forever and just keep asking for more money. But the AC's got to turn a profit soon or one of the other outfit's going to raid them."

Shay said, "You think one of the other Horsemen will be able to take Hansen down?"

Van took his bowl to the sink and wiped it clean. He wasn't that interested in Morris Hansen's wheelings and dealings, or in any of the other space entrepreneurs the media had dubbed the "Four Horsemen." He knew all he needed to know: Hansen, who once quipped that "Anybody should be willing to risk a few billion if they stand to make a trillion," was the driving force behind the Asteroid Consortium, the wide-reaching multinational that planned to exploit its two asteroids and was setting up the lunar colony as its mining camp. The other big players also reached across national borders and were headed by equally flamboyant people: Bhuresh Golgawethy of Extra-Solar; Ferdinand Garcia Vasquez Albierto of Low-Gee Processing, Ltd.; and Alistair MacInnis of Orbital Salvage & Recovery.

He interrupted Henry and Shay's discussion of international—interplanetary?—high finance. "This is fascinating, guys, but I'm beat like a bad dog, and tomorrow's only six hours away. Holler if you need me."

The other two barely missed a beat as Van headed for his rack.

CHAPTER SEVEN

Time Yet for a Hundred Indecisions

Sunday, 12 November 2034

The only warm color in the room was the red-brown ribbon of blood that flowed through translucent plastic tubing from Stormie's right arm to the scanner and back again.

The rest of the antiseptic room blazed cold under the fluorescent lights: the row of cabinets labeled with machine-like precision, the stainless steel table with its orderly array of implements, the ubiquitous anatomy poster. The IV drip into her left arm was clear as ice water. Even the scanning and filtration unit itself, squat and boxy in its cream-colored housing with sky blue faceplate, seemed unwarmed though her blood flowed through it.

Over-conditioned air bit through the hospital gown, and Stormie wished she had taken the thin blanket the nurse offered. At least the gown was a tri-fold—a wrap-around with three arm holes—even if it had to be the standard putrid green.

Nothing to be afraid of, she told herself. *Nothing but a million microscopic hunter-killers coursing through your blood.*

Stormie squirmed a little on the padded table, and the paper covering crackled loud as thunder. The tubing pulled against the tape that secured it to her arm. In places where the light hit the tubing just right, her blood looked as dark as her skin.

Dr. Nguyen's smiling face appeared in the wire-crossed glass set in the door. He waved, then came in carrying the brushed aluminum clipboard with all the release forms she'd signed. She hadn't read them, of course; she supposed no one did. Written in the most obscure dialect of legalese, their clauses and codicils were inaccessible to those uninitiated in the lawyerly arts, even people who were otherwise smart; if system administrators could erect electronic barriers as formidable as lawyers' linguistic barriers, no computer firewall would ever be breached. The papers all boiled down to I-understand-the-risks-associated-with-this-procedure-and-accept-the-improbable-but-very-real-possibility-that-it-may-result-in-my-death-or-permanent-disability. She had signed them with barely a first thought.

Dr. Nguyen's black, greasy hair stuck out above one ear, as if he'd just gotten up from a nap at his desk. "How are you doing?" he asked. He reached out his slender hand and Stormie shook it for the third time this morning. "Everything still okay? No irritation?" He bent toward her arm and examined the needle site.

"Seems okay," Stormie said. "I'm cold, though."

The door opened again and the same stout, blonde nurse who had witnessed the paperwork—Nurse Myracek—carried in a plastic transit case about the size of a six-pack cooler. The dark, almost hunter-green case contrasted with the room's stark brightness. She set the case next to the equipment on the steel table as Dr. Nguyen asked her to bring Stormie a blanket. She gave Stormie an "I told you so" look, but smiled and nodded to make it a friendly comeuppance.

"You'll want to lie back now," Dr. Nguyen said.

Stormie complied, and the clean paper sheet scrunched against her back. Her empty stomach complained about the preparatory fast. In a moment, Nurse Myracek had her expertly swaddled under a soft, robin's-egg-blue blanket and put a small pillow under her head.

Stormie remembered something in a poem about the night, lying on the table ... something about anesthesia ... she tried and failed to recall the line. It might be appropriate, somehow.

Dr. Nguyen snapped opened the clasps on the transit case. They clattered down one by one, then he took off the lid and lifted out a syringe about the size of a cigar. He started making notes on his clipboard.

"Just think," Nurse Myracek said. "That came from outer space."

Stormie smiled a little. The nurse made it sound as if the picophages in the syringe were alien creatures brought back to Earth by some survey team. They didn't come *from* outer space *per se*, they were grown and processed in the high-vacuum, medium-orbit foundry that the Low-Gee Corporation developed from the space station nanocrystalline laboratory. "Pico-" was marketing hype: they were smaller than almost any other nanomachines, but not three orders of magnitude smaller. So far they were one of only two commercial products that seemed to require low-gravity manufacture, but on that shallow foundation Low-Gee had built a small technical empire. A greater hurdle than making the things in the first place had been figuring out how to prepare them for descent into the Earth's gravity well; the shock-and-vibration-damping packaging was expensive, but still cheaper than sending people into orbit for treatment.

Stormie nodded. *They came from outer space. And you're going to put them in me.*

"That's what you and your husband are going to do, isn't it?" the nurse asked. "You're part of the Consortium, right? Like Dr. Nguyen? His wife's on the Moon right now, you know."

Stormie did know: Jovelyn Nguyen was on the setup crew that had landed just over two weeks before. "No, I'm not a 'Consort,'" Stormie said. Dr. Nguyen didn't react to her little jibe. "We're independent contractors. We'll be working on the air and water systems in the colony."

If we ever get there.

She and Frank and Jim had formed Lunar Life Engineering, LLP, shortly after Jim's water-skiing accident. Bidding and winning their three-year contract renewable to seven had taken long enough, and she intended to renegotiate and extend the contract indefinitely. But their waiting and preparation weren't over, and she needed this procedure to work if they were to make the original timeline and hang out their shingle sometime next summer. If it didn't work ... she didn't want to think about that.

"That's amazing," the nurse said. "I can't imagine living on the Moon and looking down at the Earth. Or would it be looking up at the Earth? That's so strange. How long does it take to get ready for something like that?"

"When I feel like I'm ready, I'll let you know," Stormie said. "Sometimes I think I'll never be ready, sometimes it's like I've been ready all my life. As long as I can remember, anyway."

She sometimes questioned her fascination with space; it wasn't as if she had any astronauts in her family, or had grown up with rockets launching nearby. But while her fellow environmental engineers had pictures of landscapes and glaciers on their cubicle walls, she had a copy of the Apollo-8 shot of Earth above the limb of the Moon. She and Frank would have to wait a little longer, and had to pass a few more tests yet, but if this worked they would finally get there—and they were going to stay.

Dr. Nguyen tugged a little on the tubing as he screwed the syringe onto the port.

"I thought it would have some color," Stormie said. "Something exotic, like electric lemonade."

Dr. Nguyen tilted his head to look at the syringe. "I don't know what 'electric lemonade' looks like," he said. "This has some color, but the fluorescent lights wash it out, I think. If we looked at it in the sunlight, it would be white, but very pale. More like very thin skim milk." He tilted the syringe and the light played off of it. He looked closely at her face and added, "You can still back out of this, you know."

"No," Stormie said. Give up on her life's ambition and go back to taking water samples from stagnant ponds or digging up square-foot patches of soil to separate for analysis? Go back to writing environmental impact statements and teaching truckers the rules for hazardous material hauling? Go back to looking at the full Moon and dreaming—and knowing she gave up her only chance because she was afraid? "Really, I can't."

Dr. Nguyen pulled back on the plunger and a bit of Stormie's blood colored the syringe. "Are you ready?" he asked.

Are you ever ready for something you know is going to hurt?

"Yes," she said.

"Once more, for the record, while you are lucid. Are you absolutely sure you want to proceed?" He emphasized each syllable of "absolutely sure."

Stormie was as far from absolutely sure as she was from Mercator Crater, but she understood why Dr. Nguyen asked the question now. Once they began, the nurses would administer ketamine in her IV to help manage the pain; it was the only anesthetic that had proven effective with this treatment, but they couldn't do a final, verbal verification with her under its influence. In a way she was more afraid of the ketamine than the picophages, because it was known to produce hallucinations. She feared that loss of control more than she feared the pain. Despite the doubt plaguing her, she said, "Yes."

Dr. Nguyen repeated his earlier descriptions as if he was trying to postpone the procedure. "As the fluid medium comes into your arm, you can expect it to sting a little. As it spreads out, you'll feel a little flushed. You've never had a CT scan or an IVP with a dye contrast, correct?"

"No, I haven't had the pleasure."

"This would be similar, although reportedly it's a bit more intense."

He pushed the plunger down, slowly.

A knife stabbed into Stormie's arm where the needle met her vein. Then it was a machete. Then a chain saw.

Stormie grunted. *A bit more intense?*

Warmth spread to her fingertips, up to her shoulder, and through her body, riding just ahead of a wave of pain. When the warmth and pain hit her chest, she believed her lungs would explode and her heart collapse. She struggled to breathe.

The sensation intensified until her body was being blasted by a heat gun. Then the heat gun became a blowtorch. The blowtorch became a blast furnace.

Oh, God, let them start those drugs already.

She descended into Hell.

She choked on a laugh at the irony, remembering her grand-mother's warnings of fiery doom if Stormie didn't give up her pride and cast her cares on the Lord. "Who you gonna throw in the lake of fire?" Mother MacGinnis would sing. She would say this torment, this blazing pseudo-immolation, was the price of Stormie's sin, her prideful arrogance—

Stormie gasped. She tried to scream but her breath was gone.

Nurse Myracek reached up to the IV bag as Stormie passed out.

O O O

She drifted in and out of consciousness. Thoughts struggled to break through barriers of agony, and when they finally emerged they seemed as broken and nebulous as dreams. She dreamed of pain, of a million needles piercing her body from the inside out, of acid-venomed wasps laying eggs beneath her skin, and occasionally Stormie reminded herself that the pain was only in her head: it couldn't be real, with the ketamine. Still she dreamed, of humid Carolina summers, the dry Mojave Desert, the stifling wet sulfurous surface of Venus.

She vaguely registered when they moved her from the examination room to a bed in the clinic. It seemed as if her skin sloughed off to the touch.

Gradually she was awake more often. The heat and the hurt fell on her like repeated avalanches of coals, but either the ketamine began working or her tolerance and endurance grew. She wondered how much time had passed, but that wasn't foremost in her mind.

"How's Frank doing?" she asked. She barely registered her own voice. "Is he okay?"

"I'll check on him," Nurse Myracek said. Through barely slitted eyes Stormie tried to follow the nurse's voice in the darkened room.

They'd insisted on treating them in separate rooms. They told them the procedure was uncomfortable—and the ocean was just a little wet, as far as Stormie was concerned. The first patients' experiences had ranged from embarrassing bodily releases to multi-sensory hallucinations to ravings that rivaled the worst Tourette's outbursts. Now, in the midst of the treatment, Stormie wasn't sure if shared suffering would've been better or worse.

O O O

Nurse Myracek returned after an indeterminate time. "Your husband is a character," she said. Stormie was surprised the words didn't hurt her ears, except that she barely registered them over the sound of her own rushing blood. "I love to hear him talk."

The nurse tried copying Frank's accent. "'Now I know how the English missionary felt when my ancestors cooked him,' he says. Oh, he is a gem." She laughed at her failure even to approximate the accent.

Stormie wanted to laugh. She tried, but managed only a weak croak.

"What is it, honey?"

After a moment she managed to say, "His father was a missionary in Kenya."

Nurse Myracek chuckled as she wiped sweat from Stormie's forehead. The cloth cut like coarse grit sandpaper. With a start Stormie realized that Frank shouldn't be joking about pain. Was he dreaming the pain, the way she was, or had he refused the ketamine? Stormie closed her eyes; a single tear escaped and dribbled back toward her ear. It burned.

"Why does it still hurt?" she whispered.

"Oh, dear, I don't think you're feeling anything. I think we could tie your toes in knots and you'd try to dance pirouettes," Nurse Myracek said.

"Why does it hurt at all?"

"Oh. You know about the tunneling nanotubes that your cells are always building: they pass genetic data around between cells, and viruses use them, too. The fluid suspension, from what I understand, stops your cells from making them. Or I may have it backward— maybe it forces them to make more. Apparently your nerve cells react by going into overdrive, but you should've only felt that for a short while.

"I've heard some of the doctors say it's really some electromagnetic flux stimulating nerve cells that don't normally register pain. I don't think they actually know. You're only the fifth person I've seen treated, and everybody seems to react differently. Most of them stay passed out, but you've been awake a good bit.

"If it's any consolation, your husband doesn't seem to be affected as strongly as you."

"Thank you," Stormie said.

Stormie shifted position a little, and the bedclothes tore at her skin. The hospital gown felt like a hair shirt, which she supposed would be appropriate from Mother MacGinnis's point of view.

Stormie's grandmother had been alternately kind and stern, a loving old woman whose hugs were solid as oak and soft as cotton but who was never shy about warning Stormie away from certain friends or pointing her toward her blessed Jesus. As each wave of … phantom? imagined? hallucinated? … pain and flame passed over and through her, Stormie struggled against the ghost of her grandmother who, no matter what Stormie did or said, no matter the admonishments she herself laid on Stormie, always—always— loved her.

Mother Mac, you may be right but I don't think so. This isn't the price of my pride. It's the cost of my dreams.

O O O

The next time Stormie was lucid, the room was brighter. It held the common accoutrements: oxygen port, vacuum port, blank television bolted to the wall. The track from an old bed-curtain was attached to the dropped ceiling, but no curtain hung from it. Several ceiling tiles were stained where a water pipe or the roof must've leaked. The only unusual item was the scanner unit, still tethered to her arm by the winding plastic tube of blood.

A new nurse, one she hadn't met, was checking the scanner unit.

"Blue," Stormie said.

"Pardon me?" the nurse asked.

"Blue. Sky blue, electric blue."

"I don't understand," the woman said.

"Electric lemonade," Stormie said, "is sort of a neon blue color. Dr. Nguyen didn't know that. You should tell him."

"I'll be sure to do that." Her tone was dismissive, maybe a little annoyed at being interrupted in the middle of whatever it was she was adjusting on the scanner.

Stormie lay very still. She concentrated on breathing: slow breaths, not too shallow but not deep enough to expand her chest too much. To pass the time and keep her mind active, she tried doing calculations in her head.

Her brain seemed sluggish. It took a long time to recall some factoids from a trivia game: about five liters of blood in her body, heart pumps about seventy milliliters or so with every beat. She tried to count her heartbeats, but the numbers jumbled together; she gave up and used seventy beats per minute for convenience. *So if I've done it right, all the blood in my body goes through my heart in about a minute. Maybe less, with how fast my heart's beating. So each blood cell goes through my body ... some 1440 times a day.*

And now her blood was carrying tailored, machined picophages that were coursing through her body just as often, and presumably burrowing their way throughout her tissues to latch onto disease organisms. She wasn't sure exactly how long it had been, but that wasn't as important as how much more time it would take.

The nurse was headed toward the door. Stormie asked, "How much longer?"

"We'll probably start the filtration sequence in a few hours," the nurse said. The door closed automatically behind her.

O   O   O

Stormie's consciousness peaked and ebbed. She dreamed of walking on hot coals, skiing down lava slopes into the caldera of a volcano, sunbathing on Mercury, but gradually her dreams ransacked her mind less and less. Her head, a supernova, calmed into a hot white star, dimmed further to a red dwarf.

Nurse Myracek was back.

"How are you, hon?" she asked. Stormie tried to smile, but her face hurt.

"My mouth is so dry," she said, forming the words with a tongue like a cooling ingot of lead.

"I'll get you something," Nurse Myracek said. She was gone only a few minutes, and when she came back she spooned burning cold crystals into Stormie's mouth. Stormie held the nuggets on her tongue and let the liquid, slowly cooling—warming?—to a tolerable level, soothe her throat. "There you go, hon," the nurse said. "Ice chips worked wonders for me when I was going into labor. They wouldn't let me have anything else, not until after the baby was out."

Stormie changed the subject. She had wanted children—still wanted children—but she and Frank had decided they would not be the test case for extraterrestrial pregnancy.

"Is Frank still doing okay?"

Nurse Myracek spooned some more ice into Stormie's mouth. "He's doing fine. He's not quite as far along as you are, since he's bigger. We started filtering everything about twelve hours ago for you, and Dr. Nguyen just started filtering Mr. Pastorelli a little while ago."

"How long has it been?"

The nurse appeared to study the cup of ice, as if it held the answer. She scooped out another spoonful and wiped the bowl of the white plastic spoon against the rim of the little white cup. She brought the spoon to Stormie's lips.

"Four days," she said. "We cut off the ketamine drip a few hours ago, and we'll let you go see your husband after we take out your catheter."

Stormie slept again, but only for a few hours. Her dreams calmed as the fires in her mind abated. The picophages were almost gone from her blood, though it would be another day before the treatment was complete—and another week to verify its success.

She reckoned herself a lava rock in the bottom of a gas grill, but she sat up and turned on CNN to see what she had missed. Not much; the world's troubles were the same as they ever were, only made to sound much worse—or at least more dramatic. She called Jim to tell him that if this didn't work she was going to host an old-style pig roast out at Gaviota State Park and he would be the main course.

Shortly after she put down the phone, Nurse Myracek brought her a thin sheaf of papers.

"What's this?"

"You were mumbling something the first night you were in here, and I knew I recognized it but couldn't remember from where. So I did a search and printed it out for you."

Stormie read the first lines:

> *Let us go then, you and I,*
> *When the evening is spread out against the sky*
> *Like a patient etherised upon a table;*

"Evening, not night," Stormie said. "I recited this? I'd been trying to remember it."

"You said part of it. Once I found it on the Net, I remembered seeing it in school. I read the whole thing again, but I don't understand it."

"I'm not saying I do," Stormie said. "I just thought the opening lines were appropriate to me lying on the table."

Nurse Myracek chuckled. "If you say so, hon. I did like this part later on, though. I marked it."

Stormie read,

> *Time for you and time for me,*
> *And time yet for a hundred indecisions,*
> *And for a hundred visions and revisions,*

The nurse said, "I think that means that no matter how much time we have, there's always time to do more than we think."

"I like that idea," Stormie said. "I'll keep it in mind."

"Now, what say we take you in to see your husband?"

CHAPTER EIGHT

Things Are Already Starting to Break

Friday, 24 November 2034
Lunar Setup Mission II, Day 24

Van whistled a little of "The Minstrel Boy" as he pulled into his pressure suit. And he scratched.

The worst thing about being in the suit for the next six hours was not being able to scratch very well. The few times he had worn hazardous chemical gear he had been dexterous enough to pull one arm at a time into the body of the suit if he really needed to dig, even though it left him cramped and was even harder to get unkinked and back into position. But the stiffeners, cross-weaved fabrics, and expandable safety baffles in a pressure suit made that kind of interior mobility impossible. So, he scratched everywhere he could reach as he got ready.

In the two and a half weeks since the laydown of what Grace called the "ice farm," the schedule had been redrawn at least two dozen times. The Consortium work schedule they'd started with was still theoretically intact, but it had devolved into a never-ending, ever-changing task list. *Thank you, Mr. Murphy.*

None of the other shelters they'd set up had been iced-in, so far, but problems seemed to multiply and mutate with every step in the setup plan. In one shelter, the straps came loose from an equipment stack and in the ensuing tumbles the crates broke lights, interior partitions, and even some of the ductwork; in another, a number ten can of tomatoes froze, split, and deposited a film of icy tomato juice that, thankfully, covered only a small volume.

The real problem was the lunar terrain itself: as the laydown grid got closer to the wall of Mercator Crater, it took much more time to dig trenches for the prefabs even when blasting wasn't needed. The next step, after all the prefabs were in place, would be to expand the colony infrastructure by tunneling into the crater wall— until they figured out the ins and outs of building domes.

But that would be a job for another day. For now Van whistled, and scratched. Some places he scratched more than once.

"Keep it in your cabin, will you, Van?" Jovelyn Nguyen said from across the corridor.

"Corridor" was a generous term. At the moment it was still stacked with consumables and small equipment containers, mostly left strapped and netted so they wouldn't fall if someone bumped against them. The stacks ballooned out of the compartments and left the passage not even a meter across—not that it would be much wider when it was eventually cleared. This prefab ran north from Grand Central, away from Mercator Crater, to the junction containing the main exit locks and the lock that connected to the garage.

Jovelyn was already suited, holding her helmet in one hand and trying to look stern. It wasn't in her nature, though, and after a second her smile lit up her brown face.

"Sorry, Jovie, but I've got to scratch now or I won't get the chance." Even with the scratching, which he did curtail a little, it took only a few more minutes for him to seal his suit. They started checking each other over.

The hatch at the far end of the habitat opened and Henry Crafts stepped through from Grand Central. "Good, you two are still here," he said. His voice echoed a little off the crates and cases that crammed the tunnel. He glided down the thin passageway, his slippers making gentle swishes across the floor.

"What's up?" Van asked. "You taking this shift?"

"You wish. Change in your task list. Once you're outside you'll need to download the latest when you do your radio check."

"Why not just call us over the intercom?" Jovelyn asked. "We can jack in from here."

Henry waved off the question. "Telly's got one of the comm panels open, jiggering with something. Meanwhile, no voice or data north of the Pimple. She should have it back up by the time you get done."

Van chuckled. "Just because you call the dome 'the Pimple' doesn't mean Grace will let you get away with calling her 'Telly.'"

"Why not? She loves me."

"Yeah, you say that when the intercom's down. Maybe I should ask her when we do our radio check."

Henry backed up a step and raised his hands in surrender. "That's okay, no need to put her on the spot."

"Cut it out, you two," Jovelyn said. "What's the new gig?"

Henry grinned. "Should be an easy enough survey. Our new celebrity here has to be fresh for his debut."

Damn bad luck of the draw. Van made a grab for him but Henry slid another step backward out of his reach.

"Alright," Van said, "let's get it over with."

Van took a few deep, deep breaths as the airlock cycled; no sense in being all uptight and jittery as soon as he stepped outside. Somebody had to brief the new colony candidates on how the setup was going. The obvious choice would've been Shay, but Shay had decreed that everyone should have a chance and insisted they all draw straws. Of course, Oskar and Scooter were on another foray down south so they weren't eligible. The rest drew straws—actually, cable ties—and Van drew short. He would give the would-be colonists the word from on high, as it were. Maybe, though, he could bribe one of the others to do it for him.

No time to think about that now.

Van stepped out of the airlock into as stark a desert as must exist in the universe. The Sun was angled about forty-five degrees off the horizon, off to the right, and cast crisp shadows from the equipment and the shelters, but the dead expanse of Mare Nubium stretched to infinity where it met the inky veil of space. Where Van grew up, on the edge of the Mojave Desert near Riverside, the barren expanse nearly teemed with life: tarantulas, roadrunners, desert tortoises.

Among the desert plant life, even the carcasses of dead cacti attested to life that once was: but here, nothing. Van resolved to bring a cactus or baby Joshua tree when he came back as a colonist, and when it got too big to keep in a cabin he would bring it outside, sacrifice it to the lunar desert, and leave it as a reminder of life that once was.

"Radio check, take two," Jovelyn said.

"Loud and clear, just like inside," Van said. "Me?"

"Loud and clear also. Control?"

"Read you both loud and clear." Grace Teliopolous's voice came through the same, and Van answered back with the five-by-five.

"You got new orders for us, Grace?" Jovelyn asked.

"Oh, yes. Shay worked around a couple of things on the schedule. Again."

Van nodded inside his helmet. "It won't be the last time."

"No, but it'll all work out in the end," Grace said. "I'm feeding you your new checklists on channel two right … now."

Van split the view on his head-up display, and opened the new checklist in the left panel. "Wait a minute. Henry said surveying, but he didn't say what. This is supposed to be easy?"

Jovelyn spoke up, "Here I thought Shay was going to take it easy on you, so you'd be fresh for your show later. Looks like he wants you to work off some mass, since the camera adds five kilos."

"Ha, ha. It's ten pounds, no matter what the metric police say. And I'm sticking out my tongue at you."

"If you do, you'd better be prepared to use it."

"That'll be the day," Van said. "You and Datu may have that kind of arrangement going, but Barbara would skin me alive."

"Enough, you two," Grace said. "Clock's ticking, you're breathing, let's keep it that way. Get to work."

"Yes, ma'am," said Van. "And hey, if briefers always get work details like this, I want out of the next drawing."

"Me, too," said Jovelyn.

Make that the next two drawings, Van thought a few hours later, as sweat tickled his spine and no amount of wriggling could alleviate the itch. It was still better than sweating in zero gee, where droplets could float anywhere, but the gravity was weak enough that surface tension and capillary action usually kept sweat from moving very much at all.

Their task had been worded innocuously enough in the checklist overview: "Survey and mark the westernmost end supports for the launch rail system, the transfer crane assembly, and as much of the landing pad areas and accessways as possible in the allotted time." Sure, it sounded easier than splitting down the next prefab units, but the former required a lot of moving around on the surface and the latter was mostly a matter of manipulating the machines that did the work.

Van would much rather be splitting and planting a habitat. Even with the site prep and the moving into position and the connecting, it was a breeze compared to hopping around outside, sighting in the coordinates and setting in the markers for the acceleration rail system that would stretch northeast across Mare Nubium. There was as yet no lunar equivalent of GPS to guide them, and he'd been a gentleman and let Jovelyn run the EDM transit, so he was the one hopping around with the prism pole. None of the team were licensed surveyors, and they knew only enough to be dangerous, but he was sure if they were surveying anything on Earth she would've had to move the electromagnetic distance measurement equipment at least once, if only to sight around some natural obstacles like trees. Here, where no atmosphere diffused the laser and the whole open plain was a cut line, she just stayed at the benchmark and had him range about to each new survey point.

Deep inside, he was just as happy that he didn't have to futz with the electronic gear. But most all the other surface work was machine-assisted, and this task was about to wear him down almost frictionless. He hadn't sweated so much since the summer before he and Barbara got married, when he agreed to help out for a week on her dad's ranch. He hated that ranch.

"Okay, Van, got it," Jovelyn radioed. "Need you to move fifty meters out on heading zero-three-zero."

Easy shift, my ass.

O O O

"Ready for your close-up, Mr. Richards?" Henry asked.

"Shut up," Van said. "Just sit there and don't let anybody bother me."

They were in the two-by-two-and-a-half-meter cabin that was the main Operations Center for the growing complex. That is, Van was in the cabin while Henry sat on a stool in the corridor, just outside the view of the console-mounted camera. One of the monitor screens was split into four quadrants, each of which showed a similar view: a small conference or classroom with tiny, almost indistinguishable faces. Everyone wore casual clothes, so the only way he could tell the corporate types from the colonist candidates was by the digital labels on each quadrant: "Long Beach" was the Consortium corporate office, "San Diego" was the preselection and processing center, and "Utah-1" and "Utah-2" were rooms in the underground training complex.

"Okay, I think everybody's on," someone said from Long Beach—the label momentarily turned green. "We have the feed from Mercator and the other video sites, and we have audio feeds from the candidates who are scheduled for the next session in the mountain. I'm Roger Ellsworth, chief of training, and we've arranged this briefing so our trainees can get a first-hand account of how the setup mission is proceeding. Our briefer today is Van Richards, who I understand spent six of the last eight hours out on the surface." Ellsworth prattled on for another minute or so, reminding everyone about the protocol for questions given the time delay, then asked Van to begin.

Van had read through the briefing script Shay had written, which was displayed in big letters on another monitor near the camera even though he had no intention of following it. He glanced down at his notes for what he was really going to say—they were on real paper, propped up between the top two rows of a keyboard. He wasn't going to toe the party line for Shay and say all was well in their lunar paradise. It would serve Shay right for not doing the briefing himself.

In a stage whisper, Henry asked, "Still going to go through with your little plan?"

"Absolutely," Van said.

"Have fun, buddy." Henry slid closed the partition.

Van transmitted the first slide before he even began speaking, and kept it up like a shield; he'd rather let all those people look at the plan view of the colony than at him. The slide showed a draftsman's ideal view of Grand Central and the array of prefab habitats.

"Ladies and gentlemen, greetings from the closest dirtball to dear old mother Earth," Van said, "where your best friend is the low-bid pressure suit with the broken oxygen gauge and cross-wired power system that you hope will hold together for another day in the sunlight. Or another night under the stars.

"Now, before I get into the prepared briefing, is Gary Needham still in the program? All your faces are too small on my monitor to pick him out. Over." Gary Needham had commanded the first lunar setup mission. He was back in the pipeline as a trainer while his wife Beverly went through as a trainee: not only would he be among the first colonists, but eventually he would be the colony administrator. Van's acquaintance with him went back to their days in the service, but he wouldn't waste transmission time to go into that.

Van waited while the signal traversed the distance, and then a hand went up in the third row of the crowded "Utah-2" screen. Van leaned in and squinted, but it didn't help. "Hello, Van," Gary said. Van waited a few seconds to see if he would say anything else, but he didn't.

"Howdy, Colonel," Van said. "I'll assume you've already given your cohorts a detailed account of your setup mission, including everything you left undone. We've been giving Roy a hard time about that—he says hello, by the way. Over."

After the requisite pause, Gary said, "Yeah, sorry about that. Quit picking on Roy about it, though. He doesn't deserve it. Next time I see you, I'll buy you a beer to make up for it. Over." Needham hadn't changed a bit: he still accepted responsibility for whatever went wrong on his watch, and Van guessed he was probably still as quick to share the praise for whatever went right.

"Oh, that's okay. I think we'll be buying each other a beer, at the rate we're going. And you did a good job with that first farm

71

unit—Sondstrom's plants are growing on schedule, which is a little surprising to me since he's primarily a mechanic. Anyway, we got most of your 'punch list' done, but our schedule's all hosed up. You're going to have a lot more work than you bargained for when you get up here." Van switched to the next slide, which was labeled *Mercator Colony—Actual Progress to Date*. Almost half the habitat modules were greyed out, and several others were visibly askew from the idealized version.

"Now, let me tell you what we *have* gotten done, and some problems we've run into. I want you to know full well what you'll be up against when you get here."

Van's version of the briefing lasted about five minutes before Shay was outside the closed partition, arguing with Henry. Van had already run down the worst of their problems, prioritized based on the time it had taken to fix them—or, in a few especially unfortunate cases, the time it was *going to take*.

Now, warmed up to his task, he switched the view and let the camera pick up his face. Behind him, Henry told Shay, "Just listen— he's getting to the good part." Van smiled.

"I told you all that so you wouldn't have any illusions," he said. "It's not my job to give you warm, fuzzy feelings. But it ain't all bad. Even though I've never worked harder at anything in my life, even though the gear is balky and the air reeks, and even though I feel like we're never going to get done, I don't want to be anyplace else.

"Some people talk like life is supposed to be safe and you're not supposed to take any risks, but I say you may as well climb in your coffin if that's the case. And you sure as hell don't want to come up here. But that's okay, 'cause better you back out now than you get up here and find out you can't hack it. Life is hard sometimes. Get over it. Making it through the hard parts is what makes life worthwhile.

"I read somewhere that back when Arctic explorers were planning an expedition, they ran ads in the paper asking for people to sign up and said, big and bold, that the chance of survival was slim. A certainty of adventure, a possibility of glory, and a good chance of death. Sound appealing? People signed up, they came out of the woodwork to sign up for a chance to do something monumental.

Because a chance of survival is still a chance, and worth taking the risk. So even though this is hard, by damn I think it's a chance worth taking. Dream big and dare big, I say. Take the chance.

"In a few weeks, we'll have as much done as we can do, and y'all are gonna have to pick up where we left off. You might be mad when you see how much we've left for you, and I'm sorry about that. We're all working hard to make sure this place is ready for you to arrive, but things are already starting to break and we're having to put them back together. It's slowing us down, but it ain't stopping us. And here's the kicker: it ain't chasing us away, either. Some of us are coming back, just like Gary Needham is coming back.

"As soon as we can, my wife and I will push ourselves through the training you're going through right now, and we'll join you up here. Jovelyn Nguyen will be along one of these days—her husband probably gave most of you your medical clearance, but it'll be a while before they get up here, before there's enough people here to justify a full-time doctor. We'll see Henry Crafts and some of the others, too, 'cause they'll be piloting cargo carriers or off working the asteroid mine. We're signing up for the long haul—and you better be ready for the duration, too.

"That's all I have to say. If you like, I can give you the party line briefing now, or I can answer some questions or we can shut this down and I can go to sleep. Just remember: I told you beforehand that we weren't going to get everything done, and things up here are harder than you might think. So when you get up here you're going to work your asses off. If you're still mad at me about that when I get up here, you can punch me in the face. Or tell me ahead of time, and I'll smuggle up a case of beer and let you have one. Over."

Van muted his microphone and reached back to tap twice on the partition. Shay slid it open and said, "What was that?"

Van grinned. "That was the truth," he said. "And it was fun."

CHAPTER NINE

Halfway House

Saturday, 2 December 2034
Lunar Setup Mission II, Day 32

Bright sunlight bathed the lunar highlands: along rills and near rocks, it cast short but ever-lengthening abyss-dark shadows.

It was a lot better to get this job done in the daylight than the darkness, as far as Van was concerned. As sunset approached, there would be precious few sunlit swathes left. And the big lights on the front of the rig would barely penetrate the darkness.

A chime sounded from the control panel in front of him; if Oskar had taken off on time, he should be in the area soon. Van checked the frequency and keyed his microphone. "Oskar, this is Van," he said, dispensing with all radio protocol. "You out there, Oskar?"

The radio crackled a little. In keeping with the Consortium's low-ball approach, its electronics were nothing fancy but easy to repair. Van waited a few more minutes, then repeated the call. He was about to transmit a third time when Oskar's voice blared from the speaker.

"Lima Victor November, this is Lima Sierra Oscar Victor, over."

"Hey, Oskar! Been waitin' for you to call. Where are you?"

Oskar sounded annoyed. "Roger, LVN. We're coming up on your left, Van, about a thousand meters high. I can see you clearly. Looks like you're right on time, over."

"Sure we are, Oskar. Where else would we be?" Van snuck looks out the left-hand window for the suborbital vehicle. "Hey, why don't you drop down and scout out ahead for us?"

"Negative, LVN. That's not in the flight plan. That route hasn't changed since the last time anyone drove it, over."

Van chuckled. Oskar loved flying almost as much as Henry, but he was so by-the-book that he wouldn't take a risk unless it really needed taking. If even then.

"You never know," Van said. "Some transie could've burst out, right on our path. You'll regret it if we drive right into a sinkhole."

"Negative, LVN," Oskar said.

Van chuckled again. *No, I don't suppose you would, Herr Hintener.*

"I see you now, LSOV," Van said, slurring the acronym into "ellessovee." The suborbital vehicle was about sixty degrees up and not quite abeam—call it about 8:30, moving to 9:00, on an analog clock. He was surprised he could see the vehicle at all: the bright sunlight and the lights in the cab washed out just about every outside light source. The flyer was visible only because it caught a good bounce from the Sun. The hydrogen-oxygen flame propelling the flyer burned clear, and even if he was at the right angle the glowing hot exhaust bell would be practically invisible to him. As it was, the reflected light would change and he'd probably lose sight of it before long.

Van noted the suborbital vehicle's forward progress, and frowned a little. Oskar wasn't trying very hard at all. He had enough fuel to fly nap-of-the-moon, but he'd programmed a semi-ballistic trajectory that let him coast after the initial boost. Knowing him, he'd probably programmed it close enough that he'd barely have to light the engines to touch down right at the rendezvous point. *You're sharp, Oskar, but you're not much fun.*

"Looking good, Oskar. See you at the implant point."

"Affirmative, LVN. Watch out for the transies, over."

Van switched off the microphone. "Good one, Oskar." Even if a transient lunar phenomenon had lit off recently right in the middle of their path—which he supposed they would know, since so many people back on Earth were watching the Moon these days—it wouldn't affect them that much. Whether it was outgassing or a minor impact, all it might do is raise a brief spray of dust; the big truck would just roll along pretty as it pleased.

Van switched to intercom. "Grace, you up? We're coming up on the setup site."

She answered right away, but she sounded sleepy. "Yeah, I'm up. Oskar's nearby?"

Van looked back into the sky, but as expected the LSOV was out of sight. "I had eyes-on a second ago, but not anymore. He'll be down and cooling when we get there."

"Roger. Do I have time to grab something to eat?"

"Oh, yeah, plenty. We're still about twenty-five klicks out, so it'll be over an hour."

"Okay. I'll start running the arrival checklist in about thirty minutes."

"Suit yourself, Telly."

"I will," Grace said.

"Ha-ha. Hey, leave me a little something, okay?"

"Why? You never leave me anything."

Van smiled. "I'm still a growing boy, don't you know?"

Grace didn't answer, but that was okay. And Van didn't care too much if she left him anything or not; Grace Teliopolous lived up to her Georgia Tech reputation as a "helluvan engineer," but she was not a cook.

An hour later, the LVN-1 crested a rise and Van looked down into a wide valley. In the distance a few large rock formations cast reaching fingers of shadow, but most of the low valley seemed almost to glow.

And in the middle of the glowing field stood a manmade rock that cast its own shadow in Van's direction.

Van had already set the vehicle's radio to broadcast. "I see you, Oskar."

"Roger, LVN, we have a visual on you also. Come on down and join us." Oskar sounded as if he was sitting in the cab next to Van.

"Henry and I are getting ready to exit the LSOV, over."

An "X" appeared in the box on the checklist screen to Van's left, in front of the "Establish close proximity line-of-sight communications" step.

Van smiled at his reflection in the head-up display. He puffed his chest and said, "Roger that, Lima Sierra Oscar Victor. We read your last transmission five by five, and copy your checklist telemetry. Copy your intention to commence Echo Victor Alpha and begin stabilizing Lima Papa Papa November Three and the Romeo Oscar Papa Sierra."

Van wasn't sure if it was Oskar or Henry Crafts who laughed over the radio, but it was certainly Oskar who spoke. "Alright, Van, just get your ass down here and get to work."

Van smiled. All eight members of the lunar setup team were well-trained, highly motivated, and exceptionally capable, but over the past few weeks Van had become even more convinced that sometimes they took themselves too seriously. Oskar Hintener, for example, senior engineer and nominal second-in-command, was wound even tighter than his Teutonic heritage might warrant. Although, Van reflected, it was probably a good thing to be careful—and not the time to test the limits of the colony's suborbital vehicle—when ferrying and setting up a nuclear power plant.

Van's eyes strayed to the readouts from the big truck's nuclear power source, ten meters behind him. The ARG's output was in the green.

The Consortium had shipped four Advanced Radioisotope Generators to the Moon. They were quicker to install than solar collectors and had the advantage of working throughout the long lunar nights; solar fields and flywheel storage batteries would come later as the colony needed more power. Two stationary ARGs were already operating, one near the Mercator base and the other at the bottom of Faustini Crater. A third, mobile ARG powered the truck Van was driving: the biggest truck in the colony inventory, with the descriptive but typically unimaginative nomenclature Lunar Vehicle, Nuclear. And they were on their way to set up the fourth, short name LPPN-3, just flown in by Oskar and Henry. Since the AC's lunar real estate was less "prime" than other concerns had acquired, LPPN-3 would power the remote Regolith Oxygen Processing Station, a way station between the main colony and the south pole for crews sent to retrieve ice for the colony's water supply.

Van understood the need to be careful, especially with the devices that would keep the colony running, but he wished his fellow workers weren't quite so uptight. Sometimes they almost made him the same way, and if he thought too hard about it that's how he'd end up. He took a deep breath, held it, and let it go slowly. The air tasted of air-conditioned plastic and dust warmed by the sunlight. He toggled the intercom.

"Coming up on the waypoint, Grace. What's your status?"

"All set except gloves and helmet. Ready when you say Go."

"And?"

It took Grace a moment to respond. "And I left a little chicken salad for you."

O O O

The crew compartment of the LVN-1 was smaller than the interior of a minivan on Earth, but spacious enough after six hours in the tiny control cabin up front. Although, up front there were windows.

The chicken salad was reconstituted, of course—it would be up to Gary Needham and the first full-time colonists to start raising real chickens—and there was only enough to put on three stale crackers.

"Aw, gee, Grace, you shouldn't have," Van said. He still had on his pressure suit after coming through the connecting tunnel from the cab; he had only taken off his gloves and helmet to choke down the crackers.

Grace put one gloved hand on her hip and glared at him. Her big brown eyes were captivating, even when she was hot about something. Maybe especially then. Van raised his eyebrows a little and gave her sad eyes until a bright white smile bloomed across her olive face. "I knew I couldn't stand to hear you gripe the whole rest of the way." She started to put her helmet on. "See you outside."

The concoction was mostly satisfying—the mayonnaise was a little thin and there wasn't quite enough celery for Van's taste. He washed the snack down with a little water while Grace cycled through the airlock to the outside.

Van ran through the pre-EVA checks with barely a glance at the checklist printed right on the tough suit fabric. The instructions were there if he needed them, but he didn't need them. His hands knew the routine better than his brain did as he repeated, flawlessly for the hundredth time, the function checks and seal inflations and joint inspections. He locked down his helmet and cycled through the airlock twelve minutes after Grace.

"It's about time you showed up," Henry Crafts's voice said in Van's ear. Henry and Oskar had set up reflectors to illuminate shadowed areas of the LPPN and the ROPS, and as Van had driven the LVN into range they had directed him to park the truck and its long, low trailer just behind one of the reflector stands about twenty meters away from the processing equipment and its power supply. Now, Henry was about thirty meters away pulling a power cable across the dusty basin floor. It was easy to pick Henry out because of the vertical line of dark blue duct tape he'd put down the outer edge of his suit's legs.

Van looked away long enough to eyeball his volume control on his head-up display; he blinked to activate it and turned the sound down a little. "Sorry, fancy pants. Grace had prepared me a sumptuous meal, I had to finish it."

Henry exhaled heavily as he spoke. "Grace, you cooked?" He pulled a few meters of the thick cable toward himself and curled it on the surface. He grabbed the free end and bounded away with it, toward the LPPN-3.

"'Add water. Stir,'" Grace said. "I can do that. It's the whole application of heat thing that I have trouble with."

"Right."

Oskar interrupted. "Well, at least with Van in his suit only he will have to endure the after-effects of Grace's cooking. Now, I'm sure you would like to stand in the sunshine and talk for an hour, but we are on a schedule."

"That's the beauty of radio, Oskar," Henry said. "We can shoot the shit all day and barely have to see each other."

Van turned toward the rear of the LVN-1. Grace was up on the trailer, starting to unpack the scavenger robots. Van bounded to the lift gate at the rear of the trailer. With the exertion, the first drops of sweat broke out on the center of his back. The long johns that formed the inner layer of his suit wicked them away, but others would join them soon enough.

"How do they look, Grace?" Van asked.

"Ugly," she said, "but serviceable. I'm hooked into the first one, ready to move it onto the lift. Stand by to take it down."

The scavenger robot hung off the edge of the lift gate as Van lowered it to the surface. Grace stayed on the trailer, but she left the control box on the lift. It was a simple joystick controller, and Van used it to maneuver the robot about ten meters away from the trailer.

The scavenger was a squat, ugly bug that was little more than a meter-wide X-frame with wheels on the four ends and a big pan laid out on top of the X. Secured to one section of its wire frame was a power collector and logic assembly; batteries hung under the pan, fastened to the frame; and a cylindrical nose—or tail, depending on its orientation—extended from the machine opposite the logic unit. The end of the cylinder was equipped with cutters and grinders, and inside the cylinder was a low-slope Archimedes screw. The creature worked by digging into the lunar soil with the cutter end, then moving the residue up the worm screw where it would be deposited onto the pan for transport back to the processor. It was low and wide to resist rollover, and what it collected would serve as its own ballast. The power unit combined solar cells with a microwave collector: during the long lunar night, the robots would charge their batteries off power beamed to them by the LPPN-3.

Van and Grace unloaded a dozen of the scavengers, then put each through a programmed routine to check its functions. By the time the last one reported its status, they'd been working for over four hours. Van was practically asleep on his feet. His suit had mostly done its job absorbing his sweat, but a thin film that wouldn't go away tickled the middle of his back. His skin was clammy from his chin to the soles of his feet, and twice already his eyes had closed on their own and he'd had to pop them back open. He took a sip of water from his reservoir, but his chicken salad crackers were long gone.

Of the twelve scavengers, three reported minor problems but Van was in no condition to deal with them. "Hoo, Grace, I'm beat," Van radioed. "I've got to be due for a rest.

"Break, break: Oskar, we've got three 'bots that need some tweaking, but otherwise we're done unloading. How are we doing on the overall timeline?"

It took Oskar a moment to answer, and Van wondered how many scenarios he was considering. Every day the schedule got tighter, and every day they fell a little further behind. Finally Oskar said, "How long will it take you to finish?"

Most of the faults were pretty minor. Van pulled the status reports up on his display and started to calculate the repair time, but he couldn't concentrate. It crossed his mind to tell Oskar that one of the 'bots had a "bad motivator." He bit down on his lip to keep from giggling.

Thankfully, Grace supplied the answer. "Give us forty-five minutes, an hour at most, and we'll have these last three ready to go."

"Okay," Oskar said. "Henry and I have the power hooked up to the ROPS, and he's running up the furnace. Next step on the checklist is to get the microwave beam up and running, so we need to stage all the 'bots in the holding area."

"I'll take care of moving the good ones," Van said. "Grace can take care of the bad ones. She's better at the fine work anyway."

"And I'll do even better if you're not hovering over my shoulder," she said.

And I'll do better if I'm moving around; then if I fall down, I'll have an excuse.

Van bounced to the oxygen port on the side of the LVN-1 and topped off his suit supply while he conferred with Oskar on where the holding area should be. Oskar adjusted the planned layout to avoid a rock formation west of the ARG, and transmitted the new coordinates to Van's suit. Van checked the inventory to see where the radio stakes were, then pulled away from the O₂ quick-disconnect.

The regulator unit on his suit "burped." Van froze for a second then reconnected to the oh-two port.

Damn, I really am tired.

His suit's "black box" confirmed what he'd already guessed: the sound had been the safety valve closing. He could almost hear Oskar scolding him that it wouldn't have had to do that if he'd been paying attention to the procedure.

He wanted to rub his eyes, and maybe slap himself in the face a little to wake back up, but couldn't. He focused on the chronometer and counted off fifteen seconds of deep breaths that counteracted a brief, gut-tightening sensation of fear.

He minimized the clock and called up his environment controls. The thermal systems were already taxed from working in the sunlight, but he ticked the temperature down a couple of notches in hopes that a little chill would keep him alert. He reset and then closed the valves on his suit and the LVN and disconnected again; a tiny chuff of air escaped from between the valves, confirming he'd done it right: the way he should've done it the first time.

No time to dwell on it, though. There's work to be done.

Van bounced to the rear of the LVN, found the appropriate transit case, and pulled out the four radio stakes and a hammer. "Here you go, little fellow," he muttered as he loaded the tools onto the first of the good 'bots, "you can carry these for me." He grabbed the remote console and started moving the machine to the holding area. The little scavenger, dragging its feed cylinder behind it, looked like a meter-wide trilobite.

When his suit confirmed he was close to the right spot, he disengaged the RF beacon from the first stake and left it on the 'bot's collection pan. He hammered the stake into the surface and hung the little transceiver back on it: the scavengers would use it as a reference to know the limits of the holding area, and would muster there to get recharged, or whenever they needed servicing, or if they were queued up for processing. He steered the cooperative 'bot to each corner of the area, where he hammered in the other stakes, then left it next to the last stake while he moved the other robots.

He could have commanded them to move to the holding area, now that it was set up, but instead he moved them in groups—two, then three, then three more—in little migrations across the dusty surface. The exertion woke him up a little, and he was glad of it.

Van headed back to see if the last three 'bots were ready and saw Grace bounding across the scattered sunlit dust with her own mechanical coterie lined up behind her. She looked like a twenty-first century Pied Piper leading radio-controlled rats out of Hamelin, until she stopped next to him and the critters kept moving. Van radioed, "Good work, Grace," as he shuffled out of the way.

Back at the trailer, Van rode the lift gate up and stepped onto the open-mesh metal bed. He didn't bother to call up the packing diagram: he could see what he needed to unpack next.

"Y'all ready for the tanks and such?" he asked.

Grace radioed back, "Wait a sec, Van. I want to top off my own tank before we unload anything else."

"That's a good idea," Oskar said. "Everybody take a rest, get a drink, and get some air."

"I already did," Van said. "I'm fine for another few hours." He sent Oskar his suit status to forestall any argument.

"Well, take a rest anyway, Van. I heard you tell Grace a while ago that you were tired. Henry's got the ROPS running, and I'm about to boresight the microwave emitter on the power plant. Once that's done, the LPPN can interrogate each of the 'bots and we can all start unloading the ground infrastructure."

"Whatever you say, Oskar," Van said. He leaned against the removable side panel of the trailer—it was essentially a low-gravity version of a stake bed—and sipped a little water. He leaned out enough to see Grace hooked up to the LVN. She was standing with one foot propped on the bottom rung of the ladder, as if she was about to climb up into the bed of the truck.

Their pressure suits weren't as bulky and hard to handle as the old Apollo suits, and they were padded enough that Grace's suit hid most of her curves. But Grace had prominent curves for a smallish woman, and the suit didn't hide them all. After a moment Van realized he was concentrating a bit too much on the shape he imagined under the suit—the shape he'd glimpsed often enough in the close quarters of the colony's prefabricated shelters—and he reached up and smacked his helmet.

He fought down the libido that wanted to see more of Grace, and concentrated on how good it would be to get back to Barbara. His wife's curves were more subtle than Grace's, but Van knew them very, very well—

He smacked his helmet again. This was not the time to get lost in a fantasy. He turned the heat in his suit down some more and got back to work.

O   O   O

"I thought I told you to take a rest," Oskar said.

In the last half hour, Van had unloaded two of the four storage tanks. He grunted a little as he wrestled the third into position on the lift gate. He didn't care to explain. "I am resting, Oskar. I'm sleepwalking."

"Yeah, you're going to sleepwalk yourself right off the damn trailer. Come down here and let me up there with Henry. We'll hand the rest of the stuff down to Grace."

Van didn't argue. He helped get the third tank unloaded, then bounced over to one of the reflector stands and did some twists and stretches while the others worked. He wobbled a little, and flailed his arms to keep his balance. When he tried to touch his toes, his eyes closed involuntarily.

Now that all four of them were working on the same thing, he expected the confusion and frustration to double. Oskar seemed to keep a map and a task list side-by-side in his head, though, and doled out their assignments with strict efficiency. He kept them out of each other's way for the most part, and kept them working on the support systems in good order. Van was impressed, though he would never tell Oskar that.

They worked together to set up the tanks and plumb them to the ROPS, then Oskar split the team again. Oskar and Henry hooked up a separate tank of helium and used an IR detector to examine all the valves and fittings for leaks, while Van and Grace set up the sunscreens that would keep all the tanks, pumps, and piping in shadow during the long lunar days. Some of the power of the LPPN-3 would have to go into selective heaters on valves and other components, but it was important to protect as much of the system as possible from the thermal shock of the Moon's three-hundred-degree-Celsius temperature swings. Van was just as happy to assemble the frames and stretch the aluminized Mylar to shade the equipment: it was less exacting than the leak check.

Oskar and Henry finished the leak check while Van and Grace were putting away their tools. "Dinner break," Oskar called over the radio.

Van smiled when Henry asked, "Grace isn't cooking, is she?"

O O O

Van felt slimy. His T-shirt and shorts clung to him, but so did everyone else's. He studiously avoided looking at Grace.

The LVN was cramped with all four of them inside, but still roomy enough after hours in his suit. Henry had drawn the short straw, so he cooked. He whipped together a reasonable facsimile of frittatas with reconstituted vegetables and powdered eggs. Van dozed a little while Henry cooked. The smell of the garlic and spices Henry used was almost strong enough to overpower the smell of sweat.

Grace called up some music from her collection—light Latin rhythms that reminded Van of a high-class Mexican restaurant—and they ate in relative silence.

Oskar wolfed down his portion and held up his glass of water. "Good work, everybody. Here's to the 'Halfway House.'"

Everyone raised their glasses; Henry and Van said, "Hear, hear."

After they drank, Van tucked back into his frittata. Henry said, "Why 'Halfway House,' Oskar?"

Oskar refilled his water glass. "Because it's about halfway between Mercator and Faustini."

Henry rolled his eyes at Van; his lips drew up in a wry smile. Van decided that he would not be the first to tell Oskar what a halfway house was.

"What's next on the agenda, Oskar?" Van asked.

Oskar looked down at his hand, as if there were a checklist printed on his palm. "While you were sleeping, I deployed the scavengers for their first pick-ups. I used the check-out setting, of course, so each will return with approximately one-quarter of its usual load." He turned to the wall screen and scrolled through a couple of menus. "Two of them have offloaded and returned to the holding area. One is being offloaded now, and four are in the queue. According to its telemetry," he tapped the display again, "furnace core number one accepted its first influx of aggregate about three minutes ago. It's too soon to draw any conclusions, but the furnace appears to be operating normally and the off-gassing is within expected parameters." He pulled the keyboard off the bulkhead and started typing.

"Status report time?"

"Yes," Oskar said. "The next satellite pass begins in sixteen minutes. It will be good for our report to go up with the ROPS telemetry burst."

Van caught Henry's eye, and winked. "Well, make sure you tell Shay and the gang that the Halfway House is up and running." He leaned back against the curving bulkhead—it forced his chin down to his chest, but he didn't mind—and closed his eyes.

Grace said, "You never answered Van's question. What's next?"

Oskar typed for another minute—unless Van dozed again, in which case it might've been longer—before he answered. "We will suit up for a final EVA. We will perform visual inspections of the scavenger robots, pack up the reflectors and the rest of the equipment, and then do pre-trip inspections of the LSOV and the LVN."

Van sat back up. "Then let's get this mess cleaned up," he said. "Or, on second thought, leave it. The quicker we get done, the quicker we're on our way south. It's Grace's turn to drive, so I'll clean up the mess before I rack out."

No one suggested a different plan, and Oskar didn't have to consult a checklist to agree with the idea. They suited up and cycled through the airlock, at which point Grace and Van met the 'bots in the holding area while Henry and Oskar started stowing equipment.

"Hey," Henry radioed, "since we're in the mode of naming things, I hereby dub the LVN the 'Turtle.'"

Henry must've turned one of the reflectors toward the LVN: between the sunlight cascading onto its rounded bulk and the additional light shining up onto its midsection, the truck did resemble a shiny, misshapen turtle. The body was the main living area: supported on four big metal-mesh wheels that were lost in the underbelly lighting, and covered with a shell of solar panels that provided auxiliary power two weeks out of four. On short trips, or even on long trips like this one with a fairly light load, the panels were redundant—the ARG powered the drive system, and the lights, heat, and other necessities ran off flywheel generators that the ARG recharged when the truck wasn't moving. The vehicle's cab was the creature's bulbous head, complete with windows for eyes except there were more than two. But this was a grossly mutated turtle, since the cab had wheels of its own; the LVN was not an articulated rig, but its cab could detach and operate independently for as long as its separate battery power lasted.

Henry's choice of names didn't quite describe the vehicle's complete shape, though: the ARG was in a flat, blocky section at the back where the tail would be, with two exterior cargo beds on either side of it. But Van figured Turtle at least had the virtue of being a short name.

Apparently Oskar liked the idea. "So be it, Henry," he said.

As Van and Grace finished checking the scavengers after their shakedown run—Grace had to tweak one of the 'bots she'd operated on before—Oskar said, "Grace, Van, these shades are not placed correctly."

"Which ones?" Grace asked.

"Over the holding tanks," Oskar said. "When the satellite passed over, it imaged the area and I got it downloaded just before it dropped over the horizon. The image is stored in the ROPS-laydown directory, in a subdirectory called 'verification.' Open it and you'll see what I mean."

Van swayed a little as he concentrated on finding and opening the image file. His fatigue gnawed at him again.

The image was grainy, as befit the low-bid piece of crap satellite orbiting the big rock. It looked similar to the photo survey of the route they had driven, but that had only been useful because it combined images taken over many days and the different Sun angles made it possible to estimate the heights and characteristics of obstructions. This was a one-pass image, and not a very good one.

The Consortium wouldn't pay for a good reconnaissance satellite—since the Moon doesn't change much year to year, like the Earth does, and nothing much happens on it, they figured a dedicated recon satellite would be a waste of money. Not only that, the satellite was more of a big fuel tank than anything else just to keep it from crashing: with very few stable low-altitude orbits, it frequently performed orbit corrections because the Moon's gravitational field perturbed its orbit. Henry said the Moon's gravitational field was "lumpy"—a technical term, he promised—because its composition wasn't uniform: too many mass concentrations from impacts over the millennia. So they put the satellite in a medium-altitude orbit and made it a multi-tasker, which to Van meant that it was a kludge that didn't meet anybody's requirements.

In this case, it was a multi-spectral sensor when a hyper-spectral suite wouldn't have cost that much more, but it was also underpowered and couldn't run all of its sensors and communications equipment at the same time. Its orbit wasn't optimized for remote sensing or communications, and it wasn't supposed to be the communications workhorse anyway. LunarComm had been chartered to build and deploy a twelve-satellite constellation using highly elliptical orbits to provide complete coverage; then their twelve satellites became eight, of which only one had been fielded and it was a dead orbiting rock. If LunarComm didn't make good on their promise soon, the AC said they would insert a dedicated communications link at the L-1 Lagrange point—but how long that would take, Van couldn't know. Meanwhile, they put up with intermittent communications and dreadful imagery.

"Okay, Oskar, what am I looking at?" Van asked.

"Look at the angle of the shadows," Oskar said, "and think about how the Sun angle will change through the entire lunar day. I think the canopies over tanks three and four need to be shifted."

"I don't buy that, Oskar," Van said. "The damn canopies reach almost all the way to the ground."

"I think I see what he means," Grace said. "It won't be too hard to move them. They don't have to move far."

Frustration bubbled over into Van's reply. "I don't care how easy it is, I just don't think it's necessary. But I'm not in charge." He took a breath and erased the satellite image from his helmet display. "One thing, though. Let's get everything else packed up, so that's the last thing we have to do before we leave."

Oskar agreed, to Van's surprise. The reflectors were the last things to be put away, once it was clear that none of the shadowed areas needed any more work. They left three of the reflectors with the power station and carried the rest to be re-stowed aboard the LSOV. The flyer was almost three kilometers away, which was still close enough to at least worry about flying debris when it lifted off.

"Shoot, Oskar, we should've driven all this stuff over here," Van said.

"Why? Don't you enjoy the exercise, the fresh air?"

"The air in my suit hasn't been fresh for hours."

"Days," Grace said.

Henry added, "I can smell you all the way over here."

As they loaded the folded units into the LSOV's cargo hold, Van tried mightily to think of a good name for the vehicle—but the only thing he came up with when he looked at the thing was "Horsefly."

On the way back, they switched off carrying two sets of worklights and stands. They left them by the LPPN, for future use, then the four of them met together at the base of the canopy shading the number four tank. "I've marked the new positions of the support posts," Oskar said. "It's mostly a shift in angle for each canopy. It shouldn't take us too long."

Van hopped over to the nearest post. Oskar's mark was only about twenty centimeters away. "You've got to be kidding me," Van said. "That's absolutely ridiculous. You're holding us up because of a quarter meter? Didn't you see how fuzzy that picture was?"

"That corner moves the least. The others move more, to twist the canopy to the proper position."

"No, Oskar, that makes no sense. You've gone way beyond the resolution in that image. I'm sorry. I understand you like precision—hell, your eyes are calibrated to the nearest microradian—but there's at least a half-meter slop in everything we've done here."

"No," Oskar said, "there's a half-meter slop in everything *you've* done here."

A burst of adrenaline came with the urge to hit Oskar, but Van got himself under control. He wasn't going to win the argument, and he was too tired to keep it going just for fun. He took a drink of stale suit water and set to work with the others.

An hour and a half later, Oskar said, "Good work, everyone. I think that wraps everything up."

"You wrote a good plan," Grace said.

Oskar bowed a little. "Thank you. Speaking of which, the next item is a mandatory six-hour rest period."

"You're not seriously going to hold us to that, are you, Oskar?" Van asked. "We could be fifty klicks down the trail by then. Grace is okay to drive, aren't you, Grace?"

"It does not matter," Oskar said before Grace could answer. "Everyone has worked hard, and resting now will avoid accidents later. Henry and I will preflight the LSOV and run the final checklist when we get up."

"Plus," Henry said, "we'll get a chance to verify everything's working right with the ROPS before we take off."

Van couldn't fault the logic, but he bristled at being told to wait around. Oskar said, "So go back to the LVN—excuse me, the Turtle—"

"Hey, should it be 'Tortoise' instead?" Henry said.

"No," Grace said. "Turtle is fine."

"As I was saying," Oskar said, "go back to the Turtle and do your walkaround, then get inside and sleep. We will radio you when we are ready to depart."

"Affirmative," Van said. "Come on, Grace. We've still got dishes to do."

She corrected him. "No, *you've* got dishes to do."

Van climbed on the trailer as Grace gathered the few tools she had used. The remaining load wasn't much—primarily scavenger robots for the ice collection station at Faustini—and Van rearranged it to his liking and tied everything down in about twenty minutes.

He leaned against the front corner of the trailer and rested for a second. "Okay, I think we're ready," he radioed.

Grace laughed. "Except for one thing."

"What's that?"

Her words choked out between chuckles, "You kind of painted yourself into a corner there, Van."

"No, I haven't," he said, "though it might look that way to the untrained eye." He started threading his way around the robots and tooling and crates of blasting explosives, back toward the tailgate, but down each side he quickly ran out of places to step. He could maneuver across the front of the trailer fine, but getting back to the lift gate was another matter.

"Then again, maybe I did," he said, and considered how long it would take to clear a path and tie everything down again.

Heck with that.

He climbed up the stake bed side, balanced on the corner for a second, and hopped down.

At least it was supposed to be that easy. Hopping around the surface had become second nature, but jumping down from an elevated height was a little trickier—especially when someone put a helmet-sized rock in your landing zone without telling you.

The force of impact wasn't bad, but inertia and momentum worked just like they did on Earth—mass was mass, after all. Van's foot slipped down on the rock and he stopped for an instant before his body continued its motion. His knee tore apart. He wasn't sure if he heard the sound inside his suit or if it had been transmitted through his own tissues, but he could almost distinguish between the pop of cartilage shunting aside and the snap of tendons being wrenched out of place.

Van cursed an instant before he skidded across the lunar plain.

"What's wrong?" Grace asked, and Oskar echoed her question a second later.

Van gritted his teeth as he rolled himself onto one side. He checked his systems display and verified that his suit was okay, then he muted his microphone while he tried to move his knee. A sharp pain shot through his kneecap as if a circular saw blade was slicing through his leg—not quite as bad as the time he'd taken a crackback block in the third quarter of the state championship game, but almost. He pushed himself partway up, turned his mic back on, and said, "Nothing, Oskar."

Van twisted around, keeping his right leg straight out. Grace was bouncing toward him. He waved to her that he was okay.

She didn't get the message. "Van's hurt," she said.

"Hurt how?" Oskar asked.

"It's nothing, Oskar," Van said as smoothly as he could. "Took a little tumble is all. Go ahead and get the LSOV ready and go to sleep."

"It doesn't sound like 'nothing.' I'm coming to see."

Van shook his head inside his helmet. Oskar was coming to see: that hurt worse than the pain in his knee.

CHAPTER TEN

Intrepid Adventurers and Would-Be Heroes

Saturday, 2 December 2034

Dim light bled from under the bathroom door. It barely overcame the digital clock display and the occasional red blink from the smoke alarm, and the semidarkness matched Stormie's mood.

Maybe it was because they were back in Santa Barbara, but in her dreams the tires squealed again, metal tore, and glass broke. Again that beautiful girl lay broken, people stared, and she had blood on her hands. As many times as she relived it, she always did the same thing—the only thing she could do.

She slid out of bed as gently as possible, to let Frank sleep, and curled herself into the chair by the window. Her nightgown was gossamer, and the room's chill raised goosebumps that barely counteracted the lingering fire of the picophage treatment.

She acknowledged that the memory of fire in her bones was all in her head, but she could not shake it. Her pride hurt, that she, the queen of checklists and proper procedure, had ignored every protocol about blood-borne illnesses and put pressure on a bleeding wound with her bare hands. She hadn't forgotten the precautions, hadn't exactly thrown caution to the wind, but had she made the right decision? Every time she recalled that girl's blood, pumping slower and growing colder, she knew the answer was no— she'd *almost* waited *too long*. Trying to save the girl wasn't her mistake; wasting time asking for damn plastic bags was her mistake.

Frank rolled over. He rummaged in the covers, but when he didn't find her he asked, "Have you gotten any sleep?"

"Not much. A couple of hours, maybe. I can't get my brain to shut off. I wish Jim would just give us the word and not go through all these eleventh-hour oscillations. I'll go sit in the lobby or the courtyard if I'm keeping you up."

"No, my dear, stay exactly where you are. It won't be long before we have to get up anyway. If you think it will help," he sat up and patted the mattress, "come here and let me rub your back."

"That's okay. I don't need my back rubbed."

"Very well." Frank lay down on his stomach and said, "Then come here and rub my back."

Stormie wondered at his calm. They'd had full physicals the day before, with more bloodwork than usual, but he didn't seem worried that the Consortium might rule them unfit to fly. Maybe he was just trying to calm her through osmosis.

She sat on the edge of the bed. Frank's back was broad and warm, not heavily muscled but still strong, especially through the shoulders. He relaxed under her fingers—

She sat back and clasped her hands together, resisting the urge to retreat to the bathroom and wash them. She'd taken to washing them often, as if after six weeks they might still carry some vestige of blood on them. It was an irrational fear, and didn't she have enough rational fears to worry about? She shook her head. Soon enough they would know if the dream still had a chance of coming true.

She took a deep breath, forced her hands apart, and pressed her fingers against Frank's back.

O O O

Frank sighed. He had hoped offering Stormie a back rub, and then asking for one himself, might help her put aside the fear that was ravaging her. But where her touch used to be strong and sure, now it was tentative, as if she was afraid to put forth full effort.

After a few moments, he rolled onto his side and grasped her hand. "Come with me," he said. "Get dressed, and let us walk."

She tried to pull away from him, but he held her fast. "I don't know if I'm up to that," she said.

"You will be, my love, because I am. I will help you."

The early morning was cold, and the street was comparatively quiet. Frank enjoyed the sensation of Stormie huddled next to him, his arm around her. He could try to protect her, to shield her from the world, but he wished most that he could deflect the criticism she aimed at herself.

As they drew nearer to the beach, Frank recalled their moments there before the accident. He flexed his fingers and remembered the feel of the sand Stormie had dripped into his hand. The grains were sharp, almost harsh, and he had wished for the feel of soft, rich garden soil. Peat moss. Loam. He had closed his fingers tight, to make a little ball, but the ball crumbled when he opened his hand again.

Now, lines from that poem Stormie had brought home from the hospital ran through his head:

> *Would it have been worthwhile,*
> *To have bitten off the matter with a smile,*
> *To have squeezed the universe into a ball*
> *To roll it toward some overwhelming question,*

Frank had no idea what it meant to Mr. Eliot, and was not at all sure what it meant to him. The ball of sand he had held that night would not hold together to roll toward questions or answers, but that was the nature of sand. Not all of the poetry he and Stormie quoted to each other had definite meanings; they had started their poetic sharing when they were first dating, and eventually included everything from unfamiliar verses they went out of their way to find, to songs anyone might know, to passages out of books they read.

Blake had written about seeing the universe in a grain of sand, but in his heart Frank preferred good soil to barren sand. Topsoil, and earthworms—he smiled at the name—ready to grow the engineered crops that would sustain the growing lunar colony. Crops that would not only need water but help establish and maintain the cycle that cleaned the water; crops that would help purify the air for him and Stormie and all the others to breathe. The colonization fever he had caught from her could not be quenched; it was stronger even than the artificial fever he had endured with her in the hospital. He marveled at the changes she had wrought in him. He had always had the soul of a farmer: as a young boy the magic of growing things captivated him, if only in his mother's tiny rooftop garden in Nairobi. He was twelve when his family moved to the United States, first to Louisiana and then to California, and he loved the variety of plants that thrived in the southern heat and the mild Pacific climate. When he started graduate school, he originally planned to join the Agriculture Department to help farmers get the most out of their soil, and help them replenish the Earth so she would always yield up a plentiful harvest. And possibly, he thought at the time, he might return to Kenya and continue the same work there. He still believed in that work, but Stormie's enthusiasm for space had changed his outlook: in space the only life was what mankind brought with them, and for man to survive everything he brought would have to thrive.

Lunar Life Engineering could have gotten the farming subcontract, he was sure; he would have been happy to try for it, but Stormie insisted air and water would be enough. Frank suspected that she had refused to bid for the farm because she did not want to be reminded that her thumb was far from green. But it was satisfactory to have parts of their worlds that did not overlap.

That was marriage—time shared and time apart, all the more precious as days started to pass a little quicker, as months and years began to look the same. As routines became habits.

But everything was going to change, starting tomorrow.

He was not afraid of the physical results; he trusted that they were fine, and he and Stormie would travel to Utah as scheduled. If that turned out to be wrong, he would admit his ignorance and look for another way to achieve his purpose—their purpose—in life. But for now he was confident in the future they had envisioned together.

He guessed that in that future, routine days would be rare. He craved order and schedule and routine in his life, but he would be fine so long as he could count on Stormie to keep him in synch. She was not as tempestuous as her name—nickname or her real name, Gale—indicated, and not nearly so much as she liked people to think. And where he wanted order, Stormie produced it. If making order out of chaos was God's original wonder, then Stormie was surely made in His image. •

O O O

Green garland festooned the grand entrance of the Doubletree Hotel. Christmas lights twined around the palm trees flanking the doors, but at least they weren't turned on this morning. Jim Fennerling wheeled across the hotel lobby and shook Frank's hand. Jim smiled, and Stormie took that as a good sign. She bent down to hug him.

He held up his hand as if to ward her off. "Are your hands clean?"

Stormie punched him in the shoulder. "Don't joke about that, Jim."

Now he took her hand and leaned forward to kiss it. At the last minute, he sniffed. "Yeah, I guess they're clean enough," he said.

"Jerk."

"That's me."

"Please, James," Frank said. "What did you find out?"

"You're always so formal, Frank," Jim said. "And you want to talk business before we even have breakfast? I can't imagine why you'd be so anxious. It's not like you, oh, I don't know, have a plane to catch or anything." He pulled out a datapad and retrieved a display. "Take a look."

Stormie stepped in and looked at the readout. Jim had pulled up an e-mail from Dr. Nguyen, listing both their names and next to each one the evaluation: *Cleared For Flight*. She let out a small whoop of joy and hugged Frank, and then Jim.

"Wonderful, James," Frank said, "thank you, for everything."

Jim rolled backward a half meter and looked at both of them. His expression became more serious. "But there's something else I need to tell you. Something else you need to do." He paused, looking grim, and Stormie's chest tightened. Then Jim grinned a little, shook his head, and positively beamed. In that smile, which she had seen too rarely the last couple of years, Stormie saw Meredith's natural joy and exuberance mirrored in her father. Despite Jim's obvious mirth and inability to fake them out with a serious pronouncement, Stormie's old ache returned: almost a guilty pain she carried because she and Frank were attempting what Meredith had longed to do. It crept over Stormie's heart like a heavy, dark spider; she shuddered, and missed exactly what Jim said.

"Say again, Jim?" she said.

"God, all that buildup for nothing. I said, 'You need to send me some Moon rocks, preferably blue diamonds.'"

Stormie looked at Frank. His eyes were bright, and one corner of his mouth turned up a little, then more and more.

"You bet," Stormie said. "The first ones we find."

Jim chuckled as he wheeled himself away from them, toward the hotel restaurant. The hostess led them to a table and removed one chair to make room for his.

As they opened their menus, Stormie said, "Sorry to cause so much last-minute trouble, Jim."

"What, you? Cause trouble? First of all, let's call it 'next-to-last-minute trouble,' since you've still got to get through training. At least if you have to do first aid on another colonist we won't have to worry about whether they're carrying any dread diseases." He lifted his water glass as if to toast. "Here's to my two intrepid adventurers and would-be heroes, who are going to curtail any attempted heroics for at least the next twelve hours until they are accepted into the Asteroid Consortium's loving hands ... who will excel at their training so they can depart their native world for a cold, desolate, soon-to-be-no-longer-lifeless world ... my two good friends, who having made my life more interesting than by rights it should be are about to make me, well, not rich, but at least somewhat comfortable." He took a sip, and Stormie and Frank returned the toast.

He didn't mention Meredith. And he called us his friends.

Stormie puzzled over that for a moment. She had just started grad school, and Frank was almost done, when they had enrolled separately in an astronomy class taught by Meredith, who was five years younger than Stormie and already working on her doctorate. Meredith's enthusiasm about quasars and pulsars and all the other brands of stars rubbed off on most of the class—except the few people who had been looking for an easy A—and rubbed off most on Stormie. While Frank courted Stormie, she courted the young blonde physicist in a way, and by the end of the semester had a new roommate and a friend for life. Two, actually.

I think I'll like having Jim as a friend as well as a partner.

"Shouldn't that be the other way around?" Stormie said. "We're just the brawn, you're the big business brain."

"I balance the checkbooks, that's all. But, I was disadvantaged, having grown up in the dark ages. If I'd had calculators and computers instead of slide rules when I was in school, maybe I could've hacked it with the big engineering brains."

"Come now, my friend," Frank said. "You are not so much older than we are."

"Oh, yes he is," Stormie said. "Look at that grey hair. Look at those wrinkles, and the way the skin sags at the corner of his eye. He's ancient. I think we should make sure his will is up-to-date and we're the beneficiaries."

Jim, poker-faced, sighed. He tapped his fingers against his water glass, then stuck them in the icy water and flicked droplets at Stormie. She sat back so fast her chair jumped.

"I'm not actually that old," he said, "and I'm still quick. And sneaky." He looked down into his lap and tapped one arm of his wheelchair. "Okay, not as quick as I used to be, but I'm still sneaky."

Stormie laughed. "And a good thing, too. I think that's the only reason we got bankrolled."

"And don't you forget it."

Coffee came, then breakfast, and both were excellent. Midway through his omelet, Jim asked Frank, "So how was your family?"

Frank rearranged his hashed browns. "I suppose it went well. Father did not appreciate that we did not stay through to go to Sunday service, however."

Stormie suppressed a growl; Frank was putting it mildly. Frank's father wasn't a missionary anymore but he was still a devout evangelical—too devout for Stormie's taste. She respected Benjamin for practicing his faith in practical terms—an engineer and project manager, he had started his mission work in Kenya by installing new wells and designing water purification and power plants in his off hours when he wasn't working on the renovations to the U.S. Embassy. When the Embassy project was complete, he'd stayed in country working on other infrastructure and housing projects and gradually became a full-time mission worker who also happened to be a practicing engineer. Stormie understood his devotion and even admired it, but she did not share it and didn't like when he pressed them about it—which he had at every opportunity during the past week. If he'd been prone to fits, Benjamin would've pitched one when they said they would be leaving on Friday.

"Other than that, the visit was fine," Stormie said. It was mostly true.

"Did you warn them about what we're doing this morning?"

"No."

"That's probably best—I don't think they'd appreciate you giving me power of attorney instead of one of them."

"Perhaps not," Frank said. "But at least they were more supportive of our venture than I have seen before."

"Well, that's something to be thankful for," Jim said.

They made more small talk as they ate: whether the Rams had a chance against the Falcons, whether the courts were going to allow individual freeholding on asteroids or just keep things limited to corporate and NGO holdings. They avoided speaking aloud the difficult truth that their lunar venture was a dream they all shared, but only two of them had a chance to achieve.

Stormie decided it had to be said, to keep everything clear and in the open. She put her hand on Jim's for a second. "It's too bad you can't come with us."

Jim toyed with his coffee spoon. "No, it's too bad *she* couldn't go with you," he said. "I was just thinking about Meredith last night, wondering if I would be saying goodbye to her today. I know she'd want to go with you. That's not to say that I wouldn't mind going myself, but I'm too long in the tooth and they don't need a number-cruncher up there. I'd just be in the way. No need for me to use up the air and water you guys make."

Frank squeezed Jim's shoulder. "Oh, I think perhaps we could get you a good deal. If you could afford it."

Jim chuckled. "You two do what I know you can do, and eventually we'll make enough that I *could* afford it. Even at my measly twenty-four percent."

"Are you still grousing about your share?" Stormie asked. "As I remember it, we offered you more, but you wouldn't take it." She owned fifty-one percent of their company, Frank twenty-five, and Jim twenty-four. If Frank had been the majority shareholder, they would have qualified as a minority-owned business, but with Stormie in the top spot they got minority- and woman-owned business consider-ations. Stormie had never been one to look for handouts growing up, but she was smart enough not to look at that gift horse's teeth.

Frank smiled and said, "I would have offered you only a ten percent share, but my wife has a thing for older gentlemen."

Jim brightened a little. "You know, I always suspected that. She's always asking to sit in my lap and ride in the chair with me—"

"Yeah, right," said Stormie. In reality, Frank had wanted Jim's share to be a full third of the company. Jim had refused, and suggested the odd step-down arrangement. "Actually, now that I think about it, you two have always been suspiciously close."

The two men looked at each other, and Frank said, "James, my friend, I think she has discovered our secret."

Jim sighed. "I know, but you made your choice long before we met." He failed to make his voice pitiful enough.

Stormie groaned. "Should I leave the two of you alone for a little while?"

"You wouldn't even have to offer, if you came out to the left coast more often. It shouldn't always be business and big goodbyes."

Jim's words took the rest of the conversation with them as they faded. Once Stormie and Frank had moved east, first to Indiana and then down to Texas, they had ventured back to California only infrequently, and other than business it seemed only in response to tragedies: Meredith's final days, Alyson's suicide, Jim's accident. It didn't have to be that way. Frank would've come out more often, to see his family, but he stayed clear because she preferred it; the realization ate at her regularly, but she pushed it down deep like forcing a cancer into remission. Her desire to avoid the never-ending conflict with his family warred against how much she wanted Frank to be happy, but every time she brought it up he insisted that he was fine. Frank was always fine....

Stormie spoke up before the silence extended too far. "You're right," she said, and she meant it. They should come back more often, but the chances of that were fading fast. She struggled against the somber mood and decided a little reverse psychology might be in order to salvage the conversation. She lightened her tone. "We shouldn't come back for long goodbyes. In fact, I'm not sure why we came down here at all. Frank, why didn't we just go straight to Utah and do this business by thumb?"

"Hey, come on," Jim said. "At least I'm buying your breakfast."

"Uh, huh."

"And while you're playing around in Mormon country, someone's got to hold the AC's feet to the fire to keep up with their payments, if only to cover the cost of *your* interferon."

"Playing around? Holed up underground with forty starstruck adventurers, trying to see who gives up and goes home first, is playing around?" Stormie looked to Frank for some support, but he didn't catch on to the game. He just shrugged. She shook her head, smiled, and tossed part of a biscuit at him.

Jim laughed. "I'm going to miss you guys, too," he said.

Twenty minutes later, the bill was paid and they had exchanged thumbprints on datapads to execute the powers of attorney. They walked Jim to his van and exchanged handshakes and hugs while the ramp extended from the side door.

"Do me a favor, will you?" Jim said. "Try to keep yourselves healthy. I can't be there to watch over you two every minute."

Stormie bent down and gave him a kiss. "Thanks, Jim. I'll be more careful next time."

Jim's eyes twitched just before his lips curled up into a smile. "You'd better. But I know you too well, Stormie, and I'm not going to count on it."

Jim maneuvered himself into his van; Stormie and Frank waved goodbye as he drove away from the hotel. A half hour later, they were in the hotel shuttle on the way to their next big step toward the Moon.

CHAPTER ELEVEN

Best to Shoot a Lame Horse

Saturday, 2 December 2034
Lunar Setup Mission II, Day 32

Damn it, Oskar, I said I'm fine."

Van tried to make his voice sound as normal as he could. He was standing, leaning mostly on his left leg, outside the main airlock to the Turtle. Sweat slicked his face, crawling down in slow rivulets, and he hoped Oskar couldn't see clearly through his helmet.

"Stand on one foot," Oskar said. He had made the long walk from the LSOV, just as he had threatened to do. He stood downrange, toward the flyer, and the Sun, just a little lower than when they arrived, threw crystal clear unbroken waves of light that shadowed most of the right half of his suit. Henry had tagged along, and stood a few meters to the left and behind Oskar. Grace, meanwhile, busied herself with the pre-trip inspection on the truck—but no doubt she was listening.

"And then what? Do a jig? Run forty meters and let you time me?"

"You're stalling."

"And you're just trying to make it worse than it really is. Yeah, I fell. Yeah, I twisted my knee. Yeah, it hurts, but I've had worse.

But we've got Ranger candy in the truck, and if I can't find an Ace bandage I'll strap it up with duct tape. It'll be fine. Hell, if those biocapsules came equipped to pump out painkillers, all would be well." The biocapsules were a NASA invention licensed to the Consortium: microscopic chemical factories that primarily secreted compounds to speed tissue repairs after radiation exposure. They were almost the only technology that made NASA a profit.

Oskar did not relent. "Your bull-headedness is exactly why the biocapsules do not produce painkillers. Pain is a warning, and warnings must be heeded. Stand on one foot."

"Alright, damn you." Van lifted his right foot off the dusty plain; his knee popped and cracked and complained. He counted off five seconds on his helmet chronometer and gingerly put his foot back down.

"Now the other one."

Van took a few stubborn breaths. He set his foot firmly on the ground and gradually balanced, keeping his quads and glutes as tight as he could to avoid locking out his knee. Another final, deep inhalation and he lifted his left foot. Even at one-sixth of his weight, he had to suppress a grunt. New sweat formed and clung to his face before slowly migrating down into his eyes and ears. He shut his eyes and counted in his head: three seconds, five, ten. He put his left foot back down, and swayed—he reached out to the ladder before he could stop himself.

"I am impressed that you did not pass out," Oskar said, his light accent coming through thicker than normal.

"I'm waiting until I get in the truck."

"I am not sure what to do with you—"

"We could shoot him," Henry said. "Best to shoot a lame horse."

Van laughed, and regretted doing so. His femur had become a thick, primitive spear with its chipped flint head jammed behind his kneecap.

"I'll consult with Shay. You may have to return with me, and Henry can continue on with Grace."

"Just let me get some tape on it, and I'll be fine. It's low gravity, Oskar. You'll see."

Oskar stood in the same place a moment longer, his face unreadable behind his partially shadowed helmet. Van kept still; he was sure his leg would collapse if he moved very far or very fast. Presently Oskar turned away and with loping, graceful strides headed for the LSOV.

"See you back at the base," Henry said, and followed behind Oskar.

It took Van five minutes just to climb the ladder into the airlock.

O   O   O

Grace cycled through the airlock fifteen minutes after Van. He was still in his suit—he'd only been able to get his helmet and gloves off before the relentless pain felled him and he had to medicate himself. Now he sprawled out on the seat/bunk, his leg propped up on two pillows, holding a flask of water and the bottle of 800 milligram Ibuprofen.

"Ranger candy?" Grace asked.

"You betcha," Van said, and sipped some more water. He studied the bulkhead while Grace stripped out of her suit.

"I thought you were in the Air Force," Grace said.

"Yeah. I thought about joining the military, but I joined the Air Force instead."

"So where did you learn about Ranger candy?"

"Honestly, right now I don't remember. Ranger candy, Ranger pudding—"

"What's that?"

"I may not even have the name right," he admitted, "but it's all the powdered goodness that comes with an MRE—coffee, creamer, sugar—with just enough water to turn it into a slurry."

"Sounds lovely."

"I hear it's even worse when you just dump the packets in your mouth and swish them around with water from your canteen. Probably almost as bad as what passes for coffee up here." He chanced a look, but Grace's sweat-soaked T-shirt was too much for him. He closed his eyes and willed the medicine to work its way into his blood.

"You eat anything with that?"

"Huh? No."

"You'll give yourself an ulcer. You need to eat a little something, even a couple of crackers, to give that stuff something to bind to. Otherwise it'll bind to your stomach lining, and you don't want that."

"No, I guess I don't," he agreed. He flexed his knee, just slightly, and had to grit his teeth. "What I do want is something stronger than this. We have any of that Tylenol with codeine in the truck?"

"No," Grace said. "That's locked up back at the base. So, are you going to change?"

Van couldn't resist. "Why, don't you like me the way I am?"

"Squelch that. Are you going to get out of your suit?"

"I would if I could." He opened one eye and Grace was staring at him, hard. "Yes, I will, as soon as these meds work. It hurts too much to do anything else right now."

She approached, and the way she moved mesmerized him. He forced his eyes down and into the corner of the Turtle where she had dumped her suit.

"Here, I'll give you a hand."

Impulses waged a ferocious battle within him, enough that the fray distracted him from Grace's hands and even from the pain. His groin reluctantly ceded control to his brain, just in time to save him from an embarrassing display once he was down to his skivvies.

"Jeez, I hope I don't stink as bad as you do, Van," Grace said as she hooked both their suits to miniature ventilation hoses to dry them out a little.

She was right; he was a ball of sweat and human dirt, still vaguely in human shape. Vaguely human because his knee looked quite alien: swollen to cantaloupe size, the skin so red it almost radiated heat.

"I think I need an ice pack," he said.

"Way ahead of you." She was already kneading one of the chemical packs. They didn't have many of them, and Van couldn't remember how much they cost. He assumed it would be a lot; he'd find out when they took it out of his pay. She handed him the rapidly cooling gel pack and a towel.

"Thanks, Grace, I appreciate it." He laid the towel across his knee so the ice pack wouldn't freeze his skin and strapped the pack in position, then lay back on the bunk and sighed. "I think I'm going to take Oskar up on his rest period. Reckon I'll have to build a brace if the swelling don't go down by then."

Van chanced a look at Grace and caught her in profile—an altogether pleasant sight, and almost too much for him in his fatigued state. She lay down on the other bunk and thankfully drew one of the dark blue blankets over herself.

O   O   O

Van woke up before Grace, and because of Grace: that is, because of the dream he had of Grace in her wet T-shirt. He stole a glance at her, thankful her blanket covered her most alluring parts, then dug with one hand into his bag by the side of the bunk. By touch he found and retrieved his flexi-viewer. He rolled toward the bulkhead as best he could—about a third of the way before his knee, no longer cold but still with the ice pack strapped to it, screamed "Stop"—and scrolled through pictures of Barbara.

"Sorry, babe," he whispered, and winked at a great picture of Barbara laughing at her 30th birthday party. That was three years ago, and today, after six years of marriage, she was more beautiful in his mind than in the picture. The lighting washed out some of her freckles and made her hair more orange than its usual red, but really highlighted her smile. He couldn't wait to hold her in his arms.

The radio crackled. "Turtle, Turtle, this is Rocky, over."

Van wondered if he had fallen back asleep and was dreaming nonsense. The radio call repeated, and Grace said, "Who the hell is Rocky?"

Van switched on the microphone above his head. "Last caller, say again."

"Hey, Van, wake up!" Henry Crafts said. "Time to go. How's your knee?"

Van rubbed grit out of his eyes. "Okay, Henry, we're up. The knee—" he looked down and flexed it enough to experience a fraction of the pain it had to offer. He considered lying and saying he was fine, but he couldn't do that to Henry. "The knee's bigger than it should be, about the size of a grapefruit, and hurts like the Devil's jabbing it with his pitchfork, but I'll live. I was able to sleep, and I should be able to wrap it up enough to go on it."

"Glad to hear it. We heard from Shay a little bit ago. He said it was your call whether you'd press on to Faustini or head back. Oskar figured you'd do just about anything rather than turn tail and run home, so he's going through the final preflight before he warms up the engines. Unless you decide to swap, we need you to get out of the way so we can head back to Mercator. We'll be ready in a half hour or so."

"Thanks, I think. Grace is running our pre-departure checklist over here, too." Grace was actually holding her arm over her eyes, and gave Van a rude gesture. "I don't see why I shouldn't press on from here—I'll be able to rest the knee while we drive.

"Hey, while we're sitting here chatting, who's Rocky?"

Henry's laughter crackled in the speaker. "That was in Shay's message, too. Oskar'd messaged him that we named this place the Halfway House and named the LVN the Turtle, so Shay sent back that the LSOV should be named 'The Flying Squirrel.'"

Grace shook her head, and Van keyed the mic. "I don't get it," he said.

Henry radioed, "Look it up on the 'Net, it's some antique cartoon Shay likes."

Van shrugged. His taste ran to immersive 3-D anime, none of which was about flying squirrels, and Shay was younger than he was. But accounting for taste was always ill-advised. After all, Shay played solitaire with real cards.

Van shook his head and rubbed his eyes again. "Roger that, Henry. Have a safe trip." He switched off the mic. Grace lay still, almost as if she had fallen asleep again, on the other side of the crew cabin. "Want me to drive, Grace?"

"No, I'm up," she said, even though she wasn't. "I'm running the checklist in my mind."

"Wow, that sounds like something I would say."

Grace looked at him, and little creases formed above her nose. "It does, doesn't it? That's not good. Okay, I'm really up now." She sat up, and Van scrolled through more pictures on his viewer while Grace tidied her bunk area and gathered her toiletries. On her way to the latrine, she tossed him two Ace bandages and a roll of reusable cling tape.

When Grace came out, Van had wrapped his knee as best he could. It wasn't supported very well, but it would do for the time being.

"Do we have any athletic tape in the kit?" he asked.

Grace rummaged. "No, don't see any."

"That's what I figured. Low-bid first aid kits. Looks like I'll have to use duct tape after all."

Grace studied his wrap job from across the cabin. "What for? Looks tight enough to me."

"I need sticky tape to crisscross around and really build up some support. But I'll have to shave first—it hurts bad enough without pulling my hairs out, too."

"Oooh, sexy," she said.

He shook his head and unsteadily got to his feet, one hand on the inward-curving bulkhead as pain sledgehammered his knee and his vision wavered. He regained control and limped into the latrine, every awkward step an exercise in agony, to give Grace some privacy while she put on her suit to move through the tunnel—or, if the truck was now a Turtle, the tunnel should now be the "neck"—to the cab.

Grace had gone forward when Van exited the latrine. She had left behind half of a fresh package of crackers, and he ate a few before he took another dose of Ibuprofen. Gritting his teeth every time he moved, he started cleaning up the common area; he listened in as Grace coordinated with the other two. He wasn't done with the cleanup but at least he was prepared for motion when she announced over the intercom, "Getting ready to roll, Van."

He sat down and braced himself before he switched on the mic. "Roger that. Let's go pick up some ice."

He stayed as still as possible while the truck was moving. The vehicle was stable enough—each wheel was independently mounted on controllable struts with limited range of motion, such that the Turtle could practically "walk" over small obstacles—but he didn't trust his knee to deal with an unexpected sway or bump. On this barren plain, the truck swayed more than bumped; the surface undulated in uneven waves, like an inland sea instantly frozen. The bumps would start soon enough.

He read off the speed on the nearest display: they were making about twelve kilometers an hour. "Grace, why are you babying this thing?" Van asked over the intercom. "As slow as we're moving, I think the Turtle name went to your head."

"Slow and steady," she said. "I think Turtle's a good name for her."

"I guess so. I think it ought to be a little bolder. Mean, even, like Snapper. Although the nose may not be pointed enough—"

"Whatever," Grace said. The truck jounced as one of the wire mesh wheels hit something big. "Sorry. How're you doing back there?"

"I'll live. Best you keep your eyes on the road now." He turned the volume down on the cabin speaker.

Van shifted around until he found a halfway comfortable position and retrieved his datapad. He checked the satellite overflight schedule; he needed to send a note to Barbara so she wouldn't panic if she heard he was hurt.

He wasn't sure how to compose a note to accomplish that. If he'd been at the main base, he would've ordered up a two-way and talked to her; the main antenna had plenty of power and, of course, always pointed at the Earth. The Turtle's—Snapper's—antenna was less powerful, so he'd have to spool the message, send it to the colony first, and then to Earth. The Consortium accepted the limitations because even with encryption they didn't want just anyone on Earth to be able to receive every signal transmitted by their teams. Usually that presented no problem, but in this case the increased delay would make it hard on Barbara ... and would have been unnecessary if LunarComm's system worked or an L-1 relay was available.

Van started and deleted three attempts—two voice, one writing—before the upcoming overflight got close enough to force his hand. He decided voice and video would be best, even if it did take more bandwidth. Before he began, he wiped his face with a T-shirt and smoothed his hair as best he could, but with the poor lighting and the camera angle he looked pretty dreadful.

"Hey, sweetness," he said. "I hope you get this message from me before you hear from anyone else. First thing is, I'm fine. They're going to tell you I had an accident, but that's an overstatement. Truth is, I fell over and wrenched my knee pretty good. I don't think it's torn up too bad—I've got it taped up and I can walk on it. Here, see?" He turned the camera pickup momentarily to capture the mountain range of bandage covering his knee. "No worse than what I did in the intramural soccer tournament a few years ago. So don't worry. All else up here is grand, and you're going to love it as much as I do when we get up here together. I've got to close now, the satellite overpass is coming up and I need to get this ready. I love you, sweetie, and I miss you all the time!"

Van fumbled a little with the routing instructions, but got the file compressed and in the upload queue with a few minutes to spare. He turned the cabin speaker back up.

"—make your distance eight klicks. Copy?" Oskar said.

"Affirmative, LSOV," Grace said. "You ready to rumble?"

"Roger, Grace. The next rise you crest, stop partway down, out of LOS, until we've lifted."

"Roger that. Estimate about ten minutes."

"Sounds good."

Van called up an outside view on the nearest display and toggled it until he found a camera trained back toward the LSOV. The Sun angle made the craft easy to pick out—as Snapper moved, light glinted off Rocky's reflective surfaces. The distortion of distance, the 2-D image, and the lack of reliable size references made the LSOV look tiny; likewise, the LPPN, ROPS, and miniature tank farm looked like Lilliputian constructions.

Van overlaid a schematic of the LSOV's takeoff profile on the screen. Rocky would take off primarily toward the east, between Snapper and the Halfway House—he chuckled at Oskar's name, but he didn't have a better one to offer—and overfly the route Grace had just driven. That way, it would throw most of its debris to the west across the plain. Fuel availability and the complexity of the machines weren't the main reasons why the AC had put most of its money into rolling stock: the LSOV or any other flying vehicle created hazard corridors just by virtue of the rocks they tossed around.

The Turtle shivered to a stop. Van guessed they were at the top of the crest, about to lose line-of-sight communications. Grace confirmed it when she transmitted, "Okay, Oskar, we'll hunker down on the other side of this rise. Send us a signal once you're up and away."

"Will do, Grace. You and Van have a safe trip."

"You, too."

Van watched the camera view as Snapper rolled down the gentle incline. A few seconds after the LSOV was out of view, Grace stopped the truck.

"Van, you catch all that?" Grace called over the intercom.

"Yeah, Grace. Now we wait." Van shuffled to the little basin of dirty dishes. "Since we're still for the moment, I'll do some cleaning up back here."

"You haven't cleaned up yet? You been sleeping?"

Van shook his head even though Grace couldn't see. "Honestly, Grace, my leg hurts too bad to try to move around back here while Snapper's rolling. I might be better off driving."

"Oh, no," Grace said. "You're not getting out of cooking that easy."

Thin wisps of static leaked from the speaker, followed by Oskar's voice, but he wasn't talking to Grace. If they could hear them, they must be up—

"—lock it down, Henry. Point oh-five." A loud burst of static cut him off. "—the gimbal. Need more altitude. Watch the yaw." More static.

"Grace? What's going on out there?"

"I'm not sure. I'm not getting their telemetry signal ... wait, there it is. Oh, sh—"

"LVN, LVN, this is LSOV," Oskar called. "Takeoff non-nominal. Number four gimbal actuator failed, almost pitched us over. Compensated now, but it's going to be a rough ride to base. We'll call it in, but request you relay our IFE on the next satcom pass. Over."

"LSOV, this is LVN," Grace said. "Understand you are declaring an in-flight emergency. We will back up your comms and relay status. Do you have a—what the hell is that?"

Over static that bloomed to fill the sudden silence, irregular tapping reverberated as if hail were falling on the Turtle's shell.

O   O   O

Fifteen minutes later, the bones in Van's leg seemed to have gear teeth on their ends that were systematically being snapped off and working their way deeper into the tissue around his knee. But he had his suit on.

He grabbed some Ibuprofen and swallowed them down before he locked his gloves on. He held his helmet and looked for the fifth time at the status panel.

All green.

"I'm suited, Grace, except for my fishbowl." She didn't answer. She hadn't said anything for over ten minutes, since she confirmed visually that rocks and debris were falling on top of their vehicle. She hadn't confirmed it directly to Van, but in a cursing tirade directed at the departing LSOV. He continued, "Standing by—literally standing by—to exit for a visual inspection."

The few cameras on the LVN each had limited pan and tilt, but they were primarily directed outward. They were set up so observers inside could keep track of work being done outside and could move the big truck despite its blind spots, not for visual inspections of the truck itself.

"Roger that, Van," Grace said. "Want to trade places with me? You don't have a lot of mobility. No offense."

"I have no idea what you're talking about," Van said. "I'll see you from the outside."

Stepping into and out of the airlock was no problem. Negotiating the ladder was trickier, and the slope they were parked on added to the trickiness. Van resolved to shave and tape his knee as soon as he got back inside.

"All your status lights still show green, Grace?"

"Affirm. Every system—power, environment, drive, comm, everything."

"You looking at overall power, or the individual elements?"

"I was looking at the combined system, let me switch into the power subsystem."

"You should see a drop in output from the front right solar array," Van said. "Looks like the coverglass got peppered pretty good." Actually, it looked as if a light gauge shotgun had sprayed the solar panels on that section of the Turtle, but Van didn't see the need to alarm Grace by describing it. And he was more concerned that falling rocks had damaged something else—maybe something he couldn't see.

"Yeah," Grace said, "there's a definite drop there, but it's still functional. Overall power is good."

"Glad to hear it." Van maneuvered himself toward the front of the truck, examining every joint and seam and surface from every angle. He saw no obvious dents or dings, no signs of outgassing, just a shiny new layer of dust on the truck. He resisted the urge to write "wash me" on the side of the vehicle.

"Hi, Grace," he said from directly in front of the truck.

Grace had her suit and helmet on inside, keeping to the safety rules until they were sure the truck was still airtight. Her gloved hand waved at him; her bulbous "head" didn't move. "Be careful out there, Van. If you fall and break your leg, I'm not coming out after you."

"No, Grace, that's not right. You're supposed to say, 'If you fall and break your leg, don't come running to me.'"

"But that doesn't make any sense."

"Forget it." Van moved on. The left side of the truck looked better than the right, except for one camera that got knocked off its mount. Van climbed carefully up and examined it. "Grace, you got any picture on camera … which one is this … camera three?"

"Switching. No, nothing."

"I figured. From the ground I thought maybe the mounting was hit, but looks now like the camera itself got it." He reached up and pushed at it; it resisted his gloved fingers enough that he didn't think it would shake loose and damage anything else. "I'm going to leave it in place for now. We can take it down later. Hey, while we're on the subject of cameras, are all of our cameras strictly visual?"

"I think so," Grace said. "Henry and Oskar had the IR camera in the LSOV. They used it when they leak-checked the ROPS system."

"I was afraid of that. If we had an IR camera with us, we could get a much better look at leaks—maybe see them when they're microscopic, instead of looking for gross evidence, steam or frost."

"Well, put it in the after-action report. How much longer you plan to be out there?"

"Twenty, thirty minutes maybe. Longer if I go over everything on the trailer. Why?"

"Just wondering. I sent a status report up to the satellite just a minute ago, and said we would circle back and check the ROPS and LPPN before we head further south."

Van chewed on that idea; it was distasteful, with the flavor of something that you ate because it was good for you even though it tasted horrid. Like mental Brussels sprouts. "That's going to put us further behind," he said, "but I reckon we need to."

"You don't sound like you're convinced."

"I just don't like it, is all."

"Then you're really not going to like this," Grace said. "By a strict reading of the checklist, we should go all the way back to Mercator for a full check-out."

O O O

Besides the camera, Van found nothing else wrong with the Turtle. Nor did he and Grace find anything wrong with the Halfway House facility. On every satellite pass during the seven-and-a-half hours they spent examining the LPPN and ROPS, they argued back and forth with Shay.

Van yawned as he read Shay's latest message. He'd read it twice already, and it didn't seem as if it was going to change. He adjusted the strap on the new ice pack on his knee. "Shay must be serious," Van said, "he's taken to signing his messages 'S. Nakamura, Mission Commander.'" Van checked the incoming queue again, even though he knew the result would be the same: no message from Barbara. She must be nearly as pissed as Shay.

Van lay back on the platform. Just a few more minutes of rest.

"It makes sense," Grace said as she stepped out of the latrine. A rolled-up white towel hung around her neck as she finger-combed her dark hair. "I'd hate to press on to Faustini and develop a worse problem."

Van closed his eyes. "Yeah, but if we go back now, when's the next chance to pick up a load of ice? It made sense to go down south this time, since we were coming this far—if we go back now, we're losing a lot of productive time."

"I don't deny that," Grace said. "But I'd rather be unproductive than stranded. It's not as if they can fly down to get us, either." The LSOV had made it back to Mercator, but it was out of commission until they could repair the faulty gimbal mechanism.

Van didn't like it, but it wasn't his job to like it. "Alright," he said, "I'll take the first shift. Give me twenty minutes of shut-eye and then I'll go forward. I'll tell you what, though—I'm just gonna drag my suit through the neck this time, instead of putting it on. That'll be easier on my knee."

"I won't tell anybody," Grace said. "I'll spool up a message while you rest. Satellite'll be coming over the horizon soon."

It was almost a half-hour later when Van wormed his way through the neck to the cab. He carried the ice pack with him, even though it was barely cool any more, along with his suit. He dumped the suit on the floor, under one of the fold-down jump seats, as he came through the hatch. He closed the hatch behind him and situated himself with the ice on his knee. Within five minutes, he ticked through the start-up procedure and had Snapper rolling back the way they had come: north toward Mare Nubium and Mercator Crater.

Van adjusted the view of the rearmost camera so he could see when they lost LOS with the Halfway House. The shadows, fingers of black grasping at the reflective lunar plain, were longer than when they had arrived. They would grow longer still until the lunar night—

Something popped. Not like the usual thermal expansions and contractions, this was sharper: not loud, but distinct. Van looked at all his instruments, but they indicated everything was fine, and was about to call Grace on the intercom when the barest flutter of a breeze blew past his right ear.

He turned his head up and to the right as if following the moving air. Thin white fingers of frosty vapor jetted out of one of the cab windows.

He recalled Grace's worry as he hit the intercom switch. "Grace? We have a worse problem."

CHAPTER TWELVE

A Wave of Growing Doubt

Sunday, 3 December 2034

The cold, clear, blue Montana sky looked almost close enough to touch. The Sun was still low, but its radiance cut through the chill and scattered most of the shadows.

Barbara Richards leaned against a fencepost, gazing up at clouds as white and soft as shredded cotton, and thought of ways to kill her husband.

She had plenty of time to plan; he wasn't due back for over six weeks, and that was if the mission didn't get extended. Unfortunately, the ground was getting too hard already to dig a hole so she could bury the careless jerk—and if she took her dad's backhoe and started digging trenches, he might get a little suspicious. Finally, she agreed with the old cliché: he was impossible to live with, but she couldn't really kill him.

"First thing is, I'm fine," his message said. Only Van would say he was "fine" in the same breath as mentioning the intramural soccer injury that left him on crutches for two months. *Clumsy ox.* She ought to bust his other knee so he'd limp evenly.

Serve him right for taking that setup mission and leaving me down here to milk the Bessies. If he gets hurt so bad that they ground him—

Barbara cut off that line of speculation as best she could; it would only lead to more consternation. She walked back along the fence, her boots squishing slightly in the cold slush. Winter had come early to the ranch, followed by spring-like days that melted the fresh snow and turned the paths to mud.

At the door, she pulled the soles of her boots over the scraper and swung her feet through the boot brushes before she went inside and pulled the boots off. The house still smelled of morning coffee and bacon, and her stomach rumbled in anticipation of an early lunch.

Her dad, hale and hearty at sixty-two, sat at the vintage Formica kitchen table, sleeves rolled up on his green flannel shirt, working over some of the books. The ranch was a sideline more than anything else—he got most of his income from oil wells on the property, tapping the Bakken Formation that spread east into the Dakotas and up into Canada—but he did all the bookkeeping himself, down to the penny. "How's the beef?" he asked.

"They're not beef yet," Barbara said. "They're still milk machines for the time being. And they're fine."

He put down his pen and looked closely at her in that fatherly way she both loved and hated. The set of his jaw, the way his dark eyes widened a little and then narrowed by the same degree: loving disapproval. "What's eating you?"

"What do you mean?"

He raised his eyebrows. "I can tell by the tone of your voice that something's not right."

Barbara went back through what she'd said. How had she sounded? She'd been too preoccupied to pay attention. Maybe she'd been a little too loud and quick, in the way that her mom used to call "snippy," snapping at him because Van wasn't there for her to snap at.

"My husband is an idiot," she said, deliberately keeping her voice calm and her speech even.

Her dad picked the pen back up and returned his attention to his paperwork. "Is that all? Heck, I could've told you that. In fact, I think I *did* tell you that."

The corners of her mouth turned up at her dad's light-hearted jab, then she reasserted control. She needed to talk to another woman, just to vent a little. She could saddle PennyFourYourThoughts and ride out to the family plot by the copse and talk to her mom, but today she needed someone who would talk back. And she knew just who to call.

Half an hour later, after getting shifted from number to number several times, she finally heard Beverly Needham's excited voice on the phone. "Barmaid, how are you?"

Barbara grimaced, glad her friend couldn't see her reaction. Serve drinks at one O-Club function and you're tagged for life. "I've been better, Belladonna. How about you?"

They had been friends since Vandenberg. Barbara was a junior captain, and had been working in the launch squadron as a planner for a month when she met the Needhams at one of the base's orientation sessions. Major Gary Needham was the epitome of the "steely-eyed missile man," newly arrived from a tour in North Dakota as a missile standardization/evaluation officer, and Beverly— "Belladonna" or "Bella" or "BD" because of some unspecified death-metal music connection—was a civilian nurse who had settled into the role of the ideal officer's wife. They made a great team, and even then Barbara knew the Needhams were destined for a textbook career. Gary was an instructor in the initial operational training program for missileers, on the fast track to a staff job and then an Operations Officer billet and eventually Squadron Command.

Another fresh face at that orientation session had been Van Richards: a young lieutenant who had washed out of pilot training and would shortly be Gary's student in the missile program.

Those were the days.

BD sounded happy. "We're doing well, hon. The desert's cool and crisp this time of year. We got up to Santa Fe over the weekend, and our final training is going well. I'm glad to get out of that mountain, that's for sure. But if you've 'been better,' then I need to hear what you called me about. So spill it, girl."

BD's no-nonsense attitude brought a less reluctant smile to Barbara's lips. "You sure I'm not taking you away from anything? It took me a while to track you down, but I can call back later if you need."

"Nothing here that won't wait, dear. Talk."

"I don't know if you heard, but Van's hurt."

BD didn't answer right away, and the background noise changed for a moment. Barbara thought she might be holding her hand over the phone.

"I didn't know, but I just asked Chuck Springer and he said he'd check. Do you know Chuck and Trish?"

"No, I don't think so."

"They're good people. They're going up with us, so you'll meet 'em. Now, that man of yours gave us a briefing a couple of weeks ago and he was healthy enough then. How'd he get himself hurt?"

Barbara explained about the message she'd received, and how little information Van had relayed. As she talked, Barbara discovered a kernel of doubt inside herself that she'd never noticed before.

Until this morning, excitement had been building inside her, growing the way a tree grows: rings of anticipation and hope layering one over the other, branches of enthusiasm spreading outward as homes for dreams. She'd known about the risk but with her engineering background she had accepted the mitigations. She hadn't really been concerned for Van's safety, even when she first got his message: the call had come from him, so obviously he was well enough. Now she was a little ashamed for being more irritated that his injury might keep them out of the colony project than worried for him. She *was* worried, especially that he might do something to hurt himself worse, but that feeling seemed distant compared to a new fear, one she had never acknowledged before: a creeping fear for her own safety that would rot the timbers of her resolve if she didn't fix it.

Before she knew it, a wave of growing doubt—doubt of her abilities, doubt of her fortitude, doubt even of her sanity for signing a Consortium contract—built up inside her and broke on the shore of her friendship. She had started out explaining what had happened to Van, but by the end she had dumped a bucketful of crap on her friend's head. BD, one of the most careful and caring people Barbara had ever known, didn't say a word during Barbara's rant.

Barbara breathed into the silence.

"So," BD said after a moment, "you feel better?"

"A little. Tell me something that'll make me feel a lot better."

"You are the most brilliant, most beautiful woman I know," BD said. "Other than me, of course."

Barbara laughed, and was some better: more for the laughing than for the words. "Of course," she said.

"So, other than your discovery that you really do have doubts like the rest of us, what's been going on with you?"

Barbara chuckled. "I've realized how much basic animal husbandry I've forgotten, and why I got out of dairy farming in the first place." She would never admit it to her father, but it had only taken one day of the farm routine for the old restlessness to kick in: the wanderlust that had led her to Northwestern, to Officer Training School, to Wright-Patterson and Eglin and Vandenberg. When she'd had enough of active duty life, it had been that same spirit that led her to accept Van's marriage proposal and follow him to Minot and then to Offutt and then out of the service and into the Consortium. Now, for the first time that she could remember, fear tainted that spirit and weighed it down.

"I'm not as sure as I was," she confessed to BD. "I'm worried that I won't be able to hack it, especially if something bad happens."

"Like what?"

"I don't know. Van gets hurt worse, or I get hurt. I screw up in training, or freak out when I'm in the Cave. Or I—"

BD interrupted. "Hang on, hon," she said. Again, it sounded as if the other end of the call was muffled for a moment, and Barbara held her breath. "Okay, Chuck just gave me an update. He said Van twisted his knee when they were loading equipment, after they'd set up one of the oxygen processors. They didn't think it was bad enough to send him back to base, so he and Grace were headed down to the polar station."

"That's pretty much what I knew before," Barbara said.

She could almost hear BD shaking her head. "Sorry, that's the best I have at the moment. Where were we?"

Barbara didn't want to go back into her litany of fears, so she took the chance to change the subject. "You were about to tell me how your training went. How was the Cave, really?"

"You know I'm not supposed to give you any details."

Barbara leaned forward and gripped the phone tighter, but she tried to keep her irritation at BD's reluctance out of her voice. "Oh, come on, you can give me a general impression."

Silence on the other end meant BD was considering what she would say. Barbara focused on the yellow backs of hundreds of old copies of *National Geographic* lining the shelves in her parents' living room. When she was young, before her dad joined the rest of the 21st Century and had high-speed Internet brought out to the house, they had been a fountain of adventures for her. He'd kept up the subscription as long as the magazine had lasted.

"You worked in some buildings that didn't have windows, didn't you?" BD asked. "Just think of it as a really secure building."

That didn't cheer Barbara as much as it should.

"It's very dark," BD continued. "Sometimes it's boring, and other times there's almost too much excitement to stand. It was hard, but in the end not as hard as I thought it was going to be."

Barbara considered that assessment. "You were an ER nurse, though," she said, "and that had to help during the 'exciting' times."

BD chuckled. "You might think, but that was a long time ago."

"Maybe, but I barely made it through Self-Aid and Buddy Care." The confessions and anxieties poured out of her in practically a single breath. "I'm just not sure I can handle big emergencies, you know? Little emergencies, okay, I can do those, but not big ones. Right now I know Van's hurt and I have no way to get to him … I haven't even been able to send a message, because I don't know what to say to him. I think I'm mad at him because it keeps me from panicking over him being hurt."

Barbara paused, and BD said, "I'm not sure I can help you with that, hon. Unless you want to come down to New Mexico and I'll give you a big hug."

Barbara smiled at the idea. "Just tell me it's all going to be alright, BD."

"You want me to lie to you?"

"Maybe a little."

A sigh issued from the speaker. "We've known each other a long time, Barmaid. I remember how careful you were, meticulous even, and I suspect that hasn't changed. That made you a good engineer, and it makes me pretty confident that you're going to make it through everything okay. But let me ask: right now this minute, do you think of yourself as a glass half-full or half-empty person?"

Barbara weighed herself on the optimism scale and found herself wanting. "Half empty, right now."

She imagined Beverly nodding her head, deep in thought. "In that case," her friend said, "I suspect Van is going to contract gangrene in his leg and have to have it sawed off just above the knee."

"What?" Barbara was too stunned to say anything else, but in response to her half-shouted question Beverly Needham was … laughing.

"That's not funny," Barbara said.

"It's not?" BD asked, between chuckles. "You really think it might happen?"

"No," Barbara said. A thousand different things might happen, but that wasn't one of them. Or at least not one she was willing to entertain.

"Then maybe your glass is fuller than you thought, dear." BD, her caring and concerned friend, started laughing again.

"It is going to be alright, isn't it," Barbara said.

"No guarantees, girl, but I think there's a good chance."

"That was mean, BD. I knew I should've called Maggie Stewart instead of you." She didn't mean it—Maggie was nice, but would never be as good a friend as Beverly—but Barbara wanted to get a dig in.

"Huh. Oh, really? Maggie is a sweet old lady, dear, but she doesn't have your best interests at heart the way I do. Besides, she's going in the Cave later today, so you wouldn't have reached her."

"Maybe, but she wouldn't be mean.…"

"Oh, stop whining," BD said, but Barbara could hear the smile in her voice. "Go call your big brute and tell him that if he scares you again you'll hurt him yourself and go to the Moon without him."

"Okay, I'll do that. Thanks, BD."

"Anytime, hon. Now get off the phone—I'm sure you've got some cow manure to pick up or something."

O O O

Van kept one eye on the window above him as he eased the Turtle to a halt.

"What's the problem, Van?" Grace asked over the intercom.

"Can't talk now, Grace," Van said. "I'll get back to you in a minute. Monitor status for me, okay? Sing out if anything bad happens."

Of all the times not to have my suit on.

The seriousness of the situation didn't *seep* in; it snapped Van awake and cut through his thickening fatigue. He became hyper alert.

He didn't see any obvious cracks, but with the Sun a little behind and to the left that particular window was pretty well shadowed. The interior lights played hell with the reflections, and only the fact that the water vapor was flashing to ice before it quickly sublimed into nothingness gave him a clue that he had a problem. Van shifted painfully right, left, forward, backward, looking from all angles through the glass to pinpoint the vapor source. It looked like a tiny leak had formed where the window joined the frame.

Van reached back to the bulkhead by the hatch and opened the emergency locker. He grabbed the largest stickypatch in the case, a twenty-by-twenty centimeter square, and knelt with his left knee in the driver's seat so he could better reach the window.

His ears popped. A thin whistle sounded, as if a fairy were playing the pipes.

Van considered that he probably had time to read the directions on the stickypatch, but it seemed absurd to bother with something so simple. A cross between plastic wrap, MIL-SPEC "five hundred mile an hour" tape, and an adhesive bandage, they were tough, impermeable membranes designed to stick even on the outside of a suit or other moderate-pressure enclosure. In this case, it would be sticking on the inside; the pressure inside would help seal the opening. The pressure differential wasn't great enough to worry much about, because a higher percentage of oxygen in the Turtle's atmosphere allowed the overall pressure to be kept lower than Earth normal and still be breathable. But the pressure on the other side was as close to zero as there was anywhere in the solar system, and Van intended to keep the glass and anything else he could find between him and it. He was as close to that zero pressure as he ever wanted to get.

"Yellow light, Van," Grace said through the irritating buzz of an alarm. The alarm went silent a second later; she must've acknowledged it on the status panel.

He didn't bother to look; he knew what it was.

He grabbed the hand towel he had brought forward with the ice pack and wiped the glass and the metal rib, in case any vapor had condensed or frozen there as the pressure in the cabin fell. He dropped the towel to float gracefully down and tore open the stickypatch package. He gently slapped the patch in place, half on the glass and the rest overlapping the support bracket. The center of the patch sucked up against the surface as the remaining atmosphere behind pressed in on it. He smoothed down the adhesive edges all around, to avoid any other small leaks.

Van listened for any more whistles, whines, or pops. Adrenaline enhanced his hearing so the cab was full of electrical hums and the conducted vibrations of pumps and fans, but they were all the normal sounds. As his heartbeat slowed to normal, his perceptions of the sounds attenuated. He slipped down off the seat and barely noticed the pain as his injured knee took up his mass.

He noticed the pain a moment later when he was suiting up. It was always hard to put on a suit in the small cab, even with the jump seats folded up and the driver's seat slid forward as far as it would go, but it was especially hard with one leg that didn't want to bend. Van contorted himself, his knee popping in agonizing complaint, until he was fully suited, checked out, and sealed in.

Van attached his suit to the cab's oxygen port, verified the flow was good, and only then consulted his status board.

"I see your yellow light, Grace. Thanks for shutting off the alarm."

"Anytime—I figured that's what you were working on."

"Yeah, looks like we got a pinhole leak, either in the window glass or around the frame. I got a patch on it. Cab pressure should be stable now."

"Looks that way," she said, "but it'll be a while before we can be sure."

"Roger that. Think I'll just sit tight."

"You're suited, right? You okay?"

"Yeah, I'm okay—for now. I'm worried about that panel, though. I don't want to put too much pressure on it."

Grace didn't answer immediately. Van scrolled through status displays while he waited for her to piece together the conclusion that seemed obvious to him. A moment later she said, "I don't know if I like where you're going with that."

Van smiled. It almost hurt to smile. "Where am I going with that?"

"You want to depressurize the cab."

"Yeppir."

"And drive all the way back in suits."

"Pretty much. We'll use the neck like an airlock, pump it down when we're moving back and forth."

"Won't that be fun," Grace said. She sounded as enthused about the idea as Van.

"Not as fun as trying to drive from the back," he said. It was possible to route the main drive controls to the rear compartment and use the Turtle's cameras to see, but no one really wanted to try it. "I just think it's better to do that than to risk making that panel worse."

Now Grace laughed. "I guess I was a little premature sending that last message, huh?"

"Yeah. Why don't you crank out a new one and get it ready for the next overpass? Meantime, I'm going to get this bucket of bolts moving again. The sooner I get some klicks behind us, the sooner I can come back and relax."

"Maybe I'll whip up something to eat for you," Grace said.

Van took his turn to laugh. "That's okay, Grace. I just want to get a few hours of solid sleep."

Van maneuvered himself into position behind the console. His knee complained and he answered with a curse. "Maybe after I tape up my knee better."

CHAPTER THIRTEEN

Professional Judgment

Wednesday, 6 December 2034
Lunar Colonist Group 2, Training Day 3

The lab was as functional as Stormie and Frank could get it in two busy days. It was a single bay inside mockup habitat four-A, which itself was inside what used to be the Aaronson and Hicks Mine, in the Wasatch Mountains northeast of Salt Lake City. The bay itself was about two meters wide by two and a half long, with a single small table in the center and a reasonable facsimile of a lab bench along one of the short walls. One of the long walls was a set of flat, sliding partitions like a Japanese screen; the other curved like the inside wall of one of those corrugated buildings she remembered from old military movies and *Gomer Pyle* episodes on TVLand. It was cramped, but she had already gotten used to the lack of space; the layout, on the other hand, wasn't ideal. She and Frank would probably rearrange the lab several more times before their three-month training session was over.

Frank was out gathering water samples, and Stormie idly wished she had won the coin toss. Not that she minded running the air balance calculations—her CommPact was more than up to the task, and she was a fair programmer—but she enjoyed the hands-on part of their work almost as much as he did. She was on the fifth iteration, with a new set of assumptions on the leak rate of the habitats and therefore new requirements for inputs from outside the ecosystem—resupplies that would be as rare as empty bellies at a family reunion—when a commotion on the other side of the sliding plastic partition stole her attention.

She slid open the "door" and caught Herb Crandall's eye as he jogged down the passageway. "What's going on?"

Crandall didn't break stride. "Fire in the next module," he said.

Stormie looked back the way he'd come, toward module three-A. No one else seemed to be coming from that direction, and she realized she hadn't heard an alarm or an announcement from Central Control. She yelled at Crandall's back, "Did anyone alert Central?"

He stepped through the hatch at the far end of the habitat, without acknowledging her question.

Stormie pocketed her CommPact and moved back the way Crandall had come, toward the junction to habitat three-A. She passed one of the emergency stations: a fire alarm, dual airline respirator hookup, fire extinguisher, and battery-powered emergency lights, all in a slender cabinet tower that was marked at the bottom with phosphorescent signs. The signs themselves, as well as the cabinet handles and controls, had shapes that were distinct to the touch so even if the corridor was full of smoke they could be located and used. The instruction manual had explained that the principle was borrowed from the emergency stations aboard nuclear submarines.

An odor of burned plastic tinged the air, and Stormie almost grabbed an airline mask from the cabinet. She already planned to grab a pressure suit out of the cabinet in the junction ahead.

Hacking coughs came from that direction.

She sprinted the rest of the way and hurdled the high threshold into the junction. The junction was a blocky room with little more than pressure doors and equipment lockers, with status monitoring and control panels next to each hatch. The hatch to the next module was closed, which was good, but Christine Abernathy sounded as if her lungs were trying to vacate her body. She was bending over Leonard Markov, whom she had apparently just dragged out of module three-A.

Before Stormie could stop herself, she asked the obvious question. "Are you okay?"

Abernathy nodded, coughing so hard she couldn't articulate an answer. She pointed at Markov.

"Let's get him into the next tunnel," Stormie said. Even though these were mockups of the prefabricated lunar habitats, and real tunnels on the Moon wouldn't be dug for almost a year, almost everyone had started calling the narrow habitat modules "tunnels"— in much the same way they used "hatch" and "door" interchangeably. "Is he injured?"

Christine shook her head.

"You go ahead, I'll get him," Stormie said.

"We'll get him," said a voice behind her. George Fiester stepped through the hatch, followed by Alex Bonaccio. "See if you can get some status from inside," George said.

The two men picked Markov up and wrestled him through the hatch into module four-A. Stormie turned her attention to Christine, whose coughing had started to subside.

"Is there anyone else in there?"

"Don't know," Christine said. "Don't think so."

"How did the fire start?"

"Not sure ... Markov was in his test cell ... something electrical." Her eyes started to glaze over, as if she might pass out or throw up or both. Stormie turned her and pushed her gently toward the open hatch.

"Go in there and sit down," she said. "We'll take it from here. George, Alex, we need to get suited up. I think we need to go into three-A." She turned to the communications panel and tapped in the code for Central Control. "Central, this is Pastorelli."

"Adamson here." Harmony's voice was as smooth as if she was singing a lullaby.

"Did you get word of a fire in Module three-A?"

"That's affirmative. Single alarm pull. We got the indicator, then everything went dark from there."

"I'm right outside that module, and there's no alarm sounding here. And we've got—"

"Standby, Stormie," Harmony said. A moment later the speaker crackled with an all-call public address. "Attention, attention. Fire reported in module three-alpha. Alarms appear inoperative. Responders report in on channel twelve. Repeat, fire reported...."

Stormie tuned out the repetition and switched the comm panel to channel twelve. Someone tugged on her arm, and she turned to find George holding out a pressure suit to her.

The Consortium had produced suits in three sizes that were adjustable within limits; two of each size were stored in lockers in each junction, as well as in lockers on either end of each habitat module. The locker behind George was open, and he held one medium suit for himself and a large for Stormie. The large would be baggy on her, but she was tall enough to need it. Behind George, Alex was halfway through putting his suit on.

"Central, this is Pastorelli," Stormie said.

"Go, Stormie."

"We've got Christine Abernathy and Leonard Markov, both with apparent smoke inhalation. They're at this end of tunnel four-A. Christy said she thought the fire was electrical, and she didn't think anyone else was left in the module. I'm here in the junction with George Fiester and Alex Bonaccio, and we're suiting up to go into three-A."

"Roger, Stormie, standby." Harmony announced a call for first aid response to the tunnel behind Stormie.

Stormie folded herself into her suit according to the instructions stenciled on the fabric. She ticked off the steps mentally as she completed them, and started the checkout sequence. She plugged her CommPact into the slot on the suit's interior, glad she'd automatically brought it along. She worked as fast as she could, almost faster than she dared since wearing the suit was not yet second nature to her, but she drove herself forward at the thought of someone still in module three-A. They would be hooked up to the airline and fighting the fire, and hopefully already had it under control—but if so, why weren't they on the response channel, giving status or calling for backup? Did that mean the module was empty and the fire wasn't being fought?

"Control, we'll be ready to enter in just a couple of minutes," Stormie said. "What's the status in there?"

Harmony was a few seconds responding. "We've got intermittent heat signals in the module. We've initiated pumpdown of the habitat."

Stormie frowned. Had she heard correctly? She glanced at the status readout and confirmed the pressure in three-A was falling, slowly. She clenched her jaw around a harsh rebuke and simply said into the microphone, "Pumpdown? If that fire's not out, that tunnel needs to be vented."

The silence on the other end galled her. They could not truly "vent" the tunnel in this situation, since it was a training mockup, but she was determined to play the scenario as if it were completely real. She expected everyone else to do so, too.

Stormie started her air supply and sealed herself into her suit. She tuned her radio to the response channel and hand-signaled George to do a buddy check on her suit.

As the seconds flashed away in her display and she waited for Control to answer, her throat tightened as if she were slowly strangling. Pumping down the tunnel made no sense: why force the combustion products into the equalization tanks? They'd be hell to filter out, and it would be much quicker to purge the module of its atmosphere and rob the fire of its breath. If anyone was still inside, trying to contain the fire, they should be on the air system and expect the tunnel to be vented; because they would be unlikely to have gotten fully suited, the vent procedure would avoid going all the way to vacuum. It would hurt like hell, especially their eardrums, but getting the fire out was the first priority, and Control would do their damnedest to get more pressure back in the tunnel before whoever was inside sustained too much physical damage. That's also why the procedure wasn't instantaneous: the same pylons with the emergency power and air supply hookups had lights and klaxons to warn responders so they could work their way to the ends of the module and be closer to any rescue parties.

Stormie checked George's suit seals and gave him a thumb's-up. She found it difficult to concentrate as her mind shifted from one scenario to another to another. She considered the volume of air in

139

tunnel three-A compared to the capacity of the pumps to move it; then how she and Frank would compensate when that volume was lost; then the damage inside the tunnel and the possibility of finding a person inside. A wave of vertigo struck her as her mind jumped from topic to topic, and the thought of fire on the other side of the door brought back the memory of the scorching treatment she and Frank had recently endured. She punched her own thigh through the fabric of the suit to give herself some external stimulus to consider.

"Central," Stormie said, "this is Bio. On the record, in my professional judgment, I believe the module must be vented immediately. Repeat: in my professional judgment, module three-A must be vented now."

O O O

Frank stepped through the hatch from habitat module one-A into the junction leading to module two-A. The water sample bottles clinked against the little wire mesh tray he was carrying back to their makeshift lab. In Frank's opinion, calling it a laboratory was like calling a paper wasp a jumbo jet, since their workspace was basically a closet with a cramped lab bench shoved into it.

The speaker above his head crackled to life. A female voice called for attention and reported a fire in the next module but one.

Frank stepped into module two-A. A group of people hurried toward him from the other end of the habitat. He flattened himself against the right-side wall to give them more room to pass.

Frank still had trouble keeping some of the trainees straight; he registered the tall, blonde electronics technician without recalling her name, then the Carmichael couple stepped past him into the junction. Frank said, "Where are you going?"

"Fire in tunnel three-A," Carmichael yelled over his shoulder. "We're evacuating." He ran past, with four more trainees on his heels.

Frank was alone in the tunnel, frozen not by fear but by incredulity. *Evacuating to where?*

The AC had gone to great pains to simulate the condition in which "evacuate" carried a similar meaning here as it would on the

Moon. The fake habitats were positioned inside mine tunnels, and outside hatches were sealed in such a way as to simulate vacuum on the other side. The trainees had even had to enter through a big airlock and walk into the habitats wearing pressure suits, just as they would at the colony. The layout in the mine was linear instead of the branching plan of the Mercator base, but Stormie had commented as they processed into the mine that the facility must have been absurdly expensive. One of the trainers had overheard and said, "Yeah, but Cheyenne Mountain was already taken."

Frank set down the tray of sample bottles and ran in the opposite direction from Carmichael and the others.

Voices echoed from the end of the tunnel, in the junction between modules two-A and three-A. He recognized everyone in this group: Jake Adamson, Chu Liquan, and Maggie Stewart. All of them were in the category of candidates that Stormie had called "most likely to succeed," and it was clear to see why: they weren't running away from the danger, they were putting on pressure suits to confront it. Jake, the smallest of the three, had his suit on completely except for helmet and gloves; the others lagged only a little. Liquan stepped aside gracefully from the open suit locker so Frank could get a suit for himself.

"Why did the alarm not sound?" Frank asked.

"I don't know," Jake said. "We can sort that out later. Get a suit on quick as you can, or back away and let us handle it."

One of the two suits left in the locker was a "large," and Frank pulled it out and started putting it on. He wished he'd had more orientation and more time working in the suit, but the last few days had been whirlwind enough. Thankfully, the suit design somewhat intuitive.

"What is the plan?" Frank asked.

Jake answered, and he didn't sound happy. "Damned if I know. I don't have status on the module, this panel's not reading right. The idiots who evacuated this way didn't count bodies on their way out before they dogged the door. Harmony hasn't given an update—"

He was interrupted by Stormie's report on Abernathy and Markov, and Central's announcement for first aid support to module five-A. Now Frank recognized the controller's voice as Jake's wife, though he concentrated on donning and checking out his suit.

His suit failed its self-test.

Over the intercom, Stormie called for the status inside the affected module. Frank half-listened to the answer while he traced the failure to the left glove—he hoped the diagnostic routine had correctly identified the source. It was probably something simple, like a short, but he didn't spend time wondering about it. He grabbed a new glove out of the locker, sealed it to the suit, and finally got a green light.

"Did she say pumpdown?" Frank asked. "That is not the standard procedure."

"Damn right it's not," Jake said. His face was tense, and his voice sounded as if his vocal cords needed lubrication.

Frank thought about it while he finished checking out his suit. They were pumping the atmosphere into the holding tanks? Something about that did not add up. True, lowering the pressure in the habitat would mean less oxygen to sustain the fire. And it was not a matter of pressure—the equalization tanks were rated high enough that they could hold the compressed contents of two entire modules—but a matter of composition. If the fire was small, and contained quickly, the atmosphere pumped out might contain a useful concentration of oxygen. But surely the fire was using up oxygen and creating a lot of carbon monoxide and possibly other compounds which would be better lost. Frank asked, "Why pump the habitat down? Why not open the access port and let the module vent down to the limits?"

Over the intercom, Stormie asked the same question of Central Control. Central did not respond.

Liquan said, "Your wife seems to be wondering the same thing. Perhaps Central does not believe we can afford to lose that volume of atmosphere."

"Seal up and buddy check, everybody," Jake said. "Frank, you're with me. Maggie, dog that door shut and then you and Liquan check each other out. As soon as everyone's ready, we'll pump down the junction so we can open the door and get inside the module.

Liquan, you and Maggie get extinguishers in case the fire hasn't smothered. Frank, you and I will pull out bodies if we find any. Damn, I hate not knowing what's going on."

Frank checked his oxygen supply and power, then sealed his suit. He and Jake ran through a buddy check and everyone checked in on the common response radio channel.

Stormie's voice came through inside Frank's helmet. "Central, this is Bio. On the record, in my professional judgment…" The hint of tension in her voice was vintage Stormie; she was wound tight like a spring-driven clockwork, ready for action and barely held back. He heard in her voice the passion that so captivated him. Frank stifled a chuckle but smiled so wide he caught the reflection of his teeth from his darkened head-up display.

Frank turned on the display and tried using it to pull up a status report on the module, but all he got was a schematic out of the database with dark spots where the sensors should be. Something was wrong with the electronics, probably either the sensor package or the power supply; that would account for the missing alarm and the nonfunctional status panel. With a quick glance at the air system schematic Frank took in the pumps, filters, and tanks that kept air circulating and as fresh as possible—he and Stormie knew that system as well as they knew their own names. Stormie was right— that habitat needed to be purged immediately. It should have been purged as soon as the doors were shut. Every trainee was supposed to know where the airline respirators were, where the extinguishers were, and the importance of getting people either protected or out of the danger zone so a module could be purged if needed. But Adamson had said people fled the scene without doing a basic check; if they left behind someone incapacitated, purging the module would kill them. *Did no one stay in place? Did no one fight the fire?*

Frank began to share Jake's agitation with the lack of information; it lay on the back of his neck like a warm itch. "Who is with Stormie in the other tunnel junction?" Frank asked.

He regretted the question immediately as Jake's wife overrode the signal from the Central Control station: "Cut the chatter. I need reports. Junction three-A-four, report your status."

O O O

In the junction between three-A and four-A, Stormie answered Harmony's call for the status report.

"Central, this is Pastorelli," she said, pleased that Frank was listening in the other junction cell. He was safe, and she could be sure to answer his question in her report. "Since Christy said the fire was electrical, George and Alex are going to try to pull the plug on three-A from here. The pump-down is taking too long," she resisted the urge to remind them that she had told them it would, "and I recommend shutting off the tank and purging the tunnel immediately. Regardless of whether they can get the power shut—"

"Roger," Harmony said. "I've got only intermittent signals from the heat detectors. There's still something hot there, and I don't know if it's people. I'm about to initiate the purge, but the system's screwed up and you may have to do it from there."

We should've already done it.

Stormie fought to keep her voice steady. "Understood, Central," she said. "Anybody in that module should be on an airline by now." *If someone is still inside ...* Christine hadn't reported anybody else, and Stormie'd told Central that herself. Why were they dragging their feet?

She reminded herself briefly that this was still training, but shunted that aside because they all needed to act as if it was the real thing. The brief realization that everything was a long, complicated test produced a fluttery feeling in her stomach—no, further down and deeper in—as if her guts were alternately weightless and leaden. The feeling intensified and abated in spasmodic bursts as she considered possible courses of action. Obey Control and let the fire do more damage, or do what needed to be done? A bead of sweat tickled the back of her neck as it tumbled down her spine. She hovered her hand lightly over the controls.

"Hey, Harmony," Jake said over the response channel. "Why not do a head count on the rest of us? Process of elimination—"

"What do you think I'm trying to do, Jake? Just shut up a second and let me do my job."

Normally Stormie would commend Harmony for standing up to Jake in a moment of crisis, but her voice carried a thin film of near panic. Stormie lifted her hand away from the touchscreen. If she purged the module now, it would save Harmony trying to make the decision, but that wasn't a good reason for doing so. Stormie's only turn in the Central Control "hot seat" had been in a simulation during the early computer-based phase of training. Neither she nor Frank would ever be assigned to monitor all the inputs, communications, and chaos that crashed into and filtered out of the tiny control center … control cubicle was more like it. She liked knowing what the controllers went through, because it helped her know when to talk and when to shut up, and it was part of the general approach of learning a little bit of practically everything. The frontier might need a few specialists, but most early colonists were generalists by necessity. They might not need to be able to gut a pig or handle a plow or do any of a hundred mundane earthbound tasks on the lunar frontier, but that kind of flexibility—to be able to step in and perform adequately a wide variety of tasks—could mean the difference between life and death. So Stormie *could* do the control job, but had no desire to. She endured enough stress across her shoulder blades and in the muscles running up either side of her neck—and with the stress, searing memory-heat—with just the dilemma she was facing: including, in the back of her mind, how to re-balance the whole air system once she dumped nearly an entire module's worth of atmosphere, and how to filter out any contaminated air pumped into the balancing tank. She didn't need the additional stress of monitoring and directing all of the base's routine and emergency activities. It was no wonder Harmony was stressed, but there were only forty trainees in this facility: within a year there would be more colonists than that for Control to keep track of. *If she can't handle it at this scale….*

Still, as far as Stormie could tell there was no reason to do a headcount, no reason to poll the proximity sensors to see if anyone's ID ring showed up inside that module—even if those sensors were still working, and they hadn't loaned out their ring to somebody else. On the other side of the pressure door there was, or had been, a fire. An electrical fire, which meant to some degree burning insulation, probably burning plastic, spewing out a variety of poisons. Anyone in there should've found the airline system and plugged in, even in the dark—if anything, they would be wondering why their ears hadn't popped yet from the blowdown.

Stormie looked back at the two men with her. Alex had sealed the junction and started its airlock cycle; the slack in Stormie's suit ballooned away as the good air in the smaller space was pumped out. At this rate the junction, being so much smaller, would get down to the amber line almost as fast as the module would if she purged it. George stepped away from the other control panel and waved his hand across his throat. Stormie took that to mean he'd gotten the power shut off; she confirmed it with a glance at the panel itself, and smiled because he'd had the presence of mind to cut only the noncritical circuits. George nodded behind the glass of his helmet, and Stormie took that to mean he was ready to go.

She touched the "Initiate" block on the control pad. Only five seconds had passed since Harmony had last spoken, but they seemed like five or even fifteen minutes.

Harmony came back on the air almost immediately. "Confirmed, Bio," she said, "module is clear. Heat sensors indicate the fire is out, but sensors have been intermittent. Initiating vent."

"I just did," Stormie said. "Standby to open the supply valve if we happen to find anyone in there." She watched the pressure reading fall, wondering briefly if the indicator was programmed to respond in that way. She waved George to the hatch when the inner and outer pressures read nearly the same.

Stormie pulled a flashlight out of its wall socket and moved after George into the dimly lit habitat. The rotating warning beacons were off; only the two sets of battery-powered explosion-proof emergency lights spaced down the passageway cast any light. They were sharp and distinct and their oblique reflections made the corridor seem unusually long and narrow. The emergency air stations were set just under the lights, and beneath the warning beacons were amber lights that came on when the airline systems were operating. The amber lights were dark.

George began checking the first cramped compartment on the left side of the corridor. Stormie paused just inside the hatch and radioed in their status.

"Central, we're entering the tunnel now. No one in the corridor that I can see. No lights from the e-stations. Jake, you coming in from your end?"

"That's affirm," Jake said. "Opening the hatch now."

An oval of light blossomed in the far wall of the habitat, then was obscured by a human figure stepping through the hatch.

George checked the left-hand compartments and Stormie checked the right. Had this been real, rather than in the training environment, the toilet water would have boiled away, but the ambient pressure hadn't fallen that much: the Consortium would never have invested as much money as it would take to make the mockup tunnels that realistic.

The room and the water pumping station were clear of people or damage, as were the first two multi-use compartments thereafter. The third multi-use cubicle, however, was set up as an electronics repair area, and at the moment held a collection of charred components inside a half-melted plastic shell. Stormie found the power cord and unplugged the unit. She wrinkled her nose and chuckled at herself for doing so: her brain had imagined the smell of burned plastic and her nose had reacted.

That's okay, we'll smell it when we get out of these suits.

"Central," she said, "I found one ... I think it's a signal generator or an analyzer ... that looks like it was the fire source. I unplugged it, but I think we should check the rest of the rooms before we turn the power back on."

"Roger, Stormie," Harmony said, and turned the suggestion into a set of instructions. If she was mad that Stormie had acted to purge the module before she gave instructions to do so, her voice didn't betray it.

Stormie rotated her head as far as she could inside her helmet, easing the knots in her neck and shoulder muscles. Once they got the power back on and started re-pressurizing the habitat, she could go back to work. She grinned at the fact that she was actually looking forward to cleaning air filters, then remembered that her first task would be recalculating the air exchanges based on the lost volume—

Crap. If this is the end of day three, what's going to happen at the end of day eighty-three?

O   O   O

Frank was surprised how quickly he lost all sense of normal time down inside the mountain and under the near-constant artificial light. By his watch, over two hours had passed since he entered tunnel two-A with his tray of water samples and got sucked into the response in the next tunnel. His samples were finally safe in the lab, even though he was not with them.

He leaned over and pillowed his head on Stormie's shoulder. They sat crammed practically hip to hip and nose to tail with the primary responders and a few other trainees in the temporary briefing area euphemistically called the "big room," in front of a flat-screen television, waiting for the AC evaluators to tell them how they did. Stormie wriggled a little, her attention fixed on the datapad in front of her. Frank only looked at her calculations for a second. "Will you assume the holding tank contents are useless?"

"No telling what volatilized off those components," she said.

"Very good. Wake me when the briefing, or debriefing, is over."

"Funny." Stormie nodded at the screen.

Terrance Winder, the Consortium's training manager, did not look happy. Frank was not sure he had ever seen the man truly happy, though—Winder's thin, sunken face behind his wire-rim glasses always looked sour—so he could not be sure. "Okay, folks, let's start this show so you can all get back to whatever it is you're supposed to be doing."

The debriefing worked its way chronologically from the time the fire started. Frank was surprised that the fire had not been staged for training purposes; it was a legitimate electrical fire caused by carelessness on Markov's part. Apart from that revelation, the debriefing was a tedious exercise in the difficulty of remote communication: since Winder and the other observers were elsewhere, and some of the participants themselves were tuned in from other parts of the training facility, the proceedings made Frank feel as if he were part of one of those quaint unreality television productions.

The Consortium had considered turning the training program into a television or Internet broadcast, to generate interest and money from sponsorships. Permissions had been part of the initial paperwork he and Stormie had signed. He supposed the only reason they had not done it yet was that they had not figured out how to make the everyday training regimen interesting enough for an audience to actually tune in. It would be counter-productive to initiate fires and emergencies on a regular basis just for ratings.

The training director questioned and released various people according to when their parts played out. He was especially interested in the people who fled the scene rather than fighting the fire. Frank chuckled as Winder told one couple, "I'm not sure where you thought you would escape to—'escaping' from inside a pressure vessel into a vacuum is a difficult concept for me to grasp."

Winder shut off each of the remote connections as he dismissed the trainees using them. When he sent specific people from the room Frank and Stormie were in, they left a little reluctantly. Soon the room was down to just the response team, and Frank relaxed as the creeping claustrophobia of so many bodies in such a small space faded.

"Okay," Winder said, "now that the preliminaries are over, let's figure out what went right and what went wrong with the actual response."

Frank sat up and tried to look alert. No one in the room spoke. They looked at each other across and around the small space, and Frank found himself infected by George Fiester's sly little grin. Stormie returned to her calculations.

Frank touched Stormie's shoulder, and briefly rubbed at the tension there. They had not had much time to talk after the emergency was over, but clearly she was concerned about how her reaction would be judged: whether it was a test to see if she would do the right thing and purge the habitat, or obey the orders from Central Control. Several of the other colonists as well as many of the AC brass were former military people, and she had confided that she worried that they might insist on some sort of military discipline—which made sense when people were shooting at you— or the kind of practical safety discipline that made sense even to lifelong civilians. Frank had told her that he thought it unlikely that anyone had scripted the emergency to see whether she would obey or do what she knew was right; she had nodded and thanked him without, he suspected, really hearing his words.

"Okay," Winder said from the flat screen on the wall, "I'll start. Ms. Adamson, did Bio recommend purging module three-alpha, or pumping the module down?"

Stormie put her datapad in her lap. Jake squirmed in his seat by the far wall. His wife, apparently still on duty in Central Control, answered through the speaker. "Stormie recommended purging the module."

"Indeed," said Winder. "Was that registered as a professional judgment?"

"Yes, it was."

"In those words?"

Jake spoke up before Harmony could answer. "We all heard it, Terry. And we all know what it means. So quit dragging it out and tell us the score."

Winder stared out of the screen as if he was preparing to leap through it and seize Jake by the throat. "Okay," he said, and his voice seemed an octave deeper than it had been, "why not purge the habitat right away?"

Harmony was on a vocal pickup, so only her voice could betray her emotions. She kept under careful control. "I was in the habitat emergency checklist, and it recommended attempting to pump the module down in order to preserve as much atmosphere as possible."

The Winder image nodded. "Are there exceptions to that?"

"Yes. The presence of toxic materials."

"Very well. Ms. Pastorelli, have you analyzed the air in the equalization tank?"

Stormie did not hesitate. "No, not yet."

"So you don't know if there are any toxins in the tank."

"No. Not yet."

"And what do you expect to find when you analyze the contents?"

Frank glanced over at Jake, who was looking expectantly at Stormie. The slackness in his jaw and the wide-open set of his eyes betrayed his hopefulness, almost pleading, that Stormie would salvage this situation for his wife.

"I'm not sure," Stormie said. "Some of what burned was insulation and plastic—I don't know specifically what kind of plastic, or how completely they burned—so we might get some aromatic hydrocarbons, hydrogen cyanide, any number of different things. Not great, but they should only be small amounts, and we can probably rig a filter on the tank's output to draw off the worst of the contaminants."

Frank smiled at Stormie's carefully crafted answer, but lost his smile at Winder's next question.

O   O   O

"What level of cleanliness will that leave the tank?" the training director asked.

Stormie kept her face relaxed as she glanced up into the corner of the room. She resisted the urge to put her fingers on her chin; she wasn't that good an actress. She'd expected the question, but she pretended to ponder it in order to formulate the right answer.

Not level E, that's for sure.

She couldn't say that out loud, of course.

"I don't know," she said, because it was the truth. She faced the pseudo-Winder on the screen. "Without knowing exactly what may have gone through the pumps, what might have deposited on the inside, I couldn't be sure. But I'm not overly concerned about it." The cleanliness specifications for tanks had been around for decades, and were primarily meant to ensure that a storage tank for, say, monomethyl hydrazine, didn't have some organics that would react with it and cause a fire. They were talking about a holding tank, a pressure sink for the atmospheric system, and it had to be clean enough to produce breathable gas. Stormie was concerned about what might have ended up in the tank, but "not overly" was a good way to state her level of concern.

"I see," Winder said, in that slow delivery that said what he really saw was how Stormie was talking around the issue. "Alright then. Ms. Adamson, what about Bio's professional judgment call? Why was that significant, and why didn't you respond to it?"

Harmony was slow in answering, and suddenly Stormie's CommPact was a lead weight on her thigh. *Damn.* She could've pulled up the relevant paragraph from the Lunar Life Engineering contract and e-mailed it to Harmony. It wasn't as big a deal as Winder was making it out to be....

"It was significant," Harmony said, "because we are allowed to defer decisions to Consortium contractors if they invoke professional judgment. We aren't *required* to defer decisions to them, however, and until I had a better idea that we weren't going to anoxiate someone, I wanted to stay with the checklist."

Good answer, girl. Didn't even need my help.

"Asphyxiate," Winder said. "Ms. Pastorelli, why did you believe purging the module was the best plan?"

Stormie legitimately pondered this question for a second. "Whether it was the best plan, I'm not sure. The intakes for the pumps are near the floor, so a quick pumpdown had a chance of getting breathable air with only a few contaminants. I just knew purging the module would put the fire out quicker. And spreading seven modules' worth of atmosphere through the volume of eight, temporarily, until we can arrange for replenishment, was justifiable—"

"Why eight modules?"

It seemed a stupid question to Stormie. "Because we only have eight modules down here," she said. "Right now I'm trying to balance the air for forty people in four living modules, two working modules, and two farms. When I get on station I'll worry about balancing for more people and more habitats."

The image of Winder nodded and appeared to write some notes, then he looked up. "Very good," he said. "We'll compile our notes and get back with you. Meanwhile, you're all dismissed. Bio, I will tell you that you only have to balance for thirty-two people now. We had one couple self-eliminate after the fire, and we've cut three other couples for failure to act appropriately to the emergency."

CHAPTER FOURTEEN

Rational Trepidation

Thursday, 7 December 2034
Lunar Setup Mission II, Day 37

The Turtle's lights barely cut into the shadows outside. With every hour that the LVN moved north toward Mare Nubium and the edge of Mercator Crater, the Earth-Moon system turned and the shadows lengthened until there were more shadows than light. And just as the light was the starkest, brightest, purest light Van had ever seen, the shadows were the blackest.

But not as black as the shadow he carried with him, the shadow he himself cast over the mission and his own future in the Consortium.

His knee was smaller now, only about navel-orange-sized, but it still hurt like having razor blades installed under his kneecap. Grace had teased him about his "sexy" shaved leg—shaved from the middle of his thigh down to the middle of his calf—and he had almost gotten used to the constant feel of adhesive on his skin. These last four days of relative rest had been good for it, but the overall mission schedule had fallen apart and he wasn't going to be able to do his part to set it right.

And Oskar kept reminding him of that unfortunate fact.

Barbara, at least, had grown more supportive. She'd been thoroughly ticked off at first, and even threatened to come up and hurt his other knee if he did anything else stupid, but of late her notes had been encouraging. Her smiles were easier to read in her latest messages, but looking back he could pick out a grin even underneath the gruff exterior.

He wouldn't mind if she did come up to hurt his other knee, because at least she would be there.

He was grateful that the driving routine kept him separated from Grace, because he didn't have to be distracted by her ... attributes. The close quarters were sometimes a little too close. Van wanted Barbara on station with him. Not that it would be idyllic—the two of them had their heated moments—but it would afford far fewer temptations to stray. In his experience, misbehaving like that always led to difficulties. Hell, in his experience even the perception of misbehaving like that led to difficulties—usually the kind the Security Police had to clean up after jealous spouses exacted premature revenge.

The alarm in his helmet beeped three times in quick succession. He'd set it at half-hour intervals to keep him more alert. He checked the systems and verified that everything was still in the green. Except the crack in the cab, of course, but his stickypatch was still holding the truck together.

Good as duct tape.

He was driving northwest now, skirting the northern periphery of the low range of hills known as Rupes Mercator. Not that he could see much of the hills, being on the shadow side of them; not for the first time he wished for enough atmosphere that the Moon might have a little twilight, a little color instead of the endless black that created an almost seamless bubble around his little rolling island of light. He'd heard about teams in the Arctic and Antarctic, the storms they endured and the metaphor of being inside a ping-pong ball. Did they make black ping-pong balls? With the exception of earthshine, the lunar surface at night was like being inside one.

Static in his ears, just a momentary burst, brought him out of the shrouded night and back into the instrument-lit cab. A longer, almost musical pulse told him they were nearly in clear line-of-sight of the repeater. Then as he swung the Turtle around the well-marked curve in the worn track they called a road, an unbroken symphony of static told him they were almost home.

He squelched the static and keyed his helmet mic.

"Mercator Base, Mercator Base, do you copy? This is Van and Grace, riding the back of the Turtle, heading home."

O   O   O

Shay Nakamura had a difficult time looking pissed—he was usually so jovial—but Van thought he was pulling it off admirably.

"So how far behind are we?" asked Van.

"You mean you and Grace on your return trip, or all of us on the mission schedule?"

Van shrugged his upper body out of his suit. He started toweling off and said, "Either. Or both."

"Well, you cost me fifty bucks in the pool on when you two would get here. I said you'd overshoot your original ETA by eight hours—"

"Thanks for the vote of confidence."

"—but Oskar said twelve, and he was closest."

"Great. If it was anybody else, I'd probably get a cut."

"Funny. How's your knee?"

"It's been better, quite recently. But it's been worse, even more recently." Van stripped off the rest of his suit and showed off his taping job. He flexed the joint as much as he could, glad the tape limited the range of motion. It didn't hurt too much. "Fightin' form, as my old coach used to say. So what's the next play you want me to run?"

Shay said, "The next play is chow, and then—"

Roy Chesterfield called out from behind a stack of transit cases, where he'd been pawing through some of the storage bins. "It may be dinner for us, but the next play for Van needs to be a bath." He stepped into the alleyway, carrying a small parts bin, and grinned. "I'll even donate my water ration if he'll clean some of that stink off of him." He tossed his ID ring at Van, who fumbled it a little but held on.

"Me, too," said Jovelyn Nguyen, who was helping Grace with her suit.

"Like I was saying," Shay continued, the irritation on his face now creeping into his voice, "and then we're going to sit down with the mission plan and see if we can schedule our way out of the mess we're in. Oskar's come up with a couple of different possibilities, but they're not easy. We'll have to know how much we can count on you, with your leg—"

"What are you talking about? I'm 110%, as always." One look from Shay confirmed that he really was in no mood for Van's bravado, so Van moderated his estimate. "Okay, I'm probably 90% for the first two, maybe three hours, with a gradual decline after that."

"Well, that's going to make a difference," Shay said. "We'll have an all-hands meeting when Henry and Scooter get back inside from plumbing in the latest prefab—call it 2200 hours. Meanwhile, bathe first and then eat. And if you can't get clean enough on their water chits, you can have mine, too."

O O O

Van only took a double-ration shower, and he didn't even use Roy's chit.

For one thing, his military training carried over to the point that just carrying Roy's ID ring around with him made him uneasy. Everyone had a dogcatcher chip in their neck that worked with the proximity detectors, and the colony wasn't established enough to have any restricted areas yet, so the rings didn't have to be treated like security badges. They were just payment counters for totaling up how much water you used, checking out equipment, that sort of thing. Their portability made it possible to do just what Roy had done—not that Van had to like it.

The double shower was luxury enough without being wasteful, but Van's next play wasn't chow—it was a call to Barbara. A full-up voice call, not prerecorded text or voice messages that were spooled up and sent when it was convenient for the satellites and the networks. He didn't spring for video, though, since he was paying for this call himself.

Van had booked time on the big antenna practically as soon as he made contact with the base, and he'd already warned Barbara by text message to be ready for the call anytime between noon Montana time on the 8th and dawn on the 9th. It was early evening when he made contact, but he wasn't quite prepared for Barbara's first question.

"So just how pretty is this Grace girl?"

Van let a couple of seconds build on top of the one-and-a-half-second time delay before he said, "That's a fine way to start. What about, 'Great to hear your voice live, sweetie,' and 'I hope everything's okay.'" He stopped there, not trusting his own tone to sound playful. He counted off three seconds, then five, but Barbara didn't respond. He said, "Come on, babe, what's the point of that question? Even if you hadn't met her, you could find a hundred pictures of her on the AC web site. So who have you been talking to?"

Now the delay ended with her voice. "Beverly Needham."

"Oh, Lord, Belladonna and the Barmaid, at it again."

"Heck, yeah. You know I wouldn't be coming up there if I couldn't count on having a friend with me."

"You've got me," Van said.

"Oh, who needs you?"

Underneath the thin layer of static, Van thought he heard a smile in her voice. "Thanks, that's very nice."

Now the smile became more evident. "You know I'm teasing," Barbara said. "Sort of."

"Yeah, I can tell from your voice. Except I think I may be hearing something else besides teasing."

Barbara paused, extending Van's wait. "Yeah, I guess you are."

"Do you guess you're going to tell me, or do you want to play twenty questions? Or maybe invisible charades?"

Van imagined her sitting up straight in her chair—he wondered if she was sitting in the wood-paneled den or in the ranch house's brightly-painted kitchen. She always sat up very straight when she was about to say something important. She said, "BD told me I should be honest with you, so I will be. I'm not feeling as good about this plan as I was before."

Van was glad he hadn't eaten. Deep in his gut the first tremors started. "How so?" he asked.

"Sweetie, I know you think this is your destiny ... the reason you were born, and all that. I respect the dream. And I respect you as the dreamer. But I'm getting scared. You getting hurt ... that was like when we took that hop to Okinawa, remember? And mom got sick...." Her voice trailed off.

Van remembered. There was no way they could count on a space-available flight to bring them back quickly from their leave, so Barbara had booked the first flights she could from Japan back to the states. Every flight was on time, they made every connection, but while they were somewhere over Idaho—already on descent into Montana—her mom died.

Van guessed the two things might be somewhat equivalent in her mind. And if he'd hurt himself seriously, or if he had an aggressive disease and was fading fast, he might even be able to see it himself. But it was just a little fall, and once he found the locker with the Tylenol-III then he'd be ready to roll.

And this wasn't the time for them to be discussing her damn doubts. He knew the Consortium was listening, or at least recording what they said. It was in their contract that all their communications would be monitored. He had no doubt they would mark it all down in their evaluation books.

You couldn't wait to talk about this when I got home? In private? And you called your friend who's already in the AC and talked to her about it? They probably have the psych eval half-written by now.

He didn't dare say the words aloud. Some Consortium shrink would jump on that like a mosquito on a tourist. Why would you say that? What are you afraid of? Were you trying to coerce her? They would analyze it and interpret it and use it to screw him. His lips were salty; nausea seeped into his empty stomach as if he was sweating on the inside. His view of the bulkhead and the control panel wavered as his brain spun through a few possible responses, seeking one that wouldn't get them canned.

Before he came up with anything Barbara spoke again. "I know *you're* up to it," she said. "You've been ready for anything as long as I've known you, and this is what you've lived your whole life for." She sniffed a little, but softly as if she had turned her head away from the microphone. Her voice was remarkably steady. "I just don't know if I'm cut out for it."

Van wasn't sure now either. He had been sure, until that moment, as sure as he could recite the date of the Apollo-11 landing. Barbara wasn't a delicate little flowery girl. Growing up on the ranch had made her just tough enough: smooth and supple, rather than worn or stiff. Not wound so tight that she was rigid and likely to snap, but strong and flexible and reliable.

He still didn't know what to say. Part of him wanted to say "Stop your whining" or "You better damn well figure it out soon." He told himself that was just fatigue and fear: he'd never spoken that way to Barbara before. He wanted to say something supportive, something encouraging and affirming like "It's okay, it's just cold feet," but he didn't want to sound as if he was begging her or trying to change her mind. She had to make her own decision, as much for herself as for the Consortium and the program.

As the silence grew uncomfortable, he still didn't know what to say. So he tried not to say much of anything.

"I appreciate you being honest with me," he said, a little surprised to find that it was true, "but I've got to go. Shay's got us mustering in a little while, and I need to eat first. We'll have to talk about this later."

O   O   O

Barbara played back that conversation most of the night and into the next day, which dawned cold and brutal. Overnight the Chinook wind had stalled, and cold came back down from Canada like a stampede of polar bears. The low clouds looked as if they were sculpted out of lead, but they were only visible for a couple of hours before the snow started falling. It was heavy, wet snow, and as she made her way from house to barn she longed for the days of her early childhood, of Saturday mornings when she could go back to bed after her chores and the adults would take care of all the really heavy work.

But she wasn't a child anymore, and she wondered if she'd been acting childish. It was one thing to be afraid, and another to let fear control you, right? But this was more than fear. It wasn't an irrational nervousness about the unknown—this was rational trepidation, the fear of risks that were known and could be numbered and analyzed but never eliminated. She used to perform hazard analyses in the service, for Heaven's sake, looking at the probability and severity of any event. She knew the risks, and what went into minimizing them and mitigating them.

Sometimes she thought it would be better not to know the risks. Blissful unawareness, the way the cows were unaware of their ultimate fate, at least had the advantage of being blissful; she, on the other hand, had doleful knowledge.

She tried to use menial tasks to work her way into blissful ignorance—by which she meant the bliss of ignoring Van and the Moon and everything outside the confines of the barn. Between the morning and evening milkings she made rounds, working on the myriad little things that had been neglected in recent months. She tightened the hinges and turnbuckles on the gates, greased the bearings on the ventilators, and worked her way through the milking parlor with the maintenance manuals and the big toolbox. She worked inside and out, on anything she could find, but she never attained ignorance, nor bliss.

By the time Barbara got back inside, she was so tired she could barely pull off all the layers of her clothes. She thought about starting something for supper, but decided instead to stoke up the fire and relax in its warm embrace.

Her father's voice roused her from a doze; he'd called her from the vicinity of the kitchen. "What?" she said.

"I said, you've got a message blinking in here on the phone."

It was probably from Van, and she wasn't sure she wanted to hear it. The smell of frying pork lured her into the kitchen, though: her father had two pork chops going in the pan. "Those smell good," she said.

"Yes, and I bet you want one."

She patted his bald spot. "You wouldn't want your little girl to go hungry, would you?"

"Okay, you can have one … if you make up some gravy." He pointed to a pot in which three medium russet potatoes were being boiled.

"I'll see what I can do," she said, and picked up the telephone receiver. The callback number for the message wasn't the Consortium switchboard, but a number she didn't recognize. Didn't *think* she recognized, that is. It seemed familiar … then her sluggish brain caught up with her and she realized it was the number she had called to reach Beverly Needham in New Mexico.

She punched the button on the machine and let the message play; no need to take it privately.

"Barmaid, this is Bella. Heard Van the man was back in the can, so I figured you'd had a chance to talk to him. I wanted to see how it went, and to run a little idea by you. Call when you can! Love."

Barbara suddenly felt light and refreshed, as if the Chinook wind had blown into the house and straight through her. She giggled and hugged her Father.

"You going to call her back?" he asked.

"After supper," she said. "You go in and put your feet up, I'll finish cooking."

"Alright. The applesauce is here in the fridge—"

"Go. Now. Skee-daddle, daddy."

He turned his rough, lined, scruffy face to look at her, a little smile curling the corner of his mouth. His eyes twinkled. He bowed a little and said, "Thanks, girlie. You make a papa proud."

She barely noticed the twin tears that rolled down into her smile.

O O O

"Hey, Wild West Woman! How's life on the ranch?"

Barbara, sated and bathed and wrapped in her softest robe, grimaced at the question. She wriggled down further into the recliner's cushions. "I think we got eight or ten inches of snow so far today, and it's still coming down. How's that sound?"

"At least you'll have a white Christmas."

"Shows what you know," Barbara said. "More likely an appaloosa Christmas, with little patches unmelted and everything else mud. But, we'll manage."

"I'm glad to hear it. So how did it go with Van? Did you tell him you're withdrawing from the program?"

Barbara scooted back a little, so she sat straighter in the chair. "When did I say I was withdrawing?"

"You're not? Well, that's good to hear."

"Wait a minute. You thought I was scratching us off the colony list?"

"Well ... I thought it was a possibility. You were having those serious doubts, after all."

"So? About once a month I have doubts that I was meant to be a woman, but that doesn't mean I want to sign up for surgery."

"Calm down, Barmaid. I'm just glad to hear that you're not letting your little episode get the better of you. But you did tell Van you were feeling some anxiety, didn't you? How did he take it?"

Barbara took a couple of breaths, eyes closed, to calm her heartbeat. She reduced her volume to gentle conversation. "Yes, I told him," she said, "and he took it about as well as can be expected. He didn't fly off the handle at me, but he didn't let me bare my soul, either."

"He's a man, dear. The last thing he wants you to bare is your soul."

"Huh? Oh. Well, I'm not likely to bare anything else for him anytime soon."

"Uh-huh. You say that now, but then he'll come walking out of that dropsule and you'll melt like a schoolgirl...." BD's voice trailed away in a little patter of laughter.

Barbara tried to put some fire in her tone, but she ended up giggling a little herself. "I don't know about that, but I guess things could be worse. He's not hurt that bad—probably his pride more than anything, and he's got pride to spare. And I worked my fingers to the bone today, fixing a lot of things that needed fixing, and that puts things in perspective. I guess we're destined to have problems, some bigger than others, whether we're up there or down here. And maybe it's not so important what difficulties you face, as the fact that you face them together."

"Amen to that."

"So what's the idea you wanted to run by me? Does it have anything to do with boiling oil or sharp knives?"

BD laughed louder. "It didn't, but I suppose I could think of something. No, I thought I might pop up to see you when I get done with this training stint. Looks like we'll have a week and a half or so before we have to head to Guiana, and I'd like to spend a few days with you."

"That would be great! You and Gary?"

"Heck, no, just me," BD said. "I'll see enough of him later, and it may get to be too much. I want some time *away* from him for now. Let absence make my heart grow fonder. You know what I mean."

Yes, she did.

O   O   O

Wednesday, 13 December 2034
Lunar Setup Mission II, Day 43

By Monday, Van's knee was some better, and by Wednesday he barely realized he'd been injured. His radio appointment with Dr. Nguyen had gone well, since he'd authorized Van to withdraw some of the colony's Tylenol-III; the Doc would want to see him as soon as he stepped out of the dropsule, probably. He still kept his knee taped—no use wasting all that effort he put into shaving his leg— which limited his mobility just enough to slow him down a little. That kept him from doing any more damage, while the codeine knocked out the pain.

It seemed to help his attitude some, too. It helped that he wasn't sitting under two feet of snow like Barbara was. He'd called on Sunday and Monday, and she said the forecasters promised no relief. He was just as glad to be where he was, even if he was injured; he didn't miss winter, and probably never would. A boy from southern California and Alabama didn't belong anywhere snow stood on the ground for more than a day, and their winters in North Dakota had been the worst of his life even though one of them was called "mild" by the other missileers. He grit his teeth at the realization that it would still be winter in Montana when he was done with this mission; they *had* to make it through the screening and get back up to the Moon, if only to get away from her damn ranch.

Although, maybe it was the cabin fever that had made Barbara's attitude a little better the last time he talked to her. Maybe Montana winters were good for something after all....

Shay had him on fairly light duty, mostly driving machines to scrape away trenches or wrench out boulders for setting new habitats in place. Every shift, Van told him his knee was almost back to normal, and today Shay had heard enough. Van chuckled now as he drove one of the little MPVs toward the south end of Rupes Mercator to set up another radio repeater. He'd been sure he could wear Shay down. He was a little surprised that Shay let him come so far out by himself—it was one thing to run around the complex alone, as opposed to being so far afield—but they wanted to make up lost time and the risk of this mission was pretty minimal.

The little trucks were far less comfortable than the Turtle, having only a bench seat in an unpressurized cab. They sat two people comfortably and three cramped. They had far less range, too, running on hydrazine turbines with limited fuel supplies. The turbine engines worked on the same principle as hydrazine-fueled monopropellant satellite thrusters: the hydrazine—a chemical Van had once been told was a near-impossibility in terms of structure, being basically an ammonia molecule with an extra hydrogen atom tacked on—flowed across a catalyst that caused it to expand with great heat and pressure. The catalyst beds in old satellite engines used to be good for only a few hundred seconds' operation, making each maneuver a rare and precious thing, so these monopropellant turbines wouldn't work except that a garage mechanic around 2020 had solved the catalyst problem by working carbon nanotubes or Buckyballs or something into the catalyst matrix; now they ran for hours before they needed cleaning and refurbishing.

The plain of Mare Nubium, even near the low hills of the Rima Hesiodus, was a vast darkness to Van's left as the truck rumbled down the same path he and Grace had traversed six days earlier. The line of low mountains to his right that was Rupes Mercator was equally dark, since the ambient lights in the truck and his helmet display overpowered even the nearly full earthlight. If he had time, he would stop and turn down all his lights and enjoy the earthshine; but he was on a schedule.

The line of reflectors spaced every fifty meters or so down the path kept him on it—a nice touch that Scooter had installed two days ago, after they were finally unpacked—and he trusted the laser gyroscope in the truck to tell him when he got to the unmarked side path up into the range of hills. Without the benefit of precise surveys and an equivalent to GPS, all navigation was internal; it would be years, if ever, before anyone trusted an autonomous vehicle on the Moon.

Once he was on the smaller path, it was easy enough to follow: no erosion or wind action would ever wear it away. He found the tower foundation just where Jovie and Shay had installed it the week before last.

The MPV he had been issued was essentially a flat-bed pickup truck, albeit an oversized one with metal mesh wheels. Like the others, it could be fitted with a variety of implements by way of a fifth wheel and other attachment points in the rear; however, this one was fitted with tools, sections of the tower, and the communications equipment Van would leave behind.

A light standard in the bed illuminated his work area, and Van worked quickly to set up the small tower. He fit the pieces together as it lay on the ground, clamped the bottom to a pivot driven into the lunar soil, and pushed it upright and tightened it into place. It didn't need staking against wind loads, of course, but Van installed a trio of close-in guy wires to help stabilize it in case of an accident or lunar seismic activity.

With the final support wire in place, Van stopped to take a drink. He flexed his good knee, and then his bad knee to the limit of the tape. A shot of pain, as if he'd disturbed a nest of fire ants behind his kneecap, worked its way slowly from his knee to his brain. Time for some more medi—

Van hung his head until his forehead touched his face plate.

He'd forgotten to bring any pills. He knew it was useless, but he checked the little pouch in the left side of his helmet. It tasted of plastic and salty sweat, but as far as medicine it was as empty as the vacuum outside his suit. He checked to make sure his microphone was off, and cursed so long and loud he left drops of spittle that glittered in the indicator lights of his HUD.

The pain increased as he hooked up the comm unit and the combination Bergeron heat engine and solar array that would be the repeater's power source. The sensation sharpened into that old feeling of jagged gears grinding inside his knee as he picked up and packed away his tools. It took him two tries to climb back into the cab of the little truck. His vision contracted as he twisted on the seat and hooked into the onboard oxygen supply. It took several seconds before his eyesight cleared enough that he was confident moving the truck, and it wavered enough at the edges that he crept around his new installation and back downhill.

The darkness around the shafts of light seemed a thing alive as he made his way meter by meter back along his path. It wasn't the absence of light, to be dispelled by the lumens from headlamps or flashlights, but a choking presence trying to reach into the light, to extinguish it, to smother it. To smother him.

By the time he reached the main road, sweat clung to him no matter how he adjusted his suit's environment. It was a cold, clammy sweat, as if he'd run a marathon inside a freezer. He shivered, a single violent shake, and it hurt as if his leg had snapped in two at the knee.

He cried out, and the darkness claimed him.

O O O

The MPV rode up and over something, dropping with an impulse that dwarfed the usual turbine and road vibrations and broke through Van's stupor. A half-second of panic and adrenaline dampened the pain in his leg. A rock, he figured; it must have been a rock. He slowed the truck and turned it left until his headlights found one of the reflectors. He was fifteen or twenty meters off the path.

How long was I out? He couldn't answer the question, because he couldn't remember what his helmet clock read before.

Good thing I was back on the flats, instead of still coming down the hills.

Van moderated his breathing until it was under control, then held his breath until he got the truck back on the road. Once clearly on the path again, he sighed so fully that the motion sent another radiating wave of agony out from his knee. He winced, gritted his teeth, and spent the next few minutes arranging himself on the truck seat so his leg was splayed out on the seat and loosely strapped in position. Once he was sure he could still reach the main controls and operate the steering yoke, he started off again.

He concentrated on reaching the nearest reflector, and the next, and the one after that. In fifty-meter intervals, he crept down the path toward the colony, focused like the team's surveying laser and moving slow enough that the Sun might rise before he got back. He stifled a laugh, afraid the slightest movement would send him back into the black.

Shay would chide him for getting back late, and throwing the schedule into chaos again. As if it ever came out of chaos.

Barbara would scold him for trying to do more, sooner, than he could.

But neither compared with the scorn he heaped upon himself. The slightest vibrations rippling through his leg cried out to him for more of the blessed codeine, and he answered every cry with a grimace and a growl. Van had endured pain many times, but had never been fond of it; he didn't understand the people whose bodies craved the extra endorphins generated by tattoo needles or knives or whips, but for the moment he wished for a little of that macabre gift.

He didn't get his wish. But he bore the pain manfully the rest of the long drive back.

CHAPTER FIFTEEN

A Good Argument

Tuesday, 2 January 2035
Lunar Colonist Group 2, Training Day 30

Stormie twisted herself around on the small bunk; it wobbled and creaked as she settled her back against Frank's chest. He reached around her in a full embrace, nuzzled her neck and nibbled her earlobe. Within seconds he was asleep, his slow and regular breathing a hot, comfortable breeze against her neck.

She ached to feel his love completely, but tried contenting herself with his strong arms around her and his body heat on her back. Even if they were quiet, she was sure someone would hear; the rooms were too small and the walls too thin to keep even a yawn secret. Most of the couples seemed to have given up coupling, though Stormie suspected they were finding out-of-the-way places and opportune times out of a modern sense of propriety. When she and Frank had first come underground, they'd talked about using their laboratory space, except that it was more crowded and less comfortable than their cabin—but it was the place they spent the most time together.

Their routine had evolved into overlapping fourteen- to sixteen-hour shifts, with Frank—who attributed his habits to his namesake's "early to bed, early to rise" dictum but who Stormie believed was simply cursed with an inability to sleep late—working from six a.m. to eight p.m. or later. Stormie's ten a.m. to midnight shifts suited her much better, even though by the time she crawled into their bunk Frank was fast asleep.

Since their quarters in the colony would be just as cramped and crowded as their quarters in the training area, they would eventually have to return to an older sense of propriety: specifically, the mores of the day when extended families lived together in the same poorly-built buildings and tactfully ignored any amorous encounters they overheard.

Stormie hoped Frank's comforting embrace would help her sleep, but that hope gradually fell to pieces. She was too irritated to sleep.

Being Tuesday, she and Frank had received another visit from a Consortium medical technician from outside the training area who drew more of their blood for testing, gave them shots of interferon, and left them with a week's supply of pills they each took twice a day. It was so beyond overkill that Stormie wanted to scream. Sure, the mystery princess had been exposed to her prince's hepatitis-C, but the AC seemed not to care that Stormie and Frank had gone through the picophage treatment and insisted on this useless prophylaxis. If they actually had the disease, sure, pump them full of the stuff, but not after what they'd gone through. And Stormie was sure they were either billing LLE or withholding payments to cover the cost—she hadn't generated the nerve to ask Jim yet.

The more she stewed on it, the madder she got: at herself, at the Consortium, at the reckless woman and her infected husband.

The AC had talked about putting her and Frank in isolation, as though they thought the two of them had actually developed full-blown hepatitis. Thankfully, they dropped that idea pretty quickly and just quarantined them from all food preparation. Stormie couldn't even make herself a cup of tea; or, more precisely, she wasn't supposed to. She managed to brew a cup now and then in the privacy of their laboratory.

After a half hour of lying abed, fuming, Stormie got up and went to the lab to do just that.

She checked her e-mail while the water boiled. It was so soon after she last checked that she hadn't even received any spam messages.

She called up the respiration estimates for the training habitat and began reworking her calculations. She sipped her tea and hoped the math would make her drowsy. She had rebalanced everything four times as their numbers dwindled, and two days ago had run the numbers for twenty-two candidates. The Purcells had dropped out of the program on New Year's Eve.

A soft, repetitive tapping sounded at the sliding partition. Maggie Stewart looked in the half-open door. "I saw the light on," she said. "Didn't expect anyone else to be up this late. Is everything okay?"

Maggie was almost forty, a couple of centimeters shorter than Stormie and in excellent shape. Only a few strands of grey showed in her brown hair, and her eyes were bright and alive. She spied the mug of tea on the lab bench, and smiled at Stormie's half-hearted attempt to hide it. Maggie stepped into the cramped lab and looked closely at Stormie. "No, I can see it's not. What's the matter?"

Stormie's impulse was to tell her to mind her own business, but she checked it. Maggie exuded sincerity like the aroma of a fresh-baked peach cobbler, so strong it almost made Stormie's head swim. Because of the AC's paranoia, no one else would give her the time of day if they didn't have to, and she missed friendly human contact. "Don't you know?" she asked.

Maggie stepped around the little table and sat on the other stool. "What should I know?"

"What everyone is saying about us. About me and Frank."

Maggie smiled. "People say lots of things, dear, that's why I try not to listen to gossip. But if you want to talk about it, make me a cup of that tea and I'll be happy to listen."

Are you legit? Stormie wanted to ask, but didn't. She wondered if she was being tested to see if she would stick with the quarantine. She didn't think Maggie was the type to spy or squeal, but she couldn't take any chances.

"I'm not supposed to make anything food-related," she said. "Even making this for myself is probably against the rules. But there's hot water in that beaker and tea in the little tin, if you want some. That's Frank's mug there, but we can find you something else."

Maggie looked over at the apparatus for a second. She patted Stormie's hand as she got up. "That's okay, I don't want to make you break your word. How much tea do you have left? Not much, I see. What'll you do when you run out?"

"I guess I'll go without for a while."

"Yes, and so will we all. I don't know if I trust all the promises the geneticists are making, that all their crops will produce what they say."

"Wait a minute," Stormie said. "That's your field. How can you not trust them?"

"Actually, I'm more on the animal side of things—I'll be tending the chickens and the rabbits and the fish, more than the bushes and the little miniaturized trees they're going to plant. I hope the plants yield a good crop, certainly, but I don't know that they will. And if they don't, then we're all in trouble."

"That's true."

"I mean, it's a lot to ask of a poor plant: small size, fast growth, and high yield." Maggie sat back down with a steaming mug of tea—in Frank's mug, that she had simply wiped out with a cloth. "Small and fast, that makes sense to me, but trying to get a high yield seems like breaking a law of thermodynamics or something. And it's not like we can just walk outside and scrape up some good topsoil for each crop rotation. Keeping the soil chemistry right is going to be baffling, and I don't know how well Fukuoka farming is going to work in a closed environment. I'm glad I'm not responsible for it, but I'm relying on them to get it right just like everyone else.

"They're going to charge me enough for what I feed the animals, I know that much. And of course everything starts with staples, so luxuries," she lifted her mug in a small salute, "like tea and coffee will have to wait.

"So I *hope* they can produce what they promise, but I'm not sure yet. They're human, after all, and bound to make human-type mistakes. I'm not too concerned about a catastrophe, but if they don't come through I'm not sure how long it'll be before my little venture breaks even."

Stormie fought away a yawn and resisted the urge to look at the time. It was probably close to two in the morning. "Your venture? You're not going up as a Consortium employee?"

"No, I'm an independent. Rex is AC, though, so you probably figured I would be, too. Most people do. He'll be digging tunnels for the underground habitats—he calls it 'Phase Two,' unofficially, of course—and I put in a bid to do animal husbandry, such as it is."

"But never mind that," Maggie said. "I'm more worried about how you're doing. So I ask you again, what should I know?"

Maybe it was learning that Maggie was an independent contractor like her, but Stormie was comfortable enough telling the older woman about the accident, and the picophage treatment, and the current regimen of shots and pills. As Stormie talked, she got the impression that Maggie knew a lot more than she claimed. Stormie tried to wax philosophical about the whole thing—tried to show that she understood it could be worse—but she sounded unconvincing to herself.

Maggie listened, and more than listened: she seemed to attend every word, as if Stormie were telling a fascinating story. As Stormie wound down her narrative of fear and frustration, Maggie swirled her tea in her mug, and when she spoke she drew each sentence out as if it were a fine wire extruded from a die. "That is a difficult situation you and Frank are in. It's funny to me sometimes, how you can do the right thing and still have it turn out bad. Or, at least, not very good. I don't suppose it's very funny to you, though."

"No, not really," Stormie said, and drank the last of her tea.

"Have you thought about praying for healing?" Maggie asked.

Stormie sputtered around and through the tea; a few droplets caught the very back of her nose, and she fought not to sneeze or spray. She choked a little instead, and her mug sounded very loud as she set it on the table.

"Sorry," Maggie said. "I didn't realize that would be so funny."

"No," Stormie said as she caught her breath. "That's okay. But that's one thing I haven't thought about doing."

Maggie looked at the door and around the lab, something between a smile and a smirk on her lips. "You might try it," she said. "I think the Lord does miracles every day, and most of them we never even realize."

Stormie's face suddenly warmed. Maggie sounded ... too much like Mother MacGinnis. "That's okay," she repeated, a little surprised at the venom in her own voice.

"Stranger things have happened."

Stormie grew hotter. Maggie had no right. No right to act like the woman who opened her home to Stormie and raised her, and no right to suggest the same kind of useless course of action Mother Mac would've recommended. Stranger things have happened? "Not to me," Stormie said, in as dark a tone as she could produce.

Maggie didn't flinch away from Stormie's gaze; in fact, she held her ground so securely and yet so softly that Stormie's hot anger drained away like propellant pushed out of a tank by a nitrogen purge. Maggie smiled, and again the impression of sincerity washed over Stormie. "I'm sorry if I was out of line, Stormie. I would call your 'picophage' treatment a medical miracle of sorts, but I suppose two miracles might be too much to ask for." She finished her own tea and set the mug on the table. "Thank you for the tea, it was very good. I'll leave you to your work, or to get some sleep." She touched Stormie on the shoulder as she walked to the sliding door, where she paused and said, "I didn't come to get into a fight, dear, but I wouldn't mind a good argument sometime."

Fatigue wrapped itself around Stormie now that the momentary tension had faded. Her thoughts were so unfocused and confused, she didn't understand what Maggie had said. "What?"

"It doesn't have to be tonight, but I heard someone say that if you can't get in a good discussion, get in a good argument. We'll have to have one, one of these days, about life, the universe ..."

Stormie cocked her head. "And everything?"

Maggie smiled again, and this time her eyes sparkled with a touch of mischief. "Very good," she said.

Stormie smiled, too. "I guess we're all geeks here."

Maggie said, "I prefer 'fen.'" She gave a little wave before she slipped quietly down the corridor.

Stormie shivered, as if her grandmother's ghost had just touched her on the shoulder. Mother MacGinnis would tell her to take Maggie's advice; Stormie could almost hear her singing "Take it to the Lord in prayer" as if it were hymn time inside her skull. She shook her head to clear it, and as she tried to shut out the noise she half-idly wondered: if humans made human-type mistakes, did God make God-type mistakes?

O   O   O

Thursday, 11 January 2035

It was long after hours, but Jim Fennerling was still working. He had until Monday to make Lunar Life Engineering's estimated tax payment for the last quarter of the previous year. *Beware the Ides of January, not March—and the Ides of April, June, and September.*

He rubbed his eyes and went over the balance sheet again. It wasn't pretty. He'd front-loaded the payments on Stormie and Frank's treatment, so that was paid off and could be deducted appropriately, but the interferon regimen demanded by the Consortium was like a weekly fiscal earthquake, eroding their company's foundation and making their shaky financials practically precarious. And the damn shots would go on for a year unless they could get the AC to admit that the picophage regimen had been enough.

Stubborn assholes.

It wasn't an insurmountable problem. Jim knew it as surely as he knew the Sun would rise, as he knew the current interest rate or the hard reality of his wheelchair. He didn't believe in insurmountable problems. He couldn't. He would find a way. He might be able to cut the cash reserve some more, though it was so thin it was practically transparent. First things first, he could look for ways to trim the budget.

It was too late, unfortunately, to do anything about the long-lead laboratory equipment that was shipped up as part of module eight. At least it hadn't been part of shipment three, the one that crashed on the north side of Campanus Crater; the Consortium wouldn't have helped LLE come up with money to replace a single sample kit.

Any savings would have to come out of equipment yet to be shipped. Jim thumbed through the electronic binder, skimming over the manifest without studying it since so much of it was technobabble to him. *What the hell is a spectrophotometer? Do they really need that?* Meredith would have known what it was ... but he didn't have time to go down that road.

He slid the tablet onto the desk. They'd definitely run at a loss for a while ... could possibly spread the loss over a couple of years ... he'd have to dig up some new investors to stay solvent ...

The phone beeped, and he found he was more glad than irritated at the interruption. He punched the talk button without identifying the caller. "Hello, Jim Fennerling speaking."

An automated voice said, "Stand by for delayed transmission."

Jim's momentary gladness vanished.

"James, it is Frank. Stormie is here also." He was talking on a speaker phone, which added as much to the impression of distance as the artificial time delay the AC was enforcing.

"What's gone wrong now?" he asked.

"Why do you assume something is wrong?" Frank said.

Because we can't afford what the AC is charging us for this call. That was one part of the training simulation their customer didn't simulate: charging for communications as if they were really over Earth-to-Moon satellite links. Jim bit back his first impulse and said, "It's unusual to hear from you at an unscheduled time, that's all. What's got you so excited—good or bad—that you decided to call?"

"We have a proposition," Frank said.

Before Jim could express his noncommittal reply, Stormie said, "Jim, I know the AC is charging a premium on these shots, and I'm convinced they're not really necessary. I want to see about stopping them."

"I'm pretty sure they're useless," Jim said, "but we're stuck for the moment. I've gone straight at them, I've tried end runs, but they're sticking with this decision. They won't even give me results of the blood samples they take. Once you're out, we can have our own samples taken, maybe arrange our own treatments and medications to go up with you when you launch, but there's not much we can do while you're trapped inside there."

"Yeah, I know. But it's not just that the interferon is expensive, I think the protocol is making me sick just by itself. I'm not sleeping well, and I've had more headaches the past two weeks than I had the past two years."

"That could be stress," Jim said.

"Granted," Stormie said, "but where do you think the extra stress is coming from? It's got to be connected to this whole issue."

"Frank, how about you?"

"I am, perhaps, more fatigued than usual."

Jim spun a pen around on his desk. "So what do you propose?"

"Another pico-scrub," Stormie said.

Shortly after the turn of the century, when the real estate boom peaked and started its downward slide, one of Jim's accountant friends told him he'd had a "vision of bankruptcy." Jim had always considered it a vague and poetic notion, up until that very minute. Jim's vision of bankruptcy consisted of a series of memories that came as much in words and numbers as they did in sensations or emotions: his first day at the Paszek Group, fresh out of JPL and starting his second career, still aching so shortly after Meredith died; Morris Hansen contacting him a few months after Alyson died, when Hansen was looking for ways to invest his billions and wanted Jim's advice because Jim knew finance as it related to space projects; Frank and Stormie showing up in his hospital room three weeks after his own accident, pitching their company and offering him a stake in it. It seemed as if each of the events that threatened to twist and tear him was followed by a new opportunity, a chance to occupy his mind and avoid driving himself crazy … but in this current vision he saw nothing new coming to his rescue.

"Jim, are you still there?" Stormie asked.

"Yeah, Stormie. I was just thinking."

"Hear me out, okay? I have no reason to doubt that the Consortium will demand a full year of these treatments, even though they wouldn't be that effective even if we had this brand of hepatitis. That's still nine more months after we get out of here, thirty-six or so doses of interferon each, versus a week-long treatment if we go through another pathogen scrub."

Jim shook his head, an automatic display of disbelief that went unappreciated. "I can't believe you'd sign up for another round of that. That's like a healthy person signing up for chemo. I thought the last round almost killed you."

The time delay lasted a few seconds longer than it should.

Frank said, "It was … unpleasant, yes."

"But now we know what we're up against," Stormie said. "We know what to expect, and we can be prepared for it. Like they say, what doesn't kill you makes you stronger, right?"

Jim wasn't sure "they" ever knew what they were talking about. He considered for a moment whether his accident, or the losses he had just been thinking about, made him any stronger. He didn't think so.

"Jim, I'm speaking only for myself now. Truth is, I don't know how long I can keep up with this medication. If nothing else, this is the most expedient way to go.…" Stormie's voice trailed off as, under her breath but loud enough for the microphone to pick up, she said, "This is my prayer for healing."

"I'm not so sure this is a good idea," Jim said, "but I'll run the numbers and let you know. Or better yet, if you're absolutely sure, I'll run the numbers and if they're favorable I'll start negotiations. But don't hope for too much." He hoped he sounded upbeat, though he was afraid of how the debits and credits were going to stack up.

"James," Frank said, "I am certain I share your reservations, but this seems to us to be the best way to move beyond this situation."

"You're probably right, Frank." *But you don't know how thin our margin really is.*

Jim tapped the Rolodex icon on his tablet and started pulling up the profiles and electronic business cards of people he hadn't yet tapped as investors—and a couple he already had. He would find a way to keep their company solvent, even if it meant he had to find the money to torture his friends.

But it was still *if.* Which meant he needed to do all he could to make the answer "no." He opened another part of his Rolodex. He could start with Huang—

"Let me make some calls," he said. "Give me an hour."

O   O   O

James called back forty-eight minutes later. Before Frank could ask, Stormie said, "What'd you find out, Jim?"

James's voice crackled from the speaker. "I went through four AC functionaries with your proposal. It didn't give me as much leverage as I'd hoped it would."

Frank sighed like an airlock depressurizing. "What does that mean, James?"

"Want to do the old 'good news, bad news' thing?"

"Absolutely not," Stormie said.

"Okay, then it'll be 'bad news, good news.' The bad news is that the cost of that treatment will put us out of business."

Stormie turned her head away from Frank. She rubbed her hands together as if she was washing them.

"James," Frank said, "I must ask. Are you sure?" He did not want to hear the answer.

"I'll put it this way: We would have to dig up some new investors to cover it, and I'm not sure how many people would want to sign on at this point."

"I understand."

Stormie sniffed, and said, "Is that all the bad news, or is there more? Was there ever any good news?"

"No," James said, "that's enough bad news for one day. And there is *some* good news."

No one spoke. Frank shifted his weight, and the stool squeaked on the floor. He said, "What is the good news, James?"

"I started with Huang Wenbin—I don't think you know him—and worked my way through a few more people, and I told each of them your idea. I said that rather than have their people do it, I'd contract with another hospital that would do it cheaper, and that I'd need all the lab results to turn over to the new facility. They all balked, as I figured they would, even though we're entitled to the data.

"Huang called me back right at the end. He'd received authorization to tell me that every blood test you've had has come back negative, and that Dr. Nguyen is working to convince the bosses that if you haven't shown any sign of this or any other strain of hepatitis yet, you're not going to."

Stormie stopped wringing her hands. She leaned close to the console and said, "Don't tease us like that, Jim."

James said, "No teasing, no joking, no pulling your leg. You're almost free and clear. They may press for a few more weeks of interferon and tests, but I've told them that they have to start paying for the treatments since they're unnecessary. Even any additional bloodwork that's for their convenience instead of medically necessary, I will hang the cost of it on them.

"I told you it was good news. It's your own fault that you didn't want the good news first."

Stormie leaned over and nestled against Frank. The way she leaned sideways on the little stool was awkward, but he gathered her to his chest and kissed her temple.

Stormie said, "That's a dirty trick, Jim."

Frank agreed. "Yes, James. You did not have to make up a story about an impending bankruptcy."

The delay became a pause, as if James was formulating a snappy reply. But all he said was, "Yeah, sorry about that, guys."

CHAPTER SIXTEEN

All the Proper Courtesies

Tuesday, 23 January 2035

Barbara Richards walked out of the Asteroid Consortium's unassuming little office building adjacent to the San Diego airport. She didn't miss the bracing Montana air as much as she thought she would, but she missed the open spaces. She ignored the little garden around her, with its purplish flowers that had the temerity to bloom in January; instead she turned her face to the Sun and closed her eyes, soaking in the comforting warmth. From a distance, muffled by the greenery and the low decorative wall around this break area, a plane's thrust reversers kicked in and then faded as if to say, "We've arrived."

She'd been in San Diego for a day, waiting for Van to drop out of the sky. Not that she'd be able to see it, except on video: he would splash into the Pacific far offshore. Years ago, NASA gave up on the Space Shuttle in favor of old-style capsules that landed in the desert, the way the Russians landed Soyuz spacecraft on the steppes, on the theory that simple is better. The AC had weighed the possibility of landing in the open desert, but NASA wouldn't give up range time and too much of the accessible desert was covered over with biogenerated solar arrays. And since the Consortium's operating principles were "don't invent what's already invented" and "simplest is best," they followed other companies' leads and went back to splashdown operations—only on a larger scale, since they planned on sending up more people and moving more cargo at a time. When other launch company commitments interfered with AC plans, the European Space Agency had been very accommodating in terms of adapting their newest generation of Ariane heavy lifters to the AC's vehicles, especially considering the Consortium launched an extra unit along with almost every crewed one. Barbara's first work with the AC had been doing analyses of the launch vehicle interfaces. Now they had a depot of sorts in medium-earth orbit, with a dozen "dropsules" that they could press into service fairly quickly; enough, given the constraints of orbital mechanics, to rescue a newly-launched crew stranded in low-earth orbit or even to rescue evacuees if the Clarke station had to be abandoned.

Barbara breathed in the sweet-scented air. She didn't actually have to be in San Diego; she could've stayed in Montana until Van was safely down and then flown in for his arrival at the port, but she needed a getaway. She needed time to think.

Her phone buzzed in the pocket of her windbreaker. "Hello?" she said.

"We're starting to see something, Barbara," said Datu Nguyen. He was inside, watching the video from the landing zone. His wife Jovelyn was dropping in with Van and the others.

"Thanks," Barbara said, "I'll be right there."

She carded back into the building with her Consortium ID, a little annoyed that they couldn't just program the system to recognize her datacard, and made her way down the hall to the video center. The big screen on the wall gave it the look of a theater, though the seating was standard conference room furniture. No conference table for this event, though: only rows of chairs and a single table at the back with snacks and drinks.

Barbara took in the status with a glance. The split screen showed a swath of blue sky on the left, and a graphic on the right that combined the planned trajectory with radar returns from the recovery vessel. She poured some Sprite into one of the deep blue glasses, added ice from the bucket, and sat in an empty chair along the wall.

The video feed came from the Motor Vessel *Independence*, once owned by the Air Force and intended to recover STS boosters when the Shuttle launched from Vandenberg, which it never did. The tribal chieftain—Barbara couldn't remember what tribe, though she was sure she had known it when she and Van were stationed there—had hexed that launch site pretty well for a few years, and it still wasn't as active as everyone had hoped it would be. M/V *Independence* had berthed at Port Hueneme for many years, taking turns as a research vessel and a recovery ship for Navy search and salvage missions, until the Consortium bought her, refitted her, and based her at San Diego. She was an old ship, but a good one.

They also bought a small fleet of unmanned aerial vehicles that they flew as spotters—from little seagull-sized drones that launched off the ship up to a couple of surplus, refurbished Predators they flew from the San Diego airport—and a couple of fast hydrofoils that trailed the *Indy* and were operated by remote control from the ship's bridge. It was cheaper, Barbara supposed, than paying crews for each vessel. *Simplest is best.*

The video feed wasn't great, but Barbara cheered with the rest of the gathered crowd as the cameras picked up the ungainly craft suspended by its giant parachutes, rocking slightly from side to side as it descended. She braced herself in her chair as the dropsule smacked the water, then relaxed back into the pro forma cushion and finished her drink. Someone offered her champagne, but she got up and poured herself another Sprite as the hydrofoils approached the dropsule from opposite sides and stabilized it until the *Indy* got there.

Barbara stayed at the party until the crew got off safely. They transferred one by one to the *Independence*, waving at the camera. Van was scruffy but he smiled and waved as he made his way up the temporary gangplank. She watched to see if his knee was still bothering him, but couldn't really tell: they all wobbled a little, whether from the sea or from getting used to full gravity she wasn't sure.

She said her goodbyes after the lunar setup crew was safely aboard the recovery vessel. Now they would rig everything for towing and start back, a trip that would take about seventy-two hours—a little less than their trip from the Moon had taken. More time to think before Van was back. She hoped it would be enough.

She walked through the building to the main entrance this time, and stepped outside again into the glorious California afternoon. She got in her rental car, but left the door open to feel the breeze as she looked at the area map. She had just decided to go to Tecolote Canyon and walk around the park when her cell phone rang.

She didn't recognize the number, and almost ignored the call. But just before the voicemail could grab it, she acquiesced. "Hello?"

"Hey, love of my life, it's me."

"Van? How are you calling me so quick? I just watched you land."

He laughed. "We 'spoofed' to see who got to use the sat phone first, and I got out on the initial call. The rest of them are still playing to see where they line up. So, you made it to San Diego okay?"

The connection was a little scratchy, either from the satellite link or her cell phone, but Van's excitement was clear. They all must be high on adrenaline; she was surprised they didn't arm-wrestle or something instead of playing a round of "spoof"—standing in a circle guessing how many coins they all were holding—to see what order they could make their personal calls. She always hated that game.

"Yeah, I'm fine," Barbara said. "I was about to take myself on a little hike. You think you'll get underway soon?"

"Looks like. They're working hard enough getting everything tied down." He was interrupted by some commotion in the background. "I'm being mobbed by the rest of the crew—I think they said Grace lost, so she has to go last, and she was offering sexual favors to swap places with someone else."

Barbara tightened her grip on the phone, but she tried to keep her voice light. "Then I'm glad you're already on the line. I wouldn't want you to be too tempted."

She didn't like the pause on the other end.

"Babe, I don't want to be tempted any more, either," he said, his voice low and slow. "It's hard to be away from you, and I'm glad to be coming back. You staying in town until I get back?"

For a second, Barbara wished she wasn't: his choice of words irritated and confused her. Tempted any *more*? Pressure rose from her gut as if she were getting ready to spew more than just words. A little adrenaline rush of her own hit her. She stopped the retort she was readying and took a deep breath. *Now is not the time.*

"Look for me on the wharf on Friday," she said. "I'll be wearing a red dress."

"I can't wait, babe," Van said, and the truth was clear in his voice. She breathed a little easier as he repeated, "I can't wait."

O O O

Friday, 26 January 2035

Van was at the bow when M/V *Independence* entered the harbor and the little boat came alongside and dropped off the pilot. Van had spent hours at the bow over the past few days, watching the dolphins frolicking in front of the ship; it was a lot more comfortable than walking around, which hurt his knee worse than ever since he was under full gravity again. He was glad of the knee brace he wore, but even standing still hurt, depending on how much weight he put on that leg. Having to develop "sea legs" in a hurry did not help at all.

Despite that pain and the sure knowledge that the first kick would separate his lower leg from the rest of his body, Van fought the urge to jump overboard and swim to the dock. Not that he could've found his way, of course. *That's why harbors provide pilots.*

The pilot boat pulled away and the sound of gulls took over the cool, crisp afternoon. Land slipped by the ship as it negotiated the passage, and Van stayed in the bow. He scanned the wharf as they approached their berth. About two dozen people were split up into five little groups, and as the ship's horn announced their arrival they cheered and waved.

Four of the women on the dock had on red dresses, but he picked out Barbara quick enough. Her dress was a deep, almost fire engine red, and she was wearing a light-colored shawl or cape to keep the wind off her arms.

It took twenty minutes to get the vessel secure and the gangplank in place. He limped from the ship, and smiled to cover the grimace. When he stood in front of her, she looked him up and down and nodded in approval.

"Well," she said, "who are you trying to impress?"

He smiled bigger, this time not trying to hide any pain. The AC folks had finally gotten something right.

Two days before he'd left the colony site he had ordered a new suit—navy blue pinstripes, classic lines, with dress shirts, ties, and new shoes—and had it delivered to the *Independence* with his name on it. He'd been afraid Barbara would find out and spoil the surprise, so he made arrangements for the cost to be deducted from his next paycheck instead of putting it on his credit card. Seeing her reaction, it was all worth it.

"Only you, sweetness," he said. "Only you."

His arms were built to hold her, had ached to hold her for weeks, and he hugged her a long time before giving her a light but lingering kiss. He had no illusions: she knew what he had on his mind, and probably expected him to rush her away from the welcome party and invite her into the back seat of her rental. He hoped, deep down, that she wanted him as much as he wanted her, but a little romancing was in order first. Not only because things between them had been icy the last few weeks, and not only because taking it slow and easy would put less strain on his knee, but because, deep down, he considered himself a romantic kind of guy.

The welcome party was very informal: heavy hors d'oeuvres and a wide variety of liquor that Van avoided. Barbara greeted all the other crewmembers, mostly warmly; she even gave Grace a little lady's hug and a kiss on one cheek. Van endured a few moments' questioning from Dr. Nguyen, and promised to stop in the next day for a full exam. Van was a bit disappointed that the highest Consortium representative was Aliester Whisnant, the Chief of Operations at the San Diego facility. He guessed the brass were staying away because they were upset at how much the setup crew had left undone, and the thought irritated him almost to the point of anger. But he put his arm around Barbara and breathed the salt-and-fish smell of the air and let it pass.

After they'd made their second run by the food table, Barbara caught him looking at his watch. "Are you in that much of a hurry? Do you have somewhere you're supposed to be?"

He scrunched his head down and raised his shoulders in his best innocent child look. "Actually, I do."

Barbara's smile crashed down. "Where?"

He touched her elbow, gingerly, and pointed with his other hand toward the parking lot. "In the back of that limousine, with you, going to dinner."

It wasn't a big limo, but it was big enough that she gasped. "You're kidding, right?"

Van turned and caught Shay Nakamura's attention. He waved and Shay gave him a little salute and a big smile. Van bowed a little to Barbara and steered her toward the car. "Kidding? Me? Heaven forbid. We have reservations, social commitments. We can't be spending all our time down here on the docks with the riff-raff. But we can't appear to be in too much of a hurry to escape, of course, and we must observe all the proper courtesies. So when we get to the car, before we get in, be sure to turn and wave to your adoring fans."

"My adoring fans?"

"Okay, *my* adoring fans."

"God, you're hopeless." But she played along, and the look on her face when the welcome party erupted into applause and cheers and waves was worth every penny he'd spent on the suit and the car, and every favor he'd called in from the rest of the crew. Then she ooohed her approval at the plate of chocolate-dipped strawberries on the little table in the limo, and at the bottle of champagne chilling in a silver bucket next to their table when they got to the Oceanaire. "Who *are* you trying to impress?" she asked again.

"Who, me?"

"Yeah. You look like my husband, but I would've expected him to suggest getting down and dirty in the limo. Did cracking your knee crack your brain, too?"

That comment hit a little too close for Van's comfort. It wasn't the knee injury that cracked his brain, but relying on the damn codeine and trying to do too much. When he got back from setting up the repeater, he turned in the remainder of Dr. Nguyen's prescription to Shay and told him not to give him any more—it made him feel *too* good. Shay let him go back on the Ibuprofen, and he and Henry built the nifty support brace Van had worn until he got on the ship and found a real one waiting for him. He had continued working, though, and even worked overtime like everyone else. In the service they used to say, "Pain is weakness leaving the body," and now, carrying near constant pain, Van felt very strong.

He covered his thoughts with a smile and said, "Well, I didn't want your screams of passion to distract the driver."

"Oh, right." She examined him as if she was looking for identifying marks. "And you dress nice, and you shaved, and did they give you a haircut on the ship?"

Van leaned back and grabbed the lapels of his suit, and turned his right profile and then his left to her. "Yeah, what do you think? I clean up pretty nice, huh?"

"I don't know," Barbara said, and ran her fingers through his hair. "It's still a little long in back...." She tugged on the short hairs at the nape of his neck and he leaned in to accept her kiss. They didn't come up for air until the waiter cleared his throat.

Van barely tasted the meal. He was sure it was fine, probably even excellent, but the meals he'd eaten on the *Indy* had cleansed his palate from weeks of reconstituted food and his attention was much more on his wife. He lavished attention on her all evening and into the night, and when he winced Barbara helped him relax and attended him, until both of them were exhausted and happy.

At one-thirty in the morning, Van called the front desk and ordered a wake-up call and breakfast room service, to be delivered at ten. Within minutes he was asleep, and slept the sleep of the just—sprawled out on the big bed with Barbara snuggled up to his side.

O O O

Barbara wasn't expecting Van to ask the question during their breakfast the next morning, but he did, right after he finished his sausage and flapjacks. She was still enjoying her scrambled eggs and had only eaten one slice of bacon.

"So, what are we going to do?" he said.

She knew he wanted to find out if she was still going on the mission, but she pretended otherwise. "Well, today you're going to the doctor, and I suspect there's some arthroscopic surgery in your future. If the schedule holds, day after tomorrow we've got a flight booked to Birmingham, and from there we'll drive down to see your folks."

"No, I mean after that."

"After that we go back to the ranch...." As she let her voice drop, she smiled, and coaxed a reluctant grin out of him. The ranch wasn't his favorite place, especially now—he tolerated it well enough in the summer, but he got frustrated in the winter mud and slush. He would be grateful that he'd only have to put up with a couple of days of ranch chores; if he had to stay much longer, he'd probably run out on her and camp out at the Utah training site until she showed up. There'd be no need for that, though: he would get his wish much sooner than Barbara would've liked. They reported to Utah in a week for training in the Cave.

"After that," Barbara said, "we're getting ready to go to the Moon."

The anticipation he'd tried to hide turned to relaxed contentment, and in a low, humble voice he said, "Thanks." He popped a grape into his mouth and chewed it, working the muscles in his jaw and making sloppy noises. She refrained from scolding him for his poor table manners; she found she had even missed his occasional lack of couth. He caught her looking at him and leaned toward her, still slurping around the grape. "One more thing. What are we going to do right now?"

She leaned in and almost kissed him, but that last bit with the grape was too much. She pulled away as he puckered up, and said, "I ... am going to take a bath."

"Want some company?" he asked, in that pathetic way that he thought was sexy but she just found irritating.

She bent down and kissed his stubbly cheek, and when she was sure his mouth was empty kissed him fully. "No, I want to shave my legs and you'll just get in the way."

He pulled her down to sit in his lap; his intentions, perfectly clear before, were even more apparent now. "I like getting in your way," he said, reaching for the knotted belt on the hotel robe.

Barbara pushed his hand away and fixed him with her gaze. "I know you do, and you have all night tonight to get in my way. For now, though, I need you to relax. I'm not going anywhere, and neither are you, so just take it easy and take it slow. Okay?"

He frowned a little, and a hard edge crept into his eyes, but he nodded. "Okay."

"Come in and talk to me, and maybe I'll let you wash my back."

He sat back and let her get up, and turned to the mini-buffet he'd ordered. "That's okay, I think I'll just have another bite to eat."

"Suit yourself."

He came through the bathroom door just as she was stepping into the tub. She sat back and closed her eyes as the warmth surrounded and flowed into her.

"You sure look good in there," he said.

"Uh-huh. Don't try your sweet-talking flattery on me, mister." She opened one eye to look at him, and smiled. He tried to keep his face grim, but he failed.

"So," he asked, "what made up your mind for you?"

Back to that again. "Beverly Needham came to visit."

"I knew that."

"She stayed for a week, and got out right before we had another terrific storm. She joined up with Gary in Houston. They're down in Guiana now, I think they launch tomorrow. I should send her an e-mail."

"Anyway …," Van prompted.

Barbara clenched her teeth a little at the "get on with it" tone of his voice, then focused on the water's warmth and pushed the tension away. She mostly succeeded.

"Anyway, it took me back to when we first met, when we all had big dreams and ambitious plans, and I realized I'd bottled up some of my ambition, and almost all of my exuberance. I figured out I'd started existing instead of really living.

"I thought about that for a long time, and came down here still undecided. The day you splashed down, after you called me, I went up in the park and just sat, going over different possibilities in my head." Barbara sat up, found the bar of soap, and lathered her leg. The hotel soap was soft and fruity; it smelled like raspberry with an undercurrent of vanilla, and was like rubbing a parfait on her leg. She shaved while she talked. "I went back to my room that evening and made a pro and con list, but I tore it up when I found myself weighting things differently based on what BD or anybody else would think instead of what *I* wanted.

"So every day while you were coming back on the ship, I found another place to hike and get away from people and think. I thought about you, and how upset I was at you for going up there and getting hurt. I thought about my dad, how he's always supported me going off to fulfill my dreams but how sad he's been since mom died."

"So, what about you?" Van asked.

She jumped slightly at the interruption and almost nicked herself. Irritation found its way into her voice.

"I'm getting to that. Give me a second." She took a deep breath to calm herself again. "I realized that when we originally signed up for this, I was doing it only for you. You got the bug, probably from Gary, and you're not going to shake it, and I figured if you felt that confident then I could tag along.

"After a while, though, I got the bug just as bad. *I* wanted to ride on top of the rocket; *I* wanted to see the Earth above my head every day. I was even jealous of you, getting to go on the setup mission without me. And at first when you got hurt I was mad at you for possibly messing up our plans.

"But the more I thought about you being hurt, it started scaring me. The whole idea got scary. I felt like a cow standing at a new gate, wondering what had changed and whether I was safer where I was or if I could gather the courage to walk through. And I finally asked myself what I want. I don't mean like a good family and a couple of kids and stuff like that, but what I really *want*.

"And what I decided is this: I want to *live*. I realized it when I hiked up to the top of Iron Mountain and looked around, and how good it felt to be breathing hard and how huge and wonderful the world looked from up there. Remember when the CGOC took that trip to climb Mount Whittier, and we didn't get to go? I thought about how much better that must've been than what I was seeing, and how much we missed out on by not going on that trip. And I decided I don't want to miss out again."

Barbara rinsed off leftover lather and looked up to see Van's reaction. He seemed transfixed, staring at her shiny smooth leg where it rested on the side of the tub. She put her leg back in the water and he blinked and shivered a little. She clenched her fist around the washcloth and waited to see what he would say.

He stood there a long moment without moving, then nodded his head a couple of times. "You gonna miss out on anything down here?"

"What?"

"You don't want to miss out, and I assume you mean miss out on what's going to happen up there. What about down here?"

She loosed her grip on the washcloth, and rubbed it a little between her hands. Her mind crowded with people and things she would *miss*—her dad especially; the ranch, except for the work—but would she really miss *out* on anything if they stayed? She didn't think so, but she wasn't sure. That wouldn't be what Van wanted to hear.

She could lie to him ... she instantly rejected the idea.

"I don't know," she said. "I don't know."

Van nodded, slowly, several times, his mouth puckered in an odd little thinking frown. Then he looked her in the eye and said, "I hope you figure it out soon, sweetie. You need to be sure."

He limped out of the bathroom and left her to her figuring.

CHAPTER SEVENTEEN

The Wounds You Can't See

Monday, 5 February 2035
Lunar Colonist Group 2, Training Day 64
Lunar Colonist Group 3, Training Day 1

The tons of rock above her head dogged Barbara like a phantom weight on her shoulders. The more she tried to ignore them, and the obscene feeling that every breath and every step might bring debris down on her head, the more they pressed down on her. She deliberately took shallower, slower breaths to keep herself under control. How the others coped inside their own heads she would never know, but this was the perfect weeding-out experience for the Consortium to concoct for her.

Bastards.

She was sweaty and tired. The day wasn't half over. She stank from the hour she'd spent in the pressure suit, first waiting to cycle through the big fake airlock and into the darkness of the mine, and then walking around the outside of the habitats in the dark, her lights and the lights on the other suits only penetrating a few meters into what was supposed to pass for lunar night. Squeezing between the rock wall of the mine and the outside skin of the mockup prefabricated modules only accentuated the claustrophobia she was experiencing from the mine itself.

Finally, they cycled through the tiny airlock—big enough for two people and a crate, but miniscule compared to the double doors on the front of the mine—and into the habitat itself. She wanted to smack the Cheshire cat grin off Van's face as he stripped out of his suit. Not because he lorded it over her or anyone else that he was in his element—just on general principles, so he wouldn't feel so full of himself. No one should get over leg surgery that fast; it didn't seem human. She was proud of him, and a little awestruck when she was honest about it, but concerned that if he didn't stop strutting he'd like as not hurt himself again.

As the new group cycled into the habitat, the noise and confusion grew almost exponentially: where to stow these suits, is that my bag or yours, I thought our cabin was this one instead of that one. The sixteen trainees still remaining in Group Two tried to go about their business, sliding gracefully aside to let small gaggles of newbies pass—even though a couple of those gaggles were bigger than what was left of their entire class. Aside from some cursory greetings, they left Group Three alone.

Group Two had originally been spread out through eight modules when there were forty of them, then gradually gathered into four as their numbers dwindled. The Consortium had made them move again the day before Van and Barbara's group arrived, and they were now spread back out among thirty-eight new candidates. Barbara understood why they'd be a little upset, being forced out of their "homes."

She and Van found their cabin, which was smaller than a walk-in closet. It was like a room that might be built under the eaves in an attic, but less homey; it would've been claustrophobic, but after being in the pressure suit in the dark, seemed roomy enough.

Van tossed his bag in the corner and said, "I'm going to make the rounds and see if the rest of this place looks as good as this does." He tapped on the sliding door. "Same company built these as built the real ones, and so far they seem exactly the same. But getting them this far underground must've been a bear. Want to come with me?"

Barbara looked at their schedule; they had a briefing in an hour in the "big room," two modules over. By her map it wasn't very big at all.

"No, thanks," she said. She pulled him into a hug. "You go ahead. Besides, I think I know the real reason you're going out and about."

He smiled at her, but narrowed his eyes a little as he wrapped his arms around her. "What?"

"What was it you said the other day about your adoring fans? I think you have some among our compatriots. I could see it in their eyes when we got to the airport."

From the way he squeezed her a little tighter, she knew she was right and he didn't want to admit it. "Well, they may want some advice, you know?"

"Uh-huh." She stepped back out of his embrace and matched his powerful smile. "You go ahead and see to your fans. Make sure you give them good advice—but not too good."

Van grabbed her hand and kissed it, and said, "Okay, sweetie. You take a siesta and I'll be back in a little while to get you for the briefing."

It didn't take Barbara long to unpack the few personal items she'd brought. Van's suggestion sounded good, but she decided she wanted some water before she tried a power nap.

In the kitchen, a tall black woman in a burgundy jumpsuit sat at the small table. They nodded at each other, but Barbara didn't interrupt; the woman was finishing a plate of vegetables with some kind of savory touch to it. The spicy scent was a welcome relief to the underlying locker-room odor of the training facility. The woman's face was so dark it seemed to drink in light, and her eyes shone with peculiar clarity; she was obviously a Group Two trainee and not one of the newcomers, but Barbara hadn't studied the files on the preceding group. *How do you know who to study, when over half of the group will wash out?*

Barbara picked up a mug from the counter. Most of the dishware was communal property, and worked on the "clean it if you use it" principle.

"You probably want to wipe that out first," said the woman behind her.

The mug looked clean enough.

"Just a habit we've gotten into," the woman said. "Not everyone takes the same care washing up as you might like."

Barbara said, "Thanks. Where are the towels?"

The woman held up a small baby blue towel, about the size of a washcloth. She raised her eyebrows. "Sell you this one for five hundred dollars."

"What?" Barbara's voice came out much too loud for the small space; she looked down at her feet for a second, surprised and a little embarrassed by her outburst.

The woman chuckled. "I'm kidding. Here." She tossed it, and Barbara caught the rough synthetic.

"Thanks," Barbara said, in a small voice. She turned to the sink and wiped out the mug, her face hot with an embarrassment that confused and annoyed her. She touched her ID ring to the sensor plate by the faucet—it would note the water usage on her account—filled her glass and sipped it, slowly.

Behind her, the woman said, "You act like you've been keeping a water account all your life."

Her face a little cooler now, Barbara turned back and smiled. She tossed the cloth back and said, "Thanks. I expected something like it before we ever had the briefing."

"Oh?"

"Yeah, I read a lot of science fiction when I was little. I don't remember if it was *The Moon is a Harsh Mistress*, but one of the Heinlein stories had a bit in it where a visitor to a lunar base was surprised that he had to buy an air chit when he first arrived."

"I remember that."

"Okay," Barbara said, "great. I knew somebody here would get it—I figure we're all some kind of nerds, or else we wouldn't have joined up."

"I just said the same thing the other day."

"My dad always said great minds think alike. I'm Barbara Richards." She stepped to the table and stuck out her hand.

The woman reached nearly halfway, then hesitated. She looked at Barbara's hand, then her own, then at Barbara's eyes, and her eyes were tinged with apprehension. Barbara wondered if she'd done something wrong, but gradually—tentatively—the woman completed the action. Her grip was strong.

"Stormie Pastorelli," she said, and smiled. "Pleased to meet you. Your husband was on the setup crew, wasn't he?"

"Yes."

"He was the one who did a half-gainer off the big truck, right?" Pastorelli smiled—did she mean it as a joke?

It's not funny. Barbara withdrew, slowly, to hold the mug with both hands. "Yes, he was."

Pastorelli shook her head as she got up.

Barbara turned the mug a little, afraid that if she held it still her knuckles would turn white. Her defense mode kicked in—what Van called her "adrenalestrogen."

When she reached the sink, Pastorelli asked, "So, is he okay?"

Barbara exhaled the breath she'd been holding. "He will be," she said. "He's lost a few seconds off his 40-meter-dash time, but otherwise he's fine."

Pastorelli touched her own ID ring to the tap and drew half a cup of water. She took a sip, swished it through her teeth and swallowed, then dribbled a little on the plate she had practically licked clean. She wiped the plate with the cloth she had loaned Barbara, then put the plate in the drainer. She drank the last of her water, wiped out the mug and upended it in the drainer as well. She clipped the cloth to a D-ring hanging from her jumpsuit.

"I think, if it'd been my husband, I would've been torn between smacking him for being careless and babying him to get him better."

Barbara's hand shook with released tension. She drank down the mug of bland water. "Well, I considered more drastic options than just slapping him."

Pastorelli laughed. "Yeah, I might be that irritated, too. But as long as Frank came back to me alive, I'd forgive him anything."

Barbara forced a laugh; her tension hadn't abated yet. She said, "Sometimes we love them too much, don't we?"

"I think so." Pastorelli looked at her watch. "Barbara, I'd love to stay and chat, but I've got a date with a computer. The AC didn't tell us you and your group were coming in today, so we've been scrambling to re-balance the air system to accommodate you."

"Sorry about that, Ms. Pastorelli. If I'd had your number, I would've called—"

"Don't do that. Down here, or up there, it's 'Stormie.' And it's not your problem. The trainers look for any excuse to make you work, and they'll use anything they can as a training input. And I mean *anything*. So stay bright-eyed and you'll be fine.

"But, for the time being, try not to breathe too deeply, okay?"

Barbara agreed, and Stormie left. On her way back to her cabin, Barbara succumbed to the power of suggestion. She yawned.

O O O

Tuesday, 13 February 2035
Lunar Colonist Group 2, Training Day 72
Lunar Colonist Group 3, Training Day 9

Frank daydreamed of open skies.

He had just replaced the active element of one of the bio-filters—an organic matrix with the acronym MACEF that he and Stormie couldn't agree how to pronounce. It stood for Monocellular Atmospheric Circulating Emulsion Filter; Stormie said the word "mace" and followed it with an "eff," but Frank preferred to say "massif," as in an underwater mountain. She complained that his accent made it sound like "massive," but he always knew what he meant. The filter units' single-celled inhabitants fed off of the longer-chain hydrocarbons that all the people, plants, and animals exhaled; units were in place at either end of each habitat, and had to be replenished from lab cultures at regular intervals. One of the first things Stormie did after the fire on training day three was insist that they would start two more cultures in different places in the real colony, in case the habitat with their lab lost pressure and the main cultures died.

Stiff and sore from weeks of sleeping on the training facility mattress, Frank stretched his back as he reached down for the slotted filter cover. He wrapped his hands around his ankles and pulled until his back popped. He gasped at sudden pain concentrated in his kidneys, as if he had fiery kidney stones the size of golf balls.

"You okay, old man?"

Frank did not recognize the voice, so it must be one of the new trainees. He bristled a little, but supposed he may have looked—and sounded—like an arthritic old man.

"Yes, quite all right," Frank said. "It is nothing to be concerned about." He stayed in that position, bent in half, for a little longer—he was unsure how much it would hurt to stand. He tried to remember the last time one of these minor agonies had assailed him: more than a month ago, surely. He looked in the direction of the man who had spoken to him, and was surprised to find the fellow kneeling by him.

"Need a hand?"

"No, really, it is all right. I will be fine. A spasm, it will pass."

The newcomer tipped his head to the side as if he doubted Frank's story; in fact his doubt was clear in the way he narrowed his eyes. Frank was not a good liar, but being suspected in this way was another surprise; most men he had met would accept that kind of casual lie without question. It was a social habit they got into from their youth, one that Frank had not learned until later and that still did not come naturally to him. Stormie would have read his dishonesty in his voice and his face, but Frank was not used to other people being able to read him.

The man nodded. "I'm Gabe Morera. Agronomy."

Frank stood up … it took a long time, as if he were an old steam shovel trying to lift a heavy load. Morera stood, too, and Frank matched the man's solid grip. "Frank Pastorelli. Air and water. I suspect we will work together a lot."

Morera smiled. "I hope so. Maybe I should start by helping you with whatever you're doing."

"Thank you," Frank said, and waved him off, "but the pain will pass quickly enough."

From behind him, in the hatchway, a man called, "Gabe, you coming? It's your turn in the Turtle sim." Frank turned, and recognized Van Richards from the briefings he had given to the assembled trainees.

"Yeah, I'm coming," Morera said. "I was just checking on my life sciences partner, here."

Richards gave Frank a noncommittal wave. It could have been a greeting or a dismissal, but Frank did not know.

Frank turned back to Morera. "Thank you, but please, do not let me detain you."

Alone in the corridor again, Frank screwed the cover plate in place. The close quarters of colony life would engender both the stresses of interpersonal contact and countless opportunities to help one's fellows. It could bring out the worst or the best in every person, and Frank hoped he would not only experience the best, but have the strength to demonstrate it.

He was grateful that he and Stormie had found ways to share their reserves of strength with one another. In times of need, each could count on the other to provide the extra measure to get them through any trial.

Like volunteering to take the picophage treatment again. As he considered the prospect of facing those flames, he bowed his head and thought of Shadrach, Meshach, and Abednego, the young Hebrew boys who withstood the fiery furnace. He chuckled and shook his head at the incongruity—that they endured the flames because of their purity and righteousness, as opposed to Frank and Stormie being in the wrong place on the wrong night—and the fact that Stormie would never appreciate the reference.

Thank you, Lord, that we need not endure that again.

Stormie was much improved over the last few weeks since the shots and blood tests stopped. The headaches and nausea abated, she slept better, and she had returned to her normal routines. More than that: her libido had returned, to Frank's great pleasure. And, he hoped, hers as well.

The cover plate secure, Frank turned on the MACEF fan. The small breeze cooled his face; the soft whir of the peristaltic pump was barely audible beneath the fan noise. He put away his tools, and went across the corridor to the kitchenette for a glass of water.

Scott Herbert and the Chu couple, Liquan and Marilyn, came through the hatch from the near junction. It was odd to see them together, since they were competing for the same slots in the colony. Liquan and Herbert's wife, Angela Beacon, were both electrical engineers who wanted to work on the colony's nuclear, solar, and thermal differential power plants.

Several of the remaining sixteen prospective colonists in Group Two were competing for the same jobs; Frank supposed the Group Three trainees were likely competing as well, but they did not concern him.

Herbert, for instance, was vying with Rex Stewart to be one of the foremen directing the tunnel operations that would expand the colony into the outer wall of Mercator Crater. *What kind of pressure must they be under?* Frank sipped his water, thankful that he and Stormie were not competing with any other company for the air-and-water contract. They just had to pass the training, not beat out other prospects.

"Hi, Frank," Marilyn Chu said.

She was an independent contractor, too: principle owner of Lunar Analytics. Stormie had reviewed her services and rates weeks before they entered the training phase, and Marilyn and Stormie had managed to negotiate some volume discounts for LLE's analytic work. Frank guessed that might give Chu Liquan some preference toward the position of power engineer … maybe Angela Beacon was a backup candidate, in case Liquan did not make it through the training. Or maybe … Frank set aside the automatic rundown of training area politics before it confused him further.

"Hello, Marilyn," Frank said. "Hello, Liquan, and Scott."

"Let's ask Frank," Herbert said to the others. One nodded and one shrugged, so Herbert turned to Frank.

"What do you think about turning one of these habitats into the main kitchen and recreation area for the whole lot of us? There's so few of us left, it shouldn't be a big problem." Herbert looked older than his forty-eight years, and it seemed almost comical how he puffed himself up when he talked—as if he dared anyone to contradict him. "It'd be much more efficient to have one big kitchen and do everything there."

Frank smiled down at the older gentleman. It was a harmless enough suggestion, until he considered how difficult it would be to refit the plumbing if this habitat suddenly needed more water and more waste removal. That, he decided, would be a big problem indeed—and one that he and Stormie would have to solve.

Frank nodded in a polite pause. It seemed as if Herbert and the others did not work as long hours as he and Stormie, and most of their hours were on simulators rather than doing real work, so they had the luxury of time to discuss inane ideas. Frank's pectorals flexed and his shoulders rose at this notion that might make things easier for some people but would make more work for him and his wife.

"That is an … interesting idea," Frank said, "and I am sorry I do not have idle time to stay and discuss it. I have several other MACEFs to service before the day is over." He put the mug in the drainer beside the sink and gathered his tools. "I will only say that I suspect the project may be more intensive than you realize, and I think you ignore the redundancy of the habitats. If you put all the food preparation into one habitat, what if that one is damaged? Now, if one module has a problem, the ones around it are its lifeboats."

Herbert made room for Frank to step into the corridor, but said, "Yeah, but how is that changed by rearranging the kitchens? You could still leave another one or two in place, for emergency use."

"Perhaps," Frank said.

"More than perhaps," Herbert said. "I think as soon as Angela and I get up there, I'm going to suggest it. Chu here thinks it's a good idea, don't you, Chu?" He slapped Chu Liquan on the shoulder. Liquan shrugged, and Marilyn rolled her eyes.

Frank lifted his tool belt in a farewell gesture, grateful that he had an excuse to return to work.

O O O

Friday, 23 February 2035
Lunar Colonist Group 2, Training Day 82
Lunar Colonist Group 3, Training Day 19

Stormie sat in her cabin, alone, reading e-mail before going to the lab, when the ticklish "trouble is coming" feeling crept into her stomach with clawed feet. She had just finished eating a biscuit—wishing the whole time for honey and wondering if she could get the agronomist Frank had met to convince the AC to ship up some honeybees for pollination purposes—and the pieces filled her stomach like billets of soft, hot iron. A moment or two passed, then a yelp of pain came from the direction of the module's kitchen.

She leaned out the doorway and looked down the narrow hall. "What's the matter?" she called.

Rex Stewart, the tunnel engineer, stepped into the corridor. He held one hand awkwardly at shoulder height, supported by his other. "Got a sec?" he asked, then stepped back into the kitchen.

Stormie jogged down the corridor. Big drops of congealing blood stained the floor. Rex, paler than usual, sat at the small table putting pressure on his left hand. Fresh blood seeped from between his fingers.

Stormie petrified slowly, as if she were congealing like the blood on the floor. What did he expect her to do? She knew as much first aid as anybody, and certainly wasn't afraid of catching anything from Rex—but the Santa Barbara episode left her hesitant, concerned about the smallest thing that might go wrong. She and Frank were down to single digits in terms of training days: she didn't want to do anything to risk Consortium censure, or a fine, or worse.

"Do you want me to call someone?" she said.

"No, I'd rather you help me bandage this thing."

Her feet refused to move.

"Come on, young lady," Rex said. "Today would be better than tomorrow."

"Maybe I really should call someone."

"Oh, please. Get over here and help patch me up." He laughed lightly, and smiled as if he were inviting her to afternoon tea. "I know some of the others still treat you like a pariah, but there's nothing wrong with you that a little fresh air won't cure."

Stormie let her training take over. She pulled the first-aid kit off the wall and opened it on the table. Gloves on, she reached out to take his hand. "What did you do?"

She half expected—no, more than half expected—Rex to flinch, but instead he met her halfway and put his hand in hers.

"Reliving my younger days," he said. "I used to play around with knives a lot—even before I went in the Navy. I got good at a few tricks, used to make an extra buck or two off Marines or new shipmates from time to time. That was almost twenty years ago." He winced as he opened his left hand. The meaty part between his thumb and forefinger opened with it, and new blood flowed out. It looked warm.

It was hot as lava where it touched Stormie's gloved hand.

She gasped, closed her eyes and swayed as she fought away a cascade of remembered pain. She caught herself on the edge of the table, took a deep breath, and said, "I don't know if the suturing gel will work, the way that looks. You may need real stitches, maybe more than a few."

"Okay, then, stitch me up."

Stormie looked away from the blood into Rex's blue eyes, and saw no guile. He trusted her as he would trust any of the other colonists, and she found that a precious gift. What he wanted her to do, though ...

They'd all practiced stitching wounds—on a dead pig. Faced with the need to do it on a living person, Stormie wavered. She went for the easy out. "Let's find someone who hasn't practically been quarantined down here."

Rex shook his increasingly pale head. "Call for backup, if you're nervous, but let's get started while I still have some blood in me." He grabbed a bandage and held his hand together while Stormie called Central on the intercom. He searched around the tiny kitchen.

"What are you looking for?" she asked after Central acknowledged her call.

He raised his voice above the ensuing PA announcement. "I was wondering if there was any booze tucked away in one of these cabinets. A shot of courage, you might say."

Stormie opened the sterile package of a curved needle paired with long surgical silk. She flipped the top off a can of antiseptic analgesic foam and applied a dose to Rex's hand. He sighed as the fast-acting medicine numbed the wound.

"What are you talking about?" Stormie said. "I thought you and Maggie were all religious." They were the ones who conducted services on Sunday, at least. Stormie didn't know how many people attended, and had no intention of finding out.

"Well, Paul told Timothy to take some wine to help his stomach," Rex said. "This wouldn't be too different. Although that stuff you put on there works wonders. It tingles."

"So, are you ready for this?"

"Are you?"

Stormie positioned herself in the light as best she could. She held Rex's hand with the skin pushed together, trying not to bunch it up too much. In her other hand she gripped the little pliers—forceps, she told herself—the needle pinched in its jaws. She touched the needle to Rex's hand—and backed away. White noise in her ears drowned out Rex's encouragement; his lips moved, but she wasn't sure what he said. She took a deep breath.

The needle tip pressed, dimpled, then punctured the skin; she pushed against the soft resistance under the skin, and harder until the tip emerged from the far side of the wound. It was farther than she'd intended it to go, but she let it be. Breath hissed, and she wasn't sure if it was her sigh of relief or him hissing in discomfort. She gripped the protruding end of the needle and pulled it through. The silk dragged through the skin like dental floss around a dirty tooth.

"Need any help?" Yvette Fiester asked.

"Nah," Rex said. "Stormie's doing fine."

"Like hell I am," she said as she tied the knot. It was ugly, but it would hold. "Put on some gloves and take over."

Yvette complied, as Stormie trusted she would: as a licensed radiologist, she'd done her share of stitching during her intern days and had gone through full EMT training before signing on with the program. She was another independent contractor, slated to perform nondestructive x-ray inspections and burn PROMs for different equipment applications. By necessity and by design, Yvette would multi-task as the closest thing the early colony would get to a general practitioner.

Stormie backed away and watched Yvette work. Rex grabbed Stormie's hand and squeezed it, hard. He smiled when she looked at him. She repaid in kind.

"Thanks," he said. "You did good."

"Thank you," Stormie said. It was all she could say, and it didn't say all she wanted. She glanced away and noticed that Harmony Adamson and Onata Bonaccio had crowded in the room to watch.

"Stay here and talk to me while she does her work," Rex said. "Take my mind off of it."

"That's a good idea," Yvette said, "as long as she swabs away some of this blood so I can see what I'm doing." Stormie did as asked, content to watch the smooth speed with which Yvette worked. Her stitches were smaller, tighter, and closer together than Stormie could ever have achieved.

"Okay," Stormie said. "What do you want to talk about?"

Rex sighed. "I don't know. The Consorts haven't come in to take your blood lately—I guess it's been a month or more. Did they finally admit you and Frank weren't contagious?"

The way he looked at her, he might know more than he was telling. Whatever he knew, Stormie appreciated his voice of support, especially since Onata had been one of Stormie's most vocal detractors when the Consortium thought she was infected. Stormie answered with a question that she hoped didn't sound too challenging. "Is that why you felt safe asking me to help you?"

Rex waved with his good hand. "Ah, no. Maggie and I knew you were okay. We figured they'd relent eventually."

"Thanks, Rex."

"Can't say as we would've done anything differently, from what we've heard. Might not've been the first people to help, but we've always tried to do what we could when we could. I remember we were driving to our honeymoon, we were heading down to Arkansas to the Ozarks, had barely made it past Nebraska City … we were driving in the back woods at night, and came over a hill and saw a red-orange glow at the curve coming up. When we got there, people were running around, yelling, and a big woman came up to our car and said, 'You've got to help 'em, they're burning up!' There was a car off to the right that had hit a fence post but looked okay, but on the other side was a truck down in the field, burning, and a Jeep closer in that was burning, too.

"There was a fellow just this side of the Jeep, on the ground, and I got to him and dragged him across the road. It was hot enough that just getting to him I singed the hair off the backs of my hands, but I didn't notice until later. I couldn't get near enough to the Jeep to help the person in it, on account of the heat. And I kept hearing pops every once in a while, but it took me a little while to figure out what they were."

"What were they?" Stormie asked.

"Fellows in the truck had been hunting, and their ammunition was cooking off in the fire." Rex looked down at his hand. Yvette had turned it and was working on the palm. He seemed calm and his color was better, and he nodded a little as if he had just come to a conclusion. He looked at Stormie and winked; she looked down and wiped away the last trickle of blood as Yvette tied off one more stitch.

"Thing I remember most about that night," Rex said, "is a little boy off to the side of the road, watching the truck burning in the field. He must've been about ten or eleven. Every time one of those bullets would pop off, he'd jump a little. I thought maybe he was a farmboy, just stopped by to see what happened, but he wasn't.

"Found out that it was his uncle's truck, and he'd been riding in the bed and got thrown out when the accident happened. He didn't have a scratch on him that I could see, but the look in his eyes ..." His voice faded and he shook his head. He made a show of studying the new stitches in his hand and said, "Sometimes it's the wounds you can't see that hurt the most. And sometimes the wounds you can see matter the least."

Yvette applied more antiseptic foam and started wrapping Rex's hand in a bandage. She said, "Stormie, pull off some tape so we can cover this mess, then let's get this room cleaned up. Rex, what we've done here is fine for a field dressing, but I think a good surgeon is going to have to work on your hand."

Rex narrowed his eyes. "Yeah, you're probably right. Wonder if I can get a waiver on the last few days down here."

"Not likely," Onata said from her onlooker post by the doorway.

Yvette said, "Onata, how about you and Harmony give us some room so we can get this cleaned up?"

Stormie tore off a strip of adhesive tape; the rip echoed in the small chamber. She handed the strip to Yvette, but looked at Onata. "Better yet," Stormie said, "why not grab a mop and help clean up?"

Onata laughed—a sharp, short, attacking laugh. "I don't think so, Stormie," she said. She looked around where the spatters, drops, and outright puddles were now smeared across the table, floor, and countertop. "Some of that might be your blood. It's not worth the risk."

Heat rose from Stormie's belly, through her chest and up her neck like magma building under a volcano, but it wasn't painful memory-heat: it was embarrassment mixed with slow-boiling anger. She took a step toward Onata.

Yvette grabbed Stormie's hand, and their gloves stuck together like magnets. An instant later, Harmony grabbed her arm.

"Let it go, Stormie," said Rex. "It's over."

Is it? Stormie bit back on the words, and they tasted like old collard greens that had been boiled far too long.

Onata strode out of the little kitchen. Stormie was vaguely aware of other people out in the corridor, but she registered only Rex, sitting at the little table holding his damaged hand at an angle in front of him, and the two women holding on to her.

It wasn't over, even though these few had reached out to her. Maybe they thought she was okay, like Rex said, but maybe they were afraid and just masking it.

CHAPTER EIGHTEEN

Scientific Purposes

Sunday, 25 February 2035
Lunar Colonist Group 2, Training Day 84
Lunar Colonist Group 3, Training Day 21

Van waited in his seat by the outer wall as the crowd emptied out of the "big room" after Sunday worship. Barbara walked forward to talk to the Stewart fellow who ran the service. Van was impressed by the man's resilience: just forty-eight hours ago the Consortium evacuated Stewart to Salt Lake City for surgeons to repair his hand, and here he'd been waving it about like nothing was wrong. If he'd ever been a literal Bible thumper, the big bandage on his hand must've been enough to quell that temptation. He and his wife had orchestrated a tidy little service, with some nice music played out of her datapad—one odd little number about having church on the Moon, but it was pretty—and slides everyone could download off the server if they wanted. Stewart's preaching seemed competent, and Van couldn't fault anything the man had said; but that was probably because he couldn't remember much of it.

He leaned his head back, looked up into the lights, and listened as the roar of conversation against the recorded recessional faded to a few scattered murmurs. He'd tried to follow the sermon, out of common courtesy, but his mind worked too fast and went in too many different directions. Van liked Stewart well enough to feel a little remorseful at not paying better attention. Before Stewart had sliced up his hand, Van had watched him work in the simulator, and in the actual tunneling practice in pressure suits deeper in the mine, and had decided Stewart would be good to have around—even if he was an old Navy guy.

Van chuckled. He and Barbara were the only Air Force veterans in their training class, and with Gary Needham were the only blue-suiters in the entire program so far. Paul Timmons and Nadia Capell were the only Army vets in Group Three, although a couple in the previous groups had rolled along with the caissons. Arvati Peterson, who'd gone through Group One, was the only Marine he knew of. Most of the prospective colonists were Navy types like Stewart, and most of them were submariners—already used to living in close quarters for extended periods of time. It made sense, in a way that annoyed Van and most of the blue-suiters he knew.

Ah, we shouldn't complain—it's not like we were really in the military. Most of us, anyway.

Barbara and Stewart were still talking. Part of him wanted to eavesdrop, but he ignored that part as he looked around at the makeshift chapel. He hadn't seen it, but he was sure one of the shipping crates up at Mercator was labeled in quasi-military fashion "Kit, Chapel Supply, 1 each" and had everything from crucifixes to prayer wheels—maybe even a Torah. During the setup mission he'd teased Roy Chesterfield that he could just lie on his back to face Mecca, since the Earth was always overhead, but aside from the Stewarts and a few others, he wasn't sure who of the trainees was what in terms of religion.

Three little knots of people were still in the room. Two merged and set off in one direction, while the third, still independent, moved more slowly the other way. Off to Sunday brunch?

Van stretched. He'd let them enjoy the break, because they wouldn't get many once they landed. They would learn that lesson if something went wrong here in the mountain, like what he'd dealt with in the Turtle coming back from the Halfway House; but he doubted the AC would ever let things spin that far out of control in a training environment. Which was okay by him: even with his training responsibilities, this was a damn sight easier than the sleep-deprivation and marathon work schedule he'd just finished a few weeks ago.

From the far end of the room Mercer Romero, the wiry little mechanical engineer in their training group, waved at Van to get his attention and gave him a come-with-us gesture. Van shook his head and gave Romero a maybe-next-time wave. He'd stay and wait for Barbara; besides, he liked Romero but wasn't sure he would make it through the program. He didn't seem to have the fortitude.

A slug of quiet discontent fell into Van's gut, like a glob of snot down the back of his throat. He ought to have a little more say in who passed the program. Who in this group knew better what it took to live and work there? He needed to talk to Gary about it— now that Gary was on station, and really starting to run the show, he had to have some clout with the bureaucrats.

The big room was almost empty now, and a few stragglers came in and started setting the workstations back up. Barbara headed back his way.

"So, you volunteering to run the church service after the Stewarts leave?" he asked.

"Maybe," she said, and held out her hand as if she would help him up out of his chair. He let her.

"You should've invited the preacher to lunch. We could've gotten a big dose of holiness, last us all week."

"Very funny," Barbara said. They stepped into the junction on the way toward their cabin. "Actually, he invited us to lunch but I said maybe next time."

"That's a pretty easy promise, since they'll be gone in two days."

"Don't you think I know that? But in a few months we'll all be together again."

Van smiled at her confident tone. "Yes, we will."

O O O

Friday, 2 March 2035
Lunar Colonist Group 2, Training Day 89
Lunar Colonist Group 3, Training Day 26

All eight of the remaining couples in Group Two counted down the last days. Their smiles grew wider as it became clearer that they all would graduate from this stage of the training—though Stormie still drew dark looks from a few of her classmates, including Onata Bonaccio.

After her abortive attempt at fixing Rex's hand, Stormie spent a good deal of her free time with the Stewarts during the last week. On the night of Rex's surgery, she had taken advantage of Maggie's preoccupation by trouncing her in several rounds of cribbage; to her consternation, the two of them returned the favor three consecutive nights after he got back. By then her guilt had been assuaged and their company wore thin; it had been so long since she'd spent any time with Frank's family that she had nearly forgotten how predictable and saccharine-sweet the truly devout could be. When Rex mentioned playing bridge together once they were all on station, she said she doubted their respective work schedules would mesh enough. She told herself that since she controlled her work schedule—and Frank's—she would make sure they didn't.

So she returned to her regular routines, and day followed night and their last day dawned. Not that they saw the dawn, but Stormie ached to see the Sun.

A few Group Three trainees came to see them off, but not many. The real treat was the call from four colonists at the Mercator base itself: Gary Needham, the construction foreman and superintendent; his wife Beverly, a communications technician who was also a nurse; Alice Lindsey, an electrician who also maintained pressure suits; and Chuck Springer, chief operator at the main oxygen plant. They offered congratulations and emphasized that they would, as Needham said, "leave enough work for you that you won't have to worry about being bored."

After the goodbyes and good lucks had been said, Stormie cycled with Frank through the little airlock and into the evacuated mine shaft. They waited for a few others and went through the big airlock with the Stewarts and Jake and Harmony Adamson.

On the other side, finally free of the training facility, they cheered as they stripped off the pressure suits. Stormie's face hurt from smiling as they rode the elevator to the top of the tunnel, and as they stepped outside into the clear, cold Utah evening wearing borrowed parkas and carrying the few personal belongings they'd brought with them. Snow lay thick where it had drifted or been plowed aside. The hairs in Stormie's nose crisped. The twilight glow to the west, behind the mountains, robbed Stormie of her glimpse of the Sun, but she didn't care. The eastern sky was already dark, the first few stars lighting up what would soon be thick swathes of prickly light. The Moon had set earlier in the day, and she wouldn't get a chance to see their new home unless she stayed up after midnight.

Frank looked miserable.

Stormie hugged him, and rubbed her nose against his cheek. "What's the matter?" she asked.

"I had almost hoped that we would step out of the mine and onto a plane headed to Kourou. I am not looking forward to the next few weeks."

They stowed their carefully-packed bags and found seats on the charter bus that would take them to Salt Lake City. Stormie leaned her head on Frank's shoulder and said, "I understand. I'm not looking forward to visiting your parents, either."

His look said he didn't appreciate her joke. He knew, of course, that she was only half-joking.

"Not that," he said. "The time in New Mexico. You know how much I hate the desert."

She knew. Frank's childhood recollections always contrasted the dust and haze and busy streets of Nairobi with the little garden that had been his mother's passion. And when his father brought the family to Louisiana, where he managed construction projects on the Air Force Base near Shreveport, Frank thrived in the heat and humidity and loved the occasional storms that ranged north from the Gulf of Mexico. But his dislike for the desert came primarily from the year he'd spent in Pueblo, Colorado, working on environmental compliance for the railroad association's Transportation Technology Center. He liked the job itself, since his father had introduced him to HO-scale trains years ago, and he even admitted to Stormie that the desert had its own stark beauty; but he hated the dry air that cracked his lips and the palms of his hands, and the dust that coated everything in fine brown powder. That had done as much as anything to convince him to go back to school and get his Masters.

And Stormie was grateful for that, because otherwise she never would have met him. But she was in too good a mood, with the habitat training behind them, to let Frank sink into self-pity. She thought for a few minutes about the best way to get him out of it.

She'd tease him out of it.

"Look at it this way," she said. "You ought to enjoy the desert this time, because pretty soon we'll be in the worst desert in our corner of the solar system." She grinned at him; his cheek twitched as he set his jaw against smiling.

After a moment, he shook his head. "It is not the same," he said. "I will have conditioned air with me all the time up there. I can set the humidity the way I like."

"Yeah, I guess," she said. She decided against arguing over the details of setting the humidity. "And the dust doesn't blow around up there."

"No, it does not."

"Of course, it'll be more lonely than the southwestern desert. There probably aren't as many tarantulas."

He stiffened—Frank was not on friendly terms with arachnids. After a moment he relaxed. "Go to sleep, devil woman," he said. His voice betrayed the smile his face hid. "Stop trying to cheer me up."

O O O

The dead Springer spaniel lay on the stainless steel counter. Its coat looked clean, as if the dog had recently been bathed. Its eyes, mercifully, were closed.

"You've got to be kidding," Barbara Richards said.

"Afraid not," Terrance Winder said over the open intercom. It was a voice-only feed, though they were watching her via the ubiquitous monitoring cameras.

It was three days since Group Two had left the training facility. Two couples from Barbara's group had self-eliminated in that time, so the tunnels fairly echoed, they were so much roomier than when she arrived. That was excellent for Barbara's morale.

Facing the animal on the counter was not so good.

"Why a dog?" she asked.

"It's an agreement we have with a couple of nearby animal shelters. They're going to euthanize the dogs anyway, and this is better than cremating them or landfilling them. They like the idea that the dogs are used for scientific purposes."

Scientific, right. Surely the trainers knew that she, as a rancher's daughter, had grown up with working dogs. It was possible they knew that she loved and respected the animals. If this had been a sheep or a cow, no problem—she would go to work and get the meat aging. But a dog? That was just wrong. She wondered if cat lovers had to prep a cat.

She wished she hadn't eaten breakfast.

With two desultory knocks, Gabriel Morera came into the tunnel junction. "Sorry I'm late," he said. He sounded as enthusiastic as the dog.

"No problem," Barbara said.

Winder said through the speaker, "Okay, we may as well get started. You're both familiar with the procedure?"

Barbara hummed, considering the question and the look on Morera's face. "Familiar may be too strong a term," she said. He looked at her and nodded in understanding.

"If you mean we've read through it, yes," Morera said. "And did the sim in Colony Life."

"And promptly tried to forget it," Barbara added. Morera smiled.

Over the speaker, the Consortium training manager cleared his throat and said, "That's understandable, which is why this session is proctored. We'll walk you through the procedure, step by step."

Step by step it was. The little banter with Morera had lightened Barbara's spirits, but it didn't seem to have done much for his. If they could have projected the checklist and run it themselves, in their own time, it would've been better.

Van hadn't gone through this training procedure yet, so he hadn't given her any pep talk or supposed wisdom. This training hadn't been considered necessary for the short-term setup missions, and she would probably have discounted Van's advice in favor of her own experience growing up around the ranch and the slaughter.

But, Barbara's name came up in the random selection before Van's. The AC was big on random selection. Barbara suspected they had some statistician on staff who justified his continued employment by consulting random number tables instead of using a computer. It would fit the AC's image of never using any higher technology than they absolutely had to—an attitude Van defended but which grated on Barbara. Newer technologies were inherently more reliable and longer-lasting, so why bother with older things even if they were reparable? But she wasn't being paid to make those decisions ... just to live with them.

Their first task was to prepare the vacuum chamber—the Funerary Desiccation Device, by the Consortium's parlance. The story went that the FDD was once to be named an Apparatus but the acronym FDA was considered inappropriate. It normally folded up in one corner of this tunnel junction: an end junction, currently with nothing on the other side of it except the rest of the sealed mine. It would be similar on the Moon, except there were two of the FDD chambers in two separate end junctions.

The FDD chamber was, fortunately or unfortunately, human-sized. The AC probably considered it fortunate, because they didn't have to order and install a smaller one for training on animal carcasses and because the fact of its size would remind the trainees that they might have to do this procedure on a person some day. That was the unfortunate part for Barbara—as if she needed something else to attack her overall confidence, something else to insinuate doubt into her mind. That human-sized chamber did just fine.

A chill ran through her body as she and Morera folded the chamber down from the wall like a macabre Murphy bed. It was one thing to watch it in the computer game, another to physically set up the thing. The thought of putting a real person in the chamber raised gooseflesh in places she hadn't thought possible. She gritted her teeth as her thoughts segued to Van lying in the chamber—and then to her.

That's what they want, Barbara. They want you to forget that this is an animal, and think about it being a person. Look at the dog and forget what they want. Look at the dog and pretend it's just a really big cat.

Barbara breathed more steadily and pressed on with Winder's instructions.

The chamber was intended to desiccate a body before it was transferred outside to the furnace—on the Moon, a solar furnace—for reduction and recovery of its calcium, potassium, and other elements. Vacuum tubing ran from the chamber to ports connected to the outside of the habitat, and it suited Barbara fine that they would use the natural advantage of the Moon's lack of atmosphere to evacuate this particular chamber. A standard vacuum pump would pull air out of the chamber, all right, but into the habitat, and no one ever really enjoyed the slaughterhouse smell. She had the most trouble as she considered the bulbous water traps she attached to each hose: they were specially designed for the vacuum line to trap and hold as much moisture as possible to purify and re-use later. Thinking about that as she handled them made her sick to her stomach.

Again she reminded herself that this was all part of the psychology of the training, as well as the practical instruction. They knew the risk before they signed up, of course, and if they ever pretended not to know they were reminded by the piles of forms they signed and countersigned and witnessed. Most people signed up for the standard preparation that she and Morera were practicing today; but she and Van had opted for the more expensive route of having a portion of their final crystalline ashes returned to Earth instead of recycled into the ecosphere the lunar colony was trying to create and sustain. She wanted her dad to have something to say words over.

Winder talked them through setting up the chamber, locking down the junction, and going on the airline respirators. Barbara was grateful that she would smell the dry, slightly rubberized air inside the mask instead of the dog's opened remains. Winder asked which of them wanted to make the first cuts, and neither answered right away. He suggested they do rock-paper-scissors to decide, but Barbara took another look at Morera's face and picked up the scalpel herself. Morera smiled at her, and crossed himself.

The first few cuts weren't so bad, as they were intended to drain as much fluid from the body as possible—not so much different from draining the blood from a meat animal, except that it would take more time in lower gravity. But as the cuts became more complex and attacked the eyes and inner organs, the instrument dragged her hand like a lead weight. The realization crept up on her that this operation was not designed to preserve but to hasten an orderly destruction; and even though this dog didn't look that much like the Border Collies her dad kept on the ranch, that didn't matter. Its coat was soft and once it had run and played, perhaps worked a ranch like her father's, and chased squirrels or cars or maybe sticks. And from the back of her mind, where she had safely stored it, came the knowledge that this procedure was meant for human beings.

Tears collected in Barbara's eyes and she fought against spilling them inside the face mask. She lost that fight momentarily, regained control for a time, and lost again. The delicate blade she wielded may as well have been made of roughly chipped stone, as bad as her hand started to shake. She performed mechanically, cutting where and when Winder told her, trying to shut out the sounds of slicing flesh, short bursts of air pressure as Morera blew out the contents of arteries and organs, and the occasional drip into the catch basin. She concentrated so fully on each cut that she didn't appreciate how many she had made before Winder told Morera to take over. She stepped back and looked at the eviscerated corpse, at the blood and vitreous humor and other liquids that collected in the drip pan like oil underneath a car.

She grabbed at the front of her mask.

"You don't want to do that," Morera said, his voice muffled by his own mask. Winder's voice, clear and amplified by the speaker, said the same thing an instant later.

They were right, and Barbara mentally kicked herself for even thinking of giving in to nausea. What would her dad say? She looked down and into a far corner of the junction chamber to compose herself; she clamped her jaws tight and clenched her throat and took slow, measured breaths. After a few moments, she relaxed and turned again to the task at hand. She took up the air hose while Morera took up the scalpel.

Morera crossed himself again as Winder started directing his first cut. Barbara wondered what he prayed for in that moment, though she thought she knew.

CHAPTER NINETEEN

Fallback Position

Saturday, 14 April 2035

Frank barely kept track of where the days went, but he trusted them to keep coming. At first when they left the Utah facility, everything moved in rhythm like a well-rehearsed dance: he and Stormie stepped lightly through a brief and surprisingly cordial visit with his family, six more weeks of learning the finer points of wrangling the lunar vehicles and equipment, and last-minute business arrangements with James. Frank came to wish he had an old-style page-a-day calendar instead of his datapad, so that in the physical act of ripping off the previous day and concentrating on the new day he would feel less disoriented. Family meals and restaurant meals and dining hall meals became one and the same; the faces of his fellow trainees and his relatives and his friends became interchangeable as the days sped by.

On the second Saturday of April, Frank and Stormie stepped off the plane in Guiana. Frank sighed in contentment as the air wrapped around his body like a warm, moist compress. The jungle atmosphere settled around him soft and heavy, all the more comforting after their weeks in the New Mexico desert where the lack of humidity irritated him like an atmospheric itch. The dry air on board airplanes he stood well enough, because he knew it would end, but dry air all around that would never go away, harbinger of static electricity and cracked skin, was another matter. He chuckled now at the complaints about the heat and humidity he heard from the others.

Two other couples had flown in on the same plane as Frank and Stormie: Jake and Harmony Adamson, he to be a construction laborer before he transitioned into his role as Mining Director and chief miner on the Consortium's asteroid, she to be a construction engineer, surveyor, and laborer; and George and Yvette Fiester, who would be, respectively, a vehicle mechanic and machinist, and a private laboratory services provider and colony "doctor." Frank was still impressed that the others would carry out multiple tasks, along with a myriad of additional duties they would pick up at the colony; in contrast, he was quite content that his primary, secondary, tertiary, and quaternary duties all boiled down to the same thing: keeping the air breathable and the water potable.

After clearing Customs quite easily, since none of them had much baggage or anything to declare, the AC bused their contingent to the Kourou space launch facility where they joined three other couples awaiting transport.

Sonny Peterson would be another construction foreman and in charge of power production; his wife Arvati was an electronics technician and general laborer. Chu Liquan had been selected as a power engineer and construction laborer, and his wife Marilyn Chu was a private laboratory analyst who would also help maintain water extraction equipment. And Rex Stewart, favoring his healed but still hurting hand, would be the foreman and chief laborer of the tunneling project, while his wife Maggie ran a private service tending the colony's animals and, to a lesser extent, its plants. The other would-be colonists were scheduled for later flights, or placed on waiting lists, or simply dismissed as qualified but unneeded. Frank rejoiced that he and Stormie did not have to suffer that ignominy.

All together the dozen new colonists would join the eight already on the Moon: Gary Needham, the primary construction foreman and laborer and the acting colony superintendent; Beverly Needham, who Frank had been surprised to learn had been assigned as a communications and electronics technician and primary Command Post controller rather than as a nurse; Bruce Lindsey, primary vehicle mechanic, maintenance foreman, and hydraulics and pneumatics technician; Alice Lindsey, electrical engineer in charge of pressure suit maintenance; Chuck Springer, another hydraulics and pneumatics technician and primary oxygen production supervisor; Trish Springer, mechanical engineer and primary fabrication supervisor; Eva Sondstrom, an electronics technician and geologist; and Bent Sondstrom, a vehicle mechanic, machinist, and construction laborer.

Frank's perception of time changed again, for the better, at the launch base. It had been weeks since he had experienced any residue from the picophage treatment, and he marveled at the human body's ability to "forget" pain. Occasionally twinges struck him like deep bruises—uncomfortable, but bearable—although the procedure had also produced some stiffness and lethargy. The intervals in which any real pain returned to torment him lengthened into comfortable amnesia, and did not recur even when the doctors implanted his required biocapsules, so he was able to enjoy himself.

Briefings on safety measures, training on escape and survival equipment, and dry-runs of countdown procedures came and went so quickly that Frank was left dazed, as if he had suffered through two semesters' worth of thermodynamics class in as many weeks. However, he and Stormie happily stole an hour here and there to walk, talk, relax, and dream.

To try to realize some economy of scale in the production of the new "flex-class" Ariane launch vehicles, the Consortium had originally booked an unprecedented twenty-four launches a year out of Kourou. They had never flown that many, and the European partners had happily sold the launches to other customers, with only partial credit back to the AC even when the rival Apollo-Aten Mining & Materials was launching something. But the AC maintained sway over the launch schedule, with wedges of time, orbital insertion, and payload they could manipulate as needed—within the capabilities of the launch system. As Frank and Stormie learned during the final flight preparations, the high-passenger vehicle's flight readiness still had not been approved, so the AC was limited to only eight seats per launch. In response, they split Frank, Stormie, and their fellows into two groups and arranged separate launches for them. Since they were bound first for the Clarke station to await transit to the Moon, it did not matter except to the accountants how many launches it took to get them into orbit. Jake suggested they draw straws to see who got to launch first, but the Consortium had already assigned them to their groups.

The first group launched on April 24th—Frank's birthday—but he and Stormie were not among them. They watched the launch from the fallback position and toasted their companions' voyage. Frank argued that champagne was more appropriate to wedding cake than birthday cake, but he enjoyed both.

"It would have been a nice birthday present," he told Stormie as the countdown processed through a planned hold, "to be launching today."

"If you can't have good luck, have good timing, I always say," Stormie said. She leaned in and whispered. "And if you can't have good timing, have good sex."

"That makes no sense," he said. "And I have never heard you say it before."

She leaned in and kissed him, long and deep. She tasted of champagne and chocolate. When they broke for air, she said,

"Come live with me and be my Love,
And we will all the pleasures prove,"

at which point she broke into giggles. Frank laughed with her.

The countdown continued, and at its termination, the great vehicle began its ascent. From where they stood, a white cloud billowed from the ground and a dull rumble reached them shortly thereafter as the clock counted up. When the clock reached +00:01:27, the vehicle exploded like a Fourth of July firework.

O O O

Thursday, 26 April 2035
Lunar Colonist Group 3, Training Day 81

Barbara was numb for the first thirty hours after watching the launch vehicle explode.

She realized how bad she had gotten when she had to look on her datapad to find out what day it was, besides training day 81. She tried and failed to remember what tasks she had performed the previous day; the notations on her schedule seemed written in an unfamiliar language. She hoped she hadn't made any major errors while going through the motions of training.

As soon as she thought it, she retreated from the implications and tried unsuccessfully to immerse herself in her next training task: tearing down, cleaning, and rebuilding pressure suits. She failed to occupy her mind enough, though, because she had already gone through the pressure suit rotation three times before: her hands remembered the pieces and procedure well enough that her brain was free to think about other things she'd rather not. Several times she found her hands shaking so hard she could barely fit couplings together; other times she worked so frantically that she couldn't remember afterward if she'd put everything back in the right place. And when she allowed herself to articulate her thoughts, which she only dared in the privacy of her mind, the words might change but the meaning was always the same.

I'm not going up in that thing.

She chided herself; that made no sense. She knew the launch business better than most, and deep down was impressed by how well the system worked. The inertial navigation system detected the rocket tracking off course at +00:00:26 and tried to bring it back, but thirty seconds into the mission the condition was uncorrectable. The egress system took over, and the dropsule was a safe distance from the launch vehicle when the abort system activated. What ate at Barbara was that they hadn't released exactly how the Fiester woman broke her arm and the power engineer, Chu Liquan, ended up drowned.

Over the next several days there was too much speculation about whether the Fiester couple would continue in the program and who would replace the Chus, and not enough straight reporting about what happened and why and what they were doing to fix it. And in Barbara's mind, despite all her efforts to shut the fear off and replace it with analysis, there was too much role-playing with her in Chu Liquan's position. Worse, her mind extrapolated from the few facts she knew, especially when she slept. She dreamed of fire—which was silly, since the crew had been ejected before the vehicle blew up—and falling, which made sense except she seemed to fall without a parachute or anything in her dreams—and drowning, which only intensified the smothering sensation she still experienced knowing she was so far underground.

She slept less. She started awake whenever she began to drift off, afraid to let herself slip down into dreaming. She closed herself off like an airlock, afraid to voice her fears with the AC trainers listening everywhere, afraid to join in any casual conversation lest it turn to the obvious topic that affected everyone, afraid most of all of how badly the fear was affecting her. She cut herself some slack at first, then berated herself when her attitude didn't improve, then downloaded a copy of Frank Herbert's "Litany Against Fear" onto her datapad and repeated it to herself almost hourly. "Fear is the mind-killer"—*God, how right he was.*

She tried to act normally, and shifted her schedule a little to keep herself isolated at meals and working mostly alone, but Van eventually realized something was wrong. Even he couldn't ignore the signs for days on end. He tried to talk to her several times, but she brushed him off and he let her be. By Sunday the 29th, she was starting to nod off during routine activities. She had just completed a solar flare drill when a chime from her datapad woke her from an unplanned nap. The message was brusque and chilled her: "Report to Central Control immediately."

Damn.

Now they were going to call her out, expose the fear she was trying to control. She just needed a few more days to sort through things, and then their training would be over: she and Van would graduate and be promoted out of the Cave and back onto the surface of the world along with the seven other couples who still remained. But more than time she needed to get the launch failure investigation report and read exactly what happened. The high-level executive summary was out: all the systems worked as designed, and human error was implicated in the casualties. But Barbara wanted the technical details so she could evaluate her own risk and understand if it was acceptable. It would be; it had to be.

Wanda Lorentz, a petite woman with a beautiful complexion that reminded Barbara of the Caribbean, was on duty in the tiny control center. "Hello, Barbara," she said, shattering again the island mystique: her accent was as thoroughly British as her husband, Roy Chesterfield's. They were part of training Group Four, newly arrived and settling in. "Roy and Van out gallivanting again?"

Barbara forced her lips into a wry smile. Roy's arrival had been a mixed blessing for Van at first; on the plus side, he had someone he could talk to who had really "been there" with him, but on the minus side, Roy's good-natured ribbing about Van's problems in the "done that" category were a sore point. Now they spent as much time as they could together, which was just fine by Barbara.

"I suppose so," Barbara said. "Whether they're getting into trouble or staying out of it, I'm not sure."

"Oh, I'm sure," Wanda said. "The former, almost certainly. But that's not why you're here."

Barbara held up her datapad. "No. I was summoned."

"Indeed you were, because I summoned you. You have a call."

"I'm not surprised."

"Really? Oh, very well then. You can take it across the way there." Wanda pointed to the cabin on the other side of the habitat. "It's audio only, half-duplex, and don't forget the time lag."

"I won't. I know the drill by now." She turned, and then remembered her manners. "Thanks, Wanda."

Barbara settled herself on the stool in the tiny terminal room. By the notation on the screen, the far end was standing by. She keyed the microphone, said, "Barbara Richards here, as requested, over," and waited.

"Well, you could act a little more enthusiastic, as much as this call is costing your husband. Quit moping around, Barmaid, and get your butt up here to keep me company, over."

Beverly Needham's voice slowly seeped into Barbara's consciousness, along with the realization that the time delay wasn't a Consortium-induced artificiality. BD was calling from the colony.

And Barbara was keeping her waiting extra long by not responding. But what to say?

227

"Oh, BD, it's good to hear your voice. Even though the sound quality sucks." Nothing else came to mind, so after a second she added, "Over."

BD laughed, and her laughter was a tonic to Barbara's spirit. "Get used to it, dear, it's the way things go. But it's worth it so far. I've never been so tired, and I'm getting sick of the stored food—we're still weeks away from having more than a handful of fresh vegetables to eat—but this is nothing short of amazing. Except that my husband is livid with the AC right now. They're not telling him who they're going to select to replace the Chu couple, or how they're going to make up the lost time. He heard they were going to delay the next launch, but he thinks they should go ahead and launch that group anyway. He says the rocket's already been checked out and approved, there's no reason to wait. Over."

Barbara fell into the conversation so easily she barely registered the radio protocol—though the time lag irritated her so that she wished she were talking to BD face to face.

"Come on, BD, he's done those investigations before. He knows how they run."

"Yeah, and he used to say the same thing when we were at Patrick, long before we met you."

"At least he's consistent."

"No, at most he's consistent."

It was an old joke, but Barbara enjoyed it because her friend offered it. So much so that she almost missed BD's next words.

"You're not letting this get to you, are you?"

Lying would be no use. If Van had arranged for this call, it was because he was worried and thought BD could help pull her out of her funk. And he was concerned enough to pay for the call and not to worry about anything the AC would overhear. Barbara processed that for a moment and realized it meant that Van was more worried about her state of mind than about the possibility of getting scrubbed from the program.

"I'm trying not to," she told BD. "I guess I'm not handling it too well. I think I'll be okay once I can see the full report—and maybe after the next launch goes well."

"There you go," BD said. "Shoot, you could probably write the report."

"No, not me. I'm just a cowgirl, you know that."

BD snorted; the sound was much more grotesque with the added distortion of distance and amplification. "Yeah, you keep telling people that. They're no more likely to believe you than I am."

"So, you still think I should come up there?"

"You'd better. I'm getting tired of talking to my *husband*."

Barbara laughed a little. "Okay, then. We can have a girls' night ... in, I guess. It should make Van happy, since he won't be paying for antenna time."

"Oh, I don't think he minds. In the e-mail he sent Gary, he said he thought this would be cheaper than sending you to therapy."

"He did not."

"And more effective, too, I might add."

Barbara tried to work up a retort, but instead a genuine smile grew on her face. She might have choice words for her husband later, but for now she was content to chat with her long-distance friend. *Cheaper than therapy, indeed.*

CHAPTER TWENTY

Trespassing the Sanctity

Tuesday, 8 May 2035

In the usual way that the media ignores routine events and examines aberrations with unabashed fervor, the failed Consortium launch brought more attention to Kourou than had been seen since the first manned launch from Guiana back in the early 2020s. Air traffic to Guiana surged from every direction: not only was every direct flight from Paris full, but even the little planes that hopped their way down through the Caribbean were packed with reporters, producers, camera and sound technicians.

The AC kept Stormie, Frank, and the rest of their crew sequestered from the press, except for carefully-scripted events. Stormie preferred to think that was for the crew's sanity more than saving face; it was hard enough dealing with anxious family members, let alone droves of reporters, when they were supposed to be completing their final preparations.

Slipping the launch date only freed up time for crewmembers like Stormie who had no extended family. In contrast, Frank spent hours e-mailing, web-chatting, and talking with his parents and siblings, enough that he began losing his good humor as well as sleep. They tried to convince him to withdraw from the program, or ask for further delays, or to let them appeal to Congress or the United Nations for his protection, and probably other wacky ideas that he didn't bother to share with her. Frank held firm.

Rex and Maggie Stewart planned a memorial service for Chu Liquan; Frank persuaded Stormie to attend, if only to show solidarity in front of all the cameras. Their entire contingent sat in the first two rows of uncomfortable folding chairs in the high bay of the building where the dropsules were received and inspected. The building was packed with Consortium and Arianespace workers, with reporters lining the walls and even situated on elevated work platforms. A group of local workers played the music and Rex delivered a mercifully brief eulogy.

Almost daily they sat for press conferences, where they were peppered with questions from reporters whose only knowledge of rockets seemed to be that the pointy end went up and fire came out the bottom. It surprised Stormie that so few of the reporters seemed to know any of the technical details, but it made their questions easier to answer. After all, she didn't know many details about the launch equipment herself, and didn't need to; all she had to do was ride the thing, not fly it or fix it. The AC put on a good show and a good face, explaining that they trusted Arianespace's analysis and that the next vehicle was being thoroughly checked; no, they had not negotiated a new date for the next launch; no, they had not negotiated a new price for the next launch; yes, they had recovered the "black boxes" from the dropsule and were examining the recordings; no, they had no intention of requiring future rockets to carry more instrumentation; no, they would not discuss the details of any of the insurance settlements.

The online reporters seemed more in tune with the events and technology than did the television talking heads; one of them, Jacqueline Argos, finagled a Consortium pass into the crew cafeteria and posed as a technician working on the accident investigation. Stormie learned more than she ever hoped to know about components that had been made self-healing to improve their reliability, and about analytics software—developed to mine huge data caches—that turned out to be useful in many other rapid-comparison applications, including monitoring vehicles in flight from the ground. Details of vehicle performance that used to only be available from instruments radioing signals to the ground now were reconstructed by software using feeds from transceivers that painted the ascending vehicle with radar and lidar and that took in multispectral imagery from UV to IR. The rocket still carried critical instrumentation for parameters that couldn't be read remotely, but less instrumentation meant less expensive launch vehicles and more payload capacity.

The security people weren't fooled for long; they tracked down Ms. Argos and escorted her from the cafeteria while she was eating a piece of baklava. The next day Stormie learned that analysis of the sensor net recordings had projected with something over ninety-five percent confidence that the launch vehicle tracked off course because of a small burn-through on one of the outboard rocket engine nozzles. The day after that—a week after her and Frank's original launch date—Arianespace announced they had checked the pedigree of their rocket and certified it safe for flight. The Consortium briefed the passengers on the investigation and gave them a few minutes to talk it over before they signed onto the mission roster.

Stormie looked at Frank and raised her eyebrows at him. She didn't need to talk anything over; she had no intention of backing away from the mission. They had invested too much time and money and pain to give up now. But he had been fending off his family and may have some reservations, and she was prepared to listen to them. She might not be happy about them, but she would listen and address them as best she could.

Frank's dark eyes were inscrutable in the briefing room light. He looked at her a long time without speaking, his face relaxed and betraying nothing. His silence, in the low cacophony of conversations all around them, worried her. He reached out and put his hand over hers.

"Are you ready, my dear?" he asked, and squeezed her hand.

A thin film of moisture formed along the bottom of Stormie's eyes—not enough that she was in danger of shedding tears, but enough that she noticed the feeling and the warmth of gratitude and pride and love that came with it. She smiled, slowly, and asked, "Are you?"

Frank stood and pulled her up with him, and led her to the table where Aliette Mittengard, the AC launch controller, had set the mission book. Frank picked up one of the pens, held it out to Stormie, and smiled his brilliant smile.

"I'll let you sign first," Stormie said.

"No," Frank said. "You first."

Her hand shook a little as she took the pen, her nervousness a summation of the residue of months of planning and preparation, the memory of pain and fear, and the anticipation of realizing the biggest dream she'd ever had. She took a deep breath and signed her name in the book with a slight tremble she hoped didn't show.

Frank's hand didn't shake at all.

O O O

Friday, 11 May 2035
Lunar Colonist Group 2-B Launch Day

Stormie and Frank suited up and were strapped to acceleration cushions at the top of the massive Ariane launch vehicle. Stormie had accepted a shot of Jägermeister just before they boarded the van that took them to the launch tower—a tradition started by Gary Needham before he launched on the first setup mission—but once she had been lying in place in the rocket for an hour she alternated between regret based on slow waves of shallow nausea and euphoria from the liquor taking the edge off her nerves.

The low chatter of controllers' voices as they checked subsystems and verified power and fuel levels nearly lulled her to sleep—largely because most of the calls were in French and repeated in English; plus, she could do nothing about any of the systems they mentioned—but each time she was yanked back to consciousness by the creaks and groans of the spacecraft around her as pressures built up or released, or as thermal expansion put stress on a structural member, or simply as one of her fellow passengers shifted position. Part of the display inside her helmet scrolled through views fed from the vehicle's cameras but she paid more attention to the chronometer. It silently counted down, and she found herself gripping the arms of her seat each time the clock scrolled through a multiple of ten or paused for a planned hold. Each time she forced herself to breathe and relax her grip, but when the final hold came and the controller polled the launch team she held on until her hands cramped.

She wasn't sure if she first felt or heard the vibration as the engines ignited and ramped up to full power, but soon her entire world was full of noise and every cell of her body started to shake—and then the pain began.

No, please not now.

At her preflight checkout, she had confirmed for Dr. Nguyen that she still had occasional twinges of pain. He had mentioned some instances of pre-arthritis in picophage patients, which he thought Frank might have, and also the possibility of a form of post-traumatic stress. What might trigger her nervous system to re-create the pain, he could not tell.

Now she knew.

The pain rose in intensity with the engines' roar and then it rose faster than the noise. When the launch locks released and the countdown became a countup—and the vehicle's acceleration pushed her deep into the cushions—Stormie was screaming inside her helmet. Fire pouring out of the base of the rocket awakened the latent fire in her bones, a feeling like her flesh was being torn apart and ground up like sausage. She screamed in rage as much as in agony, furious that the joy of this moment was denied her. In the deepest, still-thinking part of her brain, she was grateful her microphone was turned off.

She yelled so loud and so long she became lightheaded; the moving figures in the display in front of her face blurred. The other half of the display darkened, and she vaguely realized that meant they were passing through the upper atmosphere and into space. She turned her attention to the camera view, grit her teeth, and smiled as one view showed her a curving expanse of Earth beneath them.

Over the next few hours their orbit would be circularized and raised and matched to the Clarke station. Stormie tried to relax, to let the gentleness of freefall comfort her agonized body. She switched on her microphone to answer the controller's status query, and her voice sounded almost normal.

Her stomach protested when it didn't feel gravity come back; she took deep, slow breaths and forced herself to accept the sensation of hanging just past the apex of a roller coaster. The smell as a couple others lost the battle with their innards bothered her less than she had feared. Gradually her stomach relaxed and so too the pain started to subside; she decided to go to sleep, even as her fellow passengers started to chat and move about.

After briefly assuring her he was fine, Frank didn't chat any more, though, and Stormie forced herself alert enough to bring up his status display in her monitor. His vital signs were stable, but showed a frightening series of spikes early in the flight; curious, she displayed her own status record. Their vitals showed similar patterns of distress, and her heart ached to think that his ride had been as torturous as hers.

Oh, Frank, I'm sorry. I'll make it up to you.

She hadn't meant to say it aloud, but she must have because Frank answered, "No apologies, my love. We are here. We have 'slipped the surly bonds,' have we not? We may not hav . lifted off on 'laughter-silvered wings,' but surely we now tread the 'untrespassed sanctity of space.' Or perhaps we are trespassing the sanctity of space. I am not sure." He fell silent; his vitals slowed down and he might have snored.

"Yes, Frank," she said. "Although, I might prefer 'rushing amorous contact high in space together ... she hers, he his, pursuing.'" She closed her eyes.

From his seat, Jake said, "I almost think my Virgin Galactic flight was more exciting."

"That's always how it is," Rex answered. "We build things up with dire warnings and gloomy forecasts, but in the end, they're always anticlimactic."

Speak for yourself, Stormie thought as she let herself drift into sleep.

O O O

Nearly two weeks after Stormie and Frank launched, Jim Fennerling still couldn't stop smiling.

The lithe, olive-skinned clerk at the front counter at WellSportz noticed his grin as he wheeled himself through the front doors.

"You still happy, Mr. Jim?" she asked.

"Absolutely, Honoria."

"That's good. Your friends, they're doing okay?"

He told her yes, though he lost a fraction of his smile since it was only a partial truth. Stormie and Frank had acclimated well enough to freefall, but they were stuck on the Clarke station and it looked as if they'd be there for several more weeks. The Consortium's transport to and from the colony wasn't as regular as they'd hoped it would be at this point. Their contracts manager had told Jim it was a maintenance issue—that the vehicles were in overhaul earlier than anticipated—but his unofficial contacts had told a different story: the two ferries were making more runs to and from the asteroid instead of to and from the lunar base. That made some amount of sense, since the lunar base wasn't ready yet to house more than a few miners on rotation—the first four-person unit was due any day. He just wished the AC would be straight up with him about the transit schedule.

Jim wheeled himself into the workout room. His insurance company would've liked him to work out at the hospital, but he preferred it here: being around athletes was much better than being around sick people. The sports therapists seemed to work him harder than the physical therapists at the hospital, and he liked that. They treated him the same as any of the walk-ins who were trying to get rehabilitated.

"Hey, where's Tony?" he asked the unfamiliar but very fit redhead who was resetting one of the resistance machines. She looked up and smiled, and Jim wished the medical miracle makers would hurry up with the nano-surgery that would fix his spine: she deserved a reaction that he couldn't give her.

She picked up a clipboard and glanced at it before she answered. "You must be Mr. Fennerling. Tony said you'd be in a little early.

He's in the office, do you want me to get him for you?"

Jim waved her off. "No, you don't have to do that. But you have me at a disadvantage. You are?"

"I'm Cindy. I just started, as an intern. I'm at U.C. Santa Barbara."

"Very good—"

A familiar voice interrupted him. "Okay, Jim, you'll have plenty of time to charm the new help later." Tony Marquez smiled his usual ferocious smile as he came through the door from the back room. Ten years out of the Marines, and he still looked as if he could outrun any new recruit. "You ready to go? You feeling good?"

Jim had learned early on that Tony didn't appreciate bluster and would usually make the offender pay during the therapy session. Day before yesterday Tony had made it his mission to work the smile off Jim's face, and he'd almost succeeded. This morning Jim was tempted to hedge, but he still felt too damn good about how close Stormie and Frank were to finally putting the "lunar" in Lunar Life Engineering. "Tony, I am still so high I may as well be in orbit myself."

"Okay," Tony said, "we'll see how long that lasts. We're going to let Miss Cynthia get you going, and I've told her to ride you like she's an Apache with the cavalry on her tail. She's all impressed that you know people who are going to the Moon, but she's the only one, and I've warned her that you stink like the rest of us once you start to sweat. She doesn't believe me, of course, but she'll find out soon enough, won't she?"

"On the contrary," Jim said, barely able to keep a semi-straight face as Cindy tittered behind the clipboard she held in front of her mouth, "I expect she'll find my aroma enticing."

Tony's lips compressed into a thin line for a second, and Jim fancied he could almost hear the man growl. Through half-clenched teeth he said, "Oh, she'll find you a-ro-matic, I'm sure. Bench press, Mis-ter Fennerling. Move it."

Jim laughed and wheeled himself to the apparatus, and Cindy, now openly giggling, followed. She set up the weights while Jim pulled himself onto the bench, got situated, and strapped in. They always did the bench press first, because it was the only exercise he had to get out of the chair for: the other equipment he could roll his chair into place to use.

Cindy proved to be an able motivator, even if her approach was nearly the opposite of the run-roughshod-over-the-patient technique Tony preferred. She was firm when she needed to be, but that wasn't often: Jim worked out harder than usual without as much prodding. By the time he got through the military press and in position at the rowing machine, he realized it was because he wanted to impress her. Tony must've figured it would happen, because he slipped back to the office without once having to badger Jim about not working hard enough.

Jim got a little dizzy during the row, enough that his right eye blurred for a moment, but he still finished strong. Cindy kept him supplied with water, which he gratefully drank while she set up the curls. He blinked a few times until his vision cleared and got back to work.

The dizziness smacked him hard about five minutes into his time on the upper body ergometer, and his right hand slipped off the handle. He slowed the rotations his left hand was doing and pulled his right hand back up ... and overshot the handle. His knuckles rapped against the ergometer's white plastic case.

"Are you okay?" Cindy asked.

Jim ignored her. He turned his attention to the right handle, watching it mostly with his left eye as it moved through the air in front of him. Vaguely, gradually, he remembered that his left hand was turning the handle and he slowed it even more. He reached out and up and finally intercepted the handle with his right hand. He kept the speed slow at first, and started speeding up when he remembered that Cindy had asked him a question.

"Yeah, I'm fine," he said. "A little dizzy, that's all. It's nothing." He wanted to look at her, but he thought he might let go of the handle again if he stopped watching it closely.

"Do you get dizzy very often?"

Jim snorted out a little laugh. "Yeah, every so often. I usually don't worry about it ... it's not like I'm going to fall down or anything."

Jim's field of vision seemed to have contracted to a sphere about a meter in radius, in the center of which he struggled to keep his hand steady and the ergometer running. A vague shape entered the sphere just beyond his hands and did something to the machine; it suddenly became much easier to spin, and his hands rushed after the faster-turning handles.

His right hand slipped free of the handle and made a couple of lazy attempts to grab it before he dropped it down to his lap. The effort made him incredibly tired, and every motion seemed as if he was pushing through an invisible gelatinous barrier. He moved his fingers against something—rough, wet. He wasn't sure what it was, and it took a long time to look down and even longer for him to recognize that his hand was feeling his own leg. His leg couldn't feel his hand touching it; he thought he should be sad about that, but for the moment he wasn't sure why.

"Jim, look at me," Tony said from far away.

Jim looked to the left and swayed. Tony was suddenly right in front of him, and Jim wasn't sure how he got there that fast or what happened to the spinny thing he was using. Tony caught him and held him upright. Tony's rugged face was blurry; Jim turned his head a little to the right to see him with his left eye, but Tony pushed against his jaw and held him facing front and center.

"Jim, I want you to do exactly as I say. Right now, I want you to smile at me."

Jim wasn't sure he understood.

"Don't look puzzled, just do as I say. Think about your friends up in space, and how happy you are for them, and give me a big smile."

Frank and Stormie, his friends and partners. He was happy they were on their way, feeling weightless and trying to make themselves useful on the space station until they could get to the Moon. It must be so nice to float and to fly—

Jim grinned, but Tony frowned.

His face felt funny ... a little numb ... and Jim puzzled over that. *Maybe some nerve damage from my workout?*

"Okay, Jim, next thing," Tony said. He backed away a little and continued, "I want you to raise both arms over your head, like I'm doing right now."

Jim shrugged. *Whatever you say, Tony.*

It was harder than he anticipated; all that lifting had really weakened his right arm. Once he raised it, it kept moving back down.

"Okay, Jim, that's enough. Hang on a second." Tony leaned over to Cindy and said something to her. She ran toward the front desk. Tony said to Jim, "Alright now, repeat after me: I think the Dodgers are going to win the pennant."

"Not likely with their pitching rotation," Jim said. His tongue fought against him, as if he'd come from the dentist with a face full of Novocain.

"Just say it, exactly the way I did. I think the Dodgers are going to win the pennant."

"I think the Dodgers are going to win the pennant."

"Again."

"I think the Dodgers are going to win the pennant."

"One more time, and really listen to what you're saying."

Agitated now, Jim put his frustration in his voice as he said it. But he paid attention like Tony said, and what he heard frightened him.

"Ah thing a doggers ah gone twin a pent."

Jim looked down at his lap, at his sad legs and his hands curled atop them. He clenched his fists, but only his left fist closed. His vision clouded with unexpected tears. The smell of the antiseptic they wiped down the machines with made him dizzy.

He looked up at the trainer. "Was happing, doan ee?" He turned his head so he could see better, with his left eye. The old Marine had tears on his cheeks.

Far away, a siren wailed.

241

CHAPTER TWENTY-ONE

The King of Nubia

Saturday, 26 May 2035

Van was out of breath by the time he got to the dormitory, and it seemed too early to be sweating so heavily. But summer came early to the New Mexico desert, and while the dry air pulled the sweat from him he chafed a little at the salty film it left behind.

The dormitory was cool enough that he shivered as he ran up the stairs and down the hall. Barbara wasn't in their room, but her datapad was. One corner of the screen blinked a soft purple light, to show his absent wife that she had a message from him.

He started growing annoyed, but found that he couldn't. He transferred his ire to the kaput intercom system. If it had been working, he wouldn't be running around the training area looking for her.

He pulled up Barbara's schedule on his own datapad, just to verify that she didn't have any appointments. This morning was blocked as free time and self-study, the same as when he'd looked at it twenty minutes ago.

Think, dummy, where would you be if you were your wife?

He ran to the women's bathroom and yelled for her from the doorway; nothing. He ran to the dayroom; no luck there, either. He ran out of the building and over to the cafeteria, and there she was, having a cup of coffee and talking with Krissa bin-Alal. The two of them looked up as he shoved the doors open and ran through, and they laughed as he tried to slide to a stop next to their table and ended up on one knee, halfway under the next one.

"What are you doing?" Barbara asked. "Are you okay?"

Van disentangled himself from a chair. Instead of standing up, he leaned forward and put his hands on their table. "Hey, I tried to call you," he said, still out of breath.

"What? Is something wrong?"

"No, no, it couldn't be righter. I just got a call from Gary."

Barbara glanced at Krissa, who looked puzzled. "Gary Needham, up at the colony," she said, and turned back to Van with a half-smile on her face. "So what did Gary say that's got you all worked up?"

"We got moved up in the rotation, baby," Van said. For only the thousandth time in his life, Van wished he was a better dancer; he probably looked foolish—on his knees, waving his arms and swaying in an awkward semblance of rhythm—but he was too excited to care. He and Barbara had to work through the same training program as everyone else, yes, and he appreciated the need for it, but he'd *been there* and almost ached to go back: the waiting, playing around on mockups of equipment he'd actually handled, live and in person, was brutal to him. Once the launch schedule got buggered, he'd worried that the wait would grow long enough to drive him batty. But now he didn't have to worry: the train was coming to the end of the tunnel.

Barbara asked, "So who did you pay off, and how much did it cost us?"

"Nothing like that, babe. We're switching with George and Yvette Fiester, until her arm is healed. Gary greased the skids for us."

"For you, you mean."

Van shook his head and chuckled. "No, I mean for us: Beverly's been giving him grief about getting you up there as quick as he can.

Said she needs someone else to talk to in real time, which he said he figures means she wants to talk *about* him as much as she talks to him."

"Or more," Barbara said.

Krissa asked, "Van, did he mention any other changes to the rotation?"

"No, just that the Fiesters will go up later. I don't think it's so much a matter of her actual healing, but I guess she'll go through some physical therapy before they certify her for flight again."

"Like someone else I know," Barbara said.

Van only smiled; a few weeks ago his graceless slide onto the cafeteria floor would have left him in agony. Now he was happy enough that he could take her friendly jibe exactly as she said it, without reading any criticism into it. He leaned back at the realization.

"What?" Barbara said. "What's that look for?"

"Huh?" Van snapped out of it. "Nothing, just thinking."

"Well, don't hurt yourself."

"No chance of that."

"Don't I know it." She turned to Krissa and shook her head. When she turned back, her face was set though a little apprehension showed in her eyes. "So did Gary give you an actual launch date? How does it affect the rest of our training?"

"I tried to get him to say we could leave today—"

"What? I'm not ready. I've still got two days left on my LVN-1 orientation—"

"I know, that's okay, I've already run all the equipment—"

Barbara's voice rose a few notes. "That's fine for you, but that doesn't help me. And we were supposed to go up and see Daddy after we got done here."

Van was tempted to tell her not to whine, but instead reached over and brushed her arm with his fingers. "Don't worry, sweets, you'll still get to. No matter how much I begged, the launch date wasn't going to change."

Barbara eyed him as if he was a con man trying to score off her. "Okay, then, when's the date?"

"About three weeks—June fifteenth is the earliest date. So we'll still be able to dig your dad out of the snow before we go."

She frowned. "You know it's mud season. And don't say it with so much gusto, I might think you mean it."

"I'm not afraid of that," Van said, as the thought of shoveling anything up in the frozen north quenched his enthusiasm. "You know me too well."

O O O

"Frank, when's the last time you heard from Jim?"

Frank looked up from the air filter he was servicing. For over two weeks, ever since it became clear that they would not get to the Moon as soon as they wanted, he and Stormie had helped the Clarke station crew work on their environmental systems. The air filters were similar to the ones installed in the colony. The water systems were a different story: even reduced gravity is still gravity, so the orbiting station relied on an array of pumps to keep effluent and filtered water moving in the right direction—or moving at all. Though they continued to add inflatable modules that would eventually form a toroidal structure—Frank could hardly imagine how much more confusing the maze of passages would be as the station grew—it would still be years before the assembly was big enough to spin to simulate gravity. At least smaller scale "tin can on a string" experiments had shown promise that such simulated gravity was effective, if fraught with its own peculiarities.

He tried to remember the last message he had received from their partner. James had called—audio only—to congratulate them a few days after they had settled in on the Clarke station. Since then they had only exchanged e-mails, though for some of those messages they recorded and transmitted brief videos. Frank regularly got copies of James's correspondence with the Consortium, but because they were always business- and contract-related his datapad collected them in a separate directory and he rarely looked at them. Had it been ... a week ... since he had received anything directly from their partner?

Frank clipped the filter housing to the worktable and pulled his datapad out of his pocket.

"Here it is," he said after a moment. "A message on the twenty-first of May—Monday a week ago, as I have heard you say—with a request for an estimate of how much time we were working on station environmental equipment. James wanted to charge the Consortium for our work above and beyond our contract. I sent him an answer two days later—a week ago today. I have heard nothing since."

"Don't you think that's strange?"

"It is a bit unusual, yes," Frank said. "Why? Has your 'trouble meter' been measuring some disturbances in the Force?"

Stormie smiled; even with her face a bit rounder due to fluid distribution in freefall, Frank loved her smile. She said, "I've been picking up trouble signals almost constantly since Santa Barbara, but nothing that's pegged the meter recently. Little fluctuations now and then. I guess I'm more curious than concerned."

"I am sure James has a good reason."

Stormie pulled the rotor out of the small circulating pump she was servicing. She eyed the end of the shaft suspiciously. "I think the bearings are wearing out on this one," she said, then turned to Frank. "I'm sure Jim's working on something good—he's always working on something good—and I hope he can get us some payments for this work. I'd do it anyway, it beats sitting around and it makes us look good. But when is he going to get us on an outbound flight?"

"I do not know. Have you asked him?"

"No, I didn't want to bother him anymore. I bugged him enough at the end of our first week here, I figured I should lay off. But if he doesn't figure out something soon, I'm going to start working it from here."

"We have no control over the flight manifests. What would you do?"

Stormie raised her eyebrows a little. She put the pump parts in the tiny worktray and closed the lid. She leaned forward and wiped a bit of grease from her fingertips. She unzipped the top of her coveralls, turned a little so Frank had a nice view, and played with the lacy fringe of the cup of her bra. "I think I might have to seduce the loadmaster, or the Port Authority equivalent, or somebody."

Frank took a deep breath and held it for a second, unsure how to respond. Finally he said, "I do not think I approve of that."

Stormie laughed, took her feet out of the restraining straps, and pushed herself through the air to him. He caught her, spun her into place, and kissed her.

"No," he said, "no matter how you try to convince me, I do not think I could approve."

"Then you need to convince our partner to do his job and get us out of here."

"Very well, my dear. I will go see if I can arrange some communication time."

Stormie smiled again. "I happen to know that the comm center has a slot open in about thirty minutes." She took Frank's datapad and scrolled through a couple of screens. "No, it's not open anymore. Some outfit called Lunar Life Engineering's got it booked."

Frank frowned at her, but his frown did not last. "'More curious than concerned?' You are too clever by half, my wife."

"Which only makes you luckier that you found me," she said.

"How could I not find you? You were the only person in our class to wear a 'Bring Back Planet Pluto' tee shirt."

"And I'm glad you noticed it."

Frank slipped his hand inside her coveralls; she flinched but did not giggle as he hit a tickle spot. "Well, it was quite noticeable," he said.

She laughed and grabbed his wrist. "You can notice some more later. For now, go make a phone call."

Knowing what was best for him, Frank pushed his wife back toward her workstation—with a gentle slap on her rear—made sure all of his tools and equipment were stowed, and wormed his way to the station's communications terminus.

The Clarke station had grown enough in the past five years that it could accommodate up to two hundred people comfortably, if the aeroponic gardens were producing at full capacity. At the moment it held a little over half that, including transients like Frank and Stormie who were trapped by one circumstance or another. The other transients were orbital construction personnel on rotation from building the next asteroid prospecting vessels, and a small contingent of asteroid miners who were still rotating in and out of the space station instead of the Mercator colony. Even with so much theoretically empty space, Frank found it difficult to maneuver anywhere without literally bumping into people—he simply had not mastered snaking his way through the habitats in micro-gee.

He made it to the communications center with three minutes to spare. As Stormie had arranged, the terminal was clear and Frank was set up to dial down to whomever he chose. He synched his datapad to the communications computer, chose voice only instead of voice-and-video, and input James's home office number. He left a message.

He left a message on James's separate home number, though he thought James's home and home office both rang over to his mobile number. He tried to access the miniserver in James's office, to grab his calendar and see if he had any appointments elsewhere in Santa Barbara, but the server did not respond to his pinging.

Frank was scrolling through other contact numbers on his datapad when the "incoming call" chime sounded. It was a video call, but he did not recognize the ID. He touched the "accept" icon on the screen and said hello to the unfamiliar man wearing an Asteroid Consortium polo shirt.

"Mr. Pastorelli, I'm Wenbin Huang in the AC accounting office. My computer alerted me that you are dialing direct to Mr. Fennerling's home."

A subtle tinge of nausea crept through Frank. Of course the Consortium would keep track of their communications, but why would they care enough to break into his comm session? "Yes, I am."

"I take it, then, that you have not contacted his sister."

The tinge of nausea grew exponentially, into waves that took him back to the first hour they were in freefall.

"Mr. Wenbin, I am confused. Why should I call his sister?"

The Consortium executive's hand went to his collar, as if he wanted to straighten a tie that was not there. "I'm sorry, Mr.

Pastorelli, but I see you are used to the Chinese order of naming. I had given my name in Western order for your convenience." He laughed, as if it were funny, and Frank joined him out of courtesy despite the transmission delay. For a brief moment Frank wondered if too much social accommodation could be as bad as too little, but he was a gentleman by upbringing and disposition and decided not. He might occasionally have to clean up a bit of social grease when the machinery of life threw it out, but that was preferable to repairing stripped and broken gears when the social engine ground to a halt.

The AC man's laugh faded into a grim smile. "Did you not receive our messages about Mr. Fennerling's condition?" he asked.

Without gravitational cues, Frank had only his visual and tactile senses to orient his sense of balance. The seat braced him because his feet were pulling up against the strap on the bulkhead, and the screen in front of him was correctly positioned in relation to the chair. But a flood of vertigo hit him and he gripped the edge of the console to steady himself.

"Mr. Huang, I am sorry," Frank said. "I meant no offense. But, I am not sure what you mean." He moved aside windows and dialogue boxes on his datapad until he could open his directory of Consortium messages. The first few looked like standard contractual gibberish, but the more recent messages had ominous words in their subjects like "Emergency Room" and "Stroke" and "Next of Kin." Frank's perception narrowed to the little screen so much that he missed the first part of what Huang Wenbin was saying.

"What was that?" Frank said, grateful that the miniscule signal delay from geosynchronous orbit would stop the agent before he prattled on another couple of seconds.

"I said call me Wenbin, please," he said. "I am sorry we did not contact you directly, but we assumed Mr. Fennerling's sister would apprise you of his situation. She may have been reluctant to speak with you, but I encourage you to call her directly for more details.

"When you did not respond to our e-mails, I programmed my computer to alert me if you made any off-station calls to Mr. Fennerling or his sister. We planned to contact you by direct voice by the end of the week if we did not hear from you regarding your company's new financing arrangement." He looked at a display or datapad in front of him and continued, "Last Tuesday, the twenty-second, Mr. Fennerling suffered an ischemic stroke—a blood clot in his brain. An alert health club worker called 9-1-1 and the medical technicians confirmed his stroke symptoms. He was taken to emergency care at Santa Barbara Cottage Hospital, where they administered a tissue plasminogen activator to dissolve the clot. He was further evaluated while his next of kin was notified, but he did not respond to the drug treatment as hoped. The doctors then used a manual method to excise the clot—"

"Excuse me," Frank said. "A 'manual method'? Do you mean they operated on him?"

Huang Wenbin shook his head. "Not exactly. I do not know the technical details, but these involve devices inserted via catheters through large blood vessels—not brain surgery. I understand that several methods are available, but I'm not sure which they used."

"How is James now?"

"At last report, they had moved him from an acute care facility to an inpatient rehabilitation clinic. I am not sure how long he will have to stay there. That's another question that his sister should be able to answer for you. Do you have her contact information?"

"Yes," Frank said. He scrolled up and down the list of unread e-mails, reading the story of James's incapacitation in the subject lines but getting another message as well: something was wrong with the company's finances, and James was trying to get it fixed.

"Excuse me, Wenbin?" Frank said.

"Yes, Mr. Pastorelli?"

"Please, you may call me Frank. You mentioned a new financing arrangement, and I see that you—the Consortium—and James have exchanged some messages on financial terms. I am not aware of any new financing."

Huang Wenbin sat back slightly and raised his eyebrows even less. "I see. I believe most of the terms are in place, and Mr. Fennerling had secured the infusion of capital you needed, but I cannot speak to any details that Mr. Fennerling may have kept to himself. I suppose I can affect a slight delay in our discussions while you confer with him. I am not sure how far he has to go in his recovery. Shall we set a time to discuss it? Say, Saturday?"

Frank's mind, accustomed more to soil and water contamination than to anything financial and still trying to cope with the image of James incapacitated by a stroke, snapped into negotiating mode. "Wenbin, I have no idea if that will give me enough time to understand the arrangements James may have made. Could we make it a week from Monday?" He had no reason to believe the AC accountant would wait so long, but it seemed a reasonable counter proposal.

"Frank, I appreciate that you need more time to go over the financials, but the eleventh is too far out. What if we said Tuesday the fifth?"

That might be possible, but asking for extra time would not hurt. "I would prefer if we could do it the eighth instead," Frank said.

Huang Wenbin pursed his lips, then nodded. "Agreed. Shall I call you to discuss preliminaries, or can we rely on e-mail?"

Frank winced, but only in his mind; he kept his face as impassive as he could. "E-mail is fine, Wenbin. I will adjust my settings to allow your messages to get through. I am sorry now that I had sequestered so many messages that I ended up ignoring them. But for now, I believe I should call James's sister. And I think my wife will want to be part of that call."

"I'm sure she will. Until the eighth, then."

Frank signed off, disconnected his datapad, and started opening e-mails. He would get Stormie and call Holly later; for now, he needed to start figuring out what James had been doing with the company's finances.

O O O

"I can't believe someone didn't call us before now," Stormie said. Frank had found her running through filtration calculations with Judy Richmond, the station's environmental engineer, told her the news, and dragged her back to the comm center to call Jim's sister. She'd barely had time to process the basic situation before Holly Lawrimore, nee Fennerling, came on the line.

Stormie wished Frank had ordered a video feed, so she could see what the woman looked like. She imagined a female version of Jim—slender without being skinny, dignified features. Her voice gave away her fatigue.

Frank introduced them—Stormie said hello herself—and apologized for not calling sooner. He blamed it on a miscommunication with the Consortium, which seemed technically accurate from what he'd told Stormie. Holly replied in kind: she apologized for not calling herself, but said she'd spent most of her time the last few days attending to Jim's immediate needs. From her sniffling, Stormie guessed how much the situation had affected her.

"Where is James now?" Frank asked. "In a clinic of some kind?"

"Yes," Holly said. "It's a rehab clinic, part of the hospital system but it's smaller and they say it's more specialized."

"How long will he have to be there?"

"They said at least a couple of weeks. Maybe up to a month."

"Holly," Stormie said, "the AC didn't tell us exactly what happened. Can you tell us?"

"Only what I know, and that isn't much. He might have been having little strokes for a while now, mini-strokes—they call them transient ischemic attacks. That's what the trainer at the little gym he goes to thought he was having, but they called the ambulance anyway and it's a good thing they did. When they scanned his brain at the hospital, they found the clot quickly enough.

"He was in the hospital a day and a half before they got in touch with me. This past Saturday they moved him to the other place. It's almost just like the hospital, only smaller, and of course he doesn't like hospitals to begin with because of his accident—" she broke off for a second until she regained her composure. "He doesn't speak very well yet and he gets really agitated when we can't understand him. He still has trouble handling little things, so he can't type yet either. I hate seeing him like that...." Her voice trailed away in soft sobs.

Stormie grabbed Frank's hand; he squeezed back, and after a few seconds he said, "Holly, we are very sorry to upset you. If it would be better to call back later ..."

"No," she said, struggling with her sniffles, "it's fine. I'm just tired, so I'm not holding it together very well."

"I think you are doing fine," Frank said, "and I am sure James is grateful for your help."

"What else would you like to know?"

Frank raised his eyebrows at Stormie. She asked, "Do they know where the clot came from?"

"They think it worked up from his legs," Holly said. "One of them, anyway. He was good about working out his upper body, but he didn't do much to keep good circulation in his legs. He didn't see the point. I think he does now." Her little laugh sounded bitter.

"How bad is his condition?" Frank asked. "How long will it take for him to recover?"

"They said it was bad, but not catastrophic. When we finally got to the hospital, the doctor showed us the images from his MRI. The thing in his head looked like a little splotch, like you get if you fling a drop of spaghetti sauce on the wall by accident. Doctor said it looked like a little jellyfish to him.

"The doctor had me hold Jim's hand and trace numbers in his palm, but Jim couldn't ever tell what number I was doing. And sometimes he'll fling his arm in a funny way because he can't keep track of where his hand is unless he really concentrates. The doctor called it 'tactile neglect.' That hasn't gotten much better yet.

"They say it's going to take a while for him to get better, and he may never be completely okay. The doctor was real happy about how quick he got to the hospital and they got those drugs into him. I was surprised they would do anything for him, since he could barely sign his name on the form—I saw it, it looked like a drunk kindergartener had written a pretend name on it. Anyway, Jim had been smart enough to have some kind of pre-approval paperwork at the hospital for emergency care—I guess he did that after Alyson died—so they gave him those drugs. But they didn't dissolve the clot all the way."

She fell silent—not weeping now, just no longer communicative. Stormie mouthed "we should go" to Frank and pantomimed the cut-off signal across her throat. He signaled her to wait.

"Miss Holly," Frank said, "if James cannot return to work, I will need to take care of our business matters from here. It will be … inconvenient, but should not be too difficult. Please tell James that

254

I will handle everything as best I can. But I will need to be able to access all of the files on his computer, and I have not been able to find our network on the Web. I can access some of our shared documents in the cloud, but James had a dedicated server. Is it possible someone turned off his computer equipment? The small unit on top of the filing cabinet in his office?"

"Oh," she said. "Yes, I'm sorry. I went to his apartment Monday and picked up his tablet—I thought he might want to have it, but he hasn't been able to use it yet—and I turned off everything electrical I could find. I can go back and turn it on tomorrow. Will that be okay?"

Frank frowned, and his right hand, balled up into a fist, bobbed up and down a few times. He reached up and rubbed the back of his neck. "That will be very helpful," he said in a low voice. "If I may, what time do you think that will be? If I know, I can make arrangements to access the server and retrieve what I need."

"I can go by there at seven, on my way to work."

"Thank you," Frank said, "that will be most helpful. And again, please tell James that I will do my best to take care of all of our financial and contractual matters—and will be most happy to turn them back over to him when he has recovered."

Stormie said, "And please let us know if there are any changes, or—" and it seemed strange to be saying this from so far away, with no chance of making good on it in any meaningful way, "—if there's anything we can do."

Jim's sister's attitude toward the gesture didn't surprise Stormie at all.

She laughed. Quietly, to be sure, and not for long, but it sounded genuine.

"Thank you," she said.

O   O   O

Tuesday, 19 June 2035

Stormie could barely stand to be around Frank. He'd gotten morose, moody, and barely said two words at a time without either getting sullen or snippy. They were still helping out with the station's environmental systems, and Frank said he was tired from doing Jim's job and his, so Stormie took on a little extra technical work—she was content to leave all the business work to him—but it didn't seem to help his mood or his attitude.

It was a great relief when their names finally came up on the manifest of an outbound flight, and for a few minutes she wondered if she could go without Frank in order to have a little break from him. But she figured things would get better once they were in place and could establish a more-or-less permanent routine. Jim's condition had improved to the point that he and Frank were e-mailing back and forth, and he'd moved to his sister's house around the middle of June, but he still couldn't take back his financial role.

Just give it time, she told herself.

The last few days before they boarded the ferry were especially tight: the station seemed much smaller when their fellow colonists, the Petersons and the two replacement couples, showed up. Stormie had never particularly liked Angela Beacon and was a little disappointed when she was picked to be Chu Liquan's replacement; as for the Richards couple, he was a little too energetic and she had the shakes pretty bad when they arrived.

So Stormie's relief was palpable the Tuesday they left the station—they could have a reunion or welcoming or whatever at the colony, where they'd have a little gravity to keep from bumping into one another. Transit to the Moon took the better part of two days, and on the back side of the summer solstice they landed on its dusty surface.

"Welcome to Mare Nubium," said Maggie as she, Rex, Frank, and Stormie checked their pressure suits. The Adamsons, with whom they had left Earth, had been at the colony for two weeks already.

The landing area was on a slight rise that had been baked solid by repeated landings and liftoffs. The elevated position gave a good view of the colony area to the south; the Sun had not been up long, and its low angle left long shadows behind the soil-mounded habitats and threw the outer wall of Mercator Crater into sharp relief. High above the crater wall, the partial Earth hung in the black sky; even though it looked smaller than it had when they were on the station, Stormie turned down her helmet display so she could see it better, and involuntarily fluttered to her tiptoes as the realization hit her that she was finally here, after so much trouble and travail. She strained to stand still and soak it in; she wanted to dance, to skip, to take off running under the earthlight, across the Sea of Clouds. Mare Nubium stretched away to the horizon to the north, a uniform plain unbroken except by a few boulders and other features Stormie couldn't differentiate. Craterlets, probably.

"It feels good to have some weight on my feet again," said Rex. Stormie agreed silently.

Maggie said, "Yes, Lord. And just think: here we are, walking on the sea of clouds."

"I believe I am the only person here who can claim this," Frank said, and Stormie was surprised after weeks of grousing to hear a playful lilt in his voice, "since I have the closest ties to Nubia on Earth. But in the name of my ancestors who dwelt among the clouds, I have come to the Sea of Clouds in pursuit of peace and prosperity, and hereby name myself Frank the first, King of Nubia!"

They laughed together, and Rex said, "Bravo, your Majesty."

Stormie's radio crackled with an unfamiliar voice. "I thought you were from Kenya, Mr. Pastorelli."

With no auditory clue as to what direction the caller was, Stormie turned almost a full circle before she saw two trucks driving toward the landing area. They moved slowly, along well-worn paths.

"That is correct," Frank said.

"And the ancient land of Nubia was actually part of Egypt, wasn't it?"

Stormie tightened her gut, thankful that the status monitoring in their suits was much less comprehensive than it had been in the Apollo days. Frank sounded unperturbed, which calmed her only a little bit.

"That is true," he said. "The southern part of Egypt and the northern part of Sudan."

"Okay, I see the connection, then. Since Kenya borders on Sudan, eh?"

"That is the general idea, yes," Frank said.

"Well, then, your Highness," the sarcasm was so thick Stormie nearly choked on it, "I hope you're not one of these high-and-mighty royal types. 'Cause there's a lot of work to be done, and the little stunt you pulled with the cargo manifest means you're going to be doing more of it than you bargained for."

Before Stormie could ask what stunt the unidentified caller meant, he continued, "Attention colonists and flight personnel, this is Acting Colony Director Needham. Two Multi-Purpose Vehicles are now approaching your position. Colonists, please follow the flight personnel to the marked safety area and wait there for the vehicles to stop—do not approach until they are in position and signal you.

"New personnel, please note: wherever there is a solid path, do not deviate from it. It has been fused to reduce dust contamination on the suits."

We know all this, Stormie interrupted in the privacy of her mind.

"MPV-1 will move into position to unload cargo from the transit vehicle. Flight personnel will be taken to the reception area after the freight is secured. New colonists will collect their personal goods and board MPV-2 to be taken inside immediately. The Adamsons will meet you in the Gateway reception area and orient you to your quarters and accessible areas of the complex.

"Mr. and Mrs. Pastorelli, I would like to see you in my office one hour after you cycle through the airlock. Habitat Four-Delta. We have a lot to discuss."

Stormie shuffled over to Frank, who had accepted their two small personal bags from the flight engineer and was already standing in the safety area: a four-by-five-meter area with a curb around it. It reminded her of evaporation ponds or collection basins on Earth.

She waved to get Frank's attention and gave him the universal "I don't know" signal: hands held out, rotated palms up. The light was such that she could see Frank's face inside his helmet. He shook his head and turned away to look at the approaching vehicles.

The nugget of hot anger in her gut, that had started growing when Needham was hassling Frank, turned as cold as the shadows on their new home—and burned worse.

CHAPTER TWENTY-TWO

Razor-thin Margins

Thursday, 21 June 2035

The prefabricated habitats were laid out in a loose, open-ended grid: one primary north-south line of habitats, crossed by two main east-west lines, with branching "fingers" that provided open space for multi-purpose vehicles to drive up to every module. The east-west rows were referred to as numbered avenues, while the north-south columns were called A through E streets—often with the phonetic alphabet. If someone said, "I'll meet you at the corner of Third and Bravo," there was only one place on the colony map they could possibly mean.

Some habitats continued to take on special names. The dome at the intersection of Second Avenue and C Street was still officially Grand Central and unofficially the Pimple; the tunnel just north of Grand Central, considered the "100 block" of C Street, had taken on the name of "Gateway" since it was where most people entered and exited the main facility.

The Gateway reception area was a wide spot in the first habitat, just past the decontamination area—which was not decontamination in the true sense of the word, but retained the name because "de-dusting" area sounded odd. Stormie and Frank marshaled through according to Jake's instructions; they had learned the procedure during their training, but this was the first time doing it to combat real lunar dust.

"The dust is worse than I ever thought," Jake told them. "Really abrasive, so get as much off as you can and hope you don't react the way I have."

"How's that, Jake?" Rex asked.

"I probably shouldn't tell you. Don't want to be the psycho behind your psychosomatic hallucinations."

"Oh, come on," Rex said. "We can handle it." Maggie just smiled. Frank acted as if he hadn't heard.

"Well, alright. After I got here, I started feeling like there was dust on everything—so much so that I started to itch. But I knew it was bad when I started feeling like I had dust in my mouth, and tasted it, too." He drank from a clear polycarbonate flask and swished the water around in his mouth for emphasis. "Anyway, if that suit you wore in here fits you good, you might think about stowing it yourself. Everyone's starting to claim their own suits that they can take good care of, instead of swapping out from the lockers and trusting that routine maintenance will take care of things."

Jake briefed them on other aspects of colony life as he showed them their quarters, but everything was almost identical to the training program. Besides the obvious difference in having to be careful how they walked in the low gravity, the only differences Stormie noted were marginal. The facility was cast from the same mold as the Utah training site; the smell, for instance, was close to but less plastic than the mockups in the Cave.

By the time they got to Gary Needham's office, Stormie's anger and confusion had metastasized; the pressure was like something horrible growing inside her. If she had been able to talk to Frank alone, to find out what was going on, it might have abated.

Needham's "office" was singularly unimpressive. It was ostensibly part of Central Control—it was the room next door—but half of the compartment was stacked with containers of preserved food, some small pieces of test equipment, and several unopened transit cases.

Needham slid his stool into a corner and stood propped against the precarious-looking stacks. He motioned them into the cramped space and invited Stormie to sit. She hesitated, unsure whether to assert her independence or to accept his hospitality. She chose in favor of politeness, and sat.

"Mr. Needham," Frank began, but the acting director waved him silent.

"As much as I was being formal on the radio, because it helps me stay in control when I'm pissed off, I really don't prefer it. I'd just as soon you call me Gary."

"Very well, Gary. And I am Frank, and this is my wife, Stormie."

"Ma'am," Needham—Gary—said, and tipped a nonexistent hat. The pantomime was almost charming, but didn't lighten Stormie's mood. "You prefer 'Stormie' over your given name?"

"As long as we're being informal, yes." She did nothing to soften the edge in her voice.

Gary nodded. "Okay, then. Let's get down to business. Frank, I appreciate your desire to get up here and set up shop, but you really screwed the pooch with that swap you arranged. I don't care what kind of financial difficulty your company is in, I don't need you interfering with the cargo manifests. It just so happens that I consider those crates you bumped to be a higher priority than your living, breathing bodies."

Stormie tried to parse what she'd just heard, but hearing two revelations at once confused her. Frank "arranged" a swap, apparently to get them on the flight manifest … and what financial difficulty?

"I am sorry if I caused you any inconvenience, Gary, but on the station we were redundant with the local staff. They were kind enough to help get us on the flight, in appreciation for our help. Now that we are here, we can—"

Stormie grabbed Frank's arm. "What financial difficulties?" she asked. "And what crates? Why were they such a high priority?"

"You said you did not want to be involved in the financial discussions," Frank said.

"Well, I want to be involved now."

"Perhaps this is not the best time."

"Why the hell not?"

Gary cleared his throat to get their attention, and Stormie let Frank's arm go. "I'd love to watch the two of you go a few rounds," Gary said, "but in twenty minutes I'm due in the garage to help tear down one of our vehicles that went Tango Uniform yesterday. And I'm sure you two have plenty to keep you busy setting up your workspace.

"Besides, it'd be better if you threw some humor into your act and did it in Grand Central and charged admission. We're a little light on live entertainment just now.

"As for what the crates were, they were key parts of the EBM system. How familiar are you with it?"

"I know the basics," Stormie said. Frank nodded his assent. In the same way that she and Frank couldn't disassemble and rebuild any of the rockets they rode on, and could only do minor maintenance on the rolling vehicles operated at the colony, all the two of them knew of the Electron Beam Melting system was what it did and the barest details of how it worked. Like any 3-D printer, it fabricated complex shapes by fusing a raw material powder layer by layer, but in this case it used a metal powder under a vacuum environment. The tight computer control, the precise electron beam, and the carefully maintained environment produced distinct shapes that required minimal finish machining, were very homogeneous and practically void-free. Stormie had once done an industrial hygiene survey of a rapid-prototyping facility that had some EBM equipment, but because it was automatic and autonomous all the hazards associated with it were well-controlled.

"Part of the difficulty in keeping some of our equipment operating has been the inability to fabricate all of the spare parts on site," Needham said. He patted the stack of transit cases behind him. "The AC packed every one of these habitats as full as they could, but they couldn't send everything. We've had some things that've worked better than expected, and others that are barely holding on. Like the LSOV—we can't seem to keep the thing flying. So I arranged to temporarily change the industrial layout and set up the EBM system early, so we can use some of the native titanium— once we reduce it out of the ilmenite and grab the iron and the oxygen—to make our own parts as needed."

Stormie was thankful he didn't feel the need to explain all the chemistry of the process, but her heart panged with the realization that if she wanted to know the details she wouldn't have Marilyn Chu around to give them to her.

"But it's not like an EBM rig just magically sets itself up once we get the parts here. I was hoping that when I got the beam generator and the 3-D imaging microscope—which, that's what was in those two crates you bumped off the flight—we might be up and running in a month. If nothing went wrong with anything else, we might cut that to three weeks—say, the middle of July. And that's just to get the first parts off the line. Trial runs of simple stuff.

"But the squirrelly flight schedule to and from L-4 means we won't see those parts here until then, which puts us into August before we can start making simple things like tools, let alone the kind of complex parts we're going to need."

Stormie could think of nothing to say that would make the situation better. She wanted to come to Frank's defense—she clenched her jaw to keep from just expressing her faith in him—but she was afraid of making the situation worse. And she was still a little mad that he hadn't told her what was going on.

Frank looked at her for a second, hesitation in his eyes. He wondered if he had done the right thing. She reached out to him again, but this time she didn't grab his arm. She brushed her fingertips down his forearm and held his hand, as firm and secure as any time they had walked together. Frank smiled a tentative, lips-only smile at her.

Frank said to Gary, "Again, I am sorry for adding to the inconvenience, Gary. It was not my intention, and I would like to make up for it in some way. But, if I may: why was the EBM system not included as standard equipment for the colony?"

Gary twisted his lips into what may have been a grin, but Stormie decided was more of a grimace. "It was," he said, his voice pitched low and rumbling out of the back of his throat. "It was in the habitat module that crashed, which means right now it's useful more as metal and plastic scrap than as an operational piece of equipment. After that, even though these things were soft-landed as best they could be," he patted the outer, curving bulkhead, though the flexion in his arm and hand made it look as if he wanted to slap it, "nobody would risk putting anything delicate in them. Hell, we've dealt with enough broken things as it is. And then other shipments started taking priority, and before anyone knew what had happened the EBM rig had been pushed off eighteen months into the future. Getting those shipments moved up was just setting the schedule right as best I could."

"And we messed it up," Stormie said.

"Yeah—"

"No," Frank said, and held up his hand. "I did it. You did nothing wrong."

Stormie motioned Frank to wait and directed her words at Gary. "He may have made the actual arrangements, but I was agitating for a faster flight from the moment we stepped onto Clarke." She paused for a second at the incongruity of "stepping" onto the space station, then pressed on, her mind barely keeping up with her words. "There's a loadmaster on the station who could've shipped those crates and told us to pound sand, and there are probably a half dozen other people who could've put up barriers to what Frank did. That doesn't make it right, I know, and we will find a way to make it right. Those other people aren't here right now to account for their actions, but we will account for ours. If you think of something we can do to make things better—to make things right—I'd appreciate if you'd tell us and let us do it." Gary looked as if he was about to speak, but Stormie pressed on, "No, let me finish. I know you have another appointment, and I won't keep you from it.

"We are here for the duration, Gary. For the long haul. Our contract is only so many years, but it's renewable, and I intend to renew it over and over and over again. And while we're here, we will work night and day—ha! I mean lunar night and day—to keep this colony going. We wouldn't, and we won't, do anything to jeopardize it. I'm sorry we botched your schedule, but we will fix it any way we can."

Gary stood silent for a moment, looking back and forth at the two of them, considering her words. He waited long enough that the icy anger that had driven her outburst—at the time she didn't think it was an outburst—started to melt from a creeping fear that she'd gone too far.

"I'll think about it," he finally said. "And I'll let you know. Right now we all have work to do." He nodded at them and slipped between them into the corridor.

Stormie raised her eyebrows a little, then a little more when Frank started to smile. "That," he said, "was impressive. My wife the orator. You should run for office."

"Not likely," Stormie said, and now that they were alone her ire returned. "Like he said, we have work to do. Let's find our lab space and start unpacking." She stopped in the hallway and half turned to her husband. "And while we do, you can tell me all about these 'financial difficulties' our company is in."

O   O   O

Monday, 9 July 2035

Van took a deep breath as he unsealed his helmet. The sour-sweet smell of people packed together was delicious to him. It was good to be home.

He slid over to Barbara and helped her off with her helmet. She sighed in relief and started moving to her next task, but he held her and looked at her as if for the first time. Her hair, which had billowed around her head when they were on the Clarke station, again framed her face in soft waves. He much preferred it that way, even now when it was a little matted and mashed from the helmet.

As he concentrated on her, she smiled a tentative smile that displayed her wonder at why he should be studying her so intently. Before she could ask, he hugged her and kissed her—an awkward move because they were still encumbered by their suits, but he didn't care. Having her here with him made everything right.

Everything about being back on the Moon thrilled him: the lighter gravity under his feet, the closed-in feel of the prefab habitat around him. This was where he belonged.

He was so content just to be back that he soaked it all in, so much that he actually paid attention to Alice Lindsey, an electrical engineer in the initial group of colonists, as she talked the group through the airlock and decontamination routine. He was glad he followed it closely—they'd made some improv:ments over the routine the setup crews had used, and the new protocols should control the lunar dust better.

And when Alice announced there was a welcoming party waiting in Grand Central for all the newcomers, organized by Maggie and Rex Stewart, his contentment enveloped him like a pressure suit holding back the vacuum of despair. God was in his heaven, and Van was in his.

The spread at the welcoming party was a little thin—crackers and some reconstituted dip that resembled pimiento cheese—but they'd put out jugs of water that were already paid for. Van was on his third glass of water and his second little cheese-and-cracker sandwich when Gary Needham approached him.

"So," Gary said, "did you make sure the EBM crates came with you?"

"Nice to see you, too, bossman," Van said around his mouthful of food.

Gary made an exaggerated bow. "I'm sorry I didn't offer you the proper pleasantries. All that pampering and celebrity life must've gone to your head."

Van swallowed the last of the cracker and leaned in close so only Gary would hear him. "Shove it up your ass, old man."

Gary didn't flinch. "I don't care how much you sweet-talk me, I'm not going to sleep with you on the first date. Or ever."

Van laughed and washed down the sticky bits and cheesy aftertaste. "Yeah," he said, "I watched them get loaded myself."

"Good," Gary said, and seemed to breathe a sigh of relief. He wiped his forehead with his hand and wiped his hand on the front of the shirt. "Sorry I didn't answer your messages—been a little busy."

"I accept your apology." Van decided to pick at Gary a little bit more. "It did hurt my feelings, though."

Gary didn't take the bait. In fact, he smiled. "I tell you, Bev is sure happy Barbara's finally here."

The two of them were having their own tête-à-tête on the other side of the chamber. They were so intent on their conversation they didn't notice their husbands watching them.

"The feeling's mutual," Van said. "Barbara seemed like she wanted out of the program a couple of times, but she came around. I think Beverly being up here helped a lot, that she would have someone to talk to, you know?"

"Yeah, that can be helpful."

"So what have y'all been doing? Got all the habitats up and running now?"

"Shoot no. We haven't done nearly as much as we should. We're getting closer. I still owe you a beer, I guess."

"That's okay," Van said.

Gary pointed across the room. "You see those two over there? The Pastorellis? You know 'em?"

Van remembered the good-looking black couple from the Utah training facility. "Not well," he said. "Met 'em. Bio contingent. Contract types, right?"

"Yeah. They're part of the reason I haven't gotten much done. I've been riding herd on them the past two and a half weeks."

"Oh, don't let anyone else hear you say that."

"Why not?"

"Come on, Colonel, think about what you just said. I know you're not really that naïve."

Gary looked puzzled for a second before the realization dawned on him. "Oh, hell, Van, you know I didn't mean it that way. And don't call me 'Colonel.'"

"I don't know why not. I bet you've got your silver oak leaves somewhere in your office here, hidden away. And even if you don't, I'd say the billet you're in is at least an O-6 equivalent."

Gary drew his lips so tight it looked as if his teeth might poke through. "First of all, this isn't a government operation, so there aren't any officer equivalents even if you think there should be. Second, I don't care if it was a damn SES equivalent, don't do that to me."

Van laughed; the Gary Needham he knew would actually care quite a bit if his job was equivalent to the Senior Executive Service.

But he didn't press the subject. "Whatever you say. Is that what's eating you? Not making the schedule because you're worrying over the hired help?"

"Now look who's being condescending," Gary said.

"I learned from the best."

"Excuse me, Mr. Needham," Arvati Peterson called from across the chamber. She walked over, a little clumsy since she wasn't used to the lunar gravity yet. Her husband Sonny followed behind, carrying one of the live specimen transit cases. Arvati popped the seal on the case and opened it. The unmistakable mewling of a very frightened cat cut through the room like a siren. Conversations died and heads turned.

"We thought we should present you with the first cat on the Moon," she said.

Van watched Gary for any reaction, but he seemed very well composed, even when the struggling cat was forced into his hands. It was a smoky grey color, darker than the Siamese Van had grown up with.

Gary eyed the cat for a long moment, his face inscrutable. Finally he asked, "What's its name?"

"Not that it'll matter," Van said. "Like it'll come when you call." Gary made as if he would pass Van the cat, but Van slid back a half step.

Arvati said, "Its tag said Comet, but we thought it looked more like a Dusty."

Gary held the cat up with his left hand and looked it in the eyes; it dug its claws into his shirt sleeve. He scratched it for a second behind its ears and handed it back to Arvati, who cradled it like a child. "Then Dusty it is," he said. "I guess it'll be useful if one of the rabbits gets loose, but I better not hear about it trying to get at any of the catfish."

"Although," Van said, "if we ever need any catgut, it'll be useful for that, too."

Nobody laughed. Van found that disappointing.

As the others turned back to their conversations, Gary pulled Van partway into the westward-leading tunnel junction. "*Cats.* Just what we need when we're on razor-thin margins up here." He

268

paused, then picked up where he'd left off before. "It's bad enough that I'm coaching Frank and Stormie along on extra work details— a duty I may transfer to you now, wise ass—because their company is strapped for cash and they need the out-of-scope hours. I mean, we need the work done to get caught up, and I appreciate them doing it. But their capabilities don't match their willingness.

"I've had 'em out helping set and open the last of the prefabs, because that's freed up folks to work on the vehicles and hook up the rest of the systems. They do okay driving around and they know when to be precise and when to say, 'Good enough,' but they're not fast enough to keep us ahead of the game.

"But that's not the real trouble," he said. "Truth is, the AC itself is looking at a balance of payment problem if the asteroid shipments don't pick up, and soon."

"Really? The last P&L statement looked okay."

"That's because it didn't detail all the executive pay cuts."

"What executive pay cuts?"

Gary chuckled. "Know how much I got deposited in my account last quarter? One thousand dollars—for the whole quarter. Do that math: that's about eighty dollars a week."

Van looked for deception in his friend's eyes, but didn't see any. "That's crazy," he said.

"No, I think it's smart, that's why I went along with it when the brass pitched it to me. I'm the lowest level to take a pay cut so far. Everybody below me is making their regular salary, everybody above me is making much, much less. And I mean much less than the rank and file, Van. Kari Aliri, up at the Clarke station? She got five hundred bucks for the quarter, and it gets worse the higher you go. Instead of salary, we're getting a cost of living allowance— which doesn't mean much to me up here, but for most of the folks down below it means they're digging into savings to pay their regular bills.

"While all this is going on, they're looking at all kinds of ways to cut costs. That's why I wanted that EBM rig up here soonest, because I didn't want them selling it off or stopping the flights or anything. Possession is nine-tenths of the law, right? Plus the fact that we need the stupid thing."

"Anyway, they're looking at buying out all the independents and making them Consortium employees. They think if they can do that, it'll save them money in the long run."

Van shrugged. "Sounds reasonable to me, but Econ class was a long time ago and I didn't do that hot in it."

"Never mind. The problem is, the Pastorellis' partner, down on Earth, is in tight with Morris Hansen. Hell, Hansen contacted him personally when he decided to join the Paszek Group—for all I know, the guy has his hands in the AC's own pockets."

"Didn't I hear that their partner had an accident or something?"

"Yeah, he had a stroke. Which means that he hasn't been part of the most recent negotiations, which means that we're stuck with them as independents for the time being. Meanwhile the AC is hemorrhaging cash."

Van couldn't remember the last time he'd seen Gary so agitated. If he was this distressed, the Consortium must be frantic to get more frequent asteroid shipments moving to Low-Gee's processing facility so that revenue stream would start coming in. But if things were that strapped ...

"I'm surprised you authorized any money for this little shindig, if things are so bad," Van said.

Gary clapped a hand on Van's shoulder. "Oh, if it had been up to me, we would've put you guys to work right away. But the Stewarts paid for all this out of their own pocket. So you can thank them."

"It's that bad?"

Gary sighed. "Probably not. But if I act as if it's that bad, then hopefully I'll be pleasantly surprised."

O O O

Frank very much enjoyed the newcomers' welcome; in their time on the Moon so far, pleasant distractions had proved rare. He looked forward to speaking to the Petersons. He had found Sonny and Arvati to be an engaging couple during their training, and would like working with them. Their presentation of the little cat to Gary Needham amused him more than it did Stormie.

"I wonder if that's a male cat or a female," she said.

"Why does it matter?" he asked.

"One, male cats have a tendency to mark their territory, and I don't find that very pleasant. Two, if it's female I wonder if it's already pregnant. That would be a convenient way of increasing the cat population pretty quickly, which means we'll have to account for a bunch of cats instead of just one cat in our calculations."

He looked at her carefully and decided she was not joking. In fact she looked far too serious. "My dear," he said, "do you really think a brood of cats will make a big difference in the figures?"

She frowned. "Maybe not a big difference, but some difference. I just don't understand the point. They took cats on ocean-going vessels because they had rats. We don't have rats, and with luck we won't have any for a long time. And cats on a ship aren't competing for resources with their hosts in a hermetically-sealed environment. Even if the thing is fixed, it seems like a waste, and we don't have a lot of room for waste."

Frank wrapped her in a hug and kissed her forehead. "I am sure we will be able to handle it," he said.

"Thanks. Do you think we've done our social duty? I'd like to get started on the nutrient solution for the next batch of bio-reactant."

Frank sighed. It would be useless to tell her she was working too hard; she already knew, and did not care. Not because she was unaware of the effects of overwork, but because she rarely thought of what she did as work in the first place. He understood the feeling well, because most of the time he shared it.

"I am certain you will be missed," he said, "but just as sure that you will be excused. I, however, would like to stay for a while yet." He gave her a quick kiss and watched her exit into the south tunnel junction.

Frank was helping himself to another cracker when Sonny Peterson stepped up next to him.

"Good to see you, Frank," Sonny said. "But I must say, you look exhausted."

It did not surprise him that Sonny would make that observation. "I am very tired, yes," he said. When it looked as if Sonny wanted more detail, Frank explained that he and Stormie had, for almost three weeks straight, spent as much time outside the habitats—setting the few remaining prefabricated shelters in place so they could be hooked up—as they had inside working on the environmental equipment.

"How'd you get roped into that?" Sonny asked. "You two must be hating life."

Frank disagreed, and the more he talked about it the more he disagreed. It was hard, he would not deny it, but their role was not just to keep the colony alive—which was important in itself—but to help it thrive. If that meant long hours in pressure suits, setting up and unpacking habitat modules, so be it. If that meant driving multi-purpose vehicles to deliver rails, newly forged from native materials, for the launch acceleration system that would eventually stretch hundreds of kilometers across the Sea of Clouds, they would do it. Most things worth doing required hard work and sacrifice, and this was no different.

"No, my friend," Frank said, "quite the contrary. Life is good, and we are just trying to make it better."

"Okay, then. But maybe now that we're here, we can take some of that load off you. If you need some help, you let me know, okay?"

"Of course," said Frank, and they shook on it.

As Sonny walked away, Frank heard, "Pastorelli! Good to see you again. How the hell are you?"

Frank cringed a little at the familiar voice and turned to see Scott Herbert standing behind him at the little snack table. He had not been looking forward to this reunion.

Herbert was forceful, usually loud and obnoxious, and his brusque manner always put Frank on guard. It did not seem to matter to the man that people tolerated him more than they actually liked him, or that his main criterion for being accepted as a colonist was having married the alternate power engineer. Again Frank mourned Chu Liquan and wondered how Marilyn was doing.

Frank wiped crumbs off his hand and slowly extended it. Herbert shook hands with his usual over-exuberance, as if they had not recently spent three months in the same underground facility. He said, "Who'd have thought that two years later we'd be together here on the Moon, huh? I mean, what were the odds?"

Frank had no idea what he was talking about. "I'm sorry?" he asked.

"You don't remember? Sure you do. Today's still the ninth, right? You and your wife were at the AC orientation with me two years ago about this time, remember?"

Frank realized he did remember. It was not that he had suppressed the memory because it was bad, just that he did not find it particularly memorable. But he had actually met Herbert at one of their initial briefings at the San Diego office.

Frank smiled, not at the memory—let Herbert think so, if he wanted—but at a memory-within-the-memory.

Herbert's first words to Frank at that July meeting had been, "So how long you been married, Frank?" It was not an uncommon question among the colonists, as Frank learned; Herbert and Angela Beacon had one of the many marriages of convenience brought on by the Consortium's policy. The Consortium had caught some flak for its insistence that the first fifty lunar colonists be married couples, men and women. Commentators and activists had editorialized against and shouted down the policy since the announcement in late 2026, but the AC stuck with the program despite all interference attempts. Stormie had once done a search and uncovered an online dating service with several listings to the effect of, "Single male engineer seeks female scientist/engineer for quick marriage and possible emigration off-planet."

But Frank always smiled at that question for a different reason. The first two years of his marriage to Stormie, he always answered in terms of days. It had started just after their honeymoon. A store clerk asked him and he said with just a moment's thought, "Thirty-two days."

Stormie had chastised him. "Why can't you just say, 'a month,' like a normal person?" she said. "No one's that precise. When someone asks you a year from now, are you going to say, 'Three hundred ninety-seven days'?" But he knew her rage was all bluster.

He had continued answering in terms of days—and sometimes down to the minute—until it became harder to calculate on the spur of the moment. The temptation hit him when Herbert asked, but

Stormie was no longer close enough to react so he refrained from doing the calculation. "Four years," he said. Herbert had expressed some surprise, but Frank found himself marveling that so much time had passed.

Frank rarely played his little game anymore of calculating the elapsed time of their marriage, but the memory amused him because Stormie's "no one is that precise" excluded her. She often vied with him in terms of the precision of her calculations. In fact, they each took a bit of pleasure in finding small errors in the other's work. And small errors were usually all they found.

Frank extricated himself from the memory, reluctantly, and let go of Herbert's hand as if in a dream. He registered that the man was speaking but did not even try to perceive the words.

He was in his own world, a world he had built together with his wife, and he was content to stay in it a little longer.

CHAPTER TWENTY-THREE

Something Has to Break

Stormie usually couldn't keep track of the days of the week. She knew the date only because her datapad told her, and only vaguely comprehended that the Stewarts organized worship services and social events a few times a week. Even after LLE's temporary forced labor campaign ended, she found that her regular work filled almost all her waking hours.

So she went halfway through the first Monday in September before it dawned on her that she used to get Labor Day off as a holiday.

Colony life was a routine of long stretches of constant, repetitive work broken up by occasional minor emergencies, usually involving sewage—which, thankfully, was Frank's specialty. Once or twice since their arrival the colonists had also staged special events, some of which they invented to add significance to what would otherwise have been normal events and what should, one day, be routine. They were still eating through the stores of prepackaged foods—and looked forward to every one of the dwindling shipments of consumables—but the first harvest of the first carrot crop had become a mini-celebration. Now every new vegetable harvested was cause for excitement, though Stormie doubted the first rabbit slaughter would be celebrated as widely. The rails for the launch system were starting to creep across the plains of Mare Nubium, and she suspected every hundred meters would become a reason to celebrate. Every time the catfish or the shrimp were moved from the spawning pool to a circulation tank, every cycle of asteroid miners who arrived and then departed, every out-of-the-ordinary occurrence would be a reason to gather whoever was available to commemorate the occasion.

Maggie had become the de facto social coordinator among all the colonists, organizing little parties and remembering everyone's birthdays. Stormie would've enjoyed more of the impromptu festivities had she not been so tired so much of the time.

Stormie had known she would encounter a learning curve associated with the real habitats and the real air and water systems, but experience in the training facility hadn't prepared her quite well enough for the dynamics in the actual colony. The output of the ARPOES oxygen plant varied depending on the quality of the ilmenite brought in by the scavenging robots, and even depending on what type of alloy the metal-processing plant was trying to produce at a given time. The uptake of carbon dioxide varied as the plants in the farm modules matured, and Frank needed to confer with Maggie and the agronomists about the crop cycles once there were enough crops to cycle: balancing the air-purifying effect of the farms according to the different stages of growth among the available species was going to be a difficult prospect. And the bioreactive air filters turned out to require even more maintenance than they had anticipated in the training facility.

Stormie might have suggested hiring one of the other colonists on a part-time basis to help with cleaning filters and other tasks, but their company couldn't afford it. So she worked longer hours and did more herself. Frank did, too, balancing the water systems—which seemed at times more complex than the air systems—and dealing with the same kinds of issues with respect to the varying life cycles of the aquatic animals that filtered the water before they fed the colonists.

So much of their learning, so much of their advancement up their respective learning curves, had to do with balancing out the peaks and troughs in all of these natural cycles. Sometimes it was as if she were trying to adjust a thousand individual signals patched into a single mental oscilloscope: as long as she kept the signals out of phase with one another enough that they didn't all synch up at the same time, they wouldn't be in danger of losing a vital resource at an inopportune moment. Not that there would ever be a good time to lose a vital resource, but it might be possible to handle a shortage if some other resource were available to take up the slack. The problem was, she was responsible for maintaining air, upon which everyone depended and the supply of which could be affected by a huge number of variables. Part of her mental fatigue came from trying to figure out which of those variables she could ignore and which of them she had to pay attention to all the time.

Frank's availability also depended on how much financial work he was still doing. Jim had moved back in to his apartment weeks ago, but he still required a lot of assistance with just the basics of living so Frank hadn't turned over business matters to him yet. Stormie had backed out of the financial morass again after the initial shock of finding out that they were overextended and undercapitalized; now, she only asked Frank about once a week if the bills were being paid and if any money was going into their account. She knew the answers before she asked the questions, of course—not that she needed to check up on him, but she had as much right to see the account balances as anyone else. She just wanted to see how he answered the question.

The creditors Jim had enticed into investing in their little company—even the most recent batch he had tapped—had, so far, been content to be silent partners. She had seen a few recent messages that worried her a little bit, because they sounded as if some of them might want to cash out their investments sooner than she, Frank, and Jim were ready for them to. That was one reason she was happy to let Jim and Frank take care of the business end; she wasn't comfortable with, nor was she confident in, those kinds of negotiations.

Where she had become surprisingly comfortable and confident was with some of the other women in the colony. Beverly Needham had organized a rotating women's bridge game, and Stormie occasionally squeezed a couple of rubbers into her schedule even though bridge was not her favorite.

Her schedule was as tight as a B-nut, and her work kept her isolated much of the time, but Stormie tried to build in an extended break when she needed one and at least stop in long enough to say hello. In this manmade microcosm, where she traversed the same corridors and saw the same people over and over, she balanced between needing human contact and wanting to stay as far away from people as possible. Sometimes the card games or just being in the same area as the other ladies were perfect, and other times she wanted to be alone with music or a movie.

Occasionally one of the ladies would be watching the others play and Stormie would join her for a quick game of cribbage. She enjoyed those times even better than when she sat in for bridge: her job required enough mental energy, and cribbage took less than bridge. She missed having a real pegboard—their respective datapads tallied the scores automatically—but even so, after a quick game she could return to her little workspace and get back into whatever calculations or analysis she needed to do, with a fresh perspective.

She needed a fresh perspective, and looked forward to the evening after she realized it was Monday and Labor Day. Since it was the first Labor Day at the colony, Maggie had arranged a small party featuring the first colony-grown cucumbers, after which the Ladies' Bridge Club was going to play.

Stormie's CommPact buzzed. She finished annotating the predictive curve she had built of the rate of consumption of ethylene and other byproduct gases by the biofilters; before she finished, it buzzed two more times. She put in her earpiece and said hello before it could buzz a fourth time.

"Stormie, this is Harmony. What've you got going on the rest of the day?"

"Just the usual," Stormie said.

"Well, I hate to tell you this, but you've been tapped for," she paused, "an unpleasant detail."

Stormie looked around the tiny workspace as if the answer to the obvious question would be in plain sight. "What kind of detail?" she asked.

"You know the rotator is coming in today, right?"

Of course Stormie knew. A dozen miners would rotate in for what they had started calling a "gravity break," and if the manifests were correct the dozen who were in the colony now would rotate out. If she and Frank were lucky, the net effect on the air and water systems would be zero—at least, after the miners took their first showers in however many days.

"Yeah," she said, "and I've already done the air consumption calculations, including the flight crew."

"That's good," Harmony said. "But what you don't know is that they're bringing back a body."

The words sank in slowly, but they sank deep. Stormie guessed where this was going, and she didn't like it a bit. She said nothing, the way a child who doesn't want to be noticed will make themselves very small and very quiet.

Harmony only let the silence go on for a moment. "Guy's been dead for four days," she said. "They just wrapped him up and secured him in place until they had a flight coming this way. His family's been notified, but we didn't announce it or anything yet."

"What happened to him?" Stormie asked, surprised that she wanted to know. It wasn't morbid fascination, she decided, but data-gathering: it would help her be prepared.

"The guy was a digger, and he'd just come off a long shift," Harmony said, "and was heading back to the pressure bubble to sleep. Instead of taking the main route out of the shaft he was in, and going overland, so to speak, he decided to cut through a fissure where they'd already excavated a vein of ammonia ice. It's not well marked, apparently, and there are a lot of cracks that look alike— he got lost, and then he got stuck."

"Did he run out of air?"

"No. And he didn't run out of power, either: his suit was still warm and pressurized when they found him, but he was gone."

"How does that happen?" Stormie asked.

"They figure he panicked when he saw he was stuck. He keyed his beacon, but inside the asteroid the signal got all confused. Nobody received it until he was overdue and they started looking for him. Anyway, they're not sure if he had a heart attack or if his blood pressure spiked and he stroked out—oh, sorry, I guess I shouldn't have said that."

Stormie frowned, even though Harmony couldn't see her. "That's okay. Why me, though?"

"Gary had me run the selector," Harmony said, "and your name came up along with Barbara Richards. I already called her, and she's on her way to the Gateway."

Stormie remembered the feel of the scalpel in her gloved hand when she eviscerated the dead Labrador retriever in training. Now she had to do that on a person? Why couldn't somebody else do it? She said, "I thought only Consortium employees were supposed to be included in those lotteries."

"Well, I put everybody's name in the program, myself included, because I figured we all have the possibility of dying up here, so we all ought to have the possibility of taking care of somebody who's died."

Stormie did not argue the point; the strain in Harmony's voice told her this wasn't the time. She needed to call Frank—or, better yet, walk over to the module he was working in—to tell him what was going on. She could recite their statement of work almost verbatim, but she would still have him verify that it didn't require this type of extra duty. And since they hadn't volunteered for this duty, the way they had volunteered for the habitat-unpacking duty when they first arrived, maybe they could bill the AC at a premium rate for these out-of-scope hours.

And for this ... oh, yeah, there'll be a premium.

O   O   O

"What do you mean, you charged them a basic hourly rate?"

Frank cringed at Stormie's question. She was not yelling, not quite, but her voice was pitched a few notes higher than usual.

"I am sorry," he said. "James and I discussed it, and felt the rate was appropriate." His conversation with James had been brief: a quick call to confirm verbally what they had tossed back and forth in text form. James was not yet up to carrying on long conversations, just as he still was not up to working at the keyboard for long periods. His brain worked faster than his mouth or his hands, and he got frustrated quickly. Frank still hoped for more progress in their friend's recovery.

Stormie shook her head. "I can't believe you. Jim … okay, I can see how he wouldn't get it. But you've done that procedure, Frank, you know what it's like! Surely you can imagine what it was like to do it on a person. I won't be able to sleep for a month.

"It would be one thing if it was in our contract to do that kind of work, but," she paused, "oh, they really couldn't pay anyone enough to do it."

"As I said, I am sorry—"

"Sorry? It's one thing that you didn't volunteer to do it for me—I don't expect you to ever have to do my share of the work—but did you even think about the precedent we're setting? We've got enough work to do, our own work, without them coming to us every time they have something extra needing to be done. We ought to be making them pay through the nose for anything we do that's out of scope."

Stormie crossed her arms across her body as if she were cold. Frank recognized a cultural element in her distress; her background, like his, did not involve handling the dead. His mother's tribe had its own specific death rituals that he knew more from stories than observation; he had been fascinated one day to learn that some cultures like the Irish and the Japanese took great care to bathe their dead, but his mother had been appalled when he told her about them. Her people, she said, used to take dying people into the bush and leave them for the hyenas and the leopards because of the uncleanness of a dead body; she would never have participated in the solemn ceremonial washing of a Jewish corpse, for instance. Now was not the time to discuss anthropology, however.

Frank wanted to go to Stormie, to wrap his arms around her and try to comfort her, but it was unlikely to assuage her anger. He should be able to think of an appropriate poem, but he feared there was little he could say that would not seem flippant. She would not accept his advances or his pity, and he could not blame her, but his heart began to break at her vulnerability, at the way she was backed into that little corner, trapped where her only recourse was to attack because she had no room to escape. And he had placed her in that position.

Yes, he had agreed with James that exacting a death tax of sorts against the Consortium would be in poor taste. But he had not thought of it from Stormie's point of view, and as a result he had both disappointed and hurt her. And that terrified him.

In some ways, Frank had always been afraid: afraid of disappointing Stormie, afraid of hurting her, afraid of losing her. Now he did what he thought he should not do, though he expected she would reject it. He stepped quickly and hugged her so fast that her arms were pinned between their two bodies. She struggled against him for a few seconds, almost moaning, but to his surprise she stopped struggling and gasped a little for air.

She put her head on his shoulder. His shirt grew wet with her tears, and she trembled.

O O O

Wednesday, 5 September 2035

"BD, I believe that's the hardest thing I have ever done in my life."

Barbara's friend sat across one of the small tables from her in the southwest quadrant of the Grand Central dome. They were each drinking coffee, which had become such a luxury that people were either hoarding it in order to establish a black market in it, or actively soliciting Maggie's assistance in trying to grow coffee plants in the farm tunnels. Barbara doubted that would happen for years and years, because engineering coffee plants the way the fruit and vegetable plants had been engineered—for faster growth and higher yields in low-gravity conditions—would never pass anyone's sanity check. Not when they could be engineering real, nutritious foods.

"Honey, I have tried to imagine what you went through," BD said, "and then I do everything in my power not to imagine what you went through. I think if my name came up in the lottery to have to do that, I'd offer anyone a month's salary to do it for me."

Barbara appreciated BD trying to lighten the mood, but she couldn't laugh. "That's what I should've done. I didn't even know the guy, but now almost everywhere I look I see his face. Last night, when I tried to sleep—I was so tired Monday night right after we finished that I fell right asleep and don't think I dreamed at all—but last night I kept dreaming of different people lying on that tray. Van, you, Rex Stewart—even Stormie, since she'd been right there with me."

"What was it like, working with her? I don't mean what was it like, what you were doing—just, how was she to work with?"

"She was quiet. I think she was probably thinking a lot of the same things I was. Or trying not to think, like I was." Barbara sipped again and added, "Professional. Stepped right through the checklist, got everything done and got out of there. Why?"

"I don't get to work with her much. Hardly at all, really. Closest I came was when we were partnered in bridge about three weeks ago. I guess I'd characterize her as intense."

"Yeah, I'd go along with that."

"Does she seem like she's pretty open to new ideas and new ways of doing things?"

"I don't know," Barbara said. "I guess it would depend on what she was doing. The checklist we were running doesn't leave a lot of room for improvisation."

"No, I know. It's just that Gary is hot on the idea of wrapping all the independent contractors into the AC. I'm pretty sure he's had top-level people in the AC contact the Pastorellis' partner down on Earth. I don't think they know anything about it, and I don't know if they realize that the other independents are being brought into the fold, too."

"Sorry, BD, I just don't know," Barbara said. She sipped more of her coffee, and shivered.

"Are you going to be okay?"

"Who, me?" Barbara smiled, but she could feel her own fakery inside it. Would she be okay?

The whole lunar experience had not turned out the way she had imagined. Oh, there were momentary periods of what she may as well consider to be joy—the exhilaration of bouncing around the surface, jumping up and floating down so smoothly and gracefully; the thrill of looking up to see the shadowed Earth in all its blue and white glory—and in the eight weeks she had been here she had accomplished more in terms of building something new and important than she would ever be able to do on Earth. And her husband—how he thrived here. He seemed to work harder than anyone, and yet always to have more energy for the next thing that needed to be done, and the thing after that. It was as if, in this environment, he had no "off" switch.

She smiled, a little more genuine this time, but tentative.

BD smiled back at her. "What are you thinking about?"

"Do you ever get the feeling," Barbara said, "that things might be going too well?"

BD blinked. "Okay, you've shifted gears on me. We're going from the hardest thing you ever did to things going too well, and I got lost somewhere in between."

"No," Barbara said, "I think I might be the one who's lost. Because, have you ever been afraid that things are going so well that something has to break? Are you ever afraid to let yourself really be happy, because you know the next thing that happens is going to ruin everything? That as soon as things start getting good, the only direction for them to go is to get bad?"

BD turned away from her and scanned the area inside Grand Central. She had a faraway look in her eye, and sipped her coffee once, twice before she answered. She didn't look back at Barbara, but looked up toward the thin horizontal windows high in the wall of the dome, the windows through which only lunar darkness was visible right now.

When Beverly spoke, her voice was soft and hard at the same time—soft-toned, but with a hard edge like the tip of a cold chisel. "I think I know what you mean.

"I don't think I ever told you about Carol. It all happened before we met you. We were stationed down at the Cape. Carol was our little girl, she was four, almost five. I had her when we were up at Malmstrom, on our first assignment.

"She loved the beach. And you can imagine that after four years in Montana, I was ready for the beach, too. Everything was so good, so right. Gary was working on the base. Not too busy, because the launch schedule wasn't that frantic—I don't think it was ever frantic at the Cape, even way before we got there—and we had weekends at the beach and trips to Disney and Saint Augustine. So many good times."

Barbara wanted to tell her to stop talking, that whatever she was starting to say she didn't need to say. But she let her go on, as if she were a bystander watching in fascination as an airplane with a broken landing gear was trying to land.

"We went out on the beach one day to watch a launch. It wasn't one of Gary's programs, so we couldn't get into the official viewing areas, but that was okay because Carol didn't like loud noises. So if we were a few miles away, where we could feel a little rumble but still see it go up in the sky, that was good enough. After all, they didn't launch very often, so you had to get out to see it whenever one did.

"I think it was on Memorial Day—it's been so long ago, I may be confusing it with something else. I do remember it was in the late afternoon, and it was summertime or close to it, because it was warm and the Sun was out and the sky was beautiful. We went out in the afternoon and I had some snacks and we listened on the radio, and when it went up it was glorious. Carol loved it. She clapped, and squealed, and I don't know if it was because I was excited or if she really did like it.

"I never got to find out. I remember thinking at the time how perfect that day was, just wonderful. We got back to where we parked the car, and I was loading our stuff in the back, and … I only took my eyes off her for a second. I heard squealing tires, and all I thought was how Carol didn't like loud noises.…"

Beverly's eyes were closed and her head was tilted a little to the side as if she were still listening to that noise from so many years ago. It was quiet in Grand Central.

Barbara reached across the table and touched her friend's arm. "I'm so sorry."

BD's head tipped forward, slowly, for a second, and then she took a deep breath and opened her eyes and looked up again. She drank the last of her coffee in one long smooth pull, and put the mug on the table. She reached up to where Barbara's hand was on her arm, and she patted it.

"Yes," she said, "I know what it's like to think that things are too perfect."

CHAPTER TWENTY-FOUR

An Independent Operation

Tuesday, 2 October 2035

Frank closed his eyes and leaned back against the rigid partition. He put his feet on the small shipping container of air sampling pumps, and thought again that once they had some of their debts paid off he and Stormie should start renting two adjacent bays, to use one for storage and the other for work. But that could wait; and, he decided, so could the water sampling he was supposed to do in the western end of Second Avenue. For now, he was too tired to think and so weak it was as if he was under full gravity.

Just a little nap, and I will get back to work.

All he got was a little nap. He awoke to a light tapping on the corridor wall, and looked at the monitor to see that not quite twenty minutes had passed.

Van Richards stuck his head into the cubicle and said, "Good work yesterday."

Frank was not so sure. Yes, everything had been done by the book, as Stormie would say; however, their reaction was slow and the response took too long.

Frank raised his hand in a halfhearted wave. "Thank you," he said. "And you as well. How is Mr. Springer this morning?"

"Oh, Chuck'll be fine. Looks like a bad sprain on his wrist and maybe one broken finger, but Bev was able to get his hand warmed up easily enough. He did an okay job wrapping it up, so it wouldn't get frostbite."

Frank did not argue the point that what he would have gotten would not have been frostbite in the classic sense; rather, that his hand would have swelled somewhat from lack of pressure and, if left long enough, heat would have radiated away from it to the point that ice crystals formed in his cells. He was glad to hear that did not happen; Springer would have some pain for a while, but he would recover.

Already Frank's perception of the event was skewed: It was another one of those situations in which time sped up so that everything blurred past, and yet it dragged by. For Frank, it was as much a case of being in a particular place at a particular time as anything else—he supposed it was the right place and time, but someone else might argue the opposite.

He had been setting up air-monitoring equipment in the first garage. Inboard of the vehicle-sized airlocks the garages were essentially open bays large enough for vehicle and equipment maintenance; unfortunately, the toxic hydrazine fuel that ran the MPV turbines was often present in such concentrations that they could not allow the garage air to circulate into the rest of the colony without scrubbing it first. Were the habitats kept at higher pressure, with nearer to a terrestrial atmospheric mix, it would be less of an issue; since they were not and never would be, Stormie hoped that they could strike a balance by increasing the efficiency of the garages' water-based permeation filters.

To figure out the right ratios of air and water flow rates and establish an appropriate maintenance schedule meant they needed a comprehensive baseline of the typical hydrazine concentration. And since the polymer film detectors installed in the garage were meant only to provide warning of high levels of hydrazine, rather than time-weighted-averages of the concentration, that meant lots of sample collection and analysis. So Frank had set up the sampling gear in the garage and was getting ready to leave when the call came in about an accident at the launch rail construction site. Richards, who had been in the garage working on one of the smaller vehicles, pointed at Frank and said, "Let's go."

Frank did not argue about whether going out on a rescue was in- or out-of-scope to the Lunar Life Engineering contract; if he were hurt and called for help, he would not want someone arguing over whether or not they were going to get paid for helping him. He followed Richards to the nearest locker, suited up, and rode with him toward the site.

The Sun was low in the West, and threw long shadows behind every rock and structure. They got not quite halfway to the launch rail facility when they were met by another multi-purpose vehicle coming toward the colony complex. Sonny Peterson was driving and Springer was in the back, his left arm trussed up so thick it looked as if he was wearing one of those pads that attack-dog trainers wear. He had gotten his arm caught between one of the massive rails and one of the precast supports, and would probably have suffered little real damage had not the rail slid sideways as they winched it back up. The lateral motion, from what Frank gathered, had torn into and shredded the glove of his pressure suit.

Rather than waste time moving Springer from one vehicle to another, Frank suggested that they simply switch vehicles and drive back. Richards agreed, but insisted that he go back with Peterson and finish Springer's shift. So Frank brought Springer back in by himself and took him to the infirmary, where Beverly Needham waited to take care of him.

"I am just glad that he will recover," Frank said now to Richards. He did not mention that he was already preparing a bill to the Consortium for out-of-scope rescue work. Stormie would be particularly pleased when he told her. He continued, "We did not need another accidental death, especially so soon after the first one."

"You're right about that, brother," Richards said. "How's your wife after that?"

It had been almost exactly a month; Stormie seemed to have recovered, though she tended to avoid the tunnel junctions that held the desiccation chambers. "She is … managing."

"Yeah, that's a good way to put it. Barbara, too. She said Stormie was good to work with, but I think the whole thing still spooks her sometimes." He paused, and looked away from Frank's eyes for a moment. "Hey, uh, I have something else I want to ask you."

"Very well," Frank said around a yawn.

"You had any contact from one of the newbies, guy by the name of Karl Capell?"

Frank hesitated. Capell was coming up with the next set of colonists, either the second or third week of October depending on the flight schedule. Stormie was already running new air consumption calculations, and he had started estimating water usage as well. Capell had taken the initiative to send Frank and Stormie a message, but he had indicated that it was proprietary.

Frank spoke slowly, not so much to find the right words as to betray little emotion. "I did receive a message from Mr. Capell, yes."

"Did he ask you to sign up for his new union?"

Frank raised his eyebrows; he had never been very good at hiding his reactions. He did not know how many people received Capell's "proprietary" message, but it had seemed very passionate and pled for support in combating the Consortium's "flagrant neglect" of safety measures that had resulted in the miner's death. Capell seemed to believe that just because accidents had identifiable causes meant that accidents are caused by people whose intentions must be questioned and motives challenged. Stormie had laughed at his message and asked Frank if Capell realized he was writing to people in the health and safety business.

Frank still measured his words to Richards carefully, as if he were titrating a solution and did not want to push it too far from acid to base. "He did mention a union," Frank said, "or the possible formation of a union. I sent him a brief note in return, explaining that we are not part of the Consortium."

Richards' brow wrinkled. "I thought I heard that you were coming into the AC with everybody else."

"No," Frank said, more firmly than he intended, and shook his head. He had just had this conversation with James a week ago. The Consortium was trying to take over all the independents, and one of the new investors James had found was urging him to accept their offer. Frank had not bothered to tell Stormie about the idea because he knew she would reject it, and rightly so. They were determined to make a run at an independent operation for as long as they could; and since the AC had agreed to a three-year contract, that was at least how long they were going to go. If the Consortium wanted to replace them after three years, so be it—they would find another adventure to share. If the Consortium wanted to buy out their entire contract at once, that was a different matter; he might entertain the idea, but he would prefer to stay and do the job they had agreed to.

A mild flush washed over him, replacing his fatigue with irritation that would border on anger if he let it go too far. He probably should not be too surprised that Richards would know about the AC's offer, since he was close friends with Gary Needham. Frank was formulating an unkind response when Richards spoke again.

"That's probably good," he said, "staying independent. I don't know about this Capell character, and I know management usually gets the union they deserve, but I hope y'all can keep your business. There need to be a few people with some objectivity around here, who aren't on the direct AC payroll, to keep the AC honest.

"Y'all are good people. I hope you make it."

Frank started to revise what he was going to say, but before he could speak Richards tossed a sloppy salute and walked away.

O   O   O

Friday, 2 November 2035

Jim Fennerling had special-ordered an old-fashioned paper calendar to mark off the days of his recovery, and every time he turned the page he thought about how much better he was than the last time. Yesterday he had flipped it from October to November: five and a half months since his stroke. He still had far to go, especially with little things.

His fine motor control was better, and he had a new appreciation for video game technology, but he needed help sometimes buttoning buttons and doing other tasks. He had established a routine that was almost normal to him now: a nurse came by in the morning to help him get up and start the day, he ordered takeout for his lunch, his sister came by at dinner—usually with leftovers from her family's meal the previous day—and another nurse stopped by at night to help him close up shop. He realized how much better he was when he got annoyed at the night nurses for coming before he was ready: when he still had things to do, or at least things he wanted to do.

He had taken back almost all of the company's financial dealings from Frank, and even though Frank still worried about his ability to get it all done, he thought Frank appreciated being free to do his real job. Jim, on the other hand, didn't worry. He had wanted to take back all the financials in September, but Frank wouldn't give it up; he only relented after Jim started sending him e-mail messages at the rate of about one an hour with everything from interest rate projections, to the costs of shipping various pieces of equipment to the Moon, to a call for papers for an upcoming safety and environmental protection conference—he even told Frank he would be happy to present the paper if Frank would just write it, or have Stormie write it. So over the course of six additional weeks, he gradually took back all of his responsibilities.

Their balance sheet from the month of October was still a little unbalanced, but the trend was in the right direction now. The Consortium had made good on the first of its asteroid material shipments to Low-Gee, and with revenues coming in it seemed to be in no danger of missing any payments to Lunar Life Engineering. Jim had managed to put some money into retiring their company's debt and still make small deposits into their respective bank accounts, so the month ended on a good note.

He scooted over to the door in his new powered wheelchair when the delivery girl brought his lunch from Athena's, a little hole-in-the-wall Greek place that just opened up about a month before his stroke. Ariadna was a lovely girl, dark-haired and dark-eyed, just like her mother, who was not actually named Athena. He made a little small talk as he paid her. He could almost smell the tzatziki sauce as he maneuvered back to the dining room. The phone rang as he put the bag on the table.

Something told Jim not to answer the phone, but he had come to the point that whenever he had feelings like that he ignored them. If something was telling him not to do it, he considered that an indication of fear rather than fate—and he believed in facing his fears. When the voice on the other end of the phone spoke, however, he wished he had gone with his first instinct.

Huang Wenbin, the AC accountant, was, as always, unfailingly polite. He seemed to be the kind of person who would expect you to thank him, or maybe even tip him, as he explained to you that the sumptuous dinner he had just served you was not only dog meat, but actually made with your own dog. And then he would make you feel guilty because you didn't own a black dog, since black-furred dogs tasted better.

Jim lost his appetite as the accountant laid out his business. The AC had gotten to LLE's most recent investor—Alberto Escarro, who manufactured special-purpose radiation-hardened microchips in a high-end facility in Alamogordo, New Mexico—and simply bought him out. Unlike Escarro, the Consortium had no interest in being a silent partner. Jim suspected that the Consortium had paid a premium for Escarro's paper, and now they demanded that Lunar Life Engineering make good on it. They were willing to lose money on the deal in the attempt to make Stormie, Frank, and Jim's company insolvent—so they could step in and buy the whole thing for a song.

Jim left his souvlaki still wrapped on the table, and scooted into the office where he could think.

The AC couldn't change the terms on the paper they'd bought from Escarro, so far as Jim knew, so they were stuck with the terms that allowed LLE to pay back the investment over … Jim struggled to remember the repayment plan. He would have to look it up, and that was the sort of detail he should have at the ready. He hated having to look it up; it was another reminder of the multitude of little things that had gone wrong in his brain. They kept surfacing again and again, and drove him to distraction. He looked up in the corner of the office, where the model of Meredith's Moon moved back and forth, softly scintillating in the midday sunlight coming through the window. He clenched his fist, and struggled to compose himself.

By the time he got through to the colony communications center, and asked Ms. Needham to route the call to Stormie and Frank, Jim admitted to himself that, even though he was better, he didn't quite feel fine.

"James? I did not expect to hear from you today."

"Something's come up, Frank. Something you to need to know about."

"What is it, Jim?" Stormie asked.

Jim laid out the situation in as much detail as he could. He hadn't bothered to try to contact Escarro and find out exactly what the consortium paid him. It didn't seem important, since it wouldn't make a difference.

"If they're going to pull this kind of stunt, Jim, why did they even go through with carrying us as contractors?"

"I don't know, Stormie. I do know that they're trying to use as leverage the … fluctuations you had when the last batch of colonists arrived." Fluctuation was putting it mildly, Jim knew. But he didn't want to upset Stormie anymore than she already was. The new colonists had arrived the third week of October, and the old law attributed to Mr. Murphy had proven to still be in force. Stormie had taken it very hard that her predictions and calculations had not proven quite up to the task of integrating so many new people into the environment. It hadn't been as bad as Huang made it sound—he called it an ecological disaster, which it certainly was not, just a few people with headaches from what was basically altitude sickness—but it had taken longer to balance the air and water systems than originally anticipated.

Frank spoke up, and Jim imagined him putting a hand on Stormie's knee or shoulder to calm her. "James, that is most unfair."

"They're not playing fair. They're playing for keeps, and they're playing for the whole thing."

"They would not be able to achieve any better results. But what can we do? Do you have any suggestions?"

"Not now," Jim said, "but I'm working on it. I wanted you both to be thinking about it, too. It's not like we have to cut them a check tomorrow. We have some time, I think about six months, and we can probably stretch it out a little further without getting into too much trouble. In the meantime, if there are ways you can think of to cut costs, then cut them. I'll do what I can down here to pull some capital out of the air or out of the ground or out of the water or wherever I can get it from, and I'll have some friends of mine take a look at our original agreement with the AC and see if we can charge them with breach of contract for trying to make this end run."

"Very well, James. We will do what we can."

"That's all any of us can do, Frank." He paused, and smiled as if they were on a video link in an attempt to make himself feel better. "I'll tell you what, though. It would be really great if, while you're waltzing around up there doing whatever it is you do, you were to stumble across a vein of gold or an oil field. Or even those diamonds you were supposed to send me."

Neither of his partners laughed. He wasn't surprised, since it was a pretty pathetic joke. But hearing Frank's reply made him feel a little better.

"Yes, good idea, James. We will start looking right away."

Chapter Twenty-five

A Biological Imperative

Saturday, 17 November 2035

Barbara loved being outside. Maybe that had to do with growing up on the ranch, but it didn't matter if it was lunar daylight or lunar dark, being outside under the open sky—even when she was encapsulated in her pressure suit—was far better than being in the prefabricated habitats.

In that respect, she considered the subterranean phase of her training to be much worse than the reality of colony life. In the Cave, she had no opportunities to go outside and see the Sun or the Earth or much of anything. At least here, there were even places inside that allowed a view of the outside world. Like now, when the Sun was nearly overhead and ambient light flooded the inside of the Grand Central dome.

In these existential moments of freedom, she felt most at home on this barren but starkly beautiful world, and closest to what she guessed her husband must feel all the time. It was a pity she didn't have those moments as often as he did.

Now that the new set of colonists had been in place long enough to know their way around and actually start contributing—was it three weeks, or four? it didn't matter—Barbara was happy to turn her attention to a new work assignment. She had given over her part of the launch acceleration rail project to Al Mancuso, one of the new engineers, and today she would start scouting for the site of the first proof-of-concept dome.

She checked in with Central Control—Bent Sondstrom had the duty at the moment—and got clearance to proceed with the nearby survey. She called up the map of candidate sites on her head-up display and verified which ones she would visit. Four of the ten-to-fifteen-meter-diameter craterlets were within range of the little electric carts, and she could survey them on her own. The additional five candidate craterlets were farther afield; to visit those, she would have to check out one of the MPVs and probably enlist someone else to ride with her.

The candidate sites had been chosen based on the available overhead imagery. She would examine each one up close to see which was the best site to cover over with a dome.

This would be the closest thing to real engineering she had done since arriving at the colony. She shouldn't have been surprised, since her experience in the service had been much the same, but on-site engineering did not amount to much. Everything big had already been designed and most things had already been built, so the little bit of engineering that was required usually only amounted to fitting things together when they might not want to. There were some small opportunities, like the work stand she designed for use in the garage: she and Van actually worked together on that one, and cut up several discarded hatch covers from the prefabs to bend into supports and hold-downs. But that was less engineering than just rough craftsmanship.

The next closest full-blown on-site engineering effort was the tunneling project, since it required detailed surveys of the rim of Mercator Crater and specific adaptation to the rock formation. No terrestrial engineer would ever be able to predict ahead of time how the tunnels would have to be dug and supported. But Barbara preferred thinking about the foundations of domed structures than about digging tunnels—digging tunnels would be too much like being back in the Cave in Utah. She was happy to leave that to Rex.

She was tired and hungry by the time she returned to Gateway and cycled through the airlock, but she was pleased with her results. She had definitely rejected three of the candidate sites and taken almost a hundred digital images of the fourth. It might work, if none of the others were better, and had the advantage of being close to the main colony. The idea was to find a site where the rim of the small crater was in good enough shape to hold the footings of a dome. Once they had built a dome about ten meters in diameter, they would progress to a twenty-meter dome, and then fifty, and on up in stages. The actual size might be plus or minus ten percent, depending on the prevailing conditions, but with each step they would get better and better at building domed-over structures that one day should eliminate the need for prefabricated and tunnel habitats.

With the worst of the sweat toweled off, her pressure suit put away, and dressed in shorts and a T-shirt, Barbara moved through the junction from Gateway to Grand Central and found one of BD's Bridge Club games in progress—even though BD was working a shift in the command center. Trish Springer and Stormie Pastorelli were playing against Maggie Stewart and Alice Lindsay.

Barbara looked at the little snack table by the curved wall. She didn't find anything she particularly liked, but she didn't feel like walking farther back into the colony and rummaging through some of the food stores. She drew a mug of water from the tap, picked up a package of dried apple slices, and walked over to the Bridge table.

"You know what I wish?" she asked. "I wish somebody would bring up some candy bars or something. Every office I ever worked in had some sort of a snack bar, and people who would go buy stuff and set it out and we'd buy it and the office would make some money. I wish somebody would order some stuff up here and sell it—I'd be happy to pay a premium for it."

"Why don't you do it?" Trish asked.

"I don't want to be in charge of it," Barbara said, "but I'd be happy to patronize it."

"I would, too," said Maggie. "Know what I miss? Real cheese. I wish we had enough feed stock that we could get a family of goats up here."

Alice wrinkled her nose. "Goat cheese? Uh, no thank you."

They all chuckled as Barbara sat down behind Stormie and looked over her shoulder at the card display on Stormie's datapad. "What are you up to?" Barbara asked.

"Three diamonds," said Stormie. "And I'm with you on the snack bar thing. Not for goat cheese—" she glared at Maggie, but it was a friendly glare, "but I would pay real money for some of those orange gel things with the dark chocolate on 'em. Oh, my goodness."

The bidding went around again and ended at four hearts. The datapad display was so small there was hardly room to show the cards as they were played, but they managed. Maggie and Alice made their bid, and Alice initiated the next deal with her datapad.

Stormie turned to Barbara. "Want to take my place? I've got plenty of things I need to be doing."

"Sure, maybe in a little while."

Alice said, "Stormie was just telling us about the current water situation."

"What water situation?" Barbara asked.

"We're being wasteful," Alice said.

Stormie shook her head. "That's not quite it."

Alice grinned. "Oh, that's it in a nutshell. We're wasting water and losing water because everything leaks."

Stormie fanned through her cards on the screen; she even turned a little so Barbara could see better. She didn't have enough points to start bidding, but she was void in clubs and long in hearts with the jack and the king. She said, "Frank did some analysis of use rates, storage inventory, flow through the treatment system and the fish farm, that sort of thing. Took into account that we're up to sixteen transient miners these days, with that programmed to go up to twenty next month."

"Are there that many?" Barbara asked. The miners mostly kept to themselves, so she rarely saw more than two or three at a time. The northwest corner of the colony, habitats One-Alpha and Alpha-One, were primarily transient quarters and had been dubbed "Cripple Creek" by one of the miners from Colorado.

"Yes, there are," Stormie said. "Anyway, Frank factored in the amount of ice the teams have been bringing up from the South Pole, which isn't that much—"

"I reminded her," Trish said, "that there's water to be had all over the place. Glaciers on Mars, all over Europa—"

"The aliens told us not to go there," Maggie said.

"—and a whole ocean of water and ammonia under the crust of Titan," Trish concluded, to a chorus of light laughter.

"And I told *her*," said Stormie, "that's an awfully long way to go for water. Pulling water up from Mars doesn't make any more sense than pulling it up from Earth."

Barbara nodded. That's why the major supply missions were going to end soon, and why it was critical for the colony to be able to sustain itself.

"I'll grant you," Stormie continued, "Titan would be excellent because you'd have water plus ammonia for fuel. But how many months would it take to get there and back? And there are other pockets of water here on the Moon, except the Consortium doesn't have claim to them.

"*Anyway* ... we also looked at humidity fluctuations, everything we could think of, and if we don't do something to make our reclamation more efficient and seal this station tighter, then it looks like we're on the declining side of the curve right now. And as we bring in more people, it's just going to get worse—we're going to have to bring in more water, since we're nowhere close to being a real closed system."

"So what's the answer?" Barbara said.

"There's no one answer," Stormie said. "Karl Capell is supposed to be installing an upgrade to the water treatment system, in preparation for opening the real tunnels, but I haven't seen any plans cross my desk yet—and I don't think Frank's seen them, either. So for now we're just trying to fix little leaks where we find them, and figure out how to strengthen the aquaculture regime so it's more efficient at cleaning the water."

"Your hubby talked to me about that," Maggie said. "I think we can make that system work better. Just have to be careful with all the tinkering and tampering."

"What do you mean?" Alice asked.

"From what I've seen, every time we try to fix a problem we cause more problems in different places. I think that's because every good deed has its own unintended consequences—and maybe that's why 'no good deed goes unpunished.' But, we still try. And now that Gabe Morera is here to take over the flora, I can work more on the fauna and the ... what's the water equivalent of fauna?"

They looked at one another and shrugged, almost in unison. A cycle of laughter built around the table, and died out as the bidding began. Hearts was bid and Stormie ended up playing the hand.

Trish, with the dummy hand, laid her datapad on the table and leaned over it to watch Stormie play. She said, "Speaking of water fauna, whatever you call it, I keep hearing people say we shouldn't be trying to get at the water anywhere else in the Solar System because it might have life in it. But back me up on this, Stormie. I say it's a biological imperative for us to use whatever water we can find, no matter what algae or microbes might be in it. Survival of the fittest, right? Like the killer bees, or the rabbits in Australia. Come on, you're from down South—I don't believe the kudzu ever worried about the other plants it choked out."

Stormie took another trick and said, "I can see your point, Trish, if you think the human race should be compared to a pernicious weed."

Maggie laughed. "Oh, how the mighty have fallen, if that's the case," she said.

"Is that from the Bible?" Trish asked.

"I believe I've read something like it in there," Maggie said. "I can't tell you chapter and verse."

Alice said, "I was surprised to find out you played cards, Maggie. I thought that wasn't allowed."

Maggie laughed again. "A common misconception, dear. I don't believe you'll find any mention of 'playing cards' in the Bible. Now, if my playing cards offends you, I'll stop—because I don't want to be a stumbling block—but I don't think trying to live right means giving up simple things that are fun and don't hurt anybody."

Barbara noticed Stormie hesitate in making her next play; she took the trick, but seemed distracted. With each succeeding trick, she seemed more and more agitated. Watching her, Barbara missed some of the conversation.

"I don't know," Maggie was saying. "I think, when it comes to salvation, it's not the hundreds of things I've done that made God unhappy. It's the one thing I did that made him happy. It's not all the thousands of things I do wrong every day. It's the one thing I did right."

Stormie took the last trick and turned to Barbara with a half-smile. "Ready to play a while?" she asked. Then, *sotto voce*, "I think I've had as much fun as I can handle in one day."

Barbara leaned forward and gave her a friendly hug. "Thanks," she said. "I'd love to. You go get some work done, and keep us all alive."

Stormie transferred the game status to Barbara's datapad, said farewell to the ladies, and they replied in kind. But Barbara noticed that Stormie frowned as she left.

O O O

Monday, 3 December 2035

Frank sat cross-legged with eyes closed on the floor of the Third Avenue farm tunnel. Just as he found solace in the aeroponics modules when he and Stormie were on the Clarke station, here in the farm tunnels he found the deepest peace. He breathed in the clean smell of productive soil, soothed by the bubbling aerators in the fish tanks at the other end of the habitat. If he concentrated hard enough, he could imagine he was in an open field, with a small brook trickling over rocks in the distance. He imagined it was night, since it was nearly midnight in the long lunar sense, but a cool and comfortable night such as he had enjoyed at his family's home. As he imagined this faux night, he missed the wind: it should be rustling the leaves of the genetically engineered trees behind him. Of course, the trees should be many meters tall instead of the bush-like plants engineered for the colony. But he would still like to hear their leaves moving in a breeze.

He wished, as he thought about the rustling leaves, that he had a better sense of smell and could smell the apple blossoms. But there were limits to his perception.

He heard humming at the other end of the habitat—not the hum of machinery but a person humming a tune he did not recognize. He kept his eyes closed, though, preferring to keep this moment of respite to himself as long as he could.

After a few more minutes of quiet reflection, Frank opened his eyes and uncrossed his legs. He knelt, and started putting away the tools he had been using earlier when he was adjusting one of the air filters. The filters in the farm tunnels were similar to those in the main tunnels, but the microorganisms in these filters did not convert carbon dioxide to oxygen—the edible plants in the farms took care of that—instead, they were specially-tailored MACEFs that devoured some of the hydrocarbon byproducts of plant respiration. He saw now that Maggie Stewart was humming as she fed the rabbits in their cages at the other end of the tunnel. He waved, and she smiled and waved back.

Frank scrolled through the screens on his datapad and entered the results of his filter maintenance. He had three more farm tunnel filters to adjust before he would be through for the day. Stormie had agreed to take his place at the water treatment system design review this afternoon, which was just fine with him. He would much rather be among the plants and animals than stuck in a room looking at drawings on the big screen. It was not really anything new, and it was ridiculous to have so many meetings to discuss something for which the major engineering was already done. But, if it made people feel better to have talked about it more than they actually worked on it, he supposed he should not begrudge them their pleasure. At least they did not force him to participate.

He picked up his tool bag and glided along the length of the habitat toward Third and Bravo.

"Good afternoon," he said as he approached her. "Thank you again for the Thanksgiving feast last week."

She chuckled. "Good afternoon to you, Frank. You're welcome, even if you do exaggerate."

Frank smiled. Perhaps "feast" was a bit much to describe two small rabbits and a chicken served with the "first fruits" of the colony farms: a salad of lettuce, carrots, cucumbers, and tomatoes. They had about a spoonful of mashed, locally-grown potatoes each, augmented by reconstituted potatoes that Maggie made palatable by copious amounts of chives and parsley.

"Nevertheless, I enjoyed it," Frank said. "And I look forward to the next feast you have planned. I assume you will continue to celebrate each new harvest?"

"Oh, yes. It looks like we'll have some soybeans soon, and we've set up a darkroom to grow mushrooms. Gabe is worried about the wheat, though—he doesn't think it's going to produce the way the geneticists said it would. And then one of these days we'll have corn. And apples and pears."

"I am very glad it is going so well."

"Thank you. I hope you're having a good day."

"Any day I get to spend among the plants is a good day."

"I think so, too. And I appreciate all the help you gave me when I was trying to cultivate things on my own."

"It was not very much," Frank said, "but you are welcome. For me, working among the growing things is very therapeutic."

"Have you been helping Gabe, then?"

"No," Frank said. Gabriel Morera, the botanist who had arrived in mid-October, seemed very friendly but Frank had not wanted to intrude on his area of expertise. "It seems he has everything very well in hand, and does not need my assistance."

"Needed or not, I'm sure he'd appreciate it. Want me to ask him for you?"

Frank shook his head. "Thank you very much, but that is not necessary. Perhaps if he needs help bringing in the first big harvest." He smiled at her and gestured with his tool bag. "I hope you have a very good day." He slid by her on his way to the tunnel junction.

"Just a minute, Frank." She approached him, wiping her hands on the apron she wore. "I've got an idea for you."

Maggie glided ahead of him toward the junction, and stepped into the small storage room just before the hatch. Frank stopped next to the bubbling fish tank; the catfish looked almost big enough to eat.

A few moments later, Maggie emerged from the storage room carrying a small tomato plant growing in what appeared to be a large can. "Here," she said, "why don't you take this and put it up in your lab, or even in your and Stormie's room?"

Frank looked closely at the can-turned-planter. Maggie laughed. "I think it was a can of peaches," she said, "but this seems to be a good way to recycle it. And since you like plants so much, may as well let you have one."

Frank took the plant and put his face close to it so its tiny leaves brushed his cheek. It smelled mildly acrid, a foretaste of the fruit it would produce. "What variety is it?" he asked.

"That's a Roma. Would you rather have a different one? All we have are Romas and grape tomatoes right now."

Frank smiled. "No, this will be fine. Are you certain I can have it?"

She shrugged. "I'm not certain, but I'll make it okay. Gabe's got the idea that he'll germinate the plants and sell them to people, so they can grow whatever they want to grow. I think he expects people will be willing to grow little things like herbs, so we can have some variety. But I'll convince him that giving you one is like advertising. If it works out well, we'll start our own little farmers' market in Grand Central."

Frank thanked Maggie and took the plant. A farmers' market on the Moon; he liked that idea.

CHAPTER TWENTY-SIX

Ice Run

Friday, 4 January 2036

Frank's voice barely came through Stormie's ear buds, beneath Nat King Cole singing "Love Letters." The other colonists wouldn't hesitate to interrupt her rest with the most trivial complaint, but Frank was too much of a gentleman—one of the reasons she had married him. She figured it must be important, so she turned down the sound and said, "Say again?"

Frank shook his head and frowned. "Your number is up, as they say. You were just selected in the ice lottery." He pointed to the computer screen on the end wall of the cabin they called their "apartment." Its spacious four-square-meter living area was, at the moment, almost completely filled by their fold-down bed.

Stormie sighed. These moments of rest were few enough, she didn't want to be bothered. She didn't need to see the message to know what it said: another pseudo-random selection had her tapped for extra duty. Her first inclination was to complain since she had been picked for funerary duty … four months ago already? But that was a different lottery.

This was the regular draw to select people to wrangle the monthly load of ice from the South Pole. It would be a long trip with a lot of hard work at the far end, but more than ever that ice was critical to their survival. The colony was still grossly inefficient, as she often explained to anyone who would listen. Stormie didn't mind going, but she was concerned about Frank pulling double duty for the two weeks she'd be away.

"Report to operations Sunday afternoon for your briefing," Frank said. "Depart Wednesday the ninth, just before local sunrise." He read the notice with all the emotion that he might read a menu; he didn't sound too upset at the prospect of her being gone.

He's probably glad he didn't get picked, because he knows how ticked off I'd be. He'd be trying to figure out how to get flowers and candy as a mea culpa, with the nearest florist 400,000 klicks away. Although flowers and candy might be nice.

"Want to cut cards to see which one of us goes?" she asked.

Frank said, "I am not sure what good that would do—your name is already on the list. See? Right there. Stormie Pastorelli." He rubbed her foot for a second. "Do not worry, my dear. With only three dozen of us to choose from and a trip every lunar day, you or I were bound to be selected eventually."

"Who else is going?"

"Would you like to read the list for yourself?"

Stormie opened her eyes and glared at him, but couldn't hold it more than a second against Frank's grin. She turned off the music and said, "Okay, pass the screen down here."

"Can you not read it from there?"

"No, you've got the font too small."

Frank unclipped the screen from the end wall. He held it out to her, but pulled it away when she reached for it. "No, wait a moment. Where is your datapad?"

"In the lab."

"Then I feel sure you can wait until I am finished with my e-mail." He clipped the screen back to the wall. He turned away, but she could tell even from the back of his walnut-brown scalp that he was still grinning.

Stormie sat up a little and tried to reach past him for the screen, but Frank slapped her hand away. She punched him in the back. "Be that way, then." She lay down and put her arm over her eyes.

Frank chuckled and scratched behind her knee.

"You can stop that right now," Stormie said. "You know that doesn't work."

"Nevertheless, I am compelled to try."

Frank knew Stormie wasn't very ticklish, but never seemed to care. He probed where her tickle spots should be. Eventually she gave up ignoring him and actually smiled.

O O O

Sunday, 6 January 2036

Stormie woke to an empty bed. She thumbed the apartment computer on and a note from Frank popped up on the screen. "I left early for H2O sampling. I also worked preliminary calculations on air, H2O for your trip. Please check. Also see note from JF. Love, F." Even in a brief e-mail message, Frank's language was formal in a way she found both irritating and endearing.

Stormie tapped the wall next to the computer screen. Jim sent a message? She called up her inbox, but when she saw the subject— "Ice?"—she sent it away again.

He's probably going to tell me not to go, that it's not our job. He would support a one-off, short-duration assignment that was out-of-scope to the contract, but not a two-week trip that would make life miserable for Frank.

But more than any rescue operation or other task, this *was* their job, as much as any air sample or design review or exfiltration test. The colony had to live and breathe, and LLE couldn't make that happen without raw materials. And with eighteen new colonists due to arrive next month, and the number of transient asteroid miners going up the month after that, this resupply operation was more important than any in the past. Plus, with something as critical as water, the responsibility to keep it supplied had to be shared. How could Stormie and Frank enforce water regulations if they didn't help top off the supply? And unless they found an unknown aquifer as they dug new habitation tunnels—or hit a vein of water ice in the asteroid the AC was mining—that water would have to come from the pole.

Stormie wouldn't let Jim type her out of going on the ice run.

But she didn't want to deal with that right now. To delay reading Jim's message, she dressed, went to LLE's little lab, and ran her own set of consumption calculations for the trip to the pole and back. When she called up Frank's results, they differed from hers by about ten percent.

She did her calculations again; they were correct. Frank was usually more careful—no, Frank was *always* more careful. If anything, he was more precise about computations than she was.

She was still trying to figure out where he went wrong when he came in a half hour later. Sample bottles clinked together as he set the basket down on the little utility table. "What are you working on so feverishly?" he asked. He walked around the table and looked over her shoulder.

Stormie pointed at his result. "Trying to find out where you got this value. I ran my own set twice, figuring four people for twelve and a half days. Normal losses, normal reloads—"

Frank wrapped his arms around her and kissed her cheek. "I included an extra safety factor, my love. I added extra margin since you are going on this mission."

Stormie smiled. "Okay, that explains it. I appreciate that." She kissed him and rubbed his stubbly head. He probably wouldn't shave at all while she was gone. "You seem to be taking this awfully well, considering how much extra work it's going to be for you."

Frank raised his eyebrows. "Well, I have given that some thought. I expect that I will send you with most of our hard work for the month." He turned away and started pulling bottles out of the basket. "Since you will spend most of your time just riding in the truck, you will have plenty of time to do the air balance calculations for the next shipload of colonists, and review the plans for hooking up utilities in the next tunnel. I thought I would ask James if he would like you to balance our books and calculate cost and revenue projections for the next few months, to ensure we can pay our outstanding debt. And I thought you might want to consider some changes to our statement of work in case we get to renegotiate our contract." He looked up at her with a big grin on his face.

"Huh," Stormie said. "So what does that leave for you to do?"

"That, my dear, is the beauty of this plan. I will work very diligently while you are gone. I expect that two or three samples per day will suffice, and perhaps an air filter or two will require cleaning, but otherwise, I believe things here will be nice and quiet. It will be like a vacation."

"Very nice, for you. Thanks." She looked for something to throw at him, but nothing was suitable. She knew he was playing, so she didn't want to throw anything dangerous—or expensive.

"My pleasure," Frank said. He picked up one of the sample bottles and held it in front of the light. He swirled it and squinted at it. "And what did you think of James's message?"

"Oh, crap, I forgot about that." Stormie retrieved the message, read it, and was surprised to see that Jim didn't insist that she back out of the trip. Quite the contrary: Jim was negotiating with the Consortium that Stormie should get a bigger bonus since this trip was going to leave their shop one-deep for almost two weeks. It sounded as if he was back in fighting form, the old Jim who could squeeze money out of the tightest capitalist misers, and that made her feel good.

"That might be a tough sell," Stormie said, "but I guess it makes sense, since you'll be stuck doing my sixteen-hour days on top of your lazy-bones fourteen-hour days."

"Please, do not remind me. And Lord forbid I should get sick while you are gone. You may return to find half the colony will have contracted Legionnaire's disease, or worse."

"Then I guess I'll have to ride to your rescue," Stormie said. "As usual."

Frank grinned his perfect grin. "You can rescue me anytime, Abbey Gale," he said.

Stormie turned back to the computer screen. She sensed him behind her before his hands were on her arms, his lips on her neck. She tilted her head to give him more access. He reached around to the front of her jumpsuit and pulled the zipper down about a hand's breadth.

Stormie took his hand, brought it to her mouth and kissed his fingers. "I love you, Frank," she said, "but there's just too much to do."

Frank touched her cheek and kissed her. "I know," he said. "But I was overcome by the thought of you rescuing me."

O   O   O

The pre-trip briefing started off well, at least.

Frank was surprised how full the multi-purpose room—the "big room"—was; since neither he nor Stormie had been tapped for ice duty before, they had always submitted their pre-trip calculations and skipped the actual meeting. Did so many people usually attend?

He pulled out the chair so Stormie could sit at the unfolded conference table. He sat against the wall behind her. Gary Needham also sat at the table along with the other three selectees and Yvette Fiester, acting colony physician.

Gary had an agenda printed on real paper, on an antique clipboard; it was a not-so-subtle signal he had adopted that his status in the Consortium afforded him certain luxuries. Frank hoped he used the same agenda before every ice run and kept it filed away in between.

Gary welcomed everyone, made sure the right people were there, and skimmed through the routine administrative items. "This will be a standard five-two-five transfer operation," he said. "Five days out, two to harvest, and five days back. Team chief is Bruce Lindsey. Karl Capell is his backup. Stormie Pastorelli and Gabe Morera round out the team."

Frank caught Bruce's eye and they nodded to each other. Bruce was the resident expert on all the colony's vehicles, and very dependable. Frank still had very few dealings with Capell, who called himself a redneck plumber even though he was dual-degreed in civil and chemical engineering; his work ethic, or lack thereof, had impressed neither Frank nor Stormie, and he was still agitating to unionize the Consortium personnel. Gabe sat next to Stormie, so Frank could not catch his eye. He would approach him in the next couple of days and offer to keep watch on the gardens for him.

It seemed odd that Capell was made the backup team chief, since he had only arrived in October. But Frank did not think about it long, as Gary continued ticking his way through the briefing items.

"Bruce, how's the LVN?"

"Snapper's ready to roll," Bruce said. "Generator's running in the green, all systems are go. Consumables loading should start tomorrow."

"Nothing too volatile, I hope?" Gary asked.

"Not that I'll admit to."

"Okay, then. Doc?"

Yvette consulted her datapad. "They're all fine. Dosimetry and records show they're all close to the expected radiation exposure for how long they've been here, so their biocapsules are fine to last the trip—especially since they'll have the benefit of the magnetotail half the time they're out. Stormie's due for a physical, but we can take care of that when they get back."

The group worked their way through verifying everyone's certifications to operate the LVN—the Turtle. Stormie and Frank were both certified, and their papers were good for another three months, even though their duties usually did not require driving the big truck. Gary and Bruce checked the training records and ensured all the procedures were correct and up-to-date. The team examined the equipment calibration and maintenance records and noted the latest telemetry from the main waypoint—the Halfway House oxygen plant—and the ice plant itself.

"About ten days ago," Gary said, "the LICEOM reported that one of its scavenger 'bots crapped out. It stopped transmitting and didn't return at its programmed time. You'll be carrying one extra to leave behind, and if you have time you'll recover the bad one and bring it back for repairs." From what Frank knew, that was not unusual: about every other trip out, the ice crews delivered as many new robots as were available to the Halfway House and the ice plant, such that gradually the production capacity of each automated factory was going up. The deliveries were sporadic because new robots were not received from off-Moon on a set schedule, but were tucked into other shipments like the EBM equipment. It would be a long time before the colony could rely on robots built locally in its own machine shop and foundry; so far they had only produced a few out of local materials and sometimes out of scavenged parts, on a space- and time-available basis.

When Gary seemed satisfied that everything from the solar flare forecast to the first aid kit was green, he tried to close the meeting. "Okay, folks, looks like you're ready for a nice trip. It's just driving and grunt work, and aside from setting up the new 'bot, nothing unusual. Bag check is day after tomorrow at 2200, and we'll see you off Wednesday as soon as it's technically morning. Any questions?"

Capell raised his hand for a second. He cleared his throat and asked, "Yeah, I was just wondering … how come Bio gets an extra fifteen percent bonus for this run?" A few others in the room muttered and nodded their heads.

Stormie looked back at Frank. He shrugged, surprised that word of James's deal could have gotten out so fast.

Gary consulted his clipboard for a second, then looked at Stormie and Frank as if to say, *Look what you got me into.* He frowned, and put on his best official voice when he said, "Karl, Ms. Pastorelli is an independent contractor, not a Consortium employee. Collecting supplies has been determined to be within the bounds of her statement of work. However, the negotiation of any additional cost, bonus or not, was handled down below, and is between the Consortium and the Lunar Life Engineering Board of Directors." Frank raised his eyebrows, and wished he could see Stormie's reaction at the description of their humble company in such lofty terms. James would find it amusing as well.

Capell shook his head. His bushy black hair wobbled. "I just don't think it's right, is all. These have always been equal shares in the past."

Strange that he would reference the past … Frank could not recall if his name had been on previous ice run rosters. He doubted it; there had only been two ice runs since Capell had landed. He pulled out his datapad to check, and almost missed what Capell said next.

"And I don't see why she should get extra money when she can't seem to keep the water supply stable."

From behind her, Frank saw Stormie's jaw clench; she might take that personally. It was true that the total water supply had fallen since the last group of colonists—including Capell—arrived. But Frank was not sure why Capell would bring that up as an issue. It was also true that the reclamation processes were not as efficient as they should be, and Capell himself had not completed his work on improving the water treatment system.

Frank touched Stormie's shoulder, but she shrugged away. "Hey, weren't you supposed to get the new water plant running by now?" she said.

"You say it like it's supposed to be easy."

His voice had risen, and Stormie's rose to match. "Maybe if you stayed here and did your job, it would be."

Capell held up one hand. "Look—"

Gary Needham slammed his clipboard down on the table. "That is a topic for another day, people." He looked at Stormie again, only for an instant. "As for the bonus situation, the transport fee will still be equal shares, based on the mass of ice brought back. Bio's extra fifteen percent applies only to the hazard bonus." He wrote something on his paper. "I've noted your question, Karl, and you're free to file a dispute if you think it's important. *After* you get back. For now, I think everyone has plenty of work to do."

Frank released the breath he had been holding, and noted several other sighs throughout the small room. The next few days would be interesting.

O   O   O

Wednesday, 9 January 2036

Stormie used the next couple of days to refresh her memory on the technical instructions on ice harvesting and transport operations, with a few hours set aside to pack her kit bag and prep her suit. She left Frank to supervise the loading of air, water, and food into the Turtle. Even though the Turtle was technically big enough for four people, that was debatable if not downright misleading: it would be comfortable for two, cozy for three, and tight for four.

She showed up for the bag check a little early Wednesday evening. The team swapped bags and verified everyone had the right inventory: Bruce checked Stormie's bag, and she checked Gabe's. They piled the bags into one of the big airlocks in the first garage, until they were ready to depart.

She and Frank enjoyed a leisurely vegetarian meal, after which he surprised her with a rare treat: a bar of dark chocolate.

"Where did you get this?" she asked. She tried to make it an ordinary question, but her voice betrayed her delight.

"I arranged for it to be brought up on one of the recent flights," he said.

She laughed, and he asked why. "Just the other day I thought about getting flowers and candy." She forced the smile from her face and asked, in as serious a tone as she could muster, "What are you apologizing for?"

Frank tipped his head to one side, as if he hadn't understood her question. She couldn't maintain her demeanor, laughed again, and kissed him.

As local daybreak approached, everyone suited up. Stormie kissed Frank again before she secured her helmet and went into the big airlock with the others.

The exterior lights were close little stars in the night that barely illuminated the lower part of the Mercator Crater wall, and made the mounds of lunar soil over the prefabricated habitats look like piles of Arctic snow.

The LVN and its trailer sat fifty meters north of the garages and the Gateway; Stormie thought its resemblance to a huge, misshapen turtle might be a little exaggerated. If not for the cab sticking out the front that someone had decided was its head, the thing would look more like a wheeled horseshoe crab than a turtle. Worklights illuminated its shell of shiny, blue-black solar panels. Since they would be driving around the clock for most of five days each way, they would need solar power to keep the batteries charged and themselves alive. Thus they had to leave right around the time of local sunrise, which—she checked the chronometer in her helmet display—was within a half-hour.

Within the first few minutes inside the Turtle, shucking off her suit and stowing her gear, Stormie wished she were shorter. And even a little thinner. The living/sleeping/eating space seemed impossibly tight; it would be tolerable only so long as one of them was in the cab, driving.

But it smelled incredibly good. Stormie took a deep breath when she got her helmet off, and it almost made her dizzy. It was the freshest air she'd experienced in months, and she was prone to "testing" the air coming out of every air filter and bioreactor she maintained.

"What'd you do, Bruce, spend all last week cleaning this thing?" she asked.

Bruce, who had his helmet off but otherwise was still suited to go forward into the cab, grinned. "Nah. I used to be an auto detailer in my youth." He shook his head. "Don't get used to it, though. It won't last."

Stormie took deep breaths, enjoying it while she could. Her brain, long used to blocking out noxious odors, struggled to make sense of what her nose was telling it. She swore she could actually smell the thin plastic of the Turtle's shell's inner wall. For a little while she thought she detected the warmth from the lights, but it must've been something in the wiring she actually smelled. She gave up trying, and folded herself into as small a package as possible to get some sleep before she had to drive.

Bruce drove the first shift. As the keeper of the Turtle, he went out on every ice run; it was no secret that he was amassing a small fortune in hazard bonuses. Capell was next in the rotation, then Stormie and Gabe.

They settled into the standard excursion routine quickly. They took turns driving, four hours at a time, which seemed short until Stormie found out how taxing it could be to wrangle the big vehicle.

Her first driving shift came after they had passed alongside the 90-kilometer-long Rupes Mercator cliff face. She was a little sorry she'd slept; in the rising sunlight the ridge must've looked spectacular, like a miniature version of snow-capped Sangre de Cristos. When they were on their way back, the Sun would be behind the ridge: she guessed it would look more like a line of black teeth, with maybe a little light on some of the edges.

She took over at the southern edge of Weiss crater, and took the Turtle up from the flats into more rugged terrain. The rising Sun cast long shadows, generally left-to-right across their path. Lindsey came forward and sat in the jumpseat behind her for the first half hour of her shift; he coached her on keeping her vision a hundred meters or so in front of the truck and making all her maneuvers smooth. It had been a long while since her qualification training, and she appreciated the tips. The control yoke was responsive and had servos that gave her feedback according to what the suspension sensed, but in the end she was sweating not from exertion but from having to concentrate so hard.

Stormie nursed the truck up into what she thought of as the lunar piedmont—the hills hadn't yet become mountains, and had a stark beauty under the harsh sunlight. Not the lush, green beauty of the Carolina piedmont where she was born, dotted with cotton and corn fields; more like the barren beauty of the southwestern desert. But less colorful.

When her shift expired, she had taken them to the southeastern edge of Wurzelbauer Crater. Always one to follow the protocols, she put her helmet back on and climbed through the Turtle's "neck" back into the shell. In the neck she felt especially vulnerable. The Turtle looked substantial enough from the outside, but it was really quite flimsy—and she, along with everyone else at the colony, had been treated to Van Richards' tale of the time the cab started leaking air. *What a showman.*

Stormie climbed into the shell, and was greeted by the overwhelming smell of oranges.

Gabe smiled at her, put on his helmet, and went forward to start his shift. Stormie quickly found out he had been nominated, seconded, and confirmed by the others as the expedition cook. The standard food load for this type of trip was intentionally bland: indigestion would eventually foul the air, and food poisoning would be exponentially worse. But Gabe had turned humble ingredients into a minor culinary masterpiece. Bruce handed Stormie a plate of the colony's farm-raised catfish smothered in a fruity glaze that rivaled anything she had eaten on Earth—and certainly outshone anything she'd had in nearly seven months on the Moon.

"Why didn't I know he could cook so well?" she asked.

"None of us did," said Bruce.

"Where did he get oranges?"

Bruce said, "It's marmalade, and he wouldn't tell us. I think he's got a secret stash."

"That's probably a strategic decision on his part," Stormie said. "If word gets out, he might find the whole lot of us lining up at his kitchen."

"It's almost too bad that he's so good," Capell said. "I kind of wanted you to wait on us, Stormie."

"I'll bet you did. Like Nadia waits on you?"

Capell bellowed out a laugh. "No—Nadia wouldn't know a cook pot from a piss pot. But you look like the serving type."

"Lay off, Karl," Bruce said. He picked up his helmet, about to go forward to coach Morera a little.

"It's okay, Bruce," Stormie said. "I've learned not to expect any better from Karl and his inbred cousins." *Son-of-a-bitch.*

When she wasn't driving or sleeping, Stormie worked calculations—respiration estimates, water purification requirements, chemical hazard calculations for the machine shop, and a dozen other things—and queued them up to send back to Frank. After each overflight of the communications relay satellite, she turned on her computer to find that Frank had sent her more work to do.

As they rose above the Sea of Clouds, the driving became more challenging: even though the route had been driven many times before, they all had to pay more attention to the road and the topography. Still, Stormie took every opportunity during her driving time to watch the bright landscape change as they rolled through it and the Sun moved overhead. She looked forward to the driving, not only because the Turtle's head stayed cleaner and smelled better than its shell but because it was less of a chore than working Frank's math problems.

O   O   O

The most amazing thing about puking in low gravity was how far it went.

As Van's stomach contracted again, he weighed that initial assessment against the fact that his convulsions could actually lift him up off the floor. Maybe that was more amazing.

He'd barely made it to the bathroom at the end of the habitat in the 200 block of D Street before his stomach overrode every command his brain was sending it. In the process, he found that his brain wasn't sending very good signals to begin with: he badly misjudged the distance to the commode, and underestimated the trajectory of his vomit.

He was not unfamiliar with this particular misery—it matched in kind and character a misery he had suffered many times in his college drinking days. He hadn't had it this bad in years.

He didn't look forward to cleaning up the mess.

He wouldn't want to make anyone else clean it up, though. He would pay someone to do it, maybe.

He decided he should probably get a towel and start right away, but his strength failed him. He settled gently to the floor, put his cheek against it and let the cool sink into his face. No, that wasn't right; heat transfer didn't work that way. The heat from his face was going into the floor, warming it up and causing a sensation of cooling on his face.

I must have it really bad now, if I'm lying here trying to figure out heat flux.

He lay there for what may have been a minute or ten before he became aware of the distinctive swish of someone gliding down the corridor. Awareness of sound triggered a new awareness of smell, and his stomach reacted faster than his brain. Thankfully, he had little left to expel.

"You too?"

Van looked up to see Rex Stewart—Navy man, geologist and engineer, self-appointed Preacher Man—looking down at him.

Van shook his head. "I'll be okay."

"Oh, I'm sure you will. Here, let me help you."

Van tried to the wave the man away, but his hand was too heavy to lift. That seemed very odd considering where he was.

"I'll be okay," he said again. "I'll clean this mess up in a little while."

Stewart laughed. "Why are all the people around here so stubborn?" He helped Van to a sitting position and leaned him against the wall. It wasn't as cool as the floor. Stewart said, "It must come from being highly motivated, very competent, Type-A personalities. Nobody can admit when they're wrong, nobody can admit that they might need a little help. Are you ready to stand up now?"

"I don't think so, not right now."

"Okay, then. I'll be right back." Stewart stepped away, and true to his word he came back in a very short time with a bucket in one hand and clean towels in the other. He handed one towel to Van. "I know, like all the others you're too stubborn and proud to let me help clean you up. So you can help me by wiping yourself off."

Van's hand was heavy enough when he had nothing in it; now, it was worse. But he managed to lift the towel to his face and wipe the vomit from around his mouth. He was surprised to see that he had some on his T-shirt as well. And his pants. And his slippers.

Stewart finished toweling down the vomit-flecked wall of the main room, and started cleaning the stall Van had tried to use.

Van shook his head at the extent of the mess. He leaned forward until he could pull himself up on the basin, and rung himself up a mug of water. He dipped a clean corner of the towel in it and wiped his forehead, then swished a little water around in his mouth and spat it out. He swallowed a few drops, but was afraid to drink too much.

"You feeling better?"

"Not especially. Sorry I'm not much help, but you don't have to do that. I'll get to it."

Stewart backed out of the stall and dropped a dirty towel into his bucket. "Yes, but if I do it now then you don't have to 'get to it.' Besides, it seems like half the place is down with the same thing."

That was news to Van, but he'd spent the last few hours in the machine shop programming the EBM to make a replacement part for Rocky, the LSOV. He'd been on his way back to his and Barbara's apartment when it hit him.

"What've we got?" he asked, and wiped his forehead again with the wet corner of the towel.

"I don't know," Stewart said, "but it ain't pretty. I figure it's some kind of food poisoning—something you guys ate that the rest of us didn't. You feel up to taking a walk? We can get you in with the others."

Van let Stewart lead him down to Second Avenue and into Grand Central; that is, Van leaned on the older man as they went through the habitats and junctions and into the dome. The far side of the chamber was bright with sunlight slanting through the high windows, and the room was more crowded than Van had ever seen it. They'd shoved aside all the little tables and laid out blankets in each quadrant of the dome. Van reckoned himself the fifteenth patient in what looked to be a twenty-bed ward.

CHAPTER TWENTY-SEVEN

Faustini Crater

Friday, 11 January 2036

They drove as straight as they could toward Tycho, along one of the bright rays of ejecta that was visible from Earth. The trail before them had been blazed monthly since the first colonists landed, and with no wind or rain to erode it the track stood out clearly. Here and there previous crews had burned warnings—on rocks or on the trail itself, especially where they had fused patches of dust together—that mimicked earthside traffic signs. "Bridge Out" was a favorite, since no bridges had been built to straighten the path; the farther they went, the more often they were forced to creep around or through obstacles or ravines.

By Friday they were on the southwest side of Tycho and stopped at the Halfway House. The scavenging station was operating normally, the LPPN and ROPS producing power and oxygen within normal limits. While they hooked up the Turtle and replenished its oxygen supply, Stormie looked back toward Tycho. It would've been nice if they'd driven close enough to see the Surveyor-7 landing site, just north of the crater, but they couldn't afford a detour of over 200 kilometers. To the south, the tracks led as far as she could see and continued on, past Maginus to Clavius and beyond. Stormie chuckled at the realization that she was standing between Tycho and Clavius. As prophetic as *2001: A Space Odyssey* was, with its Clavius base and that monolith at Tycho, she didn't remember Kubrick including anyone like her as part of the starring cast.

Topped off with oxygen, they continued south. On Saturday, the fourth day out from Mercator, Stormie was engrossed in calculating the projected respiratory totals for next month's new colonists when the truck slowed and stopped. She looked at her watch; it was an hour before her sixth driving shift was supposed to start. Bruce was snoring in his corner of the commons, and Gabe had his nose in a book on his datapad, as usual. Stormie figured Capell was sick, so she started suiting up. As she was sealing up her suit, she realized how long it had been since she'd bathed. So much for Bruce's detailing job; she was glad everyone's noses were desensitized by now.

But the truck hadn't stopped because Capell needed her to drive; he had stopped because the Turtle told him it had a problem with the drive circuits. And because she was the one suited up at the time, Stormie found herself outside checking out the situation.

The first things she noticed were the shadows. Her team had traveled far enough south that the Sun cast shadows toward the pole, though it had not reached its zenith. Nor was it close enough to lunar noon for the Moon to have entered the Earth's magnetotail, but that couldn't be helped; she would try to limit her time outside, where she was less protected from the solar wind.

She pulled one of the lamps from its charging socket and started her walkaround. Capell and Bruce had done all the troubleshooting they could from inside. The truck's diagnostics were inconclusive, but they'd tracked the problem to one circuit feeding the body's number two wheel: the front wheel on the right side. Stormie crawled under the truck and used the lamp to drive back the shadows. She looked at everything from different angles and reported back what she saw, which amounted to nothing wrong. When he was satisfied, Bruce talked her through unhooking the secondary power cable for that drive circuit. Stormie capped the cable and crawled out from under the Turtle. When she was clear,

Capell applied power to number two through the redundant circuits. Stormie watched the wheel grab and try to move forward; it spun through half a rotation before Capell stopped it. He applied reverse power and the wheel complied. Stormie reported her visual confirmation, and the others verified they could feel the motion inside.

Stormie reconnected the secondary cable, then disengaged and capped the primary so they could test that circuit. Again the wheel grabbed and spun, clockwise and counter- from Stormie's perspective.

"No alarm that time," Bruce said. "Stormie, go ahead and hook that power cable back up. We'll watch it, but we need to get going again."

Stormie's fingers had stiffened a bit, and it was harder to attach the cable than it had been to detach it, but in a few minutes she was tightening the collar—

—and the truck started moving with her still under it.

"Whoa, stop!" she said. She twisted around to keep out of the way of the spinning wheels. "I'm under here!" The truck rolled almost a meter before it stopped. She watched carefully to be sure it wasn't moving any more.

Capell cursed over the radio link. "I got a green light and just reacted."

"What?" Stormie asked. "How did you get a green light? I thought you disabled that circuit."

"That's my fault," Capell said. "I reset the breaker at the wrong time. Are you okay?"

Yeah, no thanks to you. Stormie got her breathing back under control, and checked to make sure she hadn't torn her suit on something. The pressure in her suit stayed steady, and she closed her eyes for a second to let the pressure inside her escape. *Idiot could've killed me. Spend all my time keeping him and all of us alive, just to have him run me over with a truck.* Stormie reached up to her helmet, and wished she could just rest her head in her hands. "Yeah, I'm okay. I'm locking down the collar and coming out now."

Bruce said, "Good, Stormie. I slapped Karl around a little, and I'll look the other way if you want to punch his lights out." Which she probably could: she was almost a head taller than Capell. Bruce continued, "Now, when you get out from under the truck, just climb up and strap in. I want us to drive a klick or so and see if we get any more alarms."

She weighed the extra radiation exposure against getting back inside where she would encounter Capell. She decided a few extra rads wouldn't hurt that much. "Roger," she said.

The open beds on either side of the ARG were small, and crammed with gear; Stormie made herself somewhat comfortable atop a transit case. She found it almost pleasant riding in the bed of the truck. She at least had her choice of views; inside the Turtle's shell, all they got were camera views, though the cab had a good view out the front and to either side. She looked back the way they had come and the shadows reached out toward her like the fingers of a great lunar goddess—damn it, she should remember who that was ... *Minerva? no*—guarding the trail behind them.

Stormie used the trailer as a reference point to judge the distances and sizes of rocks and ridges, but that only worked within a narrow range. To the side, beyond a hundred meters it was much harder to estimate size accurately. A boulder that looked to be as big as a car, only a short distance away, could really be a kilometer away and turn out to be the size of a house. She wished her helmet had a laser rangefinder, like the new ones made for Barbara Richards' crater development team.

They drove slowly and made some maneuvers where the landscape allowed. They sped up and slowed, went up a hill and down, and for a while Stormie actually closed her eyes and let the Turtle's motion rock her. She breathed deep and tried to decompress. After about twenty minutes, they stopped.

Stormie unstrapped and climbed down. "How is it, Bruce?"

"We got the same alarm again," he said, "but that wheel seems to be turning with all the others. Come on back inside." She put the lantern back in its charger and cycled through the airlock. Once the pressure equalized, but before she moved into the common area, she did what she could in the tiny space to clean her suit; unfortunately, crawling in the dust under the Turtle's belly had made decontamination a losing proposition.

All four of them crammed into the commons. Capell, thumbing through a checklist on his datapad, didn't acknowledge her entrance. As Stormie pushed herself into one corner of the small volume, Bruce said, "Here's how I see it. The electric transmissions are all working, else number two wouldn't want to turn on any circuit. Plus, I checked the power flow on that test drive and they were all drawing within normal limits and feeding power back when we braked."

"Then what's the problem?" Stormie asked. "Is the wheel drawing more current on that one circuit than it should?"

Bruce shook his head. His blond hair settled back into place before he spoke again. "Not so it's out of tolerance. It's a problem with that particular circuit, no doubt, and it bugs me.

"So here it is. We're less than a day and a half away from the ice plant. According to the decision matrix in the checklist, we continue on. That makes sense to me. Once we get the ice loading started, I'll do what I can to troubleshoot, but we ought to be able to go the whole way even if we lose that one drive circuit completely. And that's a lot better than driving four days back empty-handed."

Bruce looked at each of them in turn. Gabe shrugged. Capell gave a thumbs-up. Stormie said, "We should have enough air to breathe, so let's go."

"Good," Bruce said. "Don't push too hard and we'll get there okay." He looked at his watch, and continued, "We'll keep to the regular rotation and stay on the original timing. Stormie, you're up."

Of course I am, that's why I didn't take off my suit. Stormie sighed, put her helmet back on, and went forward to the cab. She resisted the urge to punch Capell as she slid by.

o   o   o

Sunday, 13 January 2036

Frank had endured much worse, but his previous experience did not make this any more pleasant.

Another spasm of nausea hit him as he put away his datapad. At least it was only nausea now; at first, it had brought back the fire—the latent manifestation of the picophage blaze that he had not experienced in many glorious weeks—and he had struggled just to stay conscious.

He had been even more circumspect than usual in his last message to Stormie. Primarily because he did not want her to worry too much, but also because she would remember his earlier joke about Legionnaires' disease and chide him about his wishes. "Be careful what you wish for, you just might get it," she would say. He had not, in fact, wished for this, but making that point would not matter.

In that way, Stormie and his mother were quite alike, though Stormie would neither acknowledge nor appreciate it. His mother would also tell him he needed to be more careful about words he said, but for a different reason: she had for many years followed the pseudo-magical "name it and claim it" evangelical fringe, and had often made the point that it worked both ways. Her intention was to name and claim things that were going to do her good, in the hope that by some miracle she would experience the good; at the same time, she assiduously avoided even naming things that might bode ill, out of fear that she would experience the ill. That always seemed too much like hocus-pocus for Frank, and he had no concern that his careless speech had somehow wrought this illness.

His father never agreed with or supported his mother's insistence on naming and claiming; he firmly believed that the answer to prayer was sometimes no, and that the ways of God were, in the end, unfathomable. His father tolerated her worldview, though, and once when he had rolled his eyes at one of her claims, Frank had asked him why. His father said it was a small thing to allow, and family harmony was much more important than any small things; that had been an important lesson in Frank's life, and one he tried to apply in his own marriage.

Frank was drawn from memory and reverie when Barbara Richards knelt next to his head and put an infrared probe in his ear to register his temperature. "Are you doing any better?" she asked.

Frank swallowed the trace of saliva he had in his mouth, and said, "Not appreciably."

"Well, it's only been about twenty-four hours yet, so I guess it's got a little longer course to run."

"How many of us are sick?"

"Twenty-eight, including five transients."

"So," he said, trying to think, "twenty-three out of thirty-six permanent party and five out of eight miners." The proportions seemed about the same, but his brain was fuzzy and would not do the math.

"Actually it's twenty-three out of thirty-two," Barbara said, "since we don't have any report that Bruce and Stormie and the others have gotten sick. So whatever it is, and Yvette is leaning toward some kind of contamination in the food supply, it hit after they were gone."

Frank resolved that he would give Stormie the details in his next message to her, even though Gary may have already briefed Bruce on the situation. If it was a food issue, her team would have to be careful since they were eating food they took from the colony.

Frank hoped it was not a food issue, for Stormie's sake; but for the sake of their business, he hoped it was.

He needed to get up and get some samples taken and analyzed to rule out the water supply as a potential cause. He pulled his legs up under him and tried to kneel, but the nausea and pain came again, hard and fast, and he found himself lying on his side with his knees drawn against his chest. Barbara's hand rested on his shoulder: it was heavy and hot and it hurt.

"I don't know where you think you're going," she said. "You just need to stay here and take it easy until we get all this figured out. I've got to check on some other people now, but I'll be back—and when I come back, I want to see you lying here quietly, resting, just like everybody else."

Frank nodded, but did not speak. As she walked away, he unfolded himself like a creaky, rusty lawn chair.

He pulled his datapad close. As soon as he could get up, he needed to be ready to act fast—and not just to take samples to help isolate the cause. He was losing ground every hour on routine maintenance that had to be done. In order to be effective, he needed to make a plan. He called up the schematics of the water and air systems on his datapad, and started writing a message to

Yvette to ask for reports on where and when everyone started getting sick.

His stomach contracted around nothing, as if his bowels had activated a vacuum pump in his gut. Tears came to his eyes.

Lord, please don't let Stormie get this.

O O O

The craters they passed started to run together in Stormie's head: Gruemberger, Moretus, Short, Newton, and a hundred others unnamed until they finally drove between Malapert and Scott. They were running behind schedule now, and started pulling extra driving shifts. Stormie started her eighth rotation six days into the trip, just to the southeast of Malapert Crater. The Malapert Mountain ridge was distinct in the sunlight, the long shadow behind it dark as lunar night.

This far south, the Sun lit only the peaks of the craters. The solar cells only caught the Sun when the Turtle crested a hill, so almost all lights and nonessential equipment inside were turned off to conserve power. But the shadows below the peaks were so deep that the big lights on the truck were kept burning all the time. Stormie followed the well-worn track, angling a little away from Amundsen Crater as they approached the pole.

She found it hard to concentrate whenever her imagination took her back to the colony and the misery evident in Frank's last couple of messages. This was not the time to lose her focus, though: she had to go forward and complete this task, in order to get back to help him.

Stormie got them within one diameter of Faustini Crater—about thirty kilometers away—by the time her shift ended. She gratefully turned the driving over to Gabe. She had barely finished her supper of crackers and the cold remains of what had been a nice vegetable soufflé when Gabe reported contact with the LICEOM's radio beacon. Bruce told him to start running the arrival checklist. When Stormie started getting into her suit, Bruce told her to wait—it would be a while yet.

Gabe stopped the truck at the crest of Faustini Crater. The Sun lit the rim through most of the lunar day, so that by parking there to run the procedure they put a little charge back into the batteries, but the crater interior, thirty-five kilometers across, was completely shadowed. The same was true for the other craters at the Moon's pole.

Faustini was near but not at the pole; nineteen-kilometer-wide Shackleton Crater had that distinction. The U.N. had allocated the relatively young Shackleton as a science outpost, even though it was unlikely to have accumulated much in the way of cometary ice, but the enthusiasm of the late '20s had waned and only a five-member international team was left in the outpost NASA and ESA had set up. Shoemaker Crater, right next to Faustini, had once been considered a good candidate for resupply, with its fifty-kilometer mouth wide open to the sky; the Lunar Prospector spacecraft had crashed into it in 1999 with Gene Shoemaker's ashes on board, and by the early 2000s astronomers from Cornell along with subsequent orbital missions had ruled it out as a supply point. Faustini itself did not have huge deposits of ice, or the Consortium would not have been able to afford the rights to it, but it had enough to last for a while.

"Got confirmation yet on the power beams, Gabe?" Bruce asked.

"Not yet. All the working scavengers are accounted for and moving to safe locations. The station estimates fifteen more minutes until the beams are off."

Since the crater floor stayed perpetually dark, the power system for the scavengers was based on solar collectors on Faustini's rim. The collectors tracked the Sun as it traversed around the pole; they had the Sun in view ninety percent of the time. The energy produced was converted to microwaves and beamed to the scavengers as they moved about on the crater floor, but the beams had to be shut down before the team was allowed to drive the truck into the crater.

"Okay, Bruce, we just got the green light."

"Roger that, Gabe. You feel comfortable about taking us down?"

"Sure, as long as the route is marked."

"Oh, yeah, it's clear, especially the places we had to blast out to make the path. Once you're at the bottom, just follow the arrows and keep the centerline on the stripe. Pretend you're driving one of the big floats in the Rose Parade. The line will take you around to the loading area. You won't even have to back up the trailer."

It took over an hour to get down the hill and into position; the LICEOM was a third of the way into the center of the crater. By the time they stopped at the loading zone, Stormie and the others were suited. They piled out of the airlock into the blackest darkness Stormie had ever seen. Even the partial Earth was hidden by the crater wall, and the only light came from the Turtle's headlights. Outside the glare of the lights, with her internal displays dimmed, the stars seemed tiny, and distant, and cold.

Once they unhooked the trailer, Bruce directed Gabe to pull the truck over closer to the ice plant itself, where he could hook up work lights to ground power. Like the ROPS oxygen plant at the Halfway House, the LICEOM was powered by its own ARG, much bigger than the Turtle's. Only the scavengers ran off beamed solar power; the ice plant required so much power that it couldn't spare any to run the robots, but it wouldn't be operating at full capacity while they were there.

"Okay, everybody, back in the truck," Bruce said. "Mandatory rest period. We're behind schedule, but we can afford to take a couple hours, just not the full four. Then we need to get started."

O O O

The first hour after their rest interval, they unloaded and checked out the scavenger robot they'd brought from Mercator. They put it through a last function check, then sent it to the holding area until the power beams were turned back on.

Once that was done, they started collecting the ice.

The ice plant processed the soil the scavengers collected into blocks about forty centimeters on a side. They were grimy—the plant stripped off most but not all the lunar dust as it melted, formed, and refroze the water—but they were ice.

Stormie chuckled a little at the uniform blocks the plant produced. The ice harvesting wasn't quite as simple as scratching the soil and digging up cubes, but the scavenger-bot-and-ice-plant setup made it seem almost that easy. Still, the supply was limited both in absolute terms and in terms of extraction efficiency; they needed to make the most of everything they had. With the asteroid mining operation in full swing and finally making money, they might be able to build more scavengers and increase the ice production within the next year, but unless the colony became far more efficient it would run out of water before then.

For now she, Capell, and Gabe sweated and grunted and moved the ice block by block into place on the trailer. They slid the blocks down an adjustable ramp from the holding area, then maneuvered them into place using old-fashioned ice tongs; it was an overprecaution, since everything stayed super-cold in the lunar night, but having a block of ice freeze to a glove or part of a suit would cause problems.

Stormie had already lost count of how many blocks they had moved when Capell radioed, "Hey, Bruce, how long until we get a tanker trailer and just haul back liquid water instead of ice?"

Bruce replied from over by the Turtle. "Don't think I've seen any kind of timeline for that. Have to install tankage and plumbing here, first. A tank to fit on the trailer wouldn't be too hard, though it would have to be baffled for slosh … a lot of momentum in moving liquid. And the CG would be higher, that might be a problem."

Stormie sipped some of her suit water and nodded, thinking of some of the turns she had made during the drive south. A high center of gravity might make some maneuvers pretty precarious, and maybe even require a new route.

She was about to comment when Gabe said, "Yeah, hate to have a rollover out here. No way to call triple-A, that's for sure."

Shifting the ice blocks around was fairly easy—owing to lunar gravity, each block could be carried by one person—but their mass still gave them considerable momentum. They took their time, to avoid any accidents: about ten minutes moving and placing each block. They worked in pairs while the third rested; nominally, they got four hours' rest for each eight hours' work. They could have worked in two pairs, except that Bruce was busy examining the Turtle. He slept little and cursed a lot.

Stormie was exhausted by the tedium as much as the exertion and lack of sleep. She could tell how tired she was every time she took a break to recharge her suit's oxygen supply: she dozed on her feet until the chime rang in her helmet. So when Gabe radioed, "That's the last one," close to the end of her third eight-hour shift, she almost shouted in relief.

Until she realized the trailer was only two-thirds full.

She was about to ask when Bruce did. "What do you mean, that's the last one?" He was bounding over to the loading area, hopping in big Apollo strides.

Gabe said, "I mean, that's the last one." Stormie could almost hear a shrug in his tone of voice. "I don't see any more in the hold."

Bruce skidded to a stop with a practiced turn. "That can't be right," he said. "You've only been loading for what, thirty hours or so? How many blocks have you loaded?"

Stormie had lost count. Gabe said, "That last one should be 212."

Bruce swore. "Supposed to be more like 240 or 250. Last October we only got 235, but 212 is down to about what the setup teams got on the first couple of runs, before I even got here."

Stormie asked, "Is the plant working right?"

"Seems to be," Bruce said. "It's probably that bad 'bot, plus there's always some variation in the output. The 'bots come back with more dirt than ice sometimes. They're smart little things, and they have detectors on them, but they don't each carry a mass spec."

Gabe said, "Maybe this crater is all fished out."

Static buzzed in Stormie's ear for a few seconds. Her mouth suddenly very dry, she said, "Don't even think that."

Bruce cut in. "No, Gabe, even though there's not as much ice as we'd like in this crater, it's still close to two hundred square kilometers. It'll be a while before we scavenge the whole thing.

"But if that's all for this trip, then that's all—can't make ice out of vacuum. At least this should put us back close to our original schedule. The bad thing is, we get paid by the ton and we're not bringing back the usual tonnage." He paused, then said, "Go ahead and get that block in place, then start putting up the frame. I'll be back in a few minutes and we'll get this thing tarped."

Stormie and Gabe stowed the ice ramp before they put the poles in place for the frame around the ice blocks. Bruce came back and helped install the aluminized Mylar tarp over the frame. They ensured that no part of the frame or tarp touched any of the blocks. The ice already sat on insulation that blocked heat from the trailer bed; by keeping the ice in shadow and limiting the heat conducted into it, the blocks would mostly stay frozen while they drove back to the colony.

As they were finishing up, Capell came out of the Turtle to start his shift. He wasn't happy when they told him what had happened, but there was nothing he could do.

They replenished their oxygen supply from tanks at the ice plant, and discussed whether to load some of the ingots of metal the oxygen plant left behind from breaking down the regolith. Bruce ultimately vetoed the idea in favor of picking up the wayward scavenger robot, the location of which they determined from the LICEOM telemetry records.

They rested for a few hours and started back early Wednesday morning almost exactly a week after they left. Bruce drove the Turtle to the top of the crater and ran the checklist to switch the power beams back on, then he consulted his trip plan and decided that the regular rotation would continue, with Stormie in the driver's seat for the first shift back. Gabe spoke up and pointed out that he and Stormie had driven an extra shift each on the way out, but Bruce stuck with his decision. Stormie was too tired to argue; she just decided to log the extra hours and bill the Consortium later.

CHAPTER TWENTY-EIGHT

Mayday

Thursday, 17 January 2036

Barbara doubted the smell would ever be purged from the colony.

So many people had been sick in so many places that as she walked through the facility wafts of stench would attach themselves to her with an almost physical sensation, as if noiseless insects had landed and tickled the back of her neck. It didn't help that many of the victims had developed diarrhea in addition to nausea. It was especially bad if she had just walked through one of the garden tunnels, where the plants and the bubbling water kept the air much fresher, into one of the residential habitats. Even after they'd been cleaned as thoroughly as possible, in places they still stank.

Oh, how she longed for the open sky at the ranch, where at least she could go upwind from the cows.

She carefully slid her way into the Bio laboratory, and put the little metal basket on the worktable. The sample vials sounded like ice cubes clinking inside a glass. "Here's the latest batch," she said.

The way Frank turned, she thought he'd aged ten years in a day. But he smiled as he thanked her again for her help.

"How's your analysis going?" she asked.

"So far I have not detected any evidence of contamination," he said, "which is a good sign. I do not know what Yvette has found using the other equipment, but her specialty is radiographic inspection, not chemical analysis. I regret that Marilyn Chu was unable to join the colony. I do not know when we will have a real analytical chemistry capability."

"Do you need anything else from me?"

Frank shook his head. "Not at this time. You have been very helpful, and I appreciate all you have done. It was good for me to be able to concentrate on analyzing samples instead of having to take the time to collect them."

"It's the least I can do," Barbara said. "Call me if you need anything else."

It was late enough in the afternoon that Barbara decided to go ahead and get something to eat. She made her way from Frank and Stormie's little laboratory north to Grand Central, where Maggie had set up a temporary cafeteria. Because they suspected an issue with the food supply, Gary had decreed that independent cooking would not be allowed until everything was verified safe. They had moved the temporary sick ward out of Grand Central and into the adjacent habitats—except for the Gateway habitat—and Gary himself along with Chuck Springer had moved some kitchen equipment from the 500 block of Second Avenue into the southwest corner of Grand Central, where BD's group usually played bridge. Barbara didn't mind the new arrangement; she liked cooking, pretty much, but she'd let someone else cook for her anytime.

Grand Central seemed crowded; most of the incapacitated were ambulatory again, and the cafeteria arrangement was showing signs of strain. But at least they'd cleaned it well, so all she smelled here was the food. Barbara got in line behind Rosaria Morera and asked if she had heard from Gabe. "Oh, yes," she said, "they're on their way back. He said they picked up less than they thought they would, but they should be back on Sunday as scheduled."

Barbara smiled, and dished herself out some sad-looking vegetables. At least something was going right somewhere.

O   O   O

Shift after shift, day after day, they crept closer to home. After the first day, the mood relaxed a little: the truck was running fine—though still nursing the number two wheel along on two circuits—and everyone had accepted the fact that this trip would not pay as much as previous trips. Plus, they were driving in the right direction: back to Mare Nubium.

They were only six hours late to the Halfway House, arriving on Friday in the early afternoon. They made up a little time during the oxygen transfer.

Saturday was the eleventh day out from the colony. Stormie was engrossed in more work for Frank, which she didn't mind since he was dealing with his own problems. She was evaluating the air balance plan for expanding into the freshly dug tunnels in the wall of Mercator Crater, and didn't notice until twenty minutes into her driving shift that Capell hadn't come back at the end of his turn. It was unusual for someone to lose track of the time, with the big chronometer displayed in the cab; if anything, most of the time they stopped the truck with a few minutes left in their allotment. She considered calling him on the intercom, but Bruce was asleep and Gabe was reading. She put her suit on and went through the hatch into the neck, and from there into the cab.

She took off her helmet just before she went through the open hatch. Capell's bushy black hair stuck up above the back of the control chair. "I thought you'd never get here," he said.

"I wondered if you fell asleep," Stormie said, "or got sick." Once in the cab, she moved to the right and pulled down the jumpseat from the bulkhead. She started to sit, but paused halfway when she glanced around the control chair.

Oh, tell me he's not really naked. Stormie looked up into the left corner of the cab, then glanced down at Capell's bare arm and hairy shoulder. She looked up again, and closed her eyes.

"Sorry, Karl, you want some privacy? I'll come back in fifteen minutes, if you like." *With a towel. And some disinfectant.*

He shook his head. "No, I'm fine. Don't you mind how hot it gets in here?"

"That's what the vent system is for," she said, automatically touching the port on her suit that would hook to the hose.

"That doesn't work well at all. Anyway, I was waiting so we could talk."

"I think Nadia might have a problem—"

"Don't flatter yourself," Capell interrupted. "First, you're not my type. Second, Nadia wouldn't care if you were. We're not that committed. Married just to meet the Consortium's regs. Third," he slapped his bare chest, "this is for comfort, that's all."

So you're just inconsiderate, instead of irresponsible. Or in addition to?

Stormie finished sitting down in the jumpseat. The cab seemed extra cramped. "Okay, then, what are we going to talk about?"

"Jeez, you are a dumb bunny. I'd think that was obvious." He reached to his left and adjusted the Sun shade, then put his hand back down. The distinctive crinkle of hair and the scritch of fingernails on skin made her wince.

Capell said, "I just want to know if you plan to report me moving the truck while you were under it."

"I'd have thought Bruce already did, in his daily report."

"I think he noted it, but didn't make a big deal of it. He and I talked about it, and agreed it wasn't that serious."

Stormie closed her eyes and put her head back against the bulkhead. *Not that serious?* She couldn't believe it. For endangering her life, he deserved to have his certificate suspended.

When she opened her eyes, the little man with his mass of black hair and ten days' worth of beard was looking back at her. "Watch the road, Karl," she said. "And strictly speaking, I already reported it. I transmit my logs and other work on every satellite pass."

Capell frowned. "Damn it, Stormie, I wish you hadn't done that. I was going to offer you half my bonus money to keep quiet about it." He swung the control chair around to the front. During the interval, the path had curved right and the truck had tracked a little off to the left. Capell pulled it slowly back to the right, and as it got back on track the truck bucked and shivered. Stormie grabbed the jumpseat frame and looked over Capell's shoulder at the system displays: nothing seemed wrong, but the control yoke was oscillating in Capell's hand.

"Did we hit something?" she asked.

"I don't think so. Feels like we're dragging. But I've got green lights on all wheels."

Bruce's voice blared from the intercom. "What's going on up there? Stormie?"

"I'm driving, damn it," Capell said. "But I'm stopping at the moment."

Stormie exited the cab and went back to the others. Since she was already suited, she would go out and check. Plus, she wanted to give Capell plenty of room to get his suit back on.

O O O

Bruce Lindsey ran a hand through his hair, then rubbed his eyes. "I don't see much choice but to call in a mayday," he said.

The dragging had been the trailer itself. The trailer sat lower than the truck, and it snagged a rock when it off-tracked behind the LVN. The rock, which looked as if it massed a couple hundred kilograms, was jammed under the suspension of the trailer's leading left wheel.

When Stormie reported the obstruction, Bruce and Gabe had joined her outside. They talked briefly about prying away the rock, but were afraid pry bars would damage the suspension even more. They had Capell back up to see if that would do anything; at first the rock continued to drag, but then it broke free. The trailer rolled another couple of meters and stopped. The leading suspension collapsed and the trailer settled down, crooked.

They spent the next hour together in the commons, discussing options. They didn't have a spare suspension, but Bruce figured he could rig a way to fix and reattach the broken one—except that they didn't have a jack that would lift the loaded trailer. They rejected the idea of dropping the trailer and driving back to the colony without it, even though they might eventually be forced to do just that.

"We're out of range of the MPVs," Bruce said. "So they can't mount a rescue that way. They're sure not going to want to pay the science geeks at Shackleton for roadside assistance, so unless they can fix up Rocky right quick, my guess is they'll order us back. That'd be cheaper than having one of the AC's asteroid ferries come back out of cycle and flying it down here with a big jack."

"And some oxygen," Stormie said. The CO_2 filters in their truck were still in decent shape, but if they didn't get moving in the next twelve hours, by the time they reached the colony their air would be very stale and the oxygen level dangerously thin.

Bruce typed up the mayday message and put it in the queue. Stormie checked the satellite coverage chart: the message would go out almost immediately. The colony and Consortium bosses would decide whether to mount a rescue or tell them to high-tail it back immediately. She hated the idea of leaving the cargo behind. They all hated that idea.

"Now that we've got nothing to do but wait," Bruce said, "Karl, you mind telling me why you were driving? By my clock, we were almost an hour into Stormie's shift."

Stormie leaned back into the corner; she didn't want to get into a big fight right now. Later, when she was rested—

"Come on," Bruce continued. "What about it? You never stopped. You never called. Stormie had to go forward, I guess to wake you up—"

"Yeah, she came forward," Capell said. "I was trying to give her a little extra rest, but she comes up and distracts me."

Stormie tensed. *I'm too tired for this.* She started to speak up, but Bruce was already talking.

"I don't buy that for a second. But you must be confident to say it with her sitting right here. So what's the story, Stormie? Did you distract him?"

She sighed. "If him turning around to talk to me counts as a distraction, then I guess so."

"Huh. How long were you turned around, Karl? How far off the path did the truck get while you weren't watching?"

"Come on, Bruce, that's not fair," Capell said. He fidgeted with the straps on his suit. "She already said she distracted me."

"In a way, she did. But she said you were talking to her. What was so important that it rated higher than watching the road?"

Capell stopped fidgeting and folded his arms. Gabe looked up from his reading. Bruce cocked his head. Capell looked from one to the other, skipping past Stormie without meeting her eyes. Suddenly he flung his arms as wide as the confined space allowed. "What difference does it make? You've already decided this is my fault, and the *Nubian queen* can do no wrong."

The Turtle fell deathly quiet, despite the ambient noise of a circulating pump and a couple of fans.

Stormie shook her head, at first amused that Frank's "King of Nubia" remark had become lunar legend and made her the defacto queen. Then she replayed Capell's words and their hateful tone, and clenched her fists. Heat built up in her back, as if she could feel adrenaline pumping, flooding through ducts she could not shut down. She closed her eyes and tried to regulate her breathing, tried to match it to the rhythm of the air circulation fan.

"So that's what this is all about?" she said.

"No," Capell said. He held his hands up, palms out.

"Sure it is. You disguise it well, most of the time, but I get it now. You drag your heels on your design work, 'cause you don't want me to be the one who checks over it. You complain about me getting more bonus money, not because you're mad that your little union's not getting its cut from us, but because you don't think I deserve it." Behind the adrenaline a wave of pain crested over her, with heat like the decaying nuclei in the Turtle's ARG, but she fought it with a low laugh. "I bet you *wanted* to run me over the other day."

"No, no—"

"Oh? You just wanted to scare me?"

"Hell, no," Capell said. He waved his hands to ward off her attack. "Look, I'm sorry. We're all a little stressed. Sometimes under stress you say things you don't really mean."

"And sometimes you say things you do mean," Stormie said.

The fan motor wound down and the silence deepened. Stormie looked away from Capell, at the cool green interior of the Turtle, at her own dark hands. She remembered some lines her brother Erick had written when they were very young, only a few months before he died,

> *I am the color of the earth—*
> *Not the slimy clay of Southern hills*
> *Or the weak and lifeless brown of desert sands,*
> *I am the rich, deep dark of living lands,*
> *The strong black coal that drives the rotten mills,*
> *The secret, inside, hidden, buried worth*
> *Of all the world.*

She remembered his haunted, soulful eyes, and the look of surprise and shock and fear as the water took him. She hadn't thought of that day in years, but now she could picture the grey, heavy clouds and the rain that obscured almost all vision except the thing she least wanted to see; the rain that fell in heavy drops like her tears that smeared those agonizing, determined words on the paper.

She laughed again, on purpose now, to keep from crying. She could let herself cry later, alone or maybe with Frank, but not here. Not in front of these men—

Gabe cleared his throat and said, "I don't mean to be insensitive, but this isn't really solving our problem."

He was right, and the fact that he was right irritated Stormie all the more. She forced her hands to unclench—when had she clenched them?—and rubbed them on her thighs. Bruce was berating Capell but she couldn't hear what he was saying for the blood pounding in her head. She wanted to pace, to walk off the anger, but there was nowhere to walk—only this tiny room and the smaller cab, a miniscule island of life on the barren face of a huge dead rock.

The adrenaline rush faded. The pain stayed behind, but a duller ache than before; it suffused her and left her more tired than ever. She rubbed her eyes and the bridge of her nose, and gradually released some of the anger and tension. She exhaled a long breath, careful not to whistle like Mother Mac's old tea kettle.

It came to her.

"Bruce," she said, "all we have is a mechanical jack, right?"

Bruce looked up from whatever he had been saying to Capell. He shook his head, but said, "Right, but it won't lift the trailer when it's loaded. It's for the Turtle, since its legs articulate."

"I know, but how high do we have to lift the trailer? If we had some bracing to hold it up?"

"Not much." He backed away from Capell and held his hands in front of him, moving them in odd patterns—obviously trying to visualize the problem. "A few inches ought to do it. What've you got in mind?"

Stormie let herself grin, a little. Bruce must be tired if he'd reverted to using English units. In the old days when space commerce went international with U.S.-Russian partnerships, even U.S. space companies went metric and the Consortium, formed with international partners, naturally followed suit.

"Do we have anything we could use as a piston and cylinder?"

"I don't know. What would we use for a working fluid?"

"Steam," Stormie said. "Put some ice in a gastight box or something, with a line to a cylinder underneath the trailer. Keep the box shaded until we're ready, then concentrate enough sunlight on it to heat the ice and drive it to steam. If we rig it right, the steam should lift the trailer enough to get the brace in place."

Gabe said, "You going to use mirrors? Sounds like Archimedes at Syracuse."

"Whatever," Bruce said.

Capell said, "A piston and cylinder? You'd blow out the seals."

"Shut up, Karl," Bruce said. "It only has to hold for a few seconds. Unless you've got a better idea."

Capell shrugged. "If you think holding the pressure in isn't a problem, why bother with making steam? We've got pressurized gas on board."

"We're breathing that gas," Stormie said, trying to keep the irritation out of her voice.

"Okay, then, why not heat up some water with the generator?"

Bruce answered before Stormie. "No way to run water through it. Even if we could do it, it's a long way to run the steam lines back to the trailer."

"No, that's not what I mean," Capell said. "Set up a separate heater and run power cables out the back."

"Maybe, if we had cables that long. But you know how hot it gets in the sunlight here. Seems easier to use that, if it'll work."

"And if it doesn't?"

"Then we see what we can do differently before we head back."

The two of them fell into a two-way debate about what could be used to build the contraption. Stormie was glad to stay out of it, and noted that Gabe had steered clear of most of the arguing. *Very diplomatic, Mr. Morera.* She was surprised to see that for once Gabe wasn't hiding behind whatever book he was reading on his datapad; he was unwrapping a small block of the processed cheese everyone loved so much.

Gabe broke off a bit of cheese and ate it, but Stormie kept her attention focused on the wrapper. Capell was right about the cylinder idea: it wouldn't hold enough pressure to lift the trailer. She hated to admit it, but now she had another idea.

"Bruce," she said. The others looked at her. "It kills me to say this, but Karl's got a point. If we can't keep the pressure in, we won't get any lift."

"You got a better idea now?" Bruce said.

Stormie took the wrapper from Gabe. She folded it and blew air into it. "We need an airbag," she said.

CHAPTER TWENTY-NINE

Ice Jack

Saturday, 19 January 2036

Bruce typed and queued another message while everyone suited up. He divided duties among them, including Capell, who seemed sullen but cooperative.

Stormie's first task was to find a suitable mirror. She walked all around the Turtle and examined it closely, but all the curved metal pieces—headlight reflectors and so forth—would have too short a focal length. Even their little parabolic antenna looked too deep to serve as a good reflector. She needed something with a slight curve, or something that could be bent, and decided to take a closer look at the solar panels on the back of the Turtle's shell.

She climbed up next to the ARG, careful to make sure she was braced well; Van Richards' tale of derring-do had been repeated too many times for her not to think of the consequences of tumbling off the back of the big truck. Most of the panels were flat, as expected, but the ones at the edges were curved like the panels she'd seen on pictures of old-time Hughes satellites. She guessed curving a few good-sized panels so they'd continue producing power as the Sun tracked over them must've been cheaper than assembling a bunch of smaller, flat panels, but she didn't waste too much time wondering about it. She disconnected a single panel in the right rear section of the truck, without asking Bruce's permission first; that panel wouldn't see much sunlight during the last days of their trip. The worst that should happen, if they missed that panel's output, would be that they might have to eat a couple of cold meals.

"Just got an answer from Central," Bruce said over the radio. "They want us to drop the trailer and come back now."

Gabe said, "So are we?"

Bruce said, "Not yet. My second message went up when that message downlinked from the satellite. It'll be a while before they even know what we're doing."

Stormie carefully pried the photovoltaic substrate from the solar panel and laid it on the trailer bed. She used an aluminized sheet on the curved cover glass to complete her mirror. It wasn't a perfect mirror: the glass was curved axially, like a funhouse mirror, instead of having a single focus like a parabolic dish, and she couldn't smooth all the crinkles out of the Mylar. She hoped it would be good enough. She shone it on some nearby rocks until she found the focus and satisfied herself that she could aim it. Then she carried it around to the side of the trailer to see everyone else's progress.

Bruce and Capell were still fashioning the jack, so Stormie went to help Gabe. He had staged bracing under the trailer that would hold it up for repairs. Then he'd attached a cable and come-along to the rock that caused all the trouble in the first place, anchored the other end to a boulder several meters off the path, and dug a small trench from the rock to the side of the path. Once the trailer was lifted and braced, he and Stormie would pull the rock out of the way while Bruce and Capell saw to the suspension. Stormie helped him dig out the last few meters of the trench, then they shifted some ice blocks away from the left side of the trailer while the other two completed their task.

"Okay, Stormie," Bruce radioed, "want to take a look at your ice jack?"

They had rigged one of the empty gas-tight transit cases with a pressure transducer and a relief valve that they scavenged off who-knew-what. Inlet and outlet lines, each with control valves, ran from that transit case to another underneath the trailer. "We took a bladder from inside one of our spent water tanks," Bruce said, "and put it in that case there. The bag should expand and push the top of the box into the bottom of the trailer. The idea is that the box'll keep the bag from getting cut on the trailer. So long as the box itself doesn't cut it."

"So it's ready to go?" Stormie asked.

"Pretty much. There's a metal box inside this transfer case here. You and Gabe take it and put a block of ice in it while Karl and I get the jack in place."

They took the smaller box—it looked like a Christmas present wrapped in aluminum foil—under the tarp to the ice storage. By the time they had it loaded with ice and back inside the bigger box, the others had the jack ready.

"Pull the lid off the little box now," Bruce said.

Stormie handed the lid to Gabe, who stepped aside to make room for Bruce. "Help me get good contact between the two boxes. Okay, hang on one second." He stepped away and came back with what looked like a small scissor-jack; he held it up, compressed it and let it go: it expanded to its original size. "Need a spring to keep the ice in contact with the wall as it melts, else we won't get decent heat transfer," he said. It took a few seconds to install the device. "Okay, we'll seal the big box now. Stormie, grab your mirror. Karl, you got that monkey shit?"

Stormie stood still for a second. Bruce was referring to the two-part RTV sealant in Capell's hand, but after the argument in the truck she bristled at the common nickname.

Get a hold of yourself, Stormie. She bounced away to get the mirror.

When he had the ice case sealed, Bruce said, "Gabe, got the brace?"

"Roger."

"Okay. Let's give that RTV a minute to set, if it's going to." Bruce went over the plan. He would work the valves to the airbag. Capell's job was to watch the pressure and open the relief valve if it got too high, while Gabe braced the trailer from underneath. When it was clear that everyone understood their roles, he said,

"Stormie, whenever you're ready."

Stormie aimed the mirror at the dark area on the side of the box. It took her a few tries to find the right pitch angle, but then a bright line of light fell on her target. Seconds flashed away in the chronometer display inside her helmet.

Work, damn it.

"Got a little pressure," Capell said slowly. "Building up now." He twisted the box a little so it caught the light more directly. "Almost there. Okay, Bruce, open your valve."

A tiny jet of steam escaped the box. It didn't billow like steam in an atmosphere, it just shot out toward the trailer. It looked like a fire hydrant shooting a spray of pure snow—only without the accompanying sound.

Bruce asked, "What can you see, Gabe?"

"Nothing yet."

"Pressure still rising," Capell said.

Gabe called, "Got some movement now. Bag's pushing the box up. One centimeter. Two. Four. Almost there. Okay, it's contacted the trailer."

Another jet of steam started pouring from the corner of the box; Stormie held the mirror steady and hoped the steam wouldn't diffuse the light too much.

"Bag's bulging out the sides now," Gabe said. "Wait, I've got movement on the trailer. Up, two, three centimeters. Keep it coming, a little more, a little more ... okay, brace is in—"

"Closing the fill valve," Bruce said. "Wait just a second to make sure it holds." The flow of steam out of the box continued.

"She's settling back down now," Gabe said. "Brace seems to be holding."

"Great. Karl, how's the pressure—"

The side of the transit case opened up and a much larger jet of silent steam, bright with reflected sunlight, came straight at Stormie.

The jet of steam hit Stormie full in the facemask. She jerked back reflexively, and her helmet rang like a thick plastic bell as something struck it. Her mind conjured another sound—a rushing sound like being under a waterfall—to go along with what her vision told her. Maybe it was the blood in her ears, but it didn't drown out the reverberating pop of whatever hit her helmet.

The steam was gone in an instant. Her suit was made to withstand the lunar temperature extremes, and a little cold steam couldn't really hurt it. The steam left behind a collection of condensed droplets on her faceplate that disappeared almost immediately.

Except for one spot.

Everything in the distance blurred as Stormie focused on the spot, a couple of millimeters in diameter. It was a pit in the faceplate, rough, circular, and definitely indented. She put her hand up to it, gingerly, but couldn't feel it through her glove.

She was afraid to breathe.

She was afraid not to breathe.

A shadow moved in front of her. Karl Capell landed there, something in his hand. He reached toward her helmet—

She gasped as if she'd been knocked in the gut, pushed Capell backward and jumped over him. She had to get to the airlock before her helmet lost integrity.

The others yelled at her as she bounced back toward the Turtle. On her third bounce she came to rest two steps away from the airlock. She stumbled on the steps but got into the lock. She focused so intently on the ding in her helmet that she could barely see past it to activate the cycle.

Pressure rose until the differential with her suit was in the green. Her lungs burned; she realized she'd been holding her breath. She stepped through into the Turtle and took off the helmet, and let herself breathe. It was dank, stale air, recycled for days and full of the sweat and stink of all four of them. It was wonderful.

O   O   O

Capell was next through the airlock. Stormie was examining the front of her helmet, feeling thoroughly stupid. The pit in the faceplate was deep, but not deep enough to warrant that level of panic. *Stupid makes mistakes, and stupid gets you dead, but stupid gets lucky sometimes.*

"What the hell is your problem?" Capell asked.

Besides you? Lord help me, I know I'm an idiot but I don't need you lecturing me. Stormie closed her eyes and started counting to ten.

"Look," he said, "you don't like me and I don't like you. Okay." He dropped something on the cushion next to her. "I was out of line before. I admit it. But when somebody's coming to help you, you don't knock 'em down." He shuffled back toward the lock.

When the lock closed behind him, Stormie looked at what he'd left her.

A standard issue stickypatch, and a sealant applicator.

Stormie didn't know whom to be more upset with: herself, for panicking, or Capell, for being right. She always counted on herself to be right. She played back the event in her mind, and realized that Capell had been coming toward her with the stickypatch in his hand. It wasn't a perfect solution, but even if her helmet had been breached the patch would've held pressure well enough to let her get back inside. But what had she done? Everything wrong. She hadn't trusted him, worried she couldn't trust him, and had reacted in fear—and maybe even anger. What if she had misjudged her jump toward the lock, and fell and really cracked her helmet?

She picked up the sealant tube and tapped it against her head.

Stupid is lucky to be alive.

O O O

Gabe came in and helped Stormie find one of the spare helmets and seal it properly with her suit. The couplings were standardized up to a point, but always needed adjustment. By the time they got back outside, Bruce and Capell had moved the troublesome rock and jury-rigged the first of two additional struts to support the broken suspension.

Stormie looked at the remains of the transit case: a five-centimeter hole was blown out of the side of it, right where one of the latches should be. Bruce explained that the case had ruptured long before they thought it would; Capell hadn't been close to opening the relief valve, and the burst disk hadn't blown. He also said he had received a message from the colony approving their plan—which was good, since they were halfway done with it.

Stormie said little as she and Gabe got the rock completely off the path, then hooked the come-along to the temporary bracing and waited. About a half hour later, Bruce was satisfied with his suspension repairs and gave them the signal to pull out the brace.

The trailer trembled and fell into place. The suspension held.

Stormie's ears were flooded with cheers and laughter from the others, but she was quiet. She wouldn't let herself feel good about their success, not after her lousy performance an hour earlier.

Back inside, Bruce announced a mandatory rest period for everyone. After that, Capell would drive and the rotation would pick up again. Stormie gritted her teeth: she would, as always, be next in the driver's seat after Capell.

Before she closed her eyes, she checked her messages. Frank said he had tried to get Gary Needham to send out a rescue—even a leapfrog of trucks with extra fuel on board—but Gary wouldn't risk it. Or the Consortium wouldn't allow it; Frank wasn't clear. Stormie smiled, though: she'd joked about getting back and rescuing him, but Frank always loved playing the knight in shining armor. Sometimes she even needed it.

And as bone-weary as she was, she probably needed it really bad.

O O O

Frank knocked on the half-open sliding door into the communications center.

Gary looked up from whatever he was reading and said, "Just a second."

Frank took out his datapad and reviewed the last message from Stormie. Her team was on its way back, and Stormie was tired but pleased that they had been able to repair the trailer suspension enough to keep going, although she anticipated that they would have to travel more slowly than normal. Her message itself would not have bothered Frank, except for the telemetered data the Turtle sent along with the message traffic. The air supply usage rate was higher than it should have been. Frank believed that Stormie must have the situation in hand, but she had not mentioned it in her message. It was important enough that she should have included it, and he was not sure if her omission was intentional—an attempt not to alarm him or anyone else—or if she had not noticed the consumption rate. There was little he could do about it; still, he was worried.

"Okay, Frank," Gary said. "How are you feeling? Do we know why everybody got sick?"

Frank started. Of course, that would be Gary's first concern. "Not conclusively," Frank said, "though I have shown Yvette all the data from my sampling and we agree the cause appears to be food-related. She suspects some of the prepackaged food, and mentioned that she may recommend developing additional biocapsules for this type of situation. But that is not why I came to see you."

"Then what's up?"

"I assume you received the message that the team is on its way back?"

Gary nodded. "Yeppir. I'm glad I didn't try to send you out, like you wanted."

"Yes, I realize it was unnecessary."

"No way you could've known they'd fix the suspension that quick. I didn't think they'd be able to. But why do I get the impression that's not what you wanted to talk about, either?"

Frank allowed himself to grin just a little; he had never been good at hiding his thoughts from people. He was, as Stormie said, transparent. Frank explained his concern about the ice team's air usage rate, and offered to submit his analysis of the data from the LVN.

"No, I don't want to see your calculations. I have enough trouble keeping up with everything else." Gary gave a lazy half wave at the console where he'd been reading earlier. "You tell me you've run the numbers, that's good enough for me. But you don't think Stormie's got the same result?"

Frank hesitated before he answered. "I am not sure," he said. "It is possible that, because she is fatigued, she has not projected the utilization rate out as far as I have. It is also possible that she has done the projections, knows what they imply, and refrained from including it in a message. She may not want to alarm the others."

Gary made a curious gesture: he closed his eyes and pursed his lips and tilted his head from side to side a couple of times. Then he looked at Frank and said, "And you probably don't want to send a message either, right?"

"I considered it, but it is also possible that I am being overly conservative. If that is the case, I would not want to alarm them without reason. It would be much more convenient to be able to discuss it with her in real time."

A shadow of anger flitted over Gary's face. "I know. I've already sent my third message down below saying, 'See? We need reliable COMSATs.' But wishing for it won't make it real. So what do you want to do?"

"I would like to prepare a replenishment supply for them. I believe we will have to meet them on their way back, and I would like to be ready."

Gary turned to the console, clicked through a couple of menus on the screen. He nodded, creased his forehead, and nodded again. "One question, Frank."

"Yes?"

"Where does something like that fall under your statement of work?" Gary looked at him and raised his eyebrows.

Strictly speaking, Frank could not say that it did. He was not as creative as James or Stormie at interpreting the contents of their statement of work, and he did not intend to try to invent something on the spot.

"I do not know," he said. "And I am not sure I care. It needs to be done, and soon, so that we do not waste time when they need us. I am happy to let the accountants and lawyers work out the finer details. But whether I do it, or someone else does it, it needs to be done."

Gary nodded, and gave a little half smile. "Then by all means, Frank, get it done."

Chapter Thirty

Emergency Frequency

Sunday, 20 January 20.36

Stormie woke when Capell went forward to start driving, but let herself sleep again. Frank had taken pity and not sent any extra work. She dreaded finding out how much would be waiting when she got back.

Her datapad alarm woke her half an hour before her shift. Gabe and Bruce were sound asleep and hardly stirred. Stormie plugged her pad into the truck and downloaded how much oxygen was still in their stores. The number came back so low she queried the truck again and got the same result. She checked their position and estimated the time remaining on their trip. A twinge became a wave of nausea as she compared their oxygen usage to the trip time and came up short.

She repeated the calculation, working from the consumption over the remaining travel time backward to the amount of oxygen needed. She got the same result. She stopped short of making up creative insults for herself for missing the problem earlier. She didn't think she could spare the time for excessive self-critique.

The time … she hadn't noticed the truck had stopped, and didn't realize it was time for her to drive until Capell came through the hatch.

He didn't say anything, which suited her like satin. They were like similar magnetic poles, repulsing each other. How much did it matter that he tried to help her? She still wanted to pummel him. She bit back a question about whether he'd kept his clothes on while he drove; being spiteful wouldn't help. With only four of them in this truck—for that matter, with only the few dozen people in the whole colony—none of them could run away from fights, but they couldn't afford to prolong them, either. They had to get along to survive.

She took a deep breath and said what she had to. "Karl." He looked up. "Thanks for trying to help me. I'm sorry I shoved you."

Behind his beard it was hard to tell what he was thinking. He nodded slightly. "That was probably hard for you to say." He scratched his neck. "No harm done."

Bruce sat up in his corner. "Time for changeover?" he asked.

"I didn't know you were awake," Stormie said.

"I wasn't."

"I need you to look at this." Stormie passed him her CommPact and started putting on her suit.

Bruce rubbed sleep out of his eyes and asked, "What?"

"Not sure if we took too long to fix the trailer or we've sprung a leak," she said, "but we don't have enough air to get back."

Capell rolled his eyes. "Oh, great."

Gabe woke, propped himself on one elbow, but said nothing.

Bruce studied the screen, handed it back, then opened his own terminal and queried the truck's computer. He rubbed his eyes again. "Looks like Snapper's hurt."

"How so?" asked Capell.

"Slow pressure loss in the number three oxygen tank," Bruce said.

"Why didn't we get an alarm?" Stormie asked.

Bruce and Capell looked at each other. Neither spoke.

Stormie looked at Gabe, who sat up a little more but just shrugged. "What aren't you two telling us?" she said.

Bruce looked as sorry as a dog that'd just been scolded for chewing up the family Bible. "It's my fault. We disabled some alarms when we stripped out the water bladder for the ice jack. I

358

forgot to re-enable them." He scrolled through a couple of menus on the computer. "Not sure if we jarred loose a fitting or took a hit from something, but we're down to the dregs in that oh-two tank."

No one spoke for what seemed a very long time, then Gabe said, "Well, we're overdue enough that we'd be rationing food anyway. Don't guess we can ration air, exactly. Won't the scrubbers make up for it?"

"They're working fine," Stormie said, "but they're just three-week filters, not the bioreactors we use in the colony. And this truck isn't as airtight as you'd think. We have little losses here and there." *Like going in and out of the airlock so much.*

"So what do we do?" Gabe asked.

"Call in another mayday," Stormie said, "and request a team to meet us with a few charged oh-two bottles." She compared her calculations to their forward progress and added, "Somewhere around Wurzelbauer Crater ought to do it."

Bruce said, "Is that your professional judgment?"

"I don't think we need to be that dogmatic," she said. "But there may be another option. If, Karl," she looked at Capell, "you're as good a plumber as you claim to be."

He was still expressionless behind his beard. Stormie shivered, a quick, sharp impulse that might have been a shudder of revulsion from just talking to him.

"What do you have in mind?" he asked.

"Can you build us an electrolytic reactor?"

Capell frowned. "Oh, yeah, I can whip one up out of Mylar and chewing gum. I'll get right on that."

"Come on, Karl," Bruce said.

Stormie held up her hand for a second. *Quit being such a smartass, Karl,* she wanted to say but didn't. "It's okay. He may not be able to. It was just a thought." She worked the problem on her CommPact as she continued. "I figure we could use a little ice so we don't run out of potable water. We could use greywater, I guess, but it might foul the reactor. Anyway, you split one block of ice at fifty-some kilograms, dump the hydrogen overboard since we don't need it in the truck, and you'll get pretty close to fifty kilograms of oxygen. At our use rate, and accounting for the CO_2 filters, that'll give us two and a half extra days—plenty of margin, since it takes less than two days to get back." She left off the fact that they'd actually require more than that to keep the partial pressure up to the point that they could breathe effectively; she'd go into that later. She picked up the spare helmet and wormed her way to the hatch. "That's less than two days as long as we're moving, though, and it's my shift."

She made her way forward to the cab. She looked around carefully, but saw nothing unusual. It looked clean enough, but she wiped the seat anyway.

o o o

When her shift was over, Stormie went back to the commons. Gabe was suited and ready, and went forward to drive. He smiled at her as he went through the hatch.

Bruce and Capell had an assortment of tubing, fittings, wires, and other equipment spread over two-thirds of the area. Stormie took off her suit and sat down, careful not to disturb their arrangement. At this rate, it looked as if they would strip the truck down to the wheels before they got back.

"I sent the message," Bruce said. "I don't know if they could get all the way to Wurzelbauer with the little trucks. That's a long haul. I expect they'll meet us at the end of Rupes Mercator or thereabouts."

"I hope we have enough to breathe that far," Stormie said. "I sent my calculations to Frank with my usual log message, we'll see if he comes up with the same result." *So much for the extra margin in his calculations.*

At the mention of her log message, Capell stiffened but kept working. Bruce didn't seem to notice. He said, "Stormie, I'm up next in the rotation, but do you mind driving for me? I need to keep working on this." He gestured at the mixture of parts.

She sighed. "Sure, Bruce. Whatever needs to be done, I'll do it." That was the way she always did things. Frank, too, which was why they worked so well together. She closed her eyes and curled up on the small cushion to get what rest she could. *Just a little while longer.*

o   o   o

Stormie took Bruce's driving shift, but not before explaining that they would need to put several ice blocks through Capell's electrolytic reactor in order to keep the atmosphere at a breathable pressure. No one was happy about that: their per-kilogram ice bonus was literally evaporating. Gabe had the best take on it: he said that as much as he loved his wife, he didn't want her spending a lot of insurance money when he could be spending a little bonus money.

When Stormie's four hours were up, she stopped the truck and made her way back from the Turtle's head.

Bruce and Capell were suited up and headed out the airlock.

"They going to get some ice?" Stormie asked Gabe. He nodded and went forward into the cab.

It was strange to be alone in the Turtle. The little compartment that was usually so crowded suddenly seemed huge. Stormie shrugged out of her suit and worked her way through some stretches until she heard the airlock cycling. As the two men brought in the ice, she checked her messages and fought back tears at Frank's admission that he already had an oxygen supply prepared to transport to them. He didn't chastise her for not catching the problem, even though he'd found it before it became obvious; he just said he would be there to meet her with whatever she needed.

By the time Bruce's shift came around again, he and Capell had the electrolysis rig going. They had shut down most of the lights and even some of the active thermal control systems in order to power the thing. Bruce went forward and took his turn at the control yoke.

The next shift change, before Capell took over driving, he and Stormie brought in two more blocks of ice. She insisted on it, to minimize the number of times they'd have to cycle the airlock. The routine continued as they crawled, kilometer by kilometer, toward home.

After Capell, Stormie drove. After her, Gabe. After him, Bruce. With every passing hour, the air seemed thick with tension but dangerously thin on everything else.

Midway through Bruce's shift, his voice came over the intercom. "We've got company, folks. Suit up and let's go meet 'em." The truck slowed and stopped.

Stormie cycled third through the airlock and climbed gingerly down. The Sun cast long shadows into the shallow bowl of Weiss crater. About thirty meters away stood a half-dozen suited figures and three of the colony's smaller trucks. Her attention was drawn to one tall figure standing by a K-bottle. Her knight hadn't brought her jewelry or flowers or candy, but he had exactly what he'd promised.

It's awkward to hug somebody when you're both wearing spacesuits, but that didn't stop her. It was more important to get that contact, even through layers of insulation and polymers, than to get some of the oxygen Frank had in the bottle.

"How are you doing, my love?" Frank radioed.

Tired. Relieved. Dirty. Stormie wasn't sure what to say. She put her gloved hand up to Frank's faceplate. "Better, now," she said.

Frank hooked her suit up to the bottle. "You did well."

The pressure in her suit tank rose bit by bit, displayed in one corner of her faceplate. She looked beyond the numbers to the big ugly Turtle with its ungainly trailer and its load of life-sustaining ice.

"Thanks," she said. She breathed deep, and smiled.

A small orange LED double-blinked and caught Stormie's attention. Her stomach was suddenly heavy, as if it were under full gravity. She switched over to the emergency frequency.

Jake Adamson's voice came over her speakers. "Okay, everybody, listen up. We're going to do a poll to see if everybody's on. When you get the green light, squawk once with the button."

In a matter of seconds, the orange blinking light became a steady green, then went out when Stormie blinked her acknowledgement. As the other acknowledgements continued, she turned on the exterior spotlight mounted on her helmet. She turned Frank so that her light shone into his helmet and she could see his face. His eyes widened a little, and he shook his head. He didn't know any more than she did.

"Okay, gang," Jake said. "Sorry to break up the little reunions, but we got an emergency call. Medical assistance needed at the fuel storage area. So, Bio, transfer enough oxygen to get the Turtle folks breathing good, but save a little in case we need it at the response site. Bruce, once you've got some air, take Snapper back to the colony and start offloading. Otherwise, everybody get in your original vehicles and we're heading out quick as we can."

Stormie keyed her microphone and said, "Jake, this is Stormie. I'd like to ride back with Frank. I can charge my suit from the K-bottle while I ride in the back of the MPV." She barely registered what she was saying. When she analyzed it in the few seconds it took Jake to respond, she decided her motivation was more because she wanted to be close to Frank than because she wanted to be far away from Karl Capell.

"Fine," said Jake. "Just make sure you're in place and ready to roll."

Frank squeezed her upper arm through the layers of her pressure suit, nodded from behind his faceplate, then they got to work. She unhooked and helped load the bottle of oxygen onto the back of the truck. He pushed her up and into place and she hooked up to the bottle again—she'd take a few more liters and make sure she left a good bit for the response.

She and Frank touched gloves, briefly, palm to palm, in a slow, intimate high five. Then he sat down next to her on the truck bed. Frank radioed Scott Herbert, who was going to drive the little truck, that he wanted to ride in back with Stormie. She smiled as Frank awkwardly put his arm around her shoulder and sat as close as possible. She snuggled next to him as the vibrations from the turbine tickled their way up her legs and the truck started to roll.

CHAPTER THIRTY-ONE

Beneath What Sky Shall Be Thy Fate

Monday, 21 January 2036

On the way to the accident scene, Frank reviewed the information Jake downloaded to the responders. The oxygen plant was now the rendezvous point for the rescue effort: east of the main colony, not far north of Rupes Mercator. It was not quite a direct line from where Frank and the rescue team had met the Turtle, but close enough that it was on their way back to the colony.

A four-person team had been installing a new tank at the fuel storage area, using one of the multipurpose vehicles fitted with a small crane on its bed. Apparently the load had shifted—it was unclear whether it was human error in the rigging, not enough ballast on the MPV, or some mechanical problem—and the tank had smashed into Trish Springer. She fell and it pinned her leg. The team immediately issued a distress call, extracted her from beneath the tank, and safed the area.

However, the only other vehicle the team had, besides the crane-equipped MPV, was one of the small, limited-range electric carts that were kept adjacent to charging stations at various points in the colony complex. They took the cart from the fuel processing station—it converted asteroidal ammonia into hydrazine—and transported Trish to the oxygen plant, where the responders would retrieve her.

"Talk about bringing a gun to a knife fight," Scott Herbert said. "All of us to pick up one person."

Frank did not think that was the most appropriate cliché, but he said nothing. The colony could not send another vehicle out to pick up Trish because his resupply effort had commandeered all of the available multipurpose vehicles. Even though Gary Needham was the one who actually made it happen, Frank felt responsible, since he had put the plan together. He would feel awful if the rescue he envisioned turned into a disaster for someone else. A line surfaced from some crevice in his brain—"defeat upon defeat, disaster on disaster"—but he could not remember its source. He pushed it back into the crack from which it had emerged.

They approached the ARPOES from the south. The setting Sun threw the autonomous processing facility into sharp relief, with a distinct terminator between the blindingly bright left side and its dimmer right side, which was only partially lit by reflections from outlying equipment.

"Okay, gang," Jake said as they approached. "Here's where we split up. Let's have the Bio team pick up Trish. She's stabilized on the e-cart, over by the scavenger pen. The rest of us, let's go on to the fuels area and see if we can get that tank stabilized. If we can, we'll set it in place and help the team finish their shift. Once things are under control, we'll let most folks head back in and leave somebody behind to replace Trish."

Frank sat up straighter and prepared to acknowledge his instructions, but before he could speak Van Richards radioed, "I'll stay behind and finish Trish's shift."

"Roger that," Jake said. "Frank, if you and Stormie are up to taking care of Trish, how about let Scott come over and go with us to the fuels area."

Frank acknowledged Jake's instructions, as did Scott, who bounded over to another MPV after he parked theirs between the oxygen processor and the scavenger holding area. Sonny Peterson, who had driven the electric cart Trish was sitting on, followed close behind.

Once he was sure no other instructions would be forthcoming, Frank switched away from the general chatter back to his and Stormie's assigned channel. "Mr. Richards certainly has a lot of energy," he said. "This will not take too long, my dear. You can stay here and rest, if you wish."

Stormie laughed a sharp little laugh, and Frank imagined her shaking her head inside her helmet. "No way," she said. "If both of us do it, it'll take even less time. And maybe we can charge the AC double."

Frank did not argue. As they exited the bed of the truck, however, he looked at her suit indicator; she had taken on only a partial load of oxygen. He asked why.

"I took enough to last until we find out whether Trish needs some," she said. "I don't need a full tank right now."

Trish's leg was roughly splinted with two pieces of metal, wrapped and affixed with duct tape. It looked as if a stickypatch had been applied to her suit before they splinted her leg. Frank switched to the common channel to ask her if her suit had been breached, but Stormie was already talking to her.

"Not a very good day for you, huh, girl?" Stormie said.

"Oh, I wouldn't say that." Trish forced out the words in quick bursts, as if she was gritting her teeth. "Just in the wrong place at the right time. I don't think it's broken. At least it doesn't hurt as bad as when my uncle's horse kicked me that time."

"So what is it about you and your husband letting things fall on you?"

"Don't joke about it. I'm never going to hear the end of it as it is."

They bantered, and Frank smiled to hear the tension in Trish's voice dissipate as she and Stormie spoke. He had never thought of Stormie as having a good bedside manner, and it pleased him to find out he may have underestimated her.

A few more lines of that poem crawled up out of his memory, and he said,

> *I do not know beneath what sky*
> *Nor on what seas shall be thy fate;*

I only know it shall be high,
I only know it shall be great.

Stormie asked quickly, as if she hadn't heard, "What's that, Frank?"

"Nothing, my love," he said. He was ashamed to admit that he still did not remember the source.

"Okay, well, we need to get Trish moved."

Frank drove the little electric cart to the back of the multipurpose vehicle. He and Stormie lifted Trish as gently as they could into the truck bed. Frank drove to the oxygen plant and plugged the cart in; by the time he returned, Stormie had Trish hooked up to the K-bottle of oxygen and was climbing down to the surface. Stormie motioned with her hand, and Frank switched back to their channel.

"I'll be right back," she said. "I assume you heard Trish say that Sonny added that second splint when they stopped here. It looks like he left some metal scraps behind from where he cut that piece of tubing to length, and I want to go pick them up. No sense letting them stay there and have somebody get hurt on them, or gum up the works of a scavenger when it runs over them."

She bounced away, and Frank climbed up into the cab of the multipurpose vehicle and started running the pre-drive checklist. He had just applied power to the gauges and was reading the fuel level when a nagging sensation, almost like a breath of air against his left cheek, made him look toward where Stormie was gathering pieces of metal.

Fifty or sixty meters away, she knelt in the dust. Her left hand was holding her right shoulder.

"Frank," she said, "I have a problem."

O O O

Stormie's trouble meter tickled her again as she approached the litter Sonny had left. She didn't expect the trouble to start quite so soon, though.

It began with the light brush and whirring sound of wind inside her pressure suit. She couldn't believe it at first, because she had done nothing to damage her suit. She had just bent down on one knee, after she made sure the spot was clear and nothing there was a puncture danger, and reached out to pick up a wad of duct tape next to the cut-off end of one of Trish's splints.

It was easy enough to locate the source of the leak. The breeze blew across her face from left to right, and up her body from the depths of her suit, directly toward her shoulder.

Except that it wasn't a breeze. It was a gust. She choked back a little laugh because it reminded her of her own name.

Stormie radioed Frank that she had a problem, and told him, "Bring the biggest stickypatch you can find."

She pressed with her gloved hand on the outside of her suit, trying to close the hole wherever it might be. The shoulder joint made it hard to find exactly where the hole was. The wind's force began to fade.

She wished she had a full tank of oxygen.

She fought the temptation to hold her breath; she forced herself to breathe shallowly. She doubted it would make much difference in the long run whether the pressure differential in her lungs burst some alveoli or not, if there wasn't enough pressure in her suit for her to breathe at all. She wasn't too afraid of the bends, since they didn't breathe as much nitrogen as an Earth normal atmosphere. Higher percentage of oxygen, lower overall pressure, right partial pressure for breathing, less stress on the materials that had to keep that pressure from escaping into the vacuum.

Her thoughts scattered. Her vision blurred.

A suited figure she assumed to be Frank landed a few meters in front of her. Her eyes followed a fine spray of dust that arced in a ballistic trajectory originating at the figure's feet. The dust sparkled as it flew in the low angled sunlight. It was really quite beautiful.

She closed her eyes and held the image of the dust as she slipped forward. She put her hands in front of her to catch herself, but she wasn't sure if she succeeded. She had a vague sensation of new pressure on her shoulder and arm, but it was indistinct, as if she was growing smaller and farther away from whatever it was outside her.

The image of the beautiful dust faded to blackness in her eyes, and Stormie was sad that she hadn't gotten to tell Frank how pretty it was.

O   O   O

Frank skidded to a halt. He caught Stormie as she pitched forward, and let her settle on her left side. She had been holding her right shoulder, and that was the only place he could think to put the stickypatch. His gloved hands were clumsy trying to remove the packaging, and he hesitated a second figuring out how to orient it. He pushed it into place and pressed it down without bothering to smooth it.

"Mayday, mayday," Frank called. "I need an oxygen bottle A-S-A-P."

He rolled Stormie on her back and looked at the indicators on her suit. Too many of them were red. Too many of them were dark.

He opened the access panel on her suit and on his, found the emergency fitting, and linked their suits together. It was a survival procedure they had first learned in the mine in Utah and practiced several times in the New Mexico desert, by which they could scavenge oxygen from an incapacitated colonist—the assumption being that the colonist was already dead, and the situation was so dire that breathing air from a dead person's pressure suit was the only means of surviving. The method had the ungainly name of Emergency Life-Support Pressure Acquisition Procedure. Frank was determined to use the procedure not to his advantage, but to Stormie's.

He watched the pressure in his suit drop as their suits equalized. He wondered why no one had come to help, but that did not concern him as much as seeing the pressure between their two suits continue to fall even as he input more of his oxygen.

The stickypatch must have slowed the air loss, but not stopped it completely. It was still trickling away. He pushed down on its edges as best he could, but the reading did not stabilize. He could not leave to get more patches, and he was afraid to move Stormie lest he open the leak wider.

Frank repeated his call. His own words vibrated back to him through the connection between his suit and Stormie's. He realized then that he was still on their private channel.

Stormie's eyes flickered open. They were unfocused, and a little dim, but they were beauty to him.

Frank selected the broadcast channel and sent his distress call a third time. Even as he heard an acknowledgment, he realized with despair that as long as her suit continued to leak the air supply would not support them both until help arrived. He had not topped off his oxygen tank, and Stormie's limited supply had bled away.

Oh, wife, why could you not have thought of yourself?

The closest person was Trish; she was rebroadcasting his mayday, now that it had gone out. Everyone else was at the fuel site by now. It was not far—just over the rise to the northeast, a little farther into the Sea of Clouds. On Earth the fuel and oxidizer stations would be separated to keep their contents from mixing, but here any spill would flash to vapor in the lunar vacuum. The separation distance was not a function of chemistry or of blast overpressure—there being no air to carry a detonation shock wave—but of fragmentation distance, since pieces of a ruptured tank could fly hundreds of meters and cause more damage to nearby facilities. All these facts, so commonplace and innocuous, bombarded Frank and left him feeling more alone than he ever had. Trish was incapable of moving from the back of the truck to bring the nearest oxygen bottle, and the others were simply too far away.

The sense of isolation clung to him more tightly than his pressure suit. He had only one chance to save Stormie's life.

Frank shut off the intake to his own suit, and shunted his supply tank directly to hers. "Lord, forgive me," he said.

He shut down the circulating equipment in his suit, and it became utterly quiet. His suit creaked and moaned as he lay down next to Stormie, but then the silence descended again. Into that silence, he spoke what he expected to be his last words.

"I love you, Stormie Gale."

The atmosphere inside his suit became thick and warm with his own exhalations. He put his suit into typing mode, and wrote a few lines until tremors and then convulsions turned his thoughts and words to gibberish.

O O O

Van had once described himself to Barbara as a mental cockroach. By that he meant that sometimes he acted without

371

thinking; in the same way that a cockroach will run because it detects minute changes in air currents and sends the impulses directly to its legs without going to its brain, he tended to act on stimuli while other people were still processing them.

So when Frank's distress call came over the radio, he was in the cab of the nearest MPV and had started warming it up before Trish repeated the call.

The problem was, the catalyst bed wasn't heated up enough. When the vehicle stopped, in order to save power, they kept the catalyst warm but not hot. That put the turbine efficiency way down at the bottom of the curve, and Van found himself tapping on the control yoke to try to speed the damn thing's warmup as Frank asked for forgiveness over the radio.

He could almost run the kilometer to where they were faster than he could drive it, but it wouldn't do any good to get there empty-handed. He couldn't carry a K-bottle, even in low gravity; the thing would be too awkward.

Van hit the yoke again as the turbine labored to get up to speed. Frank told Stormie he loved her.

The hell with this.

He jumped down from the cab, stumbled a little in the powdery dust, and started loping in their direction as fast as he could carry himself. He might not be able to get the oxygen to them, but he could get to them and maybe carry them to some oxygen. He radioed Jake to follow when they could.

Time spread out in front of him. It seemed as if he ran through gelatin. Halfway there, as he crested a small rise, he decided this might not have been the best idea. His knee screamed at him that he was an idiot. He didn't disagree.

He stopped by the cab of their MPV, slick with sweat and breathing hard, and looked around. It took him a moment to find them, over by the scavenger corral, because they were both prone. With the angle of the Sun and the crazy shadows, it was hard at first to pick them out against the backdrop of dozens of scavengers waiting patiently to be sent back out to gather more lunar soil for processing.

Van landed next to them, and took in the situation with a glance.

"Jake," he said, "this is bad." He knelt down and checked their suit status and continued, "Looks like Frank rigged a dead man circuit here."

"Say again?" Jake's voice was too loud in Van's helmet; he wished they would rig the suits to mute the voice a little the farther away the speaker was.

Van worked while he talked. "Frank's got Stormie's suit rigged to scavenge off his oh-two supply. He bypassed his own intake, the way you would in the ELSPAP."

"Can you put him back on line? We're right behind you with a bottle of oxygen."

"No," Van said, and swallowed hard at the finality of his pronouncement. He didn't want to say any more, but Jake had to know the situation. "He's got no vitals, and his tank's down to almost unbreatheable anyway. I get barely anything on Stormie. We'll be lucky to save her."

"Well, get ready to unhook her from him. We're rolling up, only about thirty meters behind you now."

Van told Jake to get two big stickypatches ready, then he disconnected Stormie from Frank's suit, picked her up and carried her to the truck. He didn't notice who hooked her suit up to the oxygen bottle, because he grabbed the stickypatches from Jake and applied them to Stormie's suit over and around the patch that was already on her shoulder.

The pressure in Stormie's suit rose, stabilized, and held.

A hand touched his arm. "Good work," Jake said.

Inside his helmet, Van shook his head. "No such thing as good work on a bad day."

CHAPTER THIRTY-TWO

Salient Details

Jim was still a little nervous behind the wheel of his van, even when it was driving for him. This was the farthest out from Santa Barbara that he had gone in many weeks, and he could think of a thousand and one other places he would rather be.

He was grateful at least that he wasn't on a timetable. He took the scenic route, avoiding the Pacific Coast Highway in favor of the much smaller, slower roads. He drove through rolling hills on the other side of the mountains from the ocean, where dry brown stalks of winter grass waved lazily in the breeze. He passed towering eucalyptus trees that guarded the road and sheltered modest, mission-style homes. He wanted to drive forever and never stop.

It was almost midday when the van pulled up in front of the Pastorellis' house. A number of cars were parked along the street and in the driveway, but they had thoughtfully put up a sign designating a handicapped space for him.

A cold wind whipped through the van as the door opened and his ramp lowered. He shivered, perhaps feeling the breeze more keenly than usual, or maybe, along with it, the freezing stares of unseen eyes in the windows of the house. They were watching;

people always did, whether he dismounted the van on the street or in the hospital parking lot or at the mall. They meant nothing by it. People were programmed to pay attention to the unusual, from millennia of learning that the unusual could be dangerous.

He hated the turns his mind was taking these days. As if Frank's parents needed to be reminded of the dangers of the world, here came his paralyzed friend and financier to express his condolences.

Jim paused at the bottom of the ramp, tempted to turn around and drive back up and away. He shivered again, turned his chair up the entryway, and pushed the button on his remote to make the van lift the ramp and close the door.

Frank's parents received him cordially, and about as warmly as he had any right to expect. Frank's father, Benjamin, was only a few years older than Jim; he was a little stooped, but still a big man. He was well experienced in the difficulties of the world, having seen workers die on job sites where he was an engineer and having dealt with all manner of hardships in his years as a missionary. Ishigu, Frank's mother, was polite but not kind. Small and straight-backed, she had an accent much thicker than Frank's and eyes that did not cry, but hid none of their sorrow.

They took the pecan pie Jim had brought—he thought he remembered it being one of Frank's favorites—and retreated into the throng of family. They left Jim alone in the front room, and he wheeled himself into an unobtrusive spot and sat in silence.

When Jim had told Stormie he planned to come visit Frank's parents, she quietly and sadly warned him against it. He would not be welcome, she said.

He was content to be ignored. To the Pastorellis, he facilitated their son's demise, not their son's dream. They didn't understand—possibly they couldn't understand, and certainly had not shared—that dream. They would not want to hear, and Jim would not want to explain, that Frank's loss blasted a profound depth of grief in him that might come close to their own, because it reminded him of Meredith's death before her similar dream had a chance to be achieved.

Jim tried not to pay too much attention to the conversations taking place in the next room. He heard Stormie's name two or three times, and his own name once. The time passed more slowly than the creeping progress of any freeway traffic jam. As the silence lengthened, Jim picked up a book off the table next to him; it was a heavy, dense text, entitled *The Gospel of John*. He thumbed through it, wondering how someone could write a book so thick about a part of the Bible that was only a few pages long.

"Are you familiar with the Gospel of John?" Benjamin Pastorelli asked. Frank's father stood over Jim, not in a menacing way but in a manner that exuded authority.

Jim shrugged and lifted the little book. "Not this familiar," he said.

"In the beginning was the Word," Benjamin said. He tilted his head and looked at Jim expectantly.

That emphasis on "word" reminded Jim of something. His frustration with his broken brain returned full force, because it seemed to be something that should have come to mind immediately. He looked past Frank's father and struggled to pull the knowledge out of his mental quicksand. It was something he had learned at Pepperdine before he transferred....

"And the Logos was with God, and the Logos was God," Jim said.

Benjamin nodded approval. "My son knew the Gospels, Mr. Fennerling, and the Epistles, and the Psalms, and the Proverbs and the Prophets and the Law. I had begun to think that he had abandoned all of it, because his wife would have none of it."

"And then you read his last message."

"Yes. 'Forgive me, Father.'" The big man shuddered. He closed his eyes. For a long moment he held still; he took a deep breath and stretched his arms as if he wanted to brace himself against anything or nothing. "I suppose," he said, "I must take some small comfort that he expressed at the end what he had seemed to deny for so long."

Another phrase occurred to Jim, with a quickness that surprised him. "Train up a child in the way he should go."

Benjamin shook his head. "That is where I failed."

"I don't understand."

Mr. Pastorelli took the book from Jim, passed it from hand to hand and fanned through the pages. "There is training in righteousness," he said, "that is, in right living, that we all need. But the word 'train' has another meaning. I don't know if you were ever in the military, but you may have heard the expression to 'train your sights' on something. To aim at something.

"I don't think I aimed my son in the right direction," he said. "I saw his destiny differently than he saw it. I did not train him up in the way *he* should go, but in the way I thought he should go. I failed. I failed to convince him to take another path, a path which would have left him alive right now. That itself would have been a different kind of failure, because even though he might be alive he would be miserable.

"But I also failed to tell him how proud I was of him."

He paused, closed his eyes for a moment and opened them again, wet and shiny, and said, "No. How proud I *am* that he had the courage to have a dream and to follow it. And to achieve it, even for a short time." He hung his head.

Jim rehearsed and discarded in quick succession half a dozen platitudes. The silence stretched, and he was afraid to break it because it would come back to the fact that he was the one who helped Frank achieve that dream, and his father was the one who tried to talk him out of it.

Jim realized that he should not have been allowed in the house at all. His attendance must hurt Frank's family as much as it would for a skydiving instructor to show up at the funeral of a novice who had been killed because of a faulty parachute. His very presence must increase their sorrow and discomfort, yet they tolerated him.

Jim turned his chair toward the door, in such a way that he could slide by Frank's father without him having to move. Benjamin looked up at the motion.

"I know this is no consolation," Jim said, "but Frank had courage and character, and he had to learn them from somewhere. I think he learned them from you. He learned what was right, and how to do what was right no matter the consequences or the cost. And no matter where he went or what he decided to do—no matter what dream he chose to pursue—he would always have the courage and the character that he learned from you. And that, sir, is not a failure."

O   O   O

Stormie laid her hand on Frank's pillow. Even in the low light her dark hand contrasted with the white pillowcase. Tomorrow would be a week since Frank's death, and she was still searching in her jumbled memory for salient details about that day.

She hadn't fully understood what had happened when they got her out of her suit. She'd been groggy and disoriented when they got her inside, and not much more cognizant when they pulled Frank out of his suit; she had held Frank's still-warm hand and muttered at him to wake up, wake up, until someone pulled her away. She didn't comprehend until later that Frank's hand had been warm from being in his insulated suit rather than from its own warmth.

Yvette had given her sedatives on that first day, and dreaming and waking mixed in Stormie's mind in uncomfortable ways. She did not work, and a sense of guilt burdened her as the days passed; she thought of sampling and testing and maintenance that she was neglecting, but she could not bring herself to do it. She must have eaten, but she remembered no meals, no drinks, no conversations. She remembered hugs from various crying, sadly-smiling ladies, and the vague discomfort of knowing she hadn't properly bathed and must smell overripe. The Stewarts had convened a memorial service, but Stormie remembered the event as if it was a story someone had told her, not something she had attended; even the tunes of the songs Maggie played out of her datapad were so mixed up in Stormie's head that she didn't recognize them.

Stormie closed her eyes, took a deep breath, held it, and pushed her face deeper into her pillow. The pillowcase was cold and damp. She exhaled into it and warmth bathed her face. Against the backdrop of darkness, in either memory or dream, tiny, scintillating lights arced across her field of vision. She didn't know what they were or what they meant.

She rolled back over and looked up at the curving bulkhead. On the other side of that thin layer lay a meter or so of lunar soil, and beyond that, practically nothing but radiation and elemental hydrogen and the single oasis of life that was the Moon's big sister. Stormie turned her head toward the direction where the Earth was and counted off the days that had passed. The Earth should be almost full now. Was it shining down in approval of what they were building here, or in mockery for their attempt to tame this desert of dust?

Stormie shook her head. Part of her wanted to hide away from both the world she was in and the world she had come from. She was still technically under observation, and had a ready supply of Yvette's little pills, but if she let herself escape that way too often she would want to escape permanently.

She crawled to the edge of the bed and sat up. After a little bout of vertigo, she pulled on a blue jumpsuit and went to the Lunar Life Engineering laboratory.

The lab wasn't as clean as she'd expected it to be. Frank had a habit of cleaning everything twice and he would've been the last person in it, but the small bench was disorderly enough that Stormie knew someone had been working there within the last couple of days. The casing and guts of a water filter lay on a pale green towel on the bench; next to the towel, a tray held the screws from the case and three sizes of jeweler's screwdrivers.

On the big monitor, the digital triptych she and Frank had bought in Santa Barbara seemed to mock her as it transitioned from one frame to another. It was a fantasy landscape in vivid hues, with an unexpected sense of depth and distance, and Stormie watched it cycle twice, resisting the urge to sweep the water filter pieces onto the floor. The low gravity probably wouldn't break anything, anyway.

She wiped a sudden tear from the corner of her eye and sat down at the main terminal. She plugged her CommPact in, accessed the company's memory module, and opened the logs on the big monitor. She breathed a little easier when text replaced the images.

She went back three weeks, to the day of their pre-briefing for the ice run, skimmed her own entries and read Frank's. She became accustomed to wiping away additional tears when the words on the screen began to blur.

Starting the day she left, Frank quoted her reports from the Turtle verbatim in their company log—adding little commentaries of his own to what he cut and pasted. His log entries were routine until he was laid low by food poisoning along with a good proportion of the rest of the colony. Stormie had forgotten about that; it seemed so long ago.

She expected to see a sizeable gap in the timeline, but instead found a series of very brief entries signed by Barbara Richards. They covered filter maintenance and some water sampling while Frank was sick … but they continued after Frank's entries began again. He had mentioned getting help when he was incapacitated, and even suggested it as a rationale for exempting their company from future ice lotteries, but he hadn't said anything about Barbara continuing to help after he was better.

Stormie frowned. She would have to contact Jim to see how he and Frank paid Barbara for her time. All of Barbara's log entries were time-stamped late in the evening, so she was doing work for LLE after her Consortium shifts were over; it wouldn't be fair not to pay her.

She decided to figure it out later, and read on.

But there was so little to read. So few entries, so short, and so hard to read through tears she no longer tried to stop.

She paused at the last entry, sat back on the stool, wiped her nose, and stared into the bright little light above her. She wasn't sure she could read it again; the first time, when she was on the line with Jim, had been hard enough. It made her want to scream, so she did—but she kept the sound behind clenched teeth. The noise built inside her head, and pain and heat built along with it, and she did not care. She held on to the heat as if it were a coal from the damn burning bush, always hot and never consumed, and she fed the fire with all of her anger at Frank for what he did, and her anger at herself for being angry at him. But no matter how much pain and frustration she fed to it, no matter that it grew so hot that she could barely differentiate her tears from her sweat, it wasn't enough to fill the aching crater that Frank's loss had blown into her soul.

She shivered, licked salty residue from her lips, and then shook herself more vigorously to try to bring herself back to the present.

An amber box emblazoned "NOTAC"—"Notice to All Colonists"—flashed in the upper left corner of the monitor. Gary Needham periodically issued such reports on hazardous conditions or procedural changes or other important topics. Stormie clicked on the box and the notice filled the screen.

Nausea added to the pain and heat in her body.

The notice required all colonists to increase vigilance on pressure suit contamination and maintenance, based on analysis of her suit's failure.

An unnamed investigative team had concluded that the joints of her suit, and those of the other three ice run participants, were badly degraded from excess exposure to abrasive lunar dust. After examining the joint on Stormie's suit, they pressure-checked the other three. Bruce Lindsey's sprang major leaks in both knees and one elbow, and the others performed nearly as badly. The investigators concluded that fatigue, excessive EVAs, and insufficient time and space in the LVN combined to make proper suit decontamination impractical.

Stormie noted the word: not impossible, but impractical. Implying that they could've done better at keeping their suits clean if they'd wanted to. The notice stopped short of saying she and the others had been negligent, but the insinuation aggravated her. It was more fuel on her emotional fire.

She closed the notice, which uncovered the log queue. She stared at it for a long time before she opened Frank's last entry.

He'd typed it while he was taking his last breaths. His CommPact had recorded every letter, and held onto them for safekeeping until it automatically copied the entry to their data module when someone brought it into the lab. If she wanted, she could probably figure out a way to have the system replay the entry in the time sequence in which he typed it. It would be more like hearing the words, and more than anything she wished she could hear his voice again. But if he had spoken … to redirect that line of thought, she added a new pain to her awareness by clenching her fist so her nails dug into her palm.

The first few lines were all business, so typical of Frank, although more telegraphic than his usual complete sentences. Then it changed, and threw everything Stormie knew about her husband into disarray.

SP's suit compromised. Patch ineffective, still leaking.
No time to retrieve another.
Suits connected. Insufficient supply 4 2.
Help requested. No time.
FP tank plumbed to SP. Cut off personal supply.
Waiting.
Forgive me, Gale, for I know not what I do.
I miss you already
forgive me, father, for i know what i have done
my only choice.
bad headache
other pain all gone my love / no fire
hard er to type now. hard 2 think
hard 2 breathe
breathe
breatheonme bbreathofgod
fil me w lif

The flames of anger rose again inside her, high enough that the backs of her eyes tingled with heat. Was it petty of her to be angry more than thankful? She pushed that thought away. She didn't care.

Why, Frank?

She hated herself for her failure.

She was ashamed of ever wanting him to rescue her, like a knight on horseback set to challenge a dragon threatening a damsel. She was no damsel, and didn't deserve such a knight. Scenario after scenario—Frank going back for another stickypatch, or driving the MPV over to her, or trying to carry her to the truck—all ended with Frank still alive. Even if she ran out of time, he wouldn't. He didn't have to. Except he did.

It didn't help that she knew she would have done the same for him. If anything, that made it worse: she would've preferred it that way. Her knight deserved to live, precisely because he was so good and pure and noble.

Damn you, Frank.

But beneath her thoughtless, inconsiderate rage at him for saving her was a more profound and disturbing sense of … she had no other word for it than betrayal. The way he so blithely retreated into blind faith … if he had cried out aloud, she might think he was panicked and thrashing like a drowning man, but he had *typed* that message. Typed it, and managed to make it sound almost casual.

She couldn't understand it, and couldn't relate to it. He'd told her he wanted to have a church wedding not because he believed in it, but because his parents did; he'd nodded in silent agreement every time she pointed out the hypocrisies of the hyper-pious; he'd been as orthodox an evolutionist as any direct descendent of Darwin. But, there on the screen, what came to him in the end? A hymn as old as any Mother Mac would've sung. Had he needed some comfort at the end, and was it a comfort that he had denied himself because of her?

It was not a comfort she could share. The only comfort she took was that he said his other pain, the recurrent pain they shared, was gone. She supposed she should be grateful to the universe for that, even though she still carried the pain with her.

A miniature roar warned Stormie before Dusty the cat rubbed against her calf. The wastrel looked up at her and repeated its greeting.

She turned off the monitor, and gathered the cat up in her arms. Stormie was tired of thinking, and wondering, and wishing Frank had found a way to live. She needed to talk to someone. She thought about tracking down Barbara Richards—Frank had trusted her with some of their work, maybe Stormie could trust her, too. Central Control would know where she was, but she was probably working.

"That's what I need to be doing," she told the cat. "Working."

She didn't want to, but it would do her good.

She set the cat down and shooed it away, pulled up to the bench, and started tearing into the half-repaired filter unit.

CHAPTER THIRTY-THREE

Such Affinity for This Barren Place

The junction tunnel shone like the interior of a diamond. Every surface gleamed, and smelled of antiseptic. The FDD chamber rested, erect in its place on the wall. It loomed over the already small space, a vulture waiting to devour anyone unwary.

Barbara hated the damn thing. She sat on the floor, back against the bulkhead opposite from the torture chamber for the dead.

"Excuse me, Ms. Richards?"

Barbara cringed at the voice, and immediately regretted her reaction. She hoped Stormie didn't notice; she might not understand it. Barbara looked away from the hatch where Stormie stood, which unfortunately brought her gaze back to the desiccator.

"It's Barbara, Stormie, you know that."

"Is this a bad time?" Stormie asked.

The corners of Barbara's mouth turned up of their own accord. The question was more the type of courtesy that Frank would have offered; Stormie was known more for direct, forthright contact. More forceful than tactful.

If it was me, I probably wouldn't know how to act anymore either.

"No," Barbara said. "I'm just thinking."

Stormie came into the junction and sat cross-legged to Barbara's left. "I've been wanting to thank you for helping Frank in the lab when he got so sick," she said.

Now Barbara smiled fully. "He was so determined to keep working, he never would've gotten better. He wanted desperately to help figure out what was wrong."

"That sounds like Frank."

"After that, I just stopped by and helped with what I could."

"I appreciate it," Stormie said. She fidgeted, twisting her ID ring around and around on her finger. "I wish I'd been here to help."

"You were dealing with troubles of your own, I think."

"I wanted to pay you for your time, but we've got some company issues. Once things settle out, maybe in a couple of weeks, you can add up your hours and I'll make it happen."

Barbara shook her head. "No need for that. It's just the way I was brought up—you help your neighbor when they need a hand." She found the words hard to say; they bound up with memories of the ranch until they were as big as apples and stuck in her throat.

She changed the subject. "What company issues?"

Stormie had a hard time keeping her composure. Her response came slowly. "The insurance company refused to pay out on Frank's policy. And the Consortium is threatening again to buy out our investors. Our partner—my partner—no, *our* partner is trying to stop them. And fight the insurance company. And keep me from losing my mind." She laughed the kind of laugh you use to cover the pain of extracting a big splinter. "He's not doing a good job with any of it."

"Why won't they pay?"

Stormie took a deep breath and held it for a second. Then, almost inaudibly, she said, "Insurance policies don't pay out for suicide."

Barbara put her hands flat on the cool floor and leaned forward, tense from toes to forehead. "That's ridiculous. That's like ... not paying out for the person who pushes someone out from in front of a car, or pulls somebody out of a fire but goes back in to look for other people. That's just ... wrong." She leaned over, reached out, and grasped Stormie's hand. "Your husband was a good man. Van told me a few days ago how impressed he was with Frank's self-control. His determination. He said he didn't think he could do what Frank did, not with the same kind of composure."

Barbara knew she couldn't have done it. To have kept under control and typed out a cogent message while suffocating … she didn't think she knew anyone with that sort of will power.

Stormie hung her head, and Barbara gathered her into her arms. She shook, but Barbara wasn't sure if she was crying or struggling not to.

Barbara remained silent. It was better not to talk too much, and she probably already had; even saying good things had a way of backfiring. She reflected again, for at least the hundredth time, on how it would be for her if she was in Stormie's place. The seedling of resolution that had sprouted in her heart spread a few new branches.

"We'll help you fight this," Barbara said. "We'll call people, blast every portal on the Net. We'll make it right."

Stormie sat back and wiped her eyes. "Thank you."

"Frank was a good man," Barbara repeated. "That's why I did it myself."

"Did what?" Stormie asked.

Barbara sighed. Again she had probably said too much. She wasn't supposed to tell; she couldn't remember the details of the nondisclosure agreement, but as her resolution blossomed and grew she found she didn't care what the AC might do to her.

It was supposed to make it easier on everyone, especially the next of kin, not to know who processed a loved one's body. Barbara and Stormie's names were probably on the bottom of the list after working on the dead miner last September—Stormie would've been exempted anyway from mutilating her husband's body—but that experience had bonded her to Stormie in a way Barbara barely understood. Every other interaction she had with Stormie and Frank had been good: their first meeting in the training facility, when Stormie joked with her; the card games and parties that BD and Maggie organized; working with Frank to collect samples and keep the air and water flowing. Maybe her bond with Stormie was part of what led her to help Frank when he got so sick.

Barbara nodded at the upright coffin, the FDD, standing like an Iron Maiden against the far bulkhead. "I thought it was wrong that they would hold a lottery," she said, "so I volunteered." Tears welled up in the bottoms of her eyes; she looked up and blinked, and they traced ticklish paths down her cheeks. "I think the last person who sees you should be a friend."

Stormie stared at Barbara. Her face was devoid of emotion: no anger, no sadness, no pain showed on her dark features. She scooted back a little bit, and looked from Barbara to the recovery station and back again.

"I'm not sure what to say." Her voice, like her face, was flat and hid all feeling.

Barbara looked down, ashamed at Stormie's scrutiny. It was her turn to fidget, and she didn't waste it. "I'm not, either. I think it might have been partly because of what you said to me when we first met."

"I don't know what you mean."

"You asked me about Van's accident, and said you would forgive Frank anything as long as he came back to you alive … I said I thought—"

"—sometimes we love them too much.…"

"Yeah, but that's not really right. I mean, it's not really possible, and it's not *right*. We shouldn't conditionalize it. It should be that you would forgive Frank anything, that I would forgive Van anything.…" Barbara paused, and wiped her eyes and nose. "I'm sorry. I shouldn't lecture, and I wasn't supposed to tell you at all. I don't quite know why I did. I do know one thing: I can't ever do that again. That's why I'm leaving."

Barbara slid back until she touched the wall again, and leaned into it for support. Before the silence became any more uncomfortable, she said, "I haven't told Van yet. But when the next shipload of people gets here, I'm leaving. Whether he comes with me or not. I've already talked to my dad, and he's going to help me pay the penalty for breaking my AC contract and I'll work the ranch to pay him back.

"I thought I had what it takes to live here, but I'm going back where I can see blue sky and feel the wind and the Sun. I'm not strong enough for this. I'm not as strong as you."

Barbara turned her head to Stormie, who was still looking intently at her. She imagined all possibility of friendship evaporating around her like morning dew, and wished she was already gone, away from the immediacy of this awful place and the feeling that she had betrayed and hurt someone she liked.

Stormie stood. She stepped across the junction and rested one hand on the desiccation chamber.

Without looking back at Barbara, she asked, "Did you ... take care with him?"

The junction lights hurt Barbara's eyes. She blinked away tears. "Yes," she said. "I think so."

Stormie walked out the same way she had come in.

O   O   O

Thursday, 7 February 2036

Van wondered if this would be the last sunrise he would see on the Moon.

He was outside early for his shift. He'd driven one of the little electric carts out away from the colony complex to a clear spot for a good view of the sunrise. As the first bit of the Sun appeared, he checked his time display.

In a little over an hour he would ride out with the rest of the crew to lay another couple dozen meters of acceleration rails for the launch system. Within six months the rails would stretch another twelve kilometers across the plain of Mare Nubium. Every kilometer of new rail would reduce the amount of fuel needed to launch supply and cargo ships from the colony, because the vessels would accelerate along the rails by ground power; every kilometer meant less and less fuel consumption and more and more cargo capacity. In the end, he supposed, the fuel savings might mean more than the added cargo since the fuel could be broken down into other constituents for the colony's use. The bottom line stayed the same, though: every hour he spent working on this project was an investment in the colony's long-term survival.

And he might not be around to see it survive.

It had been a little over a week since Barbara told him she wanted to leave. She seemed as determined as he'd ever seen her, and he'd taken it all in without speaking. She'd been smart to tell him at suppertime in Grand Central with a dozen people eating and talking around them. Even though she'd been quiet and he'd been silent, everyone figured out what was going on.

When they got back to their room, she cried in his arms. Holding her gently was one of the hardest things he'd ever done. He wanted to squeeze her until she yelled. That wouldn't help, though—him or her. He held her, and she cried, and her tears evaporated on his anger and froze inside his soul.

He hated the cold feeling that developed inside him, and in the past week he'd done everything he could think of to thaw it. He started by trying to talk Barbara out of leaving, and when that didn't work he had Beverly Needham talk to her—she'd been so instrumental in keeping Barbara in the program to begin with. But Belladonna came up empty, too. He knew he'd lost the battle when she agreed that Barbara should go home—and encouraged him to go with her.

After three days of icy coldness, Gary wanted to know if he was staying or leaving. Van didn't know what to tell him.

He wasn't sure he could stay, legally, and he hadn't asked. He was afraid that, since their contract with the Consortium was a joint contract, he wouldn't have any choice.

When his alarm signaled time to go, Van drove the short way back to the colony. Around him the shadows had just started retreating. It always took so much longer than on Earth, which made it all the more exotic. He didn't know why he felt such affinity for this barren place. Why should a sunrise on the Moon affect him so? He could see the light from it, and get some of the heat through his visor, but that was it. On Earth sunrise would bring more definitive changes: wind shifting, birds waking up, fog or dew appearing or burning off. Here, nothing much … but he believed it wouldn't always be that way.

He climbed aboard the second MPV, with Paul Timmons driving, and rode out to the prep site. He assigned only part of his brain to the usual banter; he was too busy still thinking about whether he could legally stay on if Barbara left.

If she was breaking the contract … and she was … would that leave him free to negotiate his own agreement? Pretty soon the AC would be done with the silly "first fifty" rule and wouldn't require incoming colonists to be married. But did he want to be a geographic bachelor again, here? He thought back to the torment he went through on the setup mission—*damn, was that really over a year ago?*—wanting more than just to look at Grace, and at the same time not even wanting to look at her.

He didn't want to go through that again. His sense of honor wouldn't allow him to cheat, no matter how much his gonads might want to. But he was afraid that too much time and distance might degrade his honor.

What other option did he have, then, besides leaving with Barbara? Divorce? The idea left him as frigid as the bottom of Faustini Crater, and made his temporary coldness toward Barbara seem balmy by comparison. That wouldn't be an accidental broken promise or lapse of judgment, it would be an admission that the promise just wasn't that important anymore. And maybe it wasn't. Divorce would be easy enough, since they didn't have kids: he'd been the only one of his friends at school with one set of parents, and wouldn't want to put a child of his own through what his friends went through. But if his word was his bond—and maybe he was old-fashioned to think it was—would he throw away his integrity for a dream, and especially a dream he had at least partly achieved?

"Van? You going to join us?"

He hadn't noticed that the truck had stopped and Paul had dismounted. "Sorry, Paul," Van said. It had become his new normal: he could hardly concentrate on the task at hand for the twists and turns his brain made. On this crew he should be okay, though; Timmons was nuts on safety and would look out for him.

The routine was the same as every other shift: half of the team set rails in place while the other half surveyed and set the next supports. They leap-frogged across the Sea of Clouds as long as they had supports, rails, and hardware. Every third shift delivered what the next two building shifts needed, so long as the smelters in the ARPOES kept producing titanium and aluminum from the lunar soil, and so long as the rails continued to roll out of the foundry.

He took solace in the routine, and lost himself in the repetitive motions of moving, sighting in, and attaching the rails. Time slipped away in the blissful monotony.

"Hey, Van?"

The shift was only half over. Momentary static blurred the speaker's voice, but his suit indicated the signal came from George Herbert.

"Yeah, George, whatcha need?" Van asked.

"Just wondering. Is it true the Pastorelli chick never thanked you for saving her life?"

"Where'd you hear that?"

"I've got my sources," George said. "Story goes that she bitched out your old lady for disposing of Frank's body, and that's why Barbara's leaving."

"Strike one, strike two, and strike three. You're out."

"Oh, come on."

Van didn't want to go into details. He didn't think George had earned them. True, Stormie had avoided speaking to Van for almost two weeks after the incident, until the inquest that Gary convened back the fourth of February. It wasn't a real inquest, but that's what Gary called it. It was more a response to the ruckus Barbara had raised on Stormie's behalf.

Van and Barbara had both come to Frank's defense, as did Jake Adamson, the Stewarts, and a number of others. Everyone heard from Stormie's partner down on Earth, Jim something-or-other, and some high-rollers in the Consortium and a couple of government commissions. In the end, the man behind the AC's curtain—Morris Hansen himself—got on the line and personally vouched for the Jim guy and through him for Frank. He asked if they could recover from the loss of public good will their refusal to pay would cause, which Van took to mean the loss of Morris Hansen's good will.

Nobody wants to lose favor with the fifth or sixth richest man on the planet. It didn't surprise anyone that the insurance company rep agreed in short order to release the benefits to Stormie.

That was a pretty classy move on Hansen's part, he had to admit. But Van had always thought that who you are is one thing, but what you do is a lot more important.

Afterward, Stormie thanked Van for the good things he said about Frank. "That's why you should've saved him instead of me," she said.

Van shook his head. "I would've saved him if I could, but he was already gone. Truth is, I didn't save you: he did."

She touched him lightly on the arm. "Thanks anyway," she said. And that was enough.

All of the inquest stuff was public record, so Van gave George only enough additional explanation to shut him up. "Stormie thanked me on Monday, after the inquest," he said. "The same day, she thanked Barbara for taking care of Frank at the very end. And Barbara ... she just wants to go home where you can die under the open sky and the Earth will take your body in its own good time."

And nobody can blame her for that.

Van thought maybe, just maybe, he should've said those last words out loud instead of just thinking them. But that would mean he accepted, or maybe understood, why she wanted to go. Did he really? If so, he wasn't sure he wanted to admit it.

Paul Timmons said, "So what are you going to do, Van? You going back down below? Become a ground pounder again?"

"I don't know," he said. "Maybe."

"You guys keep your minds on your work," said Sonny Peterson, the crew foreman.

"I hear a couple of the asteroid miners want out," George said. "You could get put on that rotation." Under his breath, but still on the radio, he added, "It'd get you out of our hair, at least."

Van stopped in the middle of rigging a rail section for lifting. He ignored George's last jibe. He had considered asteroid mining once before; maybe it was time to consider it again.

Van smiled, and resumed rigging the rail with new enthusiasm. He'd have to look up Henry Crafts....

CHAPTER THIRTY-FOUR

To Make This Reality Match the Dream

Friday, 15 February 2036

A half-dozen flimsy red paper hearts hung around Grand Central the day after the Valentine's party. Stormie wondered where Maggie got the red paper.

She had avoided the area while the party was going on the night before, the way she avoided so many social situations lately. The aching tug that threatened to pull her heart down into her bowels intensified as she watched the simple decorations flutter in the ventilation system breeze.

Not that she had gone without a party at all, thanks to Maggie.

Maggie and the other ladies had tried repeatedly over the three weeks since Frank's death to coax Stormie back into playing cards, but she demurred. To keep up with the responsibilities she and Frank had assumed, Stormie had immersed herself in work. Even with Barbara helping for a few hours every other day or so, Stormie had to build new routines to complete all the work she and Frank together had done before. The routines had the added benefit of keeping her mind occupied; unfortunately, they were also bastions and ramparts that kept her isolated. But she was willing to pay that price, because above all she had a promise to keep to Frank: that she would not give up, and the colony would not fail.

So on Wednesday night Maggie, Harmony, Beverly, and Barbara, along with Rosaria Morera and Angela Beacon, crowded into the Lunar Life Engineering lab and wouldn't let Stormie get any work done.

"It's ten o'clock," Harmony said, "you've done enough work for the day."

Stormie started to protest. "Well, I still have—"

"No, you don't," Yvette yelled from the hallway. "Doctor's orders."

"And it's Valentine's Eve," Maggie said. "Perfect for a girls' night out. Or in. Or something."

They "kidnapped" her then, as if there were very many places to take her. They did it right, though: they blindfolded her and marched her through the tunnels for what seemed like half an hour. When they removed the blindfold, she found herself in the 600 block of Fourth Avenue, which was in the middle of being torn apart and re-built from the inside. Some of the interior partitions had been removed and the kitchen area was being reconfigured and attached to a lunch counter spanning two adjacent cubicles.

They had never tracked down the exact cause of the food poisoning that had laid everyone low while Stormie was gone, but since Gary centralized the food preparation the problem hadn't recurred; so he'd given Gabe Morera clearance to start another eatery to reduce the crowding in Grand Central. On Wednesday night, it was more a mess than a mess hall, but the girls had set up a couple of tables and a flat screen so they could eat and watch movies.

As they settled in, Beverly said, "Here, I think you could use this," and put a shot glass in Stormie's hand. She poured it a little over half full of vodka. Stormie didn't bother to ask how much it cost to get the liquor shipped up. She held her breath and tipped the vodka down her throat. She choked a little on the vapors, but the burn comforted her.

Beverly poured a bit into all the mugs and shot glasses they had, and raised her own to Stormie. "A toast," she said, and her eyes glittered, "to Franklin Jefferson Pastorelli. May our husbands love us half as much as he loved you."

"Hear, hear," the others chorused, and they all drank together.

The liquor was the same as before—its thin consistency, pale color, and faint hint of citrus—but this time her throat closed around it like a valve. She choked, and for an instant remembered the feeling of not being able to breathe. She sputtered and coughed and caught her breath, grateful for the lungfuls of air and even for the girls laughing as they pounded her on the back.

The movie night had been fun, and it had taken a little of the sting out of knowing the Valentine's Day party was the next night. Now, in the aftermath of that party, Stormie doubted anything would ever take the sting out completely. But, life was full of stings—like yellow jackets living in rotten logs, minding their own business until you walk by them through the woods. Sometimes you get a single sting, sometimes a swarm … and sometimes you develop anaphylactic shock. The stings she would have to learn how to handle; the shock she would keep trying to avoid.

Stormie nodded at Maggie, who waved from where she was standing next to Rex. They were still the unofficial welcoming committee for new arrivals, since Gary okayed it and nobody else seemed quite so well suited for the task. Stormie was still uncomfortable around them at times, but she couldn't begrudge them the effort. They had been nicer to her than she probably deserved, and never seemed offended by the cold shoulder she gave them. She smiled a little as the first newcomers came through from Gateway into Grand Central, and the Stewarts converged on them with handshakes and grins.

Stormie turned away from the greeting ritual, and almost bumped into Barbara.

"Sorry, Stormie," said Barbara. "Here to see the new arrivals?"

"I guess," Stormie said. "It doesn't happen every day. I should make sure they fit the profiles I have on them. See if my calculations are going to cover them okay."

Barbara nodded, but her face betrayed her disbelief. "And you can verify that by looking at them?"

Stormie looked back over at the newcomers, and wished her heart would lighten enough that she could make up some fantastic story about the exercise habits of the young—oh, almost absurdly young—Asian couple now talking to Rex. She stopped for a second before she decided that, no, it wasn't Marilyn Chu and another man, and in that instant she lost even the wish to carry on with any banter.

"No," she said, "I guess not."

Barbara touched her on the arm. "I'm sorry I won't be around to help you much longer," she said.

"I appreciate all you've done," Stormie said, and realized she meant it more than she intended. "Not just in the lab from time to time, which I would still like to pay you for—"

"No need."

"—but really, for everything. For taking care of Frank. For helping Maggie keep me attached to the land of the living."

"That's okay," Barbara said. "We don't leave for another couple of days, so maybe I can do some more."

"Don't worry about it. So you're really leaving on Wednesday?"

"That's the plan. Preflight briefing Tuesday evening. Are you going to be okay? You'll be able to handle everything okay after I'm gone?"

"I think so. For a while, anyway, at least until Jim finds someone we can add to our contract." They stood in silence for a moment as two more couples went through the Stewarts' receiving line. "Where's Van?" Stormie asked.

Barbara rolled her eyes. "He came in from his shift, ate supper while his suit recharged, and went out for another."

"I want to make sure to thank him again, too, before y'all leave. He is leaving with you, isn't he?"

"He's supposed to. I'll believe it when I see him suited up and in the airlock. Or maybe when I see him climb the ladder into the ferry. Until then, I don't know. I do know he's going to be looking for you before we leave, though."

"Why?"

"He's going to give you the little cactus he brought up here—there's a whole story behind it, I'll let him tell you."

"Oh," Stormie said, flooded by grief for Frank at the thought of the tomato plant Maggie had given him, on its little shelf in their room, now to be joined by a cactus. Taking care of them was something he would have loved. She caught herself before the emotion swept her away, and hoped Barbara heard the sincerity she wanted to express more than her nervous sadness. "I guess taking it is the least I can do, since he got Gary and the AC to cancel their buyout. Frank would've liked that."

"I heard Van and Gary had less to do with the AC backing off than you getting some new capital. From a real princess?"

Stormie shook her head and flushed, surprised at the depth of information that grew on the grapevine and ashamed to be reminded of Santa Barbara, where Frank implored her to be careful and after which ... it was better not to think of that.

Another pair of new colonists entered Grand Central, and she changed the subject. "I heard Van was talking about shipping out again."

Barbara nodded. "To Aten-Galliani, yeah. He thinks he wants to work inside the asteroid. I suppose I should feel lucky that he's not talking about shipping all the way out to retrieve another one. We'll see what happens."

Stormie glanced up at the lunar mid-day sunlight streaming in from the high horizontal windows. "You think you'll let him?"

Barbara laughed. "As long as he doesn't expect me to go with him." She walked to one of the little tables and grabbed a couple of small carrots. She nibbled the first one, and said, "Van wouldn't last a whole season on the ranch, it'd drive him crazy. This really is where he belongs, here or someplace very much like here, and we both know it.

"You know, when we were in the service, I used to integrate satellite payloads onto rockets and get them ready to launch. And I thought I wanted to come up here, too—that this was the place I belonged. Whenever I had my doubts, Van or BD or whoever would listen and let me work out whatever was going on in my head. They didn't push me, one way or the other, and I don't feel them pushing me now. I don't feel like they're 'letting' me go home, really ... so I don't know if I'd be 'letting' Van go off to the asteroid mine."

"I didn't really mean it like that," Stormie said.

Barbara waved a dismissive hand. "I know. I'm a little touchy about it. I've decided this isn't the place I want to make my legacy, but I know it still is that place for Van. It's the difference between a dream and reality, you know? In the dream, it's perfect and will always be perfect. And when reality doesn't match the dream, we either accept the differences and move on, or work to make the two match up, or look for another dream. If it was worth it to me, I might work to make this reality match the dream I had, but instead I'm looking for another dream. A simpler dream."

Stormie looked up again at the high windows. Dust motes—harmless lint and flakes of skin—moved in Brownian irregularity in the sunlight.

She didn't understand Barbara's attitude, and didn't want to. It reminded her of the old quatrain,

> *I'm folding up my little dreams*
> *Within my heart to-night,*
> *And praying I may soon forget*
> *The torture of their sight.*

Over a century ago, a woman had decided that she had outlived her dreams, that it was better to stash them away out of sight and live out the rest of her days without spending her strength trying to achieve them. What were her little dreams, and did she have any big dreams? Did she hide those away, too? Was that what Barbara was doing?

Stormie shook her head. She didn't want to understand, because she was afraid she might convince herself to stash away her dreams, big or small—and, by default, that would mean stashing away Frank's dream as well. She couldn't do that. Not now, not yet, maybe not ever.

Barbara had a faraway look in her eye as she chewed on the last bit of carrot. Stormie imagined that she was seeing the farm or ranch or wherever she was going. If that was her new dream, Stormie would not gainsay it; she just hoped it was a powerful enough dream to compensate for giving up this one. *We are the dreamers of dreams, and all our dreams don't have to be the same.*

"'Each age is a dream that is dying,'" she quoted, "'or one that is coming to birth.'"

"Hmm?" said Barbara. "What's that?"

"Nothing," Stormie said. "Just a poem." She reached out and took Barbara's right hand in both of hers. "Just my way of saying, I hope you find the dream that makes you happy."

"Thanks. And if I 'let' my husband come back up here, as you say, I'll have him bring you something nice. That is, assuming you're staying."

Stormie looked at the newcomers milling about, talking with some of the veteran colonists and sampling the food the Stewarts had set out. Her stomach tightened with the memory of their first day: their arrival and their summons to Gary's office. She sniffed. Was the slight staleness in the air her imagination?

"Yes," she said, "I'm staying. I can't leave now. The air systems are balanced for the new numbers, but that won't last. And then you and Van are leaving on the same flight with the next mining rotation, so I'll have to re-balance. And Bruce is bringing a new load of ice back on the Turtle in a few days, so all the water systems have to be updated...."

"I get it, I think," Barbara said.

Stormie wasn't sure Barbara got it, but doubted if she could explain it. "It's not just that there's work to be done," she said. "It's that this is the dream that Frank and I shared. And," she took a deep breath so she could continue, "this is the dream he died for. If I leave, I'm not just leaving my dream behind. I'm leaving behind him and his dream."

"A dream that is 'coming to birth'?"

Stormie smiled. "Yeah, you might say that." Maybe she did get it, after all.

The End

ACKNOWLEDGMENTS

I owe thanks to so many people for their help with this book that I can't remember them all. I could take the easy way out and say a general thank-you, but instead I will risk leaving someone out so I can publicly thank as many as possible.

The idea of writing about environmental engineers on the Moon came from my experience as Chief of Bioenvironmental Engineering and later as Deputy Director of Safety and Health at the Air Force Rocket Propulsion Laboratory at Edwards Air Force Base. With that in mind, I must thank the colleagues I worked with most: Ted Evans, Paul Mattson, Jack Sprague (to whom I owe apologies, for I was a stupid new lieutenant), Dan Berlinrut, John Coho, Jim Unmack, Rick Riccardi, John Shirtz, Scott Allen, David Williams, and Sam Burrell.

Many of my other Air Force colleagues influenced parts of the book, notably Rob Robertson and my neighbor and good friend Dave Bergeron. Double thanks to Gill Paszek not only for his influence on the story but for his careful feedback on the draft manuscript.

Keith Phillips, with whom I was stationed at the 4th Space Operations Squadron, may recognize his contribution to chapter 11. The men and women of the Secretary of the Air Force and Chief of Staff of the Air Force Executive Action Group will almost certainly recognize their part in chapter 16. And Rob Gray, whom

I knew at the Air Force Flight Test Center, should recognize his contribution to chapter 24.

Tedd Roberts (a/k/a "Speaker to Lab Animals"), with whom I've had the pleasure of serving on various science- and space-related panels at science fiction and fantasy conventions, should recognize his contributions to chapter 21.

If you recognize a contribution you made that I have not acknowledged here, please accept my thanks and my apologies for not listing you personally.

For reading the novel (or portions thereof) in draft form and providing me with helpful feedback and encouragement, I owe tremendous thanks to Ada Milenkovich Brown, Edmund Schubert, Oliver Dale, Faisal Jawdat, James Galt-Brown, Diana Rowland, KeAnne Hoeg, Kristen Minervino, and Brian Ceccarelli. Double thanks to Allen Moore for his enthusiastic feedback and for letting me adapt an experience he lived through to the needs of one of my characters. Thanks also to Kevin Smith for help with the initial idea for the pico-scrub treatment. Thanks to Bryan Thomas Schmidt for his careful, considerate, and sometimes challenging editing.

Special thanks to Orson Scott Card, whose 2003 Writing Workshop showed me what was wrong with my first novel and whose 2004 Literary Boot Camp gave me the confidence to keep putting words on paper; to Dave Wolverton, whose 2008 Novel Writing Workshop provided excellent feedback on an early part of this novel and who graciously helped me craft the final product; and to Kevin J. Anderson and the staff at WordFire Press, for taking a chance on this story.

For putting up with me as I struggled to get it all down in electrons, and then on paper, I especially thank Jill and Stephanie and Christopher. You are tremendous blessings to me.

Praise God, from whom all blessings flow.

ACRONYMS

AC: Asteroid Consortium

ARG: Advanced Radioisotope Generator

ARPOES: Automated Regolith Processor, Oxygen Extraction and Smelting

CGOC: Company Grade Officers' Council

ELSPAP: Emergency Life Support Pressure Acquisition Procedure

EVA: Extra-Vehicular Activity

FDD: Funerary Desiccation Device

LICEOM: Lunar Ice Collection and Extraction Operations Module

LLE: Lunar Life Engineering, LLP (Limited Liability Partnership)

LPPN: Lunar Power Plant, Nuclear

LSOV: Lunar Sub-Orbital Vehicle

LVN: Lunar Vehicle, Nuclear

MACEF: Monocellular Atmospheric Circulating Emulsion Filter

MPV: Multi-Purpose Vehicle

NOTAC: Notice to All Colonists

PROM: Programmable Read-Only Memory

ROPS: Regolith Oxygen Processing Station

Chapter-By-Chapter Notes

Chapter 1:

The lunar phase information here and throughout, as well as sunrise/sunset times, came from the US Naval Observatory's data services web page and from LunarPhase software. LunarPhase was made to help amateur astronomers know when they can make detailed observations of different lunar features, and in this case it was very helpful to one author as well. Highly recommended, and a lot of fun to play with.

Chapter 4:

The fictional "Meredith's Moon" satellite uses an orbit postulated by Dr. Robert L. Forward, who, in addition to being a consultant for the Air Force Rocket Propulsion Laboratory, also wrote several science fiction novels and stories. Unfortunately, Gray did not have the chance to meet Dr. Forward during the years he served at the Rocket Lab.

Chapter 5:

The poem Frank quotes is "To Anthea, who may Command him Anything," by Robert Herrick. (The poem, along with all the poetry quoted at length in the novel, is in the public domain.) Herrick is probably best known for his poem, "To the Virgins, to make much of Time."

Chapter 6:

Readers with a particular taste in music may have caught the paraphrased line from the song "Nobody Loves You Like I Do" by Emerson, Lake and Palmer.

The Advanced Radioisotope Generator introduced here is a takeoff on the Advanced Stirling Radioisotope Generator considered by NASA to power future planetary missions. Very technical readers may point out that Gray took excessive liberties with the technology and did not adequately address all of the safety issues involved. Hopefully that dramatic license did not detract too much from their enjoyment of the story.

Chapter 7:

The poem Stormie tries to remember, and Nurse Myrachek brings her a copy of, is "The Love Song of J. Alfred Prufrock" by T.S. Eliot.

The song Stormie remembers her grandmother singing, "Who You Gonna Throw in the Lake of Fire?" was by Keith Green.

Chapter 10:

The poem Frank thinks of, after reviewing a few more lines from "The Love Song of J. Alfred Prufrock," is "To See a World in a Grain of Sand" by William Blake:

To see a world in a grain of sand
And heaven in a wild flower
Hold infinity in the palm of your hand
And eternity in an hour

Chapter 11:

The biocapsules mentioned in this chapter (and later) were invented at NASA Ames Research Center, in the Space Biosciences Division.

Chapter 14:

Monopropellant thrusters, the basis for the monopropellant turbines, also work with hydrogen peroxide as a fuel. Turbines using H_2O_2 would have the advantage of producing only oxygen and water as exhaust.

Chapter 15:

"Take it to the Lord in prayer" is a key phrase in the refrain of "What a Friend We Have in Jesus."

Chapter 16:

The M/V *Independence* is a real ship, and was actually intended to recover solid rocket boosters after Space Shuttle launches from Vandenberg Air Force Base. By the time of this story it would be ancient, but it holds a special place in Gray's heart because it was used in a maritime search-and-salvage operation that he directed while part of the Titan System Program Office.

Chapter 18:

The song about having church on the Moon is "To the Moon" by Sara Groves.

Chapter 19:

"Come live with me and be my love" is the opening line of "The Passionate Shepherd to His Love" by Christopher Marlowe.

Many fans of Frank Herbert's *Dune* should be able to recite "The Litany Against Fear" from memory.

Chapter 20:

Frank recites several phrases from "High Flight" by John Magee, and Stormie counters with lines from "The Dalliance of Eagles" by Walt Whitman.

Chapter 28:

"I am the color of the earth" happens to be the first line of "Color" by Mavis Mixon, from *Bitter Fruit: African-American Women in World War II*, edited by Maureen Honey and published in 1999. The verse attributed to Stormie's brother Erick, however, is original.

Chapter 31:

"Defeat upon defeat" and "I do not know beneath what sky" are from "Unmanifest Destiny" by Richard Hovey, from *Modern American Poetry*, edited by Louis Untermeyer and published in 1919.

Chapter 32:

If it is not clear from his shorthand, the hymn Frank quotes is "Breathe on Me, Breath of God."

Chapter 34:

"I'm folding up my little dreams" is the first stanza of "My Little Dreams" by Georgia Douglas Johnson, from *The Book of American Negro Poetry*, edited by James Weldon Johnson and published in 1922.

"Each age is a dream that is dying" is the close of "Ode" by Arthur William Edgar O'Shaughnessy, from *The Oxford Book of English Verse: 1250–1900*, edited by Arthur Quiller-Couch and published in 1919. Readers familiar with the movie *Willy Wonka and the Chocolate Factory* may have recognized the line "we are the dreamers of dreams," which is from the poem's opening stanza:

> *We are the music-makers,*
> *And we are the dreamers of dreams,*
> *Wandering by lone sea-breakers,*
> *And sitting by desolate streams;*
> *World-losers and world-forsakers,*
> *On whom the pale moon gleams:*
> *Yet we are the movers and shakers*
> *Of the world for ever, it seems.*

ABOUT THE AUTHOR

Gray Rinehart is the only person to have commanded a remote Air Force tracking station, written speeches for Presidential appointees, and had music on *The Dr. Demento Show*.

Gray retired from the U.S. Air Force after a rather odd career. He began as a Bioenvironmental Engineer, became a project engineer, then became a space and missile operator. Over the course of his career, he kept rocket propulsion research operations safe, fought fires as head of a Disaster Response Force, trained Air Force ROTC cadets, refurbished space launch facilities, "flew" Milstar satellites, drove trucks, processed nuclear command and control orders as an Emergency Actions officer, commanded the Air Force's largest satellite tracking station, protected militarily critical space technologies, and wrote speeches for top Air Force leaders.

Gray is a Contributing Editor for Baen Books, and his fiction has appeared in *Analog Science Fiction & Fact*, *Asimov's Science Fiction*, Orson Scott Card's *Intergalactic Medicine Show*, and other venues. Through a quirk of fate, his story "Ashes to Ashes, Dust to Dust, Earth to Alluvium" was a finalist for the 2015 Hugo Award for Best Novelette. He is also the author of a variety of essays, articles, and other nonfiction, and a singer/songwriter with two albums that feature science-fiction-and-fantasy-inspired songs.

Gray's "alter ego" is the Gray Man, a famous ghost of Pawleys Island, South Carolina. For more information, visit:

graymanwrites.com

IF YOU LIKED ...

If you liked *Walking on the Sea of Clouds*, you might also enjoy:

Lifeline
Kevin J. Anderson and Doug Beason

Club Anyone
Lou Agresta

Climbing Olympus
Kevin J. Anderson

OTHER WORDFIRE PRESS TITLES

Our list of other WordFire Press authors and titles is always growing.
To find out more and to see our selection of titles, visit us at:

wordfirepress.com